SWEET HOLIDAY ROMANCE

Books 1 - 4

DARCI BALOGH

Knowhere Media LLC

ENCHANTING
Eve

DARCI BALOGH

To my sister, Terri, who encourages me to be myself, follow my dreams, and always believe in a little bit of magic. Here's to good health and a long life full of abundant joy and massive success!
On to the next level, sis!

Chapter One

A cold wind moaned outside Eve's kitchen window. Falling leaves, gold and orange and crisp, blew across the paint peeled porch steps, making skittering sounds until they tumbled to their final resting place in a growing pile outside her front door.

The old house creaked in the storm, but held firm and strong as it had for over 130 years. The trees that canopied the aged home were brilliant with fall color and though another cold winter was on the horizon, fall was currently in its full glory five days before Halloween.

Eve barely noticed the storm outside. Her kitchen was warm with the sweet smells of baking.

Wearing the large apron that had been her father's, her face and hands were smudged with flour. The apron featured a giant crawdad dressed as a chef. Her father had told her he'd bought the apron when on honeymoon in New Orleans with her mother. Handprints of white flour blotched the red cartoon crawdad where Eve had used the apron instead of a dishtowel during her baking frenzy.

Her straight dark hair was pulled back to stay out of her

face while she cooked, but strands of it had come loose and dangled in her eyes. She held a ceramic mixing bowl in one arm. With her other arm she used a large wooden spoon to stir the second batch of cookie dough vigorously. A platter on the counter held a fresh batch of buttery pumpkin shaped sugar cookies. When they cooled she would cover them with orange frosting and pipe them with jack-o'lantern faces.

Eve was deep in the tradition that she and her father had kept since as long as she could remember. Baking these pumpkin cookies for his 7th grade English class at Halloween had been something Albert St. Claire had done his entire 35-year career as a middle school teacher. Eve was determined that this year her father's tradition would continue, even though he was no longer with them.

A particularly strong gust of wind rattled the window-panes making Eve stop what she was doing and look up. Her two black cats, Sabrina and Hazel, also looked towards the window from where they sat on nearby kitchen stools, lazily watching her bake. Hazel, the small and skittish one, hopped down from her perch and began to rub against Eve's ankles while she worked.

"It's just a rainstorm," Eve said. "Nothing to worry about."

The slim black cat meowed at her, whether to agree or disagree was hard to tell. Sabrina, Hazel's jealous and much larger sister, was never one to be outdone. When she saw Eve reach down and scratch Hazel behind her ears, Sabrina shifted her significant cat frame and dropped to the floor with a thump, casually trotting over to Eve in order to get her own ears scratched.

"You two are keeping me from getting my work done," Eve said, but she didn't really mind. These two cats were her only company since her father had died this past spring. Her mother had passed away when she was very young, so young that Eve had no memories of her that hadn't been told to her by her father.

Eve glanced at the wedding picture of her parents that hung on the wall in the small hallway between the kitchen and the living room. For as long as she could remember that picture and others from the family photo album were her only link to her mother. And now pictures were all she had left of her father, too. Eve's eyes filled with tears and she blinked hard to control them.

"We can't get tears in the cookie batter," she said to the cats. "Cookies aren't for sadness."

That's exactly what she told herself when she decided to carry on her father's tradition and bake their annual Halloween cookies for his class. It had been five months since Albert St. Claire suffered a fatal heart attack in his sleep, and Eve figured it was high time she did something more than work and read and sleep and cry. It wasn't going to be easy, but she knew she needed to do it and that her father would want her to get back to a more normal life.

"You're young, you're beautiful, you should be going out and living a fun young person's life." Eve could almost hear his voice.

She sighed. She wasn't all that young anymore, just turned 30. She knew that her father saw her through rose-colored glasses, because she wasn't what you would call beautiful either.

She was neither tall and willowy nor short and spunky. She was average height, too pale, too thin, with dark hair that insisted on being as unbending as possible. And though her eyes were blue, they weren't the kind of eyes one might consider pretty. They were too round and not blue enough to be memorable. Nothing about her was memorable.

She looked around at the old kitchen with its high ceilings, its ancient cupboards with iron knobs, the giant ceramic sink, and the wooden kitchen table with the small blue vase in the center. If things were totally normal her father would have filled that vase with bright orange marigolds from their flowerbeds. Eve hadn't done that. She also hadn't kept up with the garden after her father's death.

She glanced out the window where she could see the volunteer pumpkin plants that had sprouted up on their own and grown into a wild mess. Since she didn't water them in the heat of the summer they had died out and not produced any of the delightful little sugar pumpkins she and her father had always loved.

Her entire backyard was a jungle of dead brown pumpkin vines. Those tangled twisted vines reflected exactly how she felt on the inside.

A knock on the door startled her out of her melodrama. The sister cats, who acted a lot like dogs in Eve's opinion, trotted quickly to the door to greet their visitor.

"Hello, is anyone in there?" A bright and cheery voice sounded through the door followed by another series of rapid knocks.

Eve recognized the voice without looking, Belinda. She pulled open the door to let her friend inside. Belinda's short, stubby frame tumbled into the foyer with the twirling wind and a few sprinkles of raindrops from the storm.

"Oh my gosh, the wind!" Belinda exclaimed, giggling like always.

Belinda was the opposite of Eve. Small and curvy, with short funky blonde hair, dramatic black frame glasses, bright red lipstick and red nails, always dressing in colors and always ready to laugh.

Eve often thought that people were surprised by their long running friendship, which had been strong since 6th grade. But Eve wasn't surprised. Who wouldn't want to be friends with Belinda? It was more surprising, she supposed, that anyone like Belinda would want to be friends with her.

"I'm having a party!" Belinda announced, wiggling her palms in the air like jazz hands.

"A party?"

Belinda reached down to scoop up the sister cats who were meowing and twisting lovingly around her feet.

"I decided that nobody in this town ever does anything fun and if I want to go to a fabulous Halloween party then I need to throw one myself!" Belinda nuzzled her face into the necks of the purring cats and made kissy sounds as she followed Eve into the kitchen, talking the whole time. "You could help me decorate and we'll play games and we'll invite everyone we know. It won't be for kids though. I want it to be a grown up party with grown up refreshments. You know what I mean?" Belinda took in the messy kitchen. "Did Betty Crocker blow up in here?"

Eve smiled. "No, I'm just making some cookies."

Belinda's eyes fell on the giant sized pumpkin cookies. She placed each cat on a stool and pulled the third stool up to the counter. "Are you making your famous pumpkin cookies?" She sounded delighted.

"Yes," Eve shrugged. "I thought maybe I would take them by my Dad's classroom tomorrow. You know, keep up the tradition."

Belinda gave her a pitiful look. "Oh, Evie, that is so sweet." She reached under her glasses and wiped away tears with her carefully manicured fingers. "Your Dad would be thrilled." She sniffed and reached out to pat her friend's hand.

"I just thought it might be..." Eve paused, not certain how to explain, "Fun...maybe."

Belinda broke into a bright smile. "Of course it will be fun! That's great! You really need to get out more."

"Well, it's a start," Eve answered, flouring the surface of the countertop to roll out the next batch.

"Have you met Mr. Murphy yet?" Belinda asked, swiping a piece of cookie dough and popping it into her mouth.

Mr. Murphy was the English teacher who had replaced her father at the middle school. Eve had heard his name, but had not gone out of her way to meet him. She shook her head 'no' and continued rolling out the dough.

"He's really nice," Belinda reassured her. "And he's pretty young and kinda cute." Her eyes flew open with what Eve knew Belinda thought was a wonderful idea. "Maybe we could invite him to the party!"

Eve made a sour face and shook her head. "I'm not sure about a party." She didn't know if she felt up to that much social interaction.

"Please, Evie!" Belinda begged, giving her friend her cutest pleading face. "I need you to help me decorate and pick out a costume and everything."

Eve kept pushing the rolling pin back and forth, meditating on the idea before committing to anything.

"Besides, Chip is going to be there," Belinda added mischievously.

Eve stopped rolling.

"Chip? Chip Hendricks?"

"Yep," Belinda nodded briskly and reached for another blob of cookie dough. "The gossip is that he may be moving back to town permanently and..." she gave a dramatic pause, "He's still single!" Belinda gobbled up the cookie dough, giving her friend an all-knowing smile as she chewed.

Eve didn't respond, but she couldn't deny the tiny butterflies in her stomach at the mention of his name.

"Come on, Evie," Belinda teased. "You're more excited than that, aren't you? We're talking about Chip."

Eve denied Belinda's question with a quick shake of her

head, causing another piece of her ultra straight hair to drop into her eyes, blocking her view. Since her hands were covered in flour and cookie dough, Eve blew at the wayward lock and flicked her head to get it back into place.

"We're not in high school anymore," she chided Belinda.

Belinda grinned naughtily and snatched another bit of dough. "And that is exactly my point."

Eve decided to ignore the teasing. She and Belinda had spent countless hours of their lives giggling over boys. She had other things to do now.

She carefully used the cookie cutter to cut out each pumpkin cookie and placed them on the waiting baking sheet while she listened to Belinda chatter about the Halloween party. Parties weren't really Eve's thing, but as she slid the cookie sheet into the waiting oven she thought maybe Belinda was right, maybe they should throw a Halloween party, maybe it would help her get back to normal.

As if to underscore her decision, a sudden gust of wind blew open the front door and sent a swirl of gold and red fall leaves tumbling into the house.

Chapter Two

The wide sidewalk in front of the school was covered with damp remains from the previous night's storm. Eve followed the familiar path, stepping carefully over multi-colored leaves that were scattered across the cement and sodden from the rain.

She wore thick black leggings, a dark orange button up shirt that hung down past her hips, her favorite black leather knee-high boots and a red fall jacket. In her arms she carried a shallow box, and out of the top of that box stuck 30 carefully wrapped giant orange pumpkin cookies with jack o'lantern faces. Belinda had helped her slide each individual cookie into a clear cellophane bag when it was completely decorated. Then they had tied the tops closed with bits of orange yarn from Eve's craft box.

As she approached the school, Eve's heart began to pound in her chest. She had not stepped foot into the middle school where her father had taught her entire life since his death. The principal and teachers, along with his students, had held a memorial for him at the end of the school year, but that had been only weeks after the tragic event and Eve had been too grief-stricken to leave her house at the time. She had sent her regrets and everybody understood. They had all been so very kind.

Eve took a deep breath to try and calm her nerves. This was a happy day. This was the beginning of Halloween celebrations for the children that her father adored teaching.

He was a popular teacher who loved literature and learning and fun. She had enjoyed popping by and surprising him during the day, always catching him in a lively conversation with a student or reading with his great booming voice to his class. Or laughing. Her father had laughed a lot.

Eve took another breath and pushed back the grief. Today was about having fun.

She opened the heavy door at the front of the school and was immediately met with the sights and smells that she remembered so well, not only from her father's tenure there, but from her own years spent as a student in these halls. Mrs. Runyon, the school secretary, spotted her through the large glass window of the front office that looked over the entrance to the school.

"Eve!" Mrs. Runyon exclaimed with pleasure after pushing the sliding glass window open.

"Hi," Eve managed a smile and stepped to the window.

"How are you, dear?" Mrs. Runyon was in her 50's and had worked at the school for over 20 years. Not as long as Eve's father, but long enough that she had been there when Eve was in middle school.

"Fine, thank you," Eve answered. She held up the box of cookies for Mrs. Runyon to see. "I thought I would bring something to Dad's, um, my father's class...for fun," she added.

Through a flutter of 'how nice' and 'isn't that sweet' comments, Mrs. Runyon gave her the front desk's blessing and a special Visitor name tag so she could deliver her goodies to the English class.

Within a few minutes she was standing at the closed door of Room 212-B. Her heart was in her throat, the palms of her hands broke out in a sweat and she felt clammy all over.

Should she knock? She had always walked straight into this room, unannounced and perfectly welcome. This was ridiculous. No reason to be so uncertain. They were just middle school kids and she only wanted to give them some cookies.

The low murmur of a man's voice filtered through the door. Eve raised her hand, made a fist and rapped lightly three times. The low murmur stopped and a few moments later the heavy door swung open with a click and a tug.

"Yes?" A tall man with a shock of dark red hair on his head and a short beard in a slightly lighter shade of red stood in the doorway, looking at her quizzically. He wore a loose crewneck sweater in hunter green, and Eve could see a pale orange shirt collar peeking out from underneath. Green and orange, festive colors for Halloween week.

She stood frozen, unable to form words and feeling like an utter fool. Her hands were so sweaty she worried the box of cookies might slip through them and fall to the floor.

Mutely, she lifted the box and offered the man she assumed was the new teacher, Mr. Murphy, the pumpkin cookies. He glanced at the cookies and back at her, his piercing blue eyes showing a glimmer of humor.

"Are those for me?" he asked.

"I, um, they're pumpkin cookies," Eve said, trying not to stammer. "For the class." She gave him a feeble smile.

Mr. Murphy's face opened with delight. He stepped back while pulling the door wider so Eve could enter and swept his arm up and out in a dramatic gesture. "Welcome, kind Miss!"

Eve heard several giggles from the children at their desks.

She stepped into the classroom and walked to the teacher's desk at the front.

Feeling like she was moving in slow motion, Eve took in the details of what used to be familiar surroundings. The rows of student desks, the laminated posters on the walls, the blackboard with various sentences and book titles scrawled in chalk, the whiteboard in the corner where it appeared children had been drawing pictures of cartoon birds.

The room smelled like she remembered, looked basically like she remembered, but was utterly and completely different.

Placing the box of cookies on the teacher's desk, Eve could see that all of her father's things were gone and had been replaced by what must be Mr. Murphy's books, paperwork and teacher knick knacks. Of course, this is what should be expected. But somehow seeing it made Eve feel like she had swallowed a bag of rocks.

"I'm Mr. Murphy," Mr. Murphy offered. He stuck out his hand to shake hers and Eve discreetly rubbed her palm on her jacket as she reached to take his, afraid that her handshake would be wet and cold.

"I'm Eve St. Claire," Eve said. There was no reaction on Mr. Murphy's part and she realized that he must not know her name. He took her hand however, and gave it a warm shake.

"Well thank you for the cookies. They look delicious."

"That's Mr. St. Claire's daughter," one of the girls, Ruby, whom Eve recognized as a regular customer at the bookstore where she worked, whispered loudly to Mr. Murphy. His eyebrows shot up as he got the hint. He was still holding Eve's hand and he looked at her with both interest and concern.

"Albert St. Claire's daughter?" he asked.

Eve nodded.

There was an awkward pause while Eve returned Mr. Murphy's rather intimate stare with what she hoped was a serene and dignified countenance. As she looked at him, she noticed that he was young, well, younger than most of the other teachers at the school.

His face was moderately handsome, his eyes a kind blue, and his build under that loose green sweater seemed trim and masculine. In general, he looked like an educated, slightly rumpled, teacherly type of person. His red hair and beard were definitely his most dramatic features. Her hand grew warm in his.

"I'm sorry." He let go of her hand and stepped around her to pull out the chair at the desk. "Please, have a seat. It's very nice of you to come by."

"Thank you." She sat down and looked towards the children in their seats. A few of them were watching her and Mr. Murphy, most of them were eyeing the cookies.

"My father and I always made pumpkin cookies for his class at Halloween," Eve felt the need to explain her presence.

"How kind of you." Mr. Murphy turned towards the box of cookies. He pulled one of the festive cellophane bags out of the box to inspect it. "These look delicious," he said as he smiled at her. "Thank you."

"You're welcome," she responded. She smiled briefly at the kids, who were now all watching Mr. Murphy, and thought she should probably make her exit. She moved to stand up.

"Don't go," Mr. Murphy requested. "Please, join us. Ruby, Michael, would you please hand out these cookies to everyone? One per person." Mr. Murphy grabbed another bag out of the box before moving a royal blue plastic chair that sat at the side of his desk into a position so he could sit next to Eve and look out over the classroom. He handed her one of the cookies. "Would you like a cup of coffee to go with that?"

Soon Eve was sitting at her father's old desk, in her father's old chair with a steaming hot styrofoam cup of coffee and a bright orange pumpkin cookie in front of her. The familiarity of the whole experience was a little overwhelming, but also comforting. There were 24 children all milling around the room, chatting happily with each other and enjoying their homemade Halloween treat. Her father would have loved the scene and that thought made her smile.

Mr. Murphy ate the first half of his cookie in two big bites. He munched quietly next to her while watching over the children. He swallowed a sip of coffee from a stainless steel travel mug.

"We were just getting started reading some Poe," he said. "Would you like to stay for that?"

Eve loved Edgar Allan Poe. It was an old family favorite at this time of year.

"Which one are you reading? The Raven? The Tell-Tale Heart?"

"The Raven, today," Mr. Murphy answered.

Eve's gaze swept over the children, who all looked quite young and innocent. She tried to remember when she first read Edgar Allen Poe.

"That's not too dark for them?" she asked.

Mr. Murphy looked at her with mild surprise. "Well, it is the season of Halloween." He cocked his head at her in a teasing manner. "This coming from a woman who lives in a haunted house?" He smiled then popped another large chunk of cookie into his mouth.

Now it was Eve's turn to be surprised. What did he mean by that? How did Mr. Murphy know where she lived, and why would he think that her beautiful old house was haunted?

"Why do you say that?"

"Isn't your house the famous haunted house?" Mr. Murphy responded, perplexed. He looked out at his class as if for verification, but they weren't paying much attention. "Sorry," he offered when he took in her discomfort. "I didn't mean to offend you." He gestured towards the children. "They told me that Mr. St. Claire and his daughter lived in the big old house at the end of Pennsylvania and that the house was haunted."

Eve sat up straighter, as if being proper would somehow diffuse this rumor. She lifted the styrofoam cup in her hands and shook her head slightly, "It's a very old, very beautiful house, but it's definitely not haunted." She took a defiant sip of her coffee.

Ruby, who had been eavesdropping on their conversation, piped up, "Mr. St. Claire told us it was haunted."

Stunned into silence, Eve stared at the little girl. A few of the girl's little friends nodded earnestly in agreement and a number of the other children spoke up at the same time.

"He always told us about it at Halloween."

"My big brother said he told them he lived in a haunted house when he took this class."

"Your house is famous."

"Your house is haunted!"

Eve felt a burning in her cheeks and she wondered why her father would tell these children, why he would tell anyone, that kind of thing. Had he been telling haunted stories about their beloved house as long as he was a teacher?

Mr. Murphy watched her carefully and when he realized she was flustered by the children's comments, he stood up and grabbed a worn book off of the desk.

"All right let's get back to work," he declared. The children made their way back to their desks, some still carrying their treat, some already done eating. "I'll read while you finish eating." Mr. Murphy gave Eve a quick smile as he instructed the class.

Eve stayed for the reading. It seemed rude to leave. She

watched as Mr. Murphy read Poe's 'The Raven' with a commanding tone and complete with a squawking raven's voice, but she wasn't really listening.

She nibbled at her pumpkin cookie and sipped her coffee, but the whole time she was wondering why her father had told those stories to the children of their town. Did the whole town think that her house was haunted? Had he meant it as a joke or had he actually believed it was true? The whole situation bothered her, but the thing that bothered her most was that she had never known. Her own father had never told her anything about them living in a haunted house.

Chapter Three

There was something comforting about a stack of old books. The stack currently in front of Eve included all different types of fiction; romance, fantasy, sci-fi, children's books. It also included some non-fiction; health books, business books, books on how to lose weight and some on how to find love. The stack of books was precariously balanced on a wheeled cart, which Eve pushed carefully through the narrow aisles of the bookstore. When she found the section that a book belonged in, she took it from the cart and added it to the shelf.

This was the only used bookstore in their town. It was the only bookstore of any kind in their town, in fact. Eve had worked here since high school. First as a part-time cashier, then after she returned from college she had taken over as manager.

As jobs went it was perfectly suited for Eve's personality and interests. As a career it was mostly dead end, but then so were almost all of the jobs in their town. For a young woman with an English Lit degree, who was not interested in being a teacher, it was about as spot on a job as she could expect.

The bookstore bought used books for pennies and turned around to sell them, either in person or online, for a few dollars. They also assisted the older generation in town with navigating online purchases of both new and used books. But their biggest draws were the comfortable chairs and sofas placed around the store and the sale of fresh coffee, tea, scones and cookies. They played classical or jazz or sometimes French bistro music, and patrons could sit and read as long as they desired. Eve loved spending time in the bookstore.

Today she was a bit preoccupied with thoughts of her father and his haunted house stories. As she made her way through each aisle, she wondered if the entire town thought her house was haunted and, if so, what exactly did they think of her? She was a single woman, admittedly introverted, a little dark in her sense of humor who loved Halloween and owned two black cats, cats that happened to be named after famous witch characters. She shook her head at the ridiculous idea that she was some kind of haunted character in a fictional story, but she had to admit, from the outside looking in, it was possible people thought of her that way.

Eve glanced at the overstuffed denim blue chair in the corner where one of their regulars, Joanna, a retired post office employee was quietly reading. Joanna spent at least three days a week munching scones and sipping tea while reading romance novels and books on exotic travel, and Eve knew she wouldn't mind an interruption. Eve pushed her cart in Joanna's direction and when the woman looked up and acknowledged her with a friendly nod, Eve sat down in the dark red chair next to hers.

"Have you ever heard the rumor that my house is haunted?" Eve asked.

Joanna let her open book rest in her lap and looked over the top of her bejeweled reading glasses at Eve.

"Yes," she said matter-of-factly. "Everyone knows that."

"What? How can everyone know that? It's not even true!"

Joanna thought for a few moments before answering, "Your Dad used to talk about it all the time. That must be where the rumors started." She gave Eve a kind smile. "You know how he liked to tell stories."

Eve opened her mouth to protest the validity of the haunting rumor, but was interrupted by the sound of bells. A small bundle of bells hung from the front door of the store and jingled when it opened. From where she sat she couldn't see who had come in, so she stood up and went to the front counter leaving Joanna to go back to her reading.

At first glance, Eve only saw a tall, dark businessman standing in the front, looking around at the store. When he turned to face her, however, she realized with more than a little surprise that the businessman was Chip Hendricks. Chip, captain of their high school football team, president of their senior class, son of one of the richest men in town, general heartthrob and Eve's school girl crush, was standing at the counter.

"Chip!" Eve was so surprised she almost shouted his name. Out of the corner of her eye, she saw Joanna leaning forward to peer at the commotion. Eve blushed slightly at her outburst. Chip smiled in a half grin, half smirk kind of way. She lowered her voice, "What are you doing here?"

"I'm back home for an extended visit. Thought I'd stop by and see if you're still here," he said. His voice was soft and smoky and sent nervous flutters through her stomach.

"Yeah," she shrugged lightly and looked around the bookstore, which suddenly seemed a little dusty and dumpy. "Still here."

Chip let his eyes wander down her body, taking her in. She felt unusually exposed under his gaze even though she wore a modest T-shirt style dress that didn't show much of her figure, not that she had much of a figure to show. Eve glanced around shyly to see if anybody was watching. Joanna was back to reading. There were only a half dozen more patrons in the store and all of them had their noses in a book. When she looked back, Chip was giving her that same smirky grin.

"You look good," he said.

She felt heat rise in her cheeks and hated the fact that she was about to appear silly and juvenile by blushing in front of him. She didn't want him to know she was flustered, so Eve took a moment to let her eyes boldly wander up and down his body. She noticed his very nice dark grey suit that was well cut to his tall, wide shouldered form. She took in his black and silver tie, his neatly trimmed, thick, dark hair, his deep brown eyes and closely shaven face that perfectly showed off his square jaw and nicely formed lips. She had to concentrate to keep from sighing.

"You too." She tried to use a confident, sensual tone. She was no longer in high school, after all.

"Catching up on your reading?" Chip nodded his head towards the book she held in her hand.

Eve looked down. It was one of the self-help books she'd been putting away and forgotten she was holding. The title was encased in a giant, bubble heart and read, 'How to Find Love in 30 Days". Eve hurriedly set it on the shelf behind the counter out of sight and ignored the teasing look in Chip's eyes. She cleared her throat and tried to think of something to say. Nothing came to her. He caught her eye and held it with a deep, smoldering gaze. They looked at each other for a long moment. Just when she thought she might start batting her eyelashes uncontrollably at him, the front door banged open, bells jingling madly.

"Chip!" Belinda exclaimed, drawing the attention of all seven book lovers in the store.

Chip lifted his eyebrows and turned to see who was

calling his name. Belinda practically danced to the front counter, her blonde hair was pulled up in an orange bandana that had small jack-o-lanterns in place of polka dots, and she wore a tight grey T-shirt that had sequins in the form of a black cat on the front. She opened her arms wide and went in for the hug. Chip had no choice but to hug her back.

"Belinda," he said, pushing her out to arms length, his calm, cool demeanor barely dented by her bubbly greeting.

"It's so good to see you!" Belinda said, still loud, still attracting everyone's attention.

Now that Belinda was safely removed from him, Chip leaned against the counter, giving Eve an amused glance. Belinda reached up and stroked the sleeve of his suit jacket.

"What are you all dressed up for on a weekday?" She cooed.

Chip straightened his tie with mock importance. "A little board meeting at the old man's company."

The Hendricks family owned a grocery store, two gas stations and a liquor store in town. Chip, it was said, had moved to Chicago after college and worked his way up the ladder at an insurance and investment company. Not too bad for the hometown heartthrob.

"Well, it's very nice. Nice enough to wear to my Halloween party and be Bruce Wayne," Belinda suggested. "You're invited." She reached into her shining patent leather purse and pulled out an index card sized invitation, handing it to him. "Or you could come as Batman!"

Chip grinned, skimming the information on the invitation. He gave Eve a meaningful look. "Are you going?"

"Of course she's going," Belinda answered.

Again, his eyes slid down the front of Eve's chest, making her pulse quicken.

"What are you wearing to the party?" He asked.

"Um..." Eve's mind had gone blank.

"It's a surprise," Belinda saved her. "You'll have to come to the party to find out."

Chip assured them that he would be at the Halloween party before leaving. As soon as he walked out the door and past the giant window at the front of the bookstore, Belinda started tiny hopping up and down with excitement.

"Now you have to come," Belinda commanded.

Eve knew she was right. Though parties weren't her strong point, the draw of Chip being there was enough for Eve to want to at least make the effort to show up.

"I don't have any idea what to wear for a costume," Eve said.

"Don't worry about that," Belinda said confidently. "I know exactly what you should wear."

Chapter Four

Dusk was falling and the lamppost in front of Eve's house was already glowing, fending off the coming night. As dark came sooner this time of year, she had taken to leaving a light on in the living room. She walked carefully across the uneven cobblestones that led up to her front door, taking in the overgrown vegetation in her front yard that had already died back for the year and turned various shades of brown.

The wild pumpkin plants from her backyard had stretched their grasping vines around the house to the front. They combined with the rose bushes she had not pruned, the ivy that had spread across the ground and up one side of the house, and other various weeds and grasses she had neglected to mow this past summer. The result was a tangled mess where there used to be a mature and stately front lawn.

The house was a Victorian built with stone. It had a swirling iron fence, high peaked roof, tall windows and a balcony over the front door where you could walk out from her bedroom upstairs and look down at the street below.

Ancient oak and maple trees loomed on either side of the house. Their leaves had turned to crimson and gold and begun dropping, leaving wispy piles all over the ground. The moon, which would reach full status in a few nights, Halloween to be exact, rose behind the roof, half hidden by the pointed peaks and narrow brick chimneys.

As she got closer she could see Hazel and Sabrina, black and beautiful, watching for her as they sat in the living room window. They were silhouetted by the lamplight that spilled out of the window and their eyes shone yellow. Eve had to admit the whole effect did look very much like your classic haunted house. She chuckled a little at the idea of her father, tall and boisterous, weaving tales of strange sounds and ghost sightings and thrilling his students with scary stories.

Eve had always had a vivid imagination. Encouraged by her father to read, she loved stories and books and movies of all kinds. She had always liked living in a house with such character. They had both loved living in this house, but Eve also had a logical streak and, imagination or not, she certainly didn't believe in ghosts.

In the kitchen, she placed the copper tea kettle on the stove and turned on the gas flame underneath. She started to reach for a mug and a single tea bag, but decided instead to make a whole pot. It had been a chilly day and was getting even chillier outside. Eve pulled down the olive green teapot that had once been her mother's, and filled the bottom with pumpkin spice herbal tea. Why not, she thought to herself, it is almost Halloween after all.

"The wind is picking up outside," she said to the cats, who were winding themselves around her ankles. "Are you hungry?"

She opened the cupboard that held their canned cat food and they both started meowing in excitement, Sabrina most of all. After filling both of their dishes, Eve fixed herself a few slices of bread with cheese on top that she popped into the oven to toast. Steam poured out of the tea kettle as a gust of wind rattled the kitchen window. Darkness had fallen. Eve gazed out of her kitchen window at the moonlit backyard, waiting for the kettle to get to full boil and thinking about Chip Hendricks.

Seeing him today, the way he talked to her, the way he looked at her, had left her in a bit of a shambles. Her stomach felt tight and there was a pleasant lightheadedness she experienced whenever she relived the moments he had smiled at her or the sound of his voice.

Eve had suffered with a mad crush on Chip ever since they were in elementary school together. He had been dark and moody then, and only grown into a darker, moodier, extremely sexy man. Nothing had ever happened between them. In fact, Eve had always thought he either didn't notice her much or thought of her like he would an ugly duckling cousin. Her heart had never given up its romantic dream of him, and even though it had been a few years since she'd seen him, she wondered if maybe this time was the time they would finally end up together. As much as she loved her home and her job and her town, Chip Hendricks was the kind of man that could make a woman seriously consider changing her whole life.

A strong gust of wind hit her house at the exact same moment the boiling kettle started to scream and a loud knocking came at her front door. Eve jumped at the sounds, as did Hazel and Sabrina. Instead of darting off and hiding under the couch as cats normally did when frightened, Hazel and Sabrina ran to the front door meowing loudly. The knocking came again. Eve turned off the gas under the kettle and went to the door, a tiny piece of her wondering if she'd somehow conjured up Chip Hendricks on her front porch.

That particular hope was squelched as soon and she saw

the shock of red hair through the small window at the top of the great wooden front door. She looked more closely through the beveled glass and could make out a semi-familiar face. It took her a few moments, then it hit her, Mr. Murphy was waiting patiently in the wind. She opened the door.

"Mr. Murphy?"

"Hello!" He exclaimed. He was dressed in a casual dark brown leather jacket that looked more like daywear than anything that would keep a person warm. He had no gloves, scarf or hat. This late October wind held a frost in it and had turned his uncovered ears bright red. "Sorry for the intrusion, Miss St. Claire."

"Come out of the wind," Eve answered, stepping back and ushering him into the foyer.

"It gets cold once the sun goes down, doesn't it?" He said as he gratefully stepped inside. He rubbed his hands together, cupped them and blew into them, trying to warm up. He was quite windblown and all the tips of him were burning a bright red from the cold. He reminded Eve of an elf. A tall, well-built elf. His blue eyes twinkled as he smiled at her then looked down at Hazel and Sabrina who were madly twisting their furry bodies around his boots and pulling at the bottom of his jeans with their claws. "And who are these lovely beasties?" He asked. As if to introduce herself, Hazel leapt from the floor to his chest where he caught her deftly.

Eve looked at him with surprise. "She's never done that before. Hazel, come here." Eve reached for her.

"I don't mind," Mr. Murphy said, smiling at the purring feline in his arms and the plumper Sabrina who still curled around his feet, meowing loudly because she was unable to make the leap up like her sister. "Cats have a thing for me. Probably because I have a thing for them."

Taking in his chilled exterior, Eve thought it best to invite him to have some tea. She poured water from the kettle into her mother's teapot as Mr. Murphy settled himself at the kitchen table. He happily entertained both cats, who continued to beg for his attention, as he took in the large cozy kitchen with its copper pots and braided rugs and the great white gas stove where Eve prepared the tea.

"You have a beautiful house," he told her as she placed a tray holding the teapot, two cups, cream, sugar and two spoons on the table in front of him.

"Thank you," she smiled, then remembered the rumors. "Do you think it seems haunted now that you've seen it?" Eve meant it as a joke, kind of, but realized too late that she may sound overly sensitive.

He gave her an embarrassed smile. "Sorry, again, for that. I took it as a sort of fun, small town legend. I thought you knew about it. I don't go in for gossip."

Now she was embarrassed. It was hardly Mr. Murphy's fault. He'd just moved into town a few short months ago.

"Actually," he said as he took another look around the kitchen, "I think it's enchanting."

She shrugged nonchalantly, wanting to move on to another subject.

"How can I help you this evening, Mr. Murphy?"

"Please call me Atticus."

"Atticus?" A literary name.

Bashful, he took the cup she offered him and didn't look up. "Yes, Atticus," he gave a wistful sigh. "My mother wanted me to be brilliant."

Eve smiled and poured some tea into his cup, then her own.

"Call me Eve," she said. Then she tried again, "How can I help you tonight...Atticus?"

Happy to be off the subject of his name, Atticus sat back a bit in his chair to look at her. His jacket hung by the front door and he sported a robin's egg blue dress shirt, rolled up at the sleeves. The blue brought out his eyes and she liked how he wore his clothes, casual and a little dressed up all at the same time.

"I was wondering...well, the class and I were wondering...if you would like to come with us to the pumpkin patch day after tomorrow," he raised his brow with the question, "to pick pumpkins?"

Eve was stirring sugar into her tea, enjoying this chat with Atticus at her cozy kitchen table as the cold night enveloped the house. She was flattered at the invitation. Every year, for so many years, she had accompanied her father and his class on their traditional pumpkin picking field trip. She had assumed all of those traditions were gone forever. She started to answer, but was overcome by nostalgia. Big tears welled up in her eyes and she couldn't meet Atticus' gaze.

"I'm sorry," she whispered, fumbling for a napkin. Atticus pulled one from the holder on the table and placed it in her hand.

"Don't be sorry," he said softly. "I didn't mean to upset you. I thought...we thought...it might be fun." He gave her a crooked, hopeful look that made her smile through her tears.

"It does sound fun," she agreed, wiping her eyes and sniffing.

"So, you'll come?" Atticus looked genuinely delighted and Eve nodded at him as she blew her nose on the napkin. Atticus' expression changed suddenly to concern as he sniffed the air, "Do I smell smoke?"

"Cheese toast!" She exclaimed, and jumped up from the table.

Smoke poured from the oven when she opened the door. Atticus waved the smoke away with a dishtowel while Eve popped on an oven mitt and pulled the cookie sheet full of bubbling, blackened cheese out of the oven. She carried the smoking mess to the back porch while Atticus opened the windows from inside the kitchen. They both did their best to fan the smoke out of the windows, but the cold, fall wind did most of the work as it swept through the room.

After the excitement was over and the kitchen was back to normal, Eve fed the two pieces of cooled burned toast that had been her dinner to the cats and fixed four new pieces. Two for her and two for Atticus.

"Toasted cheese is delicious," Atticus declared. "It reminds me of Heidi."

"Me too!" Eve replied, "I made my Dad learn how to make it after he read me Heidi when I was little."

"Are these your parents?" Atticus stood with a fresh cup of tea in his hand looking at her parent's wedding picture on the wall.

"Yes." She set the egg timer to four minutes and joined him in the tiny hallway where the picture hung. He seemed taller, maybe because they were standing in such a small space together. She looked at the image of her mother, so small and delicate, with wide, pale eyes looking so lovingly up at her young father. His strong features, dark hair that tended to curl into a wild frizzy mess, and huge beaming smile that took over the room had already been part of his giant personality, even when they were so young.

"I've heard a lot about your father," Atticus said. "The kids tell me all kinds of stories about him."

She nodded, feeling the tears coming again. She didn't want to cry a second time in front of Atticus, so she chose not to talk at all. She just smiled and nodded.

"He was a great teacher," Atticus continued.

Eve swallowed hard and managed to answer, her voice faltering the tiniest bit, "Yes, he was. He really loved teaching." That was all she could manage to say without collapsing into a weeping mess. When she finally composed herself and glanced at Atticus he was still looking at the picture, seeming to understand the intimacy of the moment. He sensed her gaze and turned towards her, the gentle kindness in his eyes made her feel warm.

"You were lucky to have each other," he said, and he was right.

Chapter Five

"But won't my skin have to be green?" Eve asked as she stood in front of the full-length mirror.

"Technically, yes," Belinda answered.

"I don't know that I want to paint myself green." Eve screwed up her face at the idea as she looked at her reflection. She wore a long sleeved, mid-calf, tight fitting black dress, which Belinda had picked out as the basis of her Halloween costume. Belinda stood next to her wearing a white glittering cocktail dress that poofed out at her waist like a 1950's prom dress. She had found both of these gems at the thrift store and was presenting Eve with her Halloween costume concept.

Belinda wanted them to have partner costumes for her party, which wasn't a totally abhorrent idea to Eve. They were to be Glinda and Elphie, from the popular musical, Wicked. Eve would be Elphie, the green skinned wicked witch in the making with a long, black dress. Belinda would be the good witch, Glinda, with a white dress, tiara and magic wand.

Belinda was a talented seamstress, who made many of her most over the top and fashionably outlandish outfits either from scratch or from altering existing pieces. There was no question Belinda could make the appropriate alterations to these thrift store dresses and turn them into the desired witch outfits. Eve just wasn't sure she wanted to paint herself green as part of the bargain.

"We'll do it in a pretty way," Belinda explained. "I'll have to wear some glitter makeup to be Glinda. We'll just tint some of it green and you can use that."

Eve looked at her friend with some uncertainty. Was one shade of green really better than another?

"Don't worry," Belinda reassured her. "I know you want to look smashing for Chip." Belinda looked at her own stocky, abundantly curvy figure in the white cocktail dress and smoothed her hand over the material. "We all do."

"We all do? That's kind of pathetic, don't you think?" Eve asked.

"It's not pathetic," Belinda answered. "He's the biggest thing to visit this town in months! It gives us all something to shoot for, even though everyone knows you're the one with the best chance of hooking him."

Eve's stomach twisted in an excited knot at Belinda's comment, then she shook her head in denial. "I don't think that's true. Besides, is hooking a man something we should be worrying about as modern, intelligent women?"

"Hooking that man is any woman's dream, no matter how modern and intelligent she is," Belinda declared. "He's tall, dark, handsome, rich, I mean what else can you ask for?"

Funny. Kind. Well-read. Intelligent. A whole slew of attributes flooded through Eve's mind, but she didn't say them out loud. Tall, dark and handsome weren't anything to sneeze at and she had to admit that the idea of hooking Chip gave her serious butterflies.

"So, are you good with your costume?" Belinda asked.

Eve sighed and took another look at their reflection. She looked meek and pale in the black dress, especially next to Belinda with her bouncing white gown and the bright makeup she always wore. Still, the black dress did fit her well and it was better than dressing up as a clown or a French maid.

"Yes, seeing as you already bought it and I have no clue what else to wear, this will be just fine," Eve said.

"Great! I'll take it home and fix it up. You can try it on again before the party to make sure it works. And I have a hat you can use!"

Perfect. A witch's hat and green glitter makeup. Eve wasn't sure if her Halloween costume would be what you'd call man magnet material.

As they shopped at the local Walgreens for party decorations, Belinda chatted happily about all of the RSVPs flooding in for her party. She picked up a fake, plastic pumpkin with an electric, blinking light inside and showed it to Eve.

"What do you think?"

Eve wrinkled her nose. "Why don't you use real pumpkins?"

"I don't have enough time to carve a bunch of real pumpkins. Besides, they're not as bright." Belinda tossed five of the plastic, blinking pumpkins into her shopping cart. "Do you have pumpkins this year? You could bring them to the party...maybe we could have a pumpkin carving contest!" Belinda became instantly jazzed at her idea.

Eve shook her head, "No. I kind of failed at the garden this year. Some volunteer pumpkin plants grew, but I didn't take care of them." Belinda looked disappointed at Eve's confession. "I am going to that pumpkin patch south of town with the school tomorrow. I could pick some up for you," Eve offered.

"You're going to the pumpkin patch with the school?" Belinda asked.

Eve felt her cheeks get hot. She knew Mr. Mur–Atticus had only asked her to come along to be nice, because he knew about her taking part in the school traditions with her father for so long. But she had a feeling Belinda would read something into his invitation, like it was a budding romance.

"Yeah," Eve shrugged nonchalantly. "They asked if I wanted to come on their field trip, since I've gone with them for so many years." Belinda seemed to accept this explanation. Either that or she was distracted by the several options of Halloween garland she was inspecting; black cats, ghosts or witch hats. "That reminds me," Eve recalled, "Did you know that my Dad told everyone our house was haunted?"

Belinda looked at her with some curiosity. "Yes, you didn't?"

"No!" Eve was half amused and half frustrated. "Since when?"

"Since...always, really," Belinda responded, searching her mind for the answer. "I've always known your house as the haunted house."

"You can't be serious," Eve flat out denied her friend's statement.

"Everyone knows it's the haunted house," Belinda continued. Suddenly, her eyes flew open. "It would be a great place for a Halloween party!" She reached out and squeezed Eve's arm as she jumped tiny jumps up and down in glee.

"No," Eve answered automatically, shaking her head to emphasize the point. She couldn't imagine anything more awful than a bunch of costumed adults drinking and playing stupid Halloween games in her house. She was not a party kind of person and it was not a party kind of house.

Belinda's face fell. "Oh, but I already gave out the invitations with my address." She looked a little heartbroken.

Relieved to be off the hook, Eve tried to cheer her up. "Your house is great for parties. You've got that big basement room and the great sound system."

Belinda perked up a little at the compliment and smiled. "You're right. My house will be fine. But next year you need to throw a party! Nothing more fun than a Halloween party at a haunted house."

"My house is not haunted," Eve insisted.

Belinda nodded condescendingly and patted her friend's arm. "Okay, Evie, whatever you say."

Later that night Eve relaxed on her lumpy yet comfortable living room sofa. Hazel and Sabrina curled up next to her, one on either side, both of them breathing deeply as they slept. With a hot cup of pumpkin spice tea in one hand and a worn copy of Dickens' Nicholas Nickleby that she had grabbed from the bookstore in the other, Eve was happily settled in for the night. The weather had cleared up today and though it was cold, almost freezing, the night sky was brilliant, thick and black and hung with a giant globe of a moon that lit up her trees and yard in a cool blue light.

Eve tried to focus on reading, but was continually interrupted by her thoughts. Foremost on her mind was Chip. This distressed her, as she believed she had spent far too much of her life dreaming and worrying and fussing over that man. This was nothing new. He had always gotten under her skin and this time was no different than when they were in school together so many years ago. What distressed her about the whole situation was she was fairly certain he hardly ever thought of her at all. All of her fantasies, good or bad, about meeting up with him at the Halloween party were just that, fantasies. It was entirely possible Chip wouldn't even show up at the party. He was famous for being aloof and noncommittal.

Eve sighed and took a sip of her tea. Sabrina rolled onto

her back and snuggled her face into Eve's thigh, asking for a tummy rub. Placing her book face down in her lap, Eve stroked the cat's rounded belly and Sabrina rewarded her with loud purring. A sound like boards creaking came from upstairs. Eve paused and listened.

The creaking stopped. It was the house settling, she was certain. This was an old house, over 130 years old. You can't live in an old house and not hear it occasionally creak and moan. She'd heard these sounds her whole life and never thought twice about them until now.

Sabrina rolled over and sat up, looking at Eve haughtily with her deep gold eyes. Her purring had stopped abruptly when Eve stopped stroking her belly. The cat butted her soft head against Eve's shoulder and pushed hard, trying to get her attention.

"Do you hear anything funny?" Eve asked Sabrina as she gently scratched behind the cat's ears. Sabrina answered with more purring. The commotion woke up Hazel who immediately wanted Eve's attention as well. Eve placed her tea on the side table and pet both cats to their great delight. She looked around her well-worn living room.

In addition to the lumpy green and yellow floral sofa where she sat, there was a giant, dark green, lumpy chair and an ottoman to match. The well made and roughly used heavy wood coffee table sat in the center of the room right in the middle of a large, blue and green Persian style rug. An antique secretary sat against one wall and the large original fireplace took up most of another wall. It wasn't usable anymore, because the chimneys were too delicate to risk starting a fire, but the deep green tiled hearth and antique wooden mantle with a long beveled mirror across the top were gorgeous even without a fire in the fireplace. Tall, fat candles were set up inside the fireplace and Eve lit them on nights like this with beautiful results. In addition to the furnishings there were various knick knacks, tons of framed photos, many of her and her father, and books, of course, books everywhere.

Eve smiled. Her home had never made her feel anything except warm and happy. There was no way it was haunted and, if it was, she had never noticed. All she could feel in this space was love, the love of her parents, the years she'd grown up here with her father reading to her and cooking and laughing, the comfort she'd felt returning home even after his death. It was a good house and she refused to let some goofy rumors make her think otherwise. In that moment, she categorically dismissed any thought of haunting. This was her home and Eve could never imagine anything bad ever happening to her here.

Chapter Six

"A field of ripe pumpkins under a bright blue sky is a true delight, wouldn't you say?" Atticus asked as they tromped across the rough surface of the harvested cornfield towards the pumpkin patch. The tall, green corn plants of summer were long gone and all that was left were the golden brown dried stalks and husks that had been chopped down and stripped of their corn by giant harvesters during their peak ripeness.

Owned by the Fischer family, this corn farm always set aside three acres to grow pumpkins and sell locally for Halloween. The pumpkins were dirt cheap compared to those sold in the store. The catch was, customers had to pick their purchases themselves and the closest anyone could get to the pumpkin patch was to park on the road and march over the uneven fields of corn surrounding it on all sides. Nobody was completely sure why the Fischers didn't plant their pumpkins along the road for easier access. Maybe it deterred late night teenage pumpkin thieves, or maybe they just thought people needed to get more exercise. Eve didn't mind, walking to the patch was part of what made it such a grand adventure.

She, Atticus, and his entire English class were on this adventure together today. The smell of turned earth, decaying corn plants and crisp, cold country air was a distinctly fall experience that she thoroughly enjoyed. From the looks on the kid's faces, they were enjoying it too. So was Atticus. The fresh air invigorated him, made him even more animated, and it turned the tip of his nose and tops of his ears pink, a look Eve was beginning to find charming.

"I see them!" He exclaimed, pointing for the other's benefit in the direction they needed to go. "Look at them, like happy orange orbs just waiting to be gathered up and taken home." He waved his long arms wildly towards the patch, encouraging his charges, "Run! Run, children, before they escape!"

Eve had to laugh as the children bounded off towards the patch in the distance, shouting and squealing. Under Atticus' direction these normally moody and sullen teenagers had turned into a gang of bright eyed, spirited explorers. On the bus ride from school, he'd led them all in silly songs until everyone was joining in the fun. He'd joked and sang and cajoled the whole lot of them into belly laughs. She couldn't remember the last time she had laughed that hard. The real delight, however, was seeing the kids lighten up and enjoy just being kids.

Atticus fell into step next to her, keeping one eye on his class from a distance.

"You're really wonderful with them," Eve said.

"Thank you." The pink from his ears spreading to his cheeks. "Coming from you that's quite a compliment."

"I'm sure my Dad would have approved of how you are with the kids." She was sure. The way Atticus engaged with this class reminded her more than just a little bit of her father, how he kept them entertained and learning all the time.

"I can't take all the credit," Atticus said. "I get very excited on field trips and I love anything orange, so for me today is a win-win!" He tilted his tousled red hair towards her and winked, making her laugh again. "And don't forget my new shoes!" He exclaimed, lifting his right foot up high in front of him so she could see his bright orange tennis shoes.

"How could I forget those shoes?"

He'd already shown them off three or four times on the bus ride only to receive protests and groans from the whole group. She couldn't tease him too much, she'd worn her own goofy Halloween sweatshirt with a giant, toothless pumpkin on the front to get in the spirit of the whole trip.

They continued walking, falling into a comfortable silence. She liked Atticus. He was funny and kind and she was glad he had taken over her father's class. Something about him made her feel like they'd known each other longer than only a few days.

"You still miss him, I imagine?" Atticus asked, breaking the friendly silence.

"My Dad?"

He nodded.

"Oh, yes, very much." A pang of grief went through her chest, but she was surprised to find she didn't start crying.

"What about your Mom?" Atticus asked.

"Oh, my Mom passed away when I was three," she responded. Atticus made a sympathetic noise, but didn't say anything. "How about you?" Eve asked, "Are your parents near here?"

Atticus shook his head 'no', "My Dad has never been around, I don't know anything about him." It was Eve's turn to be sympathetic. "And my Mom passed away about four years ago."

"I'm so sorry," Eve offered. Atticus nodded and looked into the distance as they walked.

"I have a younger sister who lives near here. That's why I transferred," he told her.

After that, there was nothing much to say, she knew. He completely understood her pain and learning this shifted something between them, it made walking quietly next to each other feel even more normal. She had an urge to reach out and touch his shoulder.

"Mr. Murphy! Mr. Murphy!" One of the boys, Simon, stood at the edge of the pumpkin patch about 30 feet away holding a bright orange pumpkin high over his head. "I found mine!"

"Excellent, Simon!" Atticus waved at the boy and turned to her, suddenly playful. "Ready to find your magic pumpkin, m'lady?" Eve nodded and Atticus gallantly offered his hand. She took it and he led her into the pumpkins like she was a princess and he was her knight in shining armor.

An hour later they were back at the school bus, laden with their round, orange bounty. Eve had realized that she couldn't buy a lot of pumpkins for Belinda's party because she didn't have any way to carry them all back to the bus. Atticus had offered to carry two for her and enlisted a few of the older boys who were only getting one for themselves to help her out by using their free arm to carry her extras. All in all she'd managed to procure six for Belinda's party and that seemed like enough.

The controlled chaos of loading two dozen teenagers and their pumpkins onto a school bus after romping outside in the fresh air was quite a sight to behold. Eve stood guard at the back end of the bus watching traffic. This road wasn't especially busy, but she felt like it was safer to make sure none of the kids stepped out past the edge of the bus, just in case. As she waited, a dark grey, shining sports car slowed down and pulled in to park behind them. The muffled thumping of music playing inside the car caught her attention. She peered at the driver who unexpectedly flashed a smile at her and instantly Eve knew who it was, Chip.

Chip turned off the engine and opened the door, emerging from the slick car looking like a man modeling a well cut suit, or the sports car itself, or a fancy brand of scotch in a magazine. He looked that good, like a scotch ad in a magazine.

"Chip," Eve greeted him, a flush of excitement making her smile like a goon.

"Hey," he said, meandering towards her.

Under his gaze she became acutely aware of her attire. She had on worn jeans, old tennis shoes and her sweatshirt, which, in addition to the smiling pumpkins, had the words 'Hocus Pocus' scrawled across the top. She hadn't put on much makeup and just swept her hair into a quick ponytail before heading to the school this morning. In short, she didn't feel quite prepared to face Chip Hendricks with his over the top, scotch ad good looks.

"You've been picking pumpkins?" He asked as he reached her, his voice was so deep and smoldering, even when he was talking about vegetables.

"Yeah." Eve had all but forgotten about the kids, the school bus, and even Atticus, when Chip got out of his car. "It's a school field trip."

"You volunteer at the school?" Chip looked over the back end of the bus and taking in the kids now visible in the windows, jumping and singing and generally being crazy.

"Oh, well not really." Eve couldn't find the words to explain exactly how she'd ended up here. "It's just a sometimes thing...and I needed some pumpkins...for Belinda's party." Over explaining was a great way to look appealing, she thought to herself.

Chip grinned and, much to her chagrin, she found herself blushing.

"All right, Eve, we're rea–" Atticus jogged around the end of the bus and stopped short when he saw Chip. Chip didn't move from where he stood, which Eve suddenly noticed was quite close to her. He only turned his head and gave Atticus a once over, pausing for a beat on his very orange tennis shoes.

"Have you met each other?" Eve tried to break the ice. Chip didn't answer and Atticus shook his head 'no'. "Atticus, this is Chip Hendricks. We grew up together." She motioned towards Chip and Atticus stepped forward as if he might try to shake Chip's hand.

"I'm Atticus Murphy–" he started.

"He's the new English teacher," Eve interrupted. "He's teaching my father's class." She wanted Chip to understand why she was on this middle school field trip, but her words only added to the awkward vibe and nobody moved or said anything for a few moments. Before she knew what was happening, her nerves overtook her senses and she started explaining even harder, "I used to go on these trips with this class and Atticus, well the class really, invited me to come today, which is great because I needed some pumpkins for Belinda's party, but I couldn't carry them all back, and now that I think about it I don't know how I'm going to carry them all home because I walked to the school..." her voice trailed off a little and she let out a nervous laugh.

"I'll give you a lift," Chip said.

Eve's stomach did a little flip.

"Oh," she tried not to stammer. "You don't need to do that. I mean, following the bus all the way back to the school, isn't that a little out of your way?"

He chuckled and shook his head. "No, I mean I'll give you a lift from here. Put the pumpkins in the trunk." He pulled a key fob out of his pocket and pushed a button. The trunk on the sports car opened smoothly. "I insist," he added.

Eve blushed at her misunderstanding. Of course he didn't need to follow the school bus back to the school. She turned to Atticus, who remained quiet nearby.

"Well, um, I guess that would be okay?" She posed the question to Atticus. It was hard to ignore the look of disappointment that flashed across his face, but it disappeared in a nanosecond and turned to one of gracious acceptance. She was thankful to him for not making her feel guilty.

"Of course, no problem," Atticus said. "I'll just get your pumpkins for you."

A few minutes later she slid into the soft, leather seat of Chip's sports car. The seat was so low she could barely see over the dashboard, but she could see Atticus standing next to the bus. She waved at him and smiled, and he smiled and waved back. Then Chip started the car, revved the engine and pulled around the school bus, leaving it behind in a flash.

Chapter Seven

By the time Chip parked the car in front of her house, Eve felt dizzy. The swift power of the car, the heavy scent of fine leather and Chip's cologne, the strangeness of watching her home town whisk by through tinted windows, people she knew gawking as they sped past them towards her house, all of this made her head spin. The thing that she couldn't wrap her mind around, the thing that put her right over the edge into a lightheadedness, was her proximity to Chip and the way he was resting his hand on her thigh after each time he shifted the car into a different gear.

The first time he'd done it, she thought surely it must be an accident. This was a small car and maybe he didn't know where her leg was positioned. After the second time, she knew he was doing it on purpose and her heart pounded in her chest even as she stayed completely cool on the outside. She was riding in an expensive sports car with Chip Hendricks. He was taking her home. Of course it was no big deal that his hand lay on her thigh, moving slowly higher and higher as they got closer to their destination. No big deal at all.

Eve didn't know what to say, so she said nothing at all. She let her body sink into the leather seat that was built for comfort, looked out the window and let Chip's hand move where it wanted. Her body reacted strongly to his touch and she felt powerless to stop him.

He parked in front of her house. As the rumble of the engine stopped, she turned to look at him, determined to invite him in for a drink or dinner or something. He was already leaning towards her and his mouth clamped on hers before she could say a word.

Her first reaction was to pull away, but Chip slipped his free hand quickly around the nape of her neck, holding her to him. The hand on her thigh pushed further between her legs and gripped her firmly. His lips were hot and insistent, but not unpleasant. Once Eve was over the initial surprise of being kissed, she relaxed into it and the pleasure of the whole thing spread through her body. All of her sensations were alive with the feel of him, the smell of him, the plushness surrounding her and the hard warmth of his hand between her legs, his mouth against hers.

"Can I come in?" He pulled away from their kiss long enough to ask her the question in a husky whisper.

"Sure." Eve tried to remember if she'd left anything embarrassing laying around in her house. He came at her again for another kiss, this time pushing his tongue into her mouth. When she responded with her tongue, he made a little sound with his throat. She attempted to keep up with his fervor, but space in the car was cramped. "We'll have more room inside," she said during a breathing spell.

Chip laughed a little and leaned back in his seat. "Right, let's go."

As they walked up the path to the door, he put his hand on the small of her back, then let it slide down until it cupped her behind. Eve flushed and glanced up and down her street, wondering if any of her neighbors could see them.

"God, your house is creepy looking," Chip said as they walked up the front steps. The afternoon was turning to dusk and the clouds in the sky were no longer white and puffy, but grey and ominous, providing a rather gothic background for the peaked roof. The antique door loomed in front of them and Hazel and Sabrina sat in the front window, meowing at them excitedly. Still, Eve didn't think it was all that creepy.

"No it's not," she answered, a little offended.

"You have cats?" He asked, an air of disgust in his tone.

"Yes," Eve unlocked the front door. "You don't like cats?" He followed her into the foyer and pulled the door shut behind him.

"I'm allergic."

"Oh," said Eve. Right at that moment, Hazel and Sabrina rounded the corner from the living room into the foyer, meowing loudly and throwing themselves at the stranger, like always. "I'm sorry, I didn't know," Eve apologized.

"No problem," Chip responded, stiffening just a little as they wrapped around his ankles.

Any moment she knew they would start lovingly caressing him with their claws and probably snagging the pant legs of his suit. Chip sneezed. Eve cringed. The dizzying feeling of their magical ride home was dissipating quickly.

"Come on, girls." Eve scooped first Hazel then Sabrina up in her arms. She took the wriggling sister cats to the kitchen and dropped them gently on the floor. She closed the door as quickly as possible, barely getting it shut before Hazel stuck her head through the opening. The door kept the cats away from them, but it did nothing to stop their wailing at being locked up against their will.

Eve whirled around to return to Chip in the foyer, but cried out when she found him standing right behind her in the cramped hallway between her kitchen and her living room.

"I couldn't stay away," he said, leaning in to kiss her. But just before their lips touched he turned his face away quickly and sneezed again. Eve winced. She looked down at the front of her sweatshirt, which was now covered in black cat hair.

"I need to change," she said.

Chip put his hand behind her ear on the wall, right next to her parent's wedding picture, effectively blocking her escape. It was a sexy move, and a little unnerving. Eve couldn't tell if she liked it a lot or didn't like it at all.

"Or," he sniffled a few times as he slipped his other hand under her sweatshirt, caressing her stomach and pushing the sweatshirt up her body. "You could just take it off."

Eve's heart was pounding out of her chest. She was frozen. The feel of his warm, heavy hand sliding up her skin held her hostage. She gazed at him, Chip Hendricks, high school heartthrob. His thick, dark hair was disheveled and falling forward over his eyes. His beautiful lips were set in that crazy smirky sexy grin he had been giving her since they were kids, and she could tell he was moving in for another kiss. She made the decision right then that she was ready. This was Chip, after all. She had wanted him to want her for as long as she could remember. There was nothing more to think about, was there?

Chip's hand reached the sensitive area just below her bra and she inhaled sharply. That's when Eve felt something move against her back and there was a bump and a loud crash of glass shattering on the wood floor at their feet. Chip jumped back as Eve gave a cry of surprise. She looked down to see her parent's wedding photo smashed on the floor. The antique wood frame was broken in three pieces and the glass lay everywhere in shards.

"Oh, no!" Eve kneeled on the floor and began gingerly removing pieces of glass from the delicate face of the photo.

"I didn't touch it, I swear," Chip said, taking a few steps back. He sneezed loudly and cursed under his breath.

Big, fat tears welled up in Eve's eyes and she wiped them away with the sleeves of her sweatshirt so she could see what she was doing. How could she be so careless? The tears came full on now, she couldn't hold them back. It was just a photo, but she was overwhelmed at the prospect of it being destroyed.

Chip sneezed again, then he cleared his throat, "Maybe I should go now."

Eve didn't look up, she was too embarrassed. She just nodded and gave him a weak wave goodbye. As soon as she heard the door click shut, she sat down carefully next to the mess on the floor and let go with a good, old fashioned, sob.

When she finally cleaned everything up, her nose was red and her eyes were puffy. She let the sister cats out of the kitchen. They were incensed at their earlier treatment and let her know in no uncertain terms that they required a lot of love and attention to make up for her actions.

Eve sat on the couch with one cat on each side of her and inspected the wedding photo. She had been able to salvage it without damaging the main part, the actual images of her smiling, joyful parents. There was only slight damage on the bottom edge of the old picture and for that, Eve was very thankful. She placed the photo carefully on the coffee table. She would either fix the broken frame or find a replacement.

"That crisis was avoided, but can I fix the mess with Chip?" She asked the sister cats as she sat back and used both hands to rub behind their ears, one hand for each cat. Sabrina turned her wide, golden eyes to Eve and made a growling sound. Eve laughed, "What? You don't like him?" Sabrina turned away, refusing to give any further opinion. "What about you, Hazel?" Eve asked the smaller cat. Hazel looked at her and blinked a few times before putting her nose in the air and turning away. "Oh, I see," Eve said. "That's two 'no' votes." She sighed. "I'm talking to my cats again. Not a good sign."

Eve had to admit to herself, after the moment had passed, she was a little relieved nothing more had happened with Chip. Even though the incident had ended in embarrassment and near disaster. Now that it was over and she had time to think about it, she would be more comfortable postponing sleeping together, if they were going to sleep together, until they at least went out on a few dates. She wasn't really a hook up kind of girl.

"I'll just have to explain that to him," she told the sister cats. "If he's looking for a hook up, he'll need to look somewhere else." This made her feel better and she decided she would sleep on it and everything would look better in the morning. Just as she stood to go upstairs and get ready for bed, a thought struck her and she declared in dismay to her cat audience, "Belinda's pumpkins!"

Chapter Eight

The message on her voicemail was charming, full of nervous pauses and an apology for being so awkward. At the first sound of a male voice in the message, Eve's senses had perked up, thinking it was Chip. Almost immediately, however, she realized it was Atticus. Not that she was completely disappointed, but her heart sank a little bit knowing that Chip still hadn't contacted her after their make out fiasco yesterday.

On the other hand, Atticus had left the message to invite her to the Halloween Pageant at the school. This was a new development that the kids had pushed to put together. He told her in the message that they specifically wanted him to call and invite her to the event.

She took off early from the bookstore and walked to the school, enjoying the fine fall afternoon. She had decided to dress up a little today and was wearing her burnt orange and black plaid miniskirt with black tights and a matching burnt orange sweater. At least her outfit looked festive, even if she was feeling a little off kilter.

The school was abuzz with kids running around in

costume and their parents and siblings waiting in line outside the auditorium. Eve stayed near the wall, not diving into the merry crowd. She'd never been one for large groups, preferring to stay on the perimeter and people watch. Eve saw Mrs. Runyon and waved 'hello'. She also saw the principal, Gary Sunder, and many of the teachers that she knew were friends of her father.

Then there was Atticus.

Taller than almost everyone there, he stood behind a table where several of the kids were handling ticket and refreshment sales. Like all school events, the Halloween Pageant was also a fundraiser and there were Rice Krispie treats, chocolate brownies and popcorn balls dyed orange with food coloring and stuffed with candy corns, all available for 50 cents each. Atticus wore a light orange dress shirt, a purple tie with a cartoon of a fat black cat down the front and jeans. She couldn't see from where she was, but she guessed he also had on his bright orange tennis shoes. His collar was unbuttoned and the tie was loose, the sleeves of his shirt were pushed up to his elbows. His arms seemed long and leanly muscled as she watched him point and direct, answering several questions at once from different directions and generally being involved and competent.

She liked watching Atticus in his teacher role. He had such good humor and being in charge made him shine.

He saw her, locked his eyes on hers and broke into a smile so wide she couldn't help but smile back. He bent down and said something to one of the ticket salesmen then stepped on and over two empty chairs that were blocking his exit. Making his way through the crowded waiting area, Atticus kept his eyes trained on her, the same beaming smile on his face. It seemed like a warm, glowing spotlight was on her as he got closer. She felt her cheeks heat up under the attention.

Then he was there, standing very close because the crowd

behind him didn't allow much room. She looked up into his face, his beard was nicely trimmed and his red hair was artfully tousled. He smelled warm and spicy, with a hint of mint. He smiled down at her, his blue eyes bright and happy.

"You're here," he said.

"I'm here!" She made a 'ta-da' movement with her hands.

"You look very nice in orange," he said.

"So do you," she responded. Without thinking, Eve reached up and flipped his tie with her finger. "Nice tie."

Something moved between them, an electrical current, a moment of intensity that was palpable. She saw it on his face and felt it in her own body. His blue eyes darkened with it. For a split second Eve was positive Atticus was going to bend down and kiss her right here in the waiting room of the school auditorium. He didn't. Instead he let his gaze move to her mouth for just a moment before it flicked back up to her eyes. Then she felt his hand take hers.

"Come with me." He led her through the crowd towards the door leading to the backstage of the auditorium.

She followed Atticus through the door, into a narrow, dark hall then behind the heavy curtains that stretched high into the catwalk above. There were excited teens everywhere, some donned headsets and were dressed from head to toe in black, some were obviously in costume wearing stage makeup, some of them wore street clothes and it was hard to determine if they were supposed to be there or if they had just snuck back to take part in the festive chaos of the pageant.

"She's here!" Atticus announced to anyone in earshot. The excited conversations ebbed for a moment as all of the students looked at Eve. She lifted a hand in 'hello', not sure why Atticus felt the need to show her off to the whole cast and crew. "Who would like to show her to her seat?" He asked. A gangly, dark haired youth with a nose he had not yet grown into, wearing a jacket he'd outgrown two years ago, stepped forward.

"I will, Mr. Murphy," the youth said. His voice was far too deep for his face and body.

"My seat?" Eve asked, confused.

Atticus looked at her, his eyes twinkling with the secret. "The kids have something special prepared." Eve started to ask what this was all about, when the gangly young man gallantly offered her his arm. "James will show you to your seat, Miss St. Claire," Atticus said formally. He squeezed her hand warmly as he passed her off to James. She politely took the boy's arm and let him lead her out onto the stage, down the stairs that led into the half filled audience and to a chair that was one of four marked off with orange crepe paper located front row, center stage.

James cleared the crepe paper from one of the chairs and swept his arm dramatically towards it, indicating she should sit down.

"Thank you," she said.

"You're very welcome, Madame. Enjoy the show." James gave her a half bow and bounded back onto the stage, disappearing behind the curtain.

The theatre behind her filled quickly as the crowd from the waiting area continued to file in and choose their seats. A headset wearing teen walked onto the stage and tested the mic that stood on a stand in the middle. The spotlights went through a series of tests and the seated audience buzzed with conversation. Principal Sunder and his wife were shown by James to two of the crepe paper chairs, which left one open next to Eve. She wondered who was supposed to sit there. She could take a guess, but decided not to let her imagination get away with her, she would just wait and see.

A few minutes went by as Eve made small talk about the weather with Mrs. Sunder. The house lights blinked off and on and a young girl's voice came over the speakers asking that everyone take their seats as the Halloween Pageant was about to begin. The audience obeyed, conversations tapered off and almost everyone got settled. Still the seat next to Eve remained empty.

Then it was time. The house lights turned off, leaving them in total darkness for a few seconds. A spotlight flicked on, illuminating Atticus standing at the microphone.

"Good evening," Atticus spoke into the mic, his voice booming through the room. "Thank you for coming." He looked into the unlit audience as he continued, "Tonight we are happy to present the very first annual Halloween Pageant at Fielding Middle School." A ripple of applause and a few random hoots from students rose from the crowd. "This is an event that the students voted for, planned and are performing today," Atticus dropped his gaze so he was looking directly at Eve in the front row, "in loving memory of Albert St. Claire. We hope you enjoy the performance."

Eve gasped at the mention of her father. Atticus stepped away from the mic as applause and cheers filled the room. He walked quickly across the stage, hopped off the front and landed right in front of Eve. He sat in the chair next to her and even though they were virtually in the dark, she could feel his smile. She blinked back tears.

James approached the microphone from backstage. A few kids shouted his name from the audience and he waved sheepishly in their general direction. He adjusted the microphone to his height and pulled a piece of paper out of his too small jacket pocket.

"I am going to read from this cause I don't want to mess it up," he said into the mic, more cheers from his buddies in the crowd. He waved them off, cleared his throat and began, "School sucks." Laughter erupted from the audience. James waited for it to quiet down then began again, "School sucks."

He held up a finger to stop any reaction. "Not always...just sometimes. But there are teachers who have a gift for making school fun." Here he grinned at the audience. "Not always...just sometimes." More laughter. "Seriously, though, sometimes you get a teacher who makes learning interesting, that makes you look forward to going to class and even makes homework exciting. For many of us here at Fielding Middle School, Mr. St. Claire was that teacher."

Eve's heart swelled with pride and she had to swallow hard to hold down her tears.

"Why Halloween?" James continued, gesturing towards a backdrop that lit up behind him showing a huge moon with the silhouette of a witch on a broom, a few giant jack-o'lanterns and an old house that looked a lot like hers painted to look like it was in the distance. "Mr. St. Claire loved Halloween. Even more than Christmas! He taught English and he loved stories. He loved the scary ones and the sad ones and the funny ones. He wasn't afraid to let us write things that weren't pretty and happy. He taught us to not be afraid of anything and to read and learn and express ourselves in whatever ways worked for us."

Tears rolled down Eve's cheeks. She couldn't stop them. She felt Atticus pat her hand with his and she turned her palm up so she could hold his hand and share this moment with him.

"But more than anything," James said, putting his paper back in his pocket. He knew the next bit by heart. "We dedicate this Halloween Pageant to the memory of Mr. St. Claire, because the biggest reason he loved Halloween was he believed, and he wanted us to believe, that life is full of magic."

And with that, the pageant began.

It was brilliant. There were paper mâché pumpkins, witches and warlocks, ghosts and goblins, a group of robots for some reason, skits, jokes, singing performances by the school choir and a rather frightening reading by James himself of The Tell Tale Heart. Eve took it all in with enormous pleasure. Atticus did too, and he held her hand until it was time to applaud.

Afterward, her heart was full in many ways. Memories of her father wrapped together with scenes from the pageant and the powerful feeling of having been raised by such a good man lifted her spirits. Her hand still felt the warmth of Atticus' touch and she allowed a sparkle of romantic possibility to flicker across her mind. He was attractive and fun and kind, but was she interested in him romantically? Was he interested in her? She wore a quiet smile as she approached her house, ready to spend some time with the sister cats and think about her day. As she got closer, her smile faded.

Six orange pumpkins had been placed in a line by her front door. Belinda's pumpkins.

Eve looked around for signs of Chip or his car, but didn't see any. Her mood fell and she was inexplicably bothered by the sight of the perfectly innocent pumpkins. Was he trying to be cute? Or sexy? Was he trying to seduce her or dump her? She didn't know and, what was most confusing, she found that she didn't really care.

Chapter Nine

Halloween fell on Saturday this year, which always made for the most fun possible. Kids were out of school and able to attend whatever festivities they desired and go trick-or-treating until as late as they desired, because there was no school in the morning. Most adults had the weekend free, so their parties tended to be more boisterous than a weekday Halloween party. Plus, they had all day to decorate and get their costumes in order.

That's what Eve was doing. It was just before noon on Saturday and she was getting ready to go to Belinda's house and help her decorate for the big Halloween blast. The day was a perfect Halloween day, overcast and windy with the hint of a storm brewing, exactly what you would expect to conjure up some trouble.

Trouble wasn't something Eve was hoping for, however. She had some trepidation about seeing Chip at the party. He still hadn't called her or come by after dropping off the pumpkins at her door. She wasn't sure how she was supposed to interpret his behavior, but she knew it put her a little on edge. There was nothing she could do about it now, though.

Belinda was expecting her to be at the party and Eve had no real excuse not to go. She owed it to her friend, even if Chip showed up or didn't show up and ruined her evening one way or another.

Eve had packed everything she needed to change into her costume, which Belinda had finished sewing for her and had ready at her house. All that was left was to load the pumpkins into her car. She was saying goodbye to the sister cats in the kitchen where they'd just eaten a special treat of tuna fish when both of them perked their ears and ran to the living room window, meowing like crazy.

"What is it?" She asked them, following them to the window to see what had grabbed their attention. She pulled back the curtain just in time to see Atticus climbing her front steps. He wore jeans and a brown sport coat, an orange and black striped scarf wrapped jauntily around his neck and, of course, those orange sneakers. He saw her in the window and waved, holding up a book for her to see. A tiny thrill shimmered through her and she went to the door to let him in, the sister cats were already there.

"Happy Halloween!" Atticus greeted her, beaming. Hazel immediately leapt into his arms like she had the first time she'd met him. "Hello, you beautiful beasties!" He scooped Sabrina up so he could hold both purring cats. Eve watched in amazement.

"I've never seen them take to someone like they've taken to you," she said, stepping back so Atticus could come in the house.

"Well, I must admit, today I'm carrying a secret weapon." He handed her the book he was carrying. It was a well worn edition, covered in a blue, cloth like material with gold lettering across the front that read 'To Kill a Mockingbird'. "I brought that for you. I found it in the bottom drawer of your Dad's desk and thought you might want it."

Eve took the book and smoothed her hand over the cover. "To Kill a Mockingbird," she laughed in surprise at the coincidence of Atticus sharing the name of the main character. "How ironic!"

"I know, that's what I thought," Atticus said with a chuckle. He maneuvered the sister cats around in his arms so he could pull a small bag out of his jacket pocket. Hazel and Sabrina started purring so hard Eve could almost feel the vibrations from where she stood. "And this," he turned the bag so she could see it, "Is my secret weapon. I got these for my sister's cat. I'm going by there tomorrow. I thought maybe you wouldn't mind if I gave your beauties some." The bag read 'Catnip Puffs' and the sister cats were climbing all over the poor man trying to get at it.

"Yes, that's fine," Eve laughed at their crazed reaction. "You better give it to them soon, before they eat you alive!"

After he distributed a few puffs on the living room floor for the cats to attack and tucked the rest of the bag neatly back into his jacket pocket, Eve invited him to have a cup of tea. She figured she had time for a cup of tea before leaving for the party. Standing at the kitchen counter, Atticus took note of the remains of the picture frame that lay there waiting to be glued.

"Have a little accident?" He asked.

"Yes," Eve felt suddenly uncomfortable talking about the picture falling off the wall with Atticus, given what she'd been doing when it fell. She pulled the kettle off of the stove and poured hot water into their mugs. Atticus picked up the largest piece of the picture frame.

"Next time you could try taking out the screws before pulling it off the wall. That way the frame won't break," he offered, inspecting the back of the broken frame.

"I didn't pull it off," Eve said, blushing a little. "I just, kind of, bumped it."

"Really?" Atticus peered at the screws sticking out the back of the frame. "Is this the frame from your parent's wedding picture?" She nodded and he stepped into the small hallway holding the broken frame up next to where it had detached from the wall. "Hmm," he mumbled to himself, looking puzzled.

"What is it?" Eve joined him in the cramped hallway and immediately became very aware of how close their bodies were to touching. She had wild mixed feelings, remembering kissing Chip right here in this spot, and experiencing a tiny thrill from standing so near Atticus with his warm, spicy scent.

"It's just..." Atticus looked once again at the back of the picture frame and at the holes in the wall where it had hung, "I don't know how it could have possibly fallen off with these screws put in this way. It looks like it was very sturdy. Normally you would have to yank on it with two hands to pull this kind of mounting out of the wall like this."

"You would?" Eve hadn't taken time to look over the damage yet. She'd assumed the picture had hung like a normal picture on a wire or hanging on a single nail in the wall. She inspected what Atticus was looking at more closely. There were two long screws that had been screwed straight through the top two corners of the frame and into the wall. Sturdy. Very sturdy.

"Well, maybe it was the old plaster," Atticus shrugged. "Do you need any help hanging this back up?" He turned towards her when he asked and their faces were very near. He waited for her to answer, and while he waited his blue eyes wandered to her lips and back. Eve was frowning, still wondering what could have made the picture fall the other evening. She hadn't touched it and Chip, even if he had bumped it, which he denied, definitely hadn't grabbed hold of it and pulled with two hands. His hands had been other places. She noticed Atticus was still waiting for a reply.

"Oh, no thank you," she said, letting her eyes wander down his jaw line to his mouth. She noticed how nicely his beard was trimmed and felt a tingle up her spine. "I think I'm going to buy another one." Because they were so close, she spoke softly. She saw something flicker through his eyes. Desire?

"Was the picture damaged?" He asked, his own voice low and a little husky.

"No."

"That's good."

They stood there for a few moments, the air crackling between them. Eve wondered what it would be like to kiss him. Then Atticus seemed to make a decision. He took a deep breath and pushed gently past her back into the kitchen.

"I'm glad nothing got ruined," he said as he carefully placed the broken frame back on the counter.

Eve remained in the small hallway, breathless, trying to compose herself. Something caught the corner of her eye and she turned to see the sister cats sitting in the opening to the living room, staring at her. They were both completely still, their eyes glowing yellow, their tails flicking in unison behind them. They had the same odd expressions, as if they were asking her a silent question.

"What?" Eve whispered at them. Then Hazel looked at Sabrina and Sabrina looked back. They came to a mutual decision, turned their backs on her, and trotted back into the living room. "Crazy cats," Eve muttered to herself.

"Do you have plans for Halloween?" Atticus asked her from the kitchen. Eve returned to answer him.

"Yes, I'm going to a party my friend is throwing," she

answered. She wondered if Belinda had ever gotten around to inviting Atticus to the party.

His face fell a bit. "So you're busy all night."

"Yes, mostly, why?"

Atticus fiddled with his cup of tea nervously, avoiding her gaze. Then he took a deep breath and lifted his eyes to meet hers. "I was wondering if you might want to go to a movie with me tonight? Scary or not scary, whatever you like. Kind of a Halloween...date."

"Oh." The tingling returned to her neck and shoulders. "I can't, I–" Just then, a heavy gust of wind hit the house and the front door blew open. The door banged against the wall and dried leaves swept into the foyer. "For heaven's sake," Eve exclaimed. "I thought I shut that."

She rushed into the foyer to close the door, Atticus right behind her. He ducked past her to grab the door and stood in the doorway as if to leave. Dismayed at the idea of Atticus going as well as missing out on a Halloween date with him, Eve took hold of the door as well.

"You don't have to go," she said.

"It's okay," he answered. "You've got plans. Maybe another time." He stepped backwards through the door onto the front porch. Giving her a quick wave he said in an overly cheery tone, "Have a Happy Halloween, Eve."

Then he was walking quickly away and another cold wind blew through her front door. Eve felt a pang of regret. Why didn't she invite him to the party? Why didn't she stop him from leaving? The way his shoulders had hunched down and he shoved his hands in his pockets as he walked away made him look sad and lonely and made her feel like a jerk.

Turning back into her house and shutting the door firmly, Eve saw the sister cats sitting squarely in the wide doorway that went to the living room. Their catnip puffs lay ignored on the floor behind them. Both of them looked at her with disapproving glares.

"What do you want me to do? Tackle him?" Eve asked them, exasperated. The sister cats turned their black, furry rumps to her and stalked away.

Chapter Ten

Belinda's house was a bustle of energy, much like her personality. There were decorations to put up, snacks to prepare, punch to mix, music to set up on her sound system and when they were finished with that, they had to get dressed in their costumes.

Belinda, true to her word, had made brilliant alterations to her thrift store finds and Eve thought they both looked the part of the witches from Wicked. Belinda brushed glitter onto her face in her upstairs bathroom while Eve inspected her green makeup options.

"Don't forget your hat," Belinda reminded her. Eve took up the black pointed hat and placed it on her head, studying her reflection. She had curled her long, dark hair upon Belinda's suggestion and with much of her friend's help. "No need to be an unattractive witch," her friend had said. Belinda could work magic with hair just like she did with clothes and seeing her wavy locks tumbling out from under the black hat and around her shoulders, Eve was happy with the look. Her dress was form fitting, fairly low cut and had an abundance of black silk and taffeta strips attached to her wrists so when she moved, she fluttered. The only part about her costume she wasn't crazy about was the green makeup.

"You don't think my eyes will be too pale if my skin is green, do you?" Eve asked.

"I thought of the color of your eyes when I bought it, which is why I got the paler green. I think it will make them brighter," Belinda answered. "Just try it, if you really hate it you have time to wash it off." The doorbell rang and Belinda finished her bright pink lipstick quickly. "Trick-or-treaters are starting! The red lipstick is for you." Belinda pointed at a tube of lipstick next to the green glitter makeup and disappeared out the door.

"May as well go for it," Eve said to her reflection. She dipped her fingers into the pot of green makeup and smeared it on her cheeks. By the time she was done, every inch of her face and neck and ears was a pale, shimmering green. Her lips were a beautiful poppy red and she silently blessed Belinda for her fashion sense. The color of the green did bring out her pale blue eyes, making them a deeper blue/green color. Eve took one last look in the full-length mirror. She looked transformed into someone else, which was what a costume was supposed to do, wasn't it?

Downstairs, the party had already started. When Eve descended the stairs it was not into the suburban home she had entered earlier in the day. Belinda's house was now a full on Halloween blowout. All of the best music, including Monster Mash, Ghostbusters and Time Warp, blasted over the sound system. The fog machines were working double time to keep a mystical layer of fog floating around the feet of the guests who continued to stream through the front door. The rooms were dark except for glowing white globes that looked like moons and strings of purple and orange lights hung along the walls. Everyone was decked out in full costumes and Eve was continually surprised at not recognizing old friends until they revealed who they were as she walked through the crowd. She found Belinda by the punch bowl that was flowing over with dry ice mist.

"This is great!" Eve shouted to Belinda over the music.

"You look fantastic!" Belinda responded, "The green looks really cool in this light. And doesn't it make your eyes look brilliant?" Belinda was obviously delighted with her costume creation.

"Yes, you were right." Eve took a cup of the punch Belinda offered. "Did you invite Atti—Mr. Murphy?" Eve asked, wondering if she might see him tonight after all.

Belinda continued pouring punch into cups, "No, I didn't. I don't really know him and I never ran into him this week. Should I have?"

"No," Eve tried to seem nonchalant. "Not really, I guess."

"Have you seen Chip?" Belinda asked. Eve's stomach tightened at the question. She shook her head 'no', not sure she wanted to find him. "Me neither," Belinda said, her eyebrows screwing into a knot.

Eve shrugged, "It doesn't matter, this is a great party with or without him!" She lifted her cup and toasted Belinda's in a toast. She took a drink and immediately felt the burn of vodka in her throat. She coughed.

"It's spiked," Belinda told her, grinning before taking a big swig of her own drink.

Between the spiked punch, the loud music and the crowd of dancing characters that ranged from a giant Winnie the Pooh to a sexy devil lady who by day sold car insurance at the local State Farm, this was definitely an epic Halloween event. Eve couldn't think of the last time she'd been to such a wild party, if ever. After chatting with some of her friends and downing a couple of glasses of punch, Eve took up her favorite position at any party, in the most out of the way place she could find. Nestled into the darkest corner, she perched on a stool, munched steaming hot cheese puffs from a paper plate and people watched.

Not long after taking her place as resident wallflower, Eve felt a melancholy wash over her, a sad kind of loneliness that she couldn't explain. She popped the last cheese puff into her mouth and chewed it thoughtfully. For one thing, the number of couple's costumes in the room was a little depressing. She saw a sailor and a mermaid, Danny and Sandy from Grease, Barbie and Ken, Little Red Riding Hood and the Big Bad Wolf, a priest and a nun and Wesley and Buttercup from The Princess Bride. This last one made her especially moody, such a romantic story. She wondered what Atticus was doing right now. Had he found someone else to take on a Halloween date? That thought made her even more depressed.

"Do you want to dance?" The unmistakable gravelly voice came from the darkness beside her. She jumped, losing her balance on the stool. A hand clad in a black glove grabbed her arm to steady her. "Whoa, I didn't mean to scare you."

Eve looked up into the face of...Batman.

She peered into the mask, trying to see the man's eyes before she blurted out his name. It was no use, there wasn't enough light and she realized she had drank her punch a little too fast and could not see completely clearly at the moment. She could make out the man's mouth through the opening in the mask, however, and after a few moments of concentration she recognized the smirky grin.

"Chip?"

"Do you want to dance?" He asked again, moving his hand under her elbow to guide her to the middle of the living room where a strange blend of characters were bouncing and gyrating to Michael Jackson's 'Thriller'.

"Sure," she said, even though she didn't think he could hear her answer. They were already halfway into the dancing mob.

Batman, or Chip—she was pretty sure it was Chip—had pretty good moves. The music and the punch got to her and Eve lost herself in dancing. She was no longer Eve St. Claire, bookworm, cat lady in the making. She was a sexy witch and she was dancing with Batman. She was, in fact, dirty dancing with Batman now that he'd grabbed her around the waist and pulled her into him. She found it easy to match his rhythmic pelvic moves and when the song finished, they were almost in a full embrace. The music shifted to a slow song, Love Song for a Vampire, Eve recognized it immediately.

"Stay," Chip said when she started to back away. He took her by the waist and she wrapped her arms around his neck and they swayed to the music. Eve saw Belinda notice them from the other side of the room. Belinda's mouth dropped open, then she lifted her hands and gave Eve two thumbs up.

The rest of the night she was his. Chip stayed by her side, bringing her snacks and refilling her punch several times. He stood by her as they made small talk with other guests and they danced with each other exclusively. Eve felt dizzy from the attention. She felt claimed, like they were one of those couples that had dressed to match each other at the party. He took off his mask so he could talk and he was easily the handsomest man in the room. She blushed under his attention, letting him hold her close and kiss her neck during more slow dances. After a while she had drank too much and told him so. He asked if she wanted to go home and said he would drive. She agreed.

Eve found herself once again sunk deep in the leather passenger seat of Chip's car. The wind had picked up and briefly cleared the hazy clouds so there was just cold, black sky where the giant moon hung. Perfect for Halloween. She turned to say something to Chip about it and took in his Batman outfit, then thought about her own witch costume and green face. She touched her head, she still had her hat on.

The idea of what they must look like driving around in his sleek sports car tickled her funny bone so completely that she burst out laughing.

"What?" Chip asked as he shifted gears and placed his hand proprietarily on her thigh.

Eve started to answer, then looked down at his hand and was reminded of the fiasco of the last time he took her home. His sneezing fit and the way her parent's wedding picture had mysteriously fallen off the wall and interrupted them. She started laughing even harder. She couldn't stop, and after a few minutes Chip grew annoyed.

"What is so funny?" He asked, turning onto Pennsylvania, her street.

"Next stop, the haunted house!" Eve blurted out, sending herself into another bout of hysterical laughter. She had a blurred idea that perhaps she had drank too much punch and tried to explain to Chip, "I had too much spooky brew!" She heard the slur in her words and collapsed into the door handle, giggling uncontrollably.

Chip didn't say anything. They pulled up to her house and he helped her out of the car then to her front door. The old house loomed dark and empty next to them. She had forgotten to leave a lamp on in the living room. Eve fumbled in her purse for her keys, still chuckling quietly, when a sudden cold wind whipped by them, whisking her hat off of her head.

"Whoops!" She cried as she lunged for it, dropping her keys in the process.

"I'll get it," Chip said. He sounded exasperated and it took him a few long minutes and more than a little effort of feeling around the porch to find both lost items. Finally, he stood up and handed her the keys and the hat. "Can we get inside? This costume is flimsy and that wind is cold."

Eve bit her lip and didn't make any comment, even

though the idea of Batman shivering on her porch was really, really funny. She tried to get the key in the hole three different times, but missed. Finally, Chip put his flimsy, fake Batman gloved hand over hers and put the key in, turning the lock. Eve pushed on the door, but nothing happened. It stayed stubbornly closed. She pushed it again, nothing. Chip tried the door and it wouldn't budge.

"Give me the key, maybe it's still locked," he said brusquely.

Eve handed him the key and watched as he used it to lock and unlock the door several times, pushing it each time to try and open it, to no avail. The chilling wind continued to blow and Chip sighed and grunted in irritation.

"It doesn't normally get stuck," Eve explained, half apologizing, half wondering what was wrong with the door.

"Are you sure this is the unlocked position?" Chip asked. Eve checked the key placement and nodded 'yes' earnestly. "Stand back," Chip commanded. She stepped back and watched him walk to the edge of the porch, turn around, lower his shoulder and run at the door, slamming his shoulder into it with a loud bang before bouncing backwards.

"Oh!" She exclaimed, "Be careful." Even as she said it she had to giggle at the look of him getting thrown backwards.

"I felt it move," he said with confidence, stepping back to the edge of the porch to try again. All in all, Chip ran at her door four times. The first three ended in the same banging sound and with him being thrown back, unable to move the door. The fourth time the door opened, Eve saw it, or at least that's what she thought she saw. She wasn't completely sure, because it seemed to open just moments before Chip hit it with his shoulder. It sort of slipped open a tiny crack all on its own. She tried to tell him, but it was too late, he was already in full on attack mode and he hit the slightly open door with all of his weight, slamming it so hard that it crashed against the inside wall and his momentum hurled him into the foyer where he slipped and fell, sprawling onto the floor.

Eve ran in after him, afraid he might have hurt himself. A bitter cold wind followed her, making the strands of the silk and taffeta on her costume flutter madly. She flipped on the light to see Chip laying face down on the floor, his arms and legs still spread wide, his Batman cape twisted in disarray around him. She also saw the sister cats placed in odd positions, glaring at Chip with frightful anger. Hazel stood at the top of the staircase, her back arched, her tail shooting straight up behind her, yellow eyes glowing. And Sabrina, she was almost directly in front of Chip's head, her front and back legs set wide apart, her back hunched with her jet black hair sticking up straight all along her spine, making her look even bigger than her already large size. Her great yellow eyes were slits and she emitted a terrible, guttural, growling sound. It made a shiver go down Eve's spine.

"Holy shit!" Chip shouted as he struggled to get up, his tangled cape causing him to slip and slide across the foyer floor before he finally managed to stand. He stared at Sabrina as he straightened his cape. The cat continued to growl. "What in the hell is the matter with your cat?"

"Nothing...I don't know," Eve answered, surprised at the cat's behavior, but even more bothered at Chip's angry reaction. "They're just cats. We scared them. It's probably the full moon."

Chip scoffed and ran his hand through his hair, trying to smooth it after his tumble. "What, because you're a witch for Halloween you think you know all about the full moon?"

Eve didn't like his tone. It was sarcastic and belittling.

"You think you can break down doors because you're dressed like Batman?" She quipped.

"Excuse me for trying to help you," he replied. Sabrina growled again. "Are you gonna get those cats locked up bef—"

suddenly Chip opened his mouth into a wide yawn that went on forever and ended in a massive sneeze. Both cats bolted. Eve watched in shocked curiosity as Chip sneezed five more earth shattering times. Tears streamed from his eyes, his nose was bright red and he had to lean against the wall to keep his balance.

"Are you all right?" She asked.

"No, I'm not all right," he said. "I just wanted to have a little fun tonight, get in a little action before I head home on Monday and this is what I get for my trouble?"

Eve felt her hackles rise, just like the sister cats. She was still a little drunk, but she wasn't too drunk to misunderstand his meaning. She was his Halloween hook up. He was going back home to Chicago in two days and he only took her home tonight because he wanted to get laid.

"You're going back to Chicago on Monday?" Eve asked icily.

"Yes," Chip answered with a scowl. "Thank God. I can't stand this stupid town. I don't know how anyone still lives here. The whole place is full of losers."

There was such disdain in his voice Eve was almost at a loss for words. Almost. She stepped to the door and swung it all the way open, gesturing outside with a wide sweep of her arm.

"Then you better go home and get packing," she told him.

Chip Hendricks, her high school crush, teenage heart-throb of their town, wearing a cheap Batman outfit and suffering from watery eyes and extreme sniffles, stood in her foyer with his mouth agape.

"You're not serious," he said. Apparently, Chip wasn't familiar with rejection, especially from a 'loser' in this 'stupid town'.

"I'm dead serious," Eve told him, letting her eyes narrow like Sabrina's. Another cold wind blasted through the door as if to emphasize her words. He gave her one last look of disgust, then stormed out the door to his car and out of her life, hopefully forever.

Eve stood at the door with her shoulders back and her head held high, watching him drive away.

"Good riddance," she said, expecting Hazel and Sabrina to hurry to her side in support. But they didn't. In fact, they were nowhere to be seen.

Eve's stomach dropped with a sickening realization. It was midnight on Halloween, her front door had been wide open for several minutes while she and Chip argued, and the sister cats were gone.

Chapter Eleven

It had been stupid to leave the house without a coat. Eve knew that now. Not only that, but her purse and her phone sat on the small table in her foyer where she'd put them after Chip fell through the door. She'd been in such a frenzy of worry she hadn't thought anything through, just ran outside looking for Hazel and Sabrina. She'd hoped to find them exploring in the wooded area behind her house, or maybe frolicking with other cats in her neighbor's yards, or maybe even on a wild adventure in Sander's Park whose entrance was just four blocks from her house.

She hadn't found them in any of those places. As she searched, calling their names, the futility of finding two completely black cats in the middle of the night sunk in. The wind had picked up and the giant, glowing moon looked a lot creepier than it had earlier in the evening. Thick clouds were moving over it, giving it an eerie quality and quickly blotting out its light. The trick-or-treaters and their families had gone home a long time ago. It was too late for little kids to be out. All of the scariest stories she'd ever read flew through her mind as she trudged through the park. Trees swayed, moaning in the wind, their bare limbs scratching against each other. Houses everywhere were dark, shuttered against the storm and maybe against the frightening forces of Halloween night. Not one jack-o-lantern had been left glowing on anyone's stoop. Eve felt utterly alone. It took all of her concentration to control the icy fear that crept up from her belly.

That's when it started to rain.

Cold splinters of water carried by the wind whipped into her face. She stopped, turning around slowly to orient herself. In her frantic searching, she'd lost track of how far she'd gone. She was on the far side of Sander's Park now. It was almost a thirty minute walk home from where she stood and the sister cats were nowhere in sight. Her car was still at Belinda's, whose house was even farther away. Fat, hot tears welled up in her eyes and started rolling down her face. She had to go home without Hazel and Sabrina, and it was her own fault.

She'd been such a fool. There were so many red flags that she should have noticed with Chip. She'd ignored every one of them, because she'd been, what? Flattered by his attention? Finally getting a shot with her high school crush? Ridiculous. Even her beautiful old house had given her a sign that Chip wasn't right for her, and she hadn't listened. And this is what she got for it, missing cats and a long walk home in the rain in the middle of the night. There was nothing to do but give up for now. The sister cats were nowhere nearby and whether the fear she felt in her belly was from something real or something imagined, she wanted to go home.

Eve's hat was already pulled down hard around her ears so she wouldn't lose it in the wind again. Her witch costume wasn't the cheap, thin costume you might buy in a store, but it still wasn't terribly warm and it definitely wasn't water-proof. She wrapped her arms around her body to try and control her shivering and made towards home as the rain began in earnest.

By the time she got within a half block of her driveway, Eve was soaked to the bone. Her witch hat and dress were soggy, as was her hair and shoes. Though the wind had died down now that the rain was going full force, her shivering was even more out of control because she was so wet.

Her house was completely dark, as was every house along her street. Even the street lamps were out. Her heart beat wildly at the creepy possibilities this total blackout held on a Halloween night. Of course, logically, it was probably just a powerful outage, but still. Through the rain she saw a faint light flash across her front porch. She paused for a moment, trying to remember if she'd locked her front door in her rush to leave, then cursing silently when she realized her keys were inside her purse, which was inside the house.

A form moved on the porch. Eve took a step back. The form was large enough to be a man, but through the rain and without any light coming from the moon or anywhere else, it was difficult to tell what it was.

"Eve?" A man's voice sounded from the porch, then the light came again, a flashlight. It swept across the ground in front of her then across her dress and into her face, blinding her for a moment. She shielded her eyes with her hand.

"Hey!" She shouted, trying to sound less scared than she felt.

"Sorry." The light shone on the ground then swept up to fall on the form holding it. She was right, it was a man. It was Atticus. "It's me!" He waved one hand at her. "Your front door was open..." his voice trailed off as she made her way up the front steps and he got a better look at her. "Jeez, what happened? Are you all right?"

"I'm j-j-just cold," she stammered, relieved as he grabbed her arm pulling her under the small porch roof then swung the front door open and led her inside. She was dripping and shaking and crying. Atticus' flashlight lit the foyer sporadically as he moved. He shut the door behind her.

"Do you have candles? The power's out," he asked.

Eve nodded, pointing towards the kitchen. "D-d-drawer by the sink."

He disappeared and she could hear him moving around in the kitchen. She took off her shoes, grateful for the warm, dry house. She imagined she heard a muffled meow from upstairs and felt another ache of grief over the sister cats being lost out in this storm. Atticus returned, carrying a lit candle in front of him. The candle illuminated her entire foyer, including the staircase where two black cats with yellow eyes sat watching her. When the light hit them they both stood up and trotted down the stairs, meowing at her loudly.

"Hazel! Sabrina!" Eve exclaimed, dropping to her knees so she could wrap them in her arms. "Where did you come from? I thought you were lost!" Both cats purred loudly and let her caress them even though she was still wet and they normally shied from all forms of water.

"I found them. Well, actually, they found me," Atticus said.

"Where were they?" Eve buried her face in their soft, black fur.

"They ran in front of my car," Atticus explained. "I was coming back from the movie and two black cats shot out in front of me and I thought, what bad luck! And then I thought wait a minute, those cats look familiar."

Eve cringed a little when he mentioned the movie, the same movie she'd refused to go to with him. Atticus continued without pause.

"I stopped the car and when I got out to look for them they ran right to me. I figured you'd be looking for them so I brought them here. Your door was wide open and the power had gone off. I put the cats in the house and then noticed your purse was sitting right there and..." here he kind of shuffled his feet, "I got a little worried. So I thought I'd wait a bit on your porch just to see if you made it home safely."

Good Lord, she thought, *he is an angel.*

Overcome at his story and the return of the sister cats, Eve stood up and hugged him, crying and sniffling as she did.

"Thank you, thank you so much," she mumbled into his shoulder. He only hesitated a moment before wrapping his long arms around her and holding her tight. She relaxed into his strong embrace. He was so warm.

"You're shivering," he said softly.

"I know."

Atticus pulled out of her arms. He lifted the candle that he still held with one hand closer to her face and looked her over carefully. "Are you sure you're all right? Did anything happen to you?"

"No," she said, sniffling a little. "I just got caught in the rain and I was so worried about Hazel and Sabrina." Her lip trembled when she spoke.

"Here," Atticus handed her the candle. "Go change into something dry. I'll make you some tea. Everything's fine now."

The sister cats followed her upstairs and laid on her bed as she changed by candlelight. She put on black fleece pants, heavy socks, a white long sleeve cotton shirt and her burnt orange sweater. When she took the candle into the bathroom to brush out and pull up her hair, she was shocked at her reflection.

All of the crying and walking in the rain had made her eye makeup run in black streaks down her face and blend with the green face makeup making a muddy swirl of strange colors. In all of the distress of the evening, she'd completely forgotten she had green makeup on at all. She looked like she'd fallen into a mud puddle face first or had tried to go undercover with the navy seals and come to a tragic end. No wonder Atticus had been so shocked at her appearance.

Eve scrubbed the makeup off with soap and warm water then brushed her damp hair and pulled it back into a loose ponytail at the nape of her neck. She studied her appearance and decided she didn't look great, but she definitely looked better.

Meanwhile, Atticus had apparently located all of the candles in the house. As Eve descended the stairs with her candle in hand and the cats right on her heels, she gasped in delight at the scene in her living room. Several candles on the coffee table, mantle, side tables and shelves were lit, their light dancing off of the glass knick knacks and the large beveled mirror over the fireplace. The tall candles she kept in the fireplace were also lit, making it feel cozy and romantic.

"Hot tea," Atticus announced coming from the kitchen. He carried two mugs of steaming tea and gave her one once she was settled onto the couch. He placed his mug on the coffee table and took the throw from the back of the couch, covering Eve with it before he sat down next to her.

"Thank you," Eve said. "This is beautiful."

"You're even more beautiful in candlelight." His eyes twinkled at her. "So, it's entirely my pleasure."

Eve blushed at the compliment, but couldn't help smiling. She spotted a smear of glittery green on his shoulder and reached out to touch it, dismayed. "I got makeup on your shirt."

Atticus dipped his chin down and to the side to try to see the spot, telling her, "Don't worry about it."

"I'm sorry," Eve said. She let her hand slide from his shoulder down his arm and finally to rest on top of his hand. "I'm also sorry I didn't go on a Halloween date with you."

His eyes, those piercing blue eyes, locked onto hers. She

had stopped shivering from cold when she put on dry clothes, but now, she felt that delicious tingle along her shoulders and neck. The candlelight deepened the richness of his red hair and beard, making her want to reach out and touch it with her fingers. She ran her eyes along his nose to the corner of his firm mouth where his mustache curled just a little.

"That's okay," Atticus said, his voice low and soft. "This is better than what I had planned for us."

Us. What a simple little word. Yet the sound of it filled her heart with joy. She lifted her hand and let her fingers touch his temple and push up into his fiery red hair.

"Us?" She asked sweetly.

"If you want there to be," he answered, leaning towards her, pulled into her by the feel of her fingers in his hair. "Do you?"

"Yes, I want there to be an us," she said as his lips touched hers.

That was it, what he'd been waiting for, and with this encouragement, Atticus kissed her. He was so gentle as they pressed their lips together for the very first time, savoring the first taste. Then, as the moments passed, his mouth was firmer, more insistent, and he reached around her waist, pulling her closer. Eve pushed her fingers into his hair and around the back of his neck, sensually massaging the muscles down his neck and along his shoulders. She opened her mouth ever so slightly and he touched his tongue to hers, tasting her, wanting more, but holding himself in check.

She had never felt so safe and so wanted. His whole body was reacting to her, rippling with desire, tuned in to her and only her, she could feel it, sense it in the air. Yet he had such a gentle touch, kissed her so tenderly, respect and longing wrapped into one. The effect was dizzying.

Atticus pulled her into the crook of his arm and she rested her head there where she could hear his heart beating fast in his chest. They didn't speak for a while, just cuddled, his fingers played with the ends of her hair sending more tingles along her neck and shoulders.

"This is so nice," she said, almost whispered.

"Mm-hmm," he answered, the sound rumbling through his chest.

The rain still drummed on the roof and spattered against the windows. The wind blew wildly outside, but the door remained closed and the sister cats lay together in the armchair nearby, sleeping quietly. Peace and contentment surrounded them and in that moment she had a thought.

"You know what?" Eve lifted her head and looked at Atticus in the eye.

"What?"

"I think the house likes you."

"Does it?" He smiled.

"Yes." Eve looked around at the calm living room. Nothing had fallen, no candles had blown out, everything had stayed in its place.

"Does the house actually have an opinion?" He asked, still smiling.

"I didn't used to think it did, but over the past few days I may have changed my mind. Maybe my Dad was right, maybe this house is haunted," she answered.

Atticus looked around the room, considering this comment before answering. Then he said, "It's too beautiful to be haunted. This is a lovely home. Maybe instead of haunted we should say it's enchanted."

Another shiver went down Eve's spine, then back up again. Goosebumps covered her arms. He was right. She knew he was right. Everything about Atticus Murphy was right.

"Enchanted...I like that," she answered.

"Good," he said, and kissed her again.

THANK you for reading Enchanting Eve! If you enjoyed this book you may enjoy the other books in the series...

Love is at the Table - Thanksgiving Romance

Mistletoe Madness - Christmas Romance

New Year in Paradise - New Year's Eve Romance

OR YOU MAY ENJOY Darci's Dream Come True series. The first book, Her Scottish Keep is a fun and flirty romance set in the Scottish Highlands...a clean and wholesome contemporary Scottish love story :)

Epilogue

"Eve, honey, did you get the popcorn?" Atticus called to her from the kitchen just as Eve placed the giant bowl of hot, salted popcorn on the coffee table.

"Yes," she answered. "The hot chocolate is still on the counter." She stood up in time to see Atticus walking through the hallway, not carrying two mugs of hot chocolate, but instead holding a tiny orange ball of fur. She smiled, the man hadn't put their new kitten down for more than two minutes since they picked him up yesterday at the animal shelter.

"Merlin," Atticus spoke to the orange fluff sticking out of his cupped hands. "These are your grandparents." Atticus stopped in front of Eve's parent's wedding photo and held the tiny kitten up to see.

"Merlin isn't old enough to understand about grandparents," Eve pretended to scold her boyfriend—correction, fiancé—as she gingerly took the beautiful little kitty from him. Merlin mewed in protest, his blue eyes blinked and he stuck his big ears high into the air as if to say he was, indeed, interested in grandparents. "Now go get the hot chocolate, please," Eve said.

"Of course!" Atticus leaned over and kissed her before turning towards the kitchen. Merlin mewed again.

"Not in front of the children, darling," Eve teased, then held Merlin's tiny body carefully to her chest as she carried him into the living room. The sister cats perked up and took notice when she sat down with him on the couch. They didn't go so far as to get up from their comfortable spot on the fat armchair, but they knew Merlin was a new member of the family. They would deign to play with him when he was a little older.

"When will the trick-or-treaters get here?" Atticus asked as he carried in the hot chocolate. He was almost as excited as a child was about trick-or-treating. "Is the candy out?"

"Yes," Eve said calmly. "I got it ready earlier just in case." She looked out the living room window to the grey light of dusk. "I think they will be coming any time, the little ones at least."

"Those are my favorite," Atticus declared as he took some popcorn and popped it into his mouth, chewing happily.

He had been over the top elated for the past few days, she had too. She looked into her hands where she held their new pink nosed, blue eyed orange tabby cat, and was surprised once again at the diamond engagement ring that now graced her left ring finger. They had been engaged for just over three days and she wasn't quite used to seeing the beautiful ring on her hand yet.

He'd proposed in the middle of the Fischer pumpkin patch because that's where he said he had fallen head over heels for her. The kids from the classroom had assisted him with the surprise proposal while they were on the annual pumpkin picking field trip. They had secretly brought rolled up poster boards in their jackets with colorful letters drawn on them spelling out 'MARRY ME EVE' and held them up in line behind Atticus as he got on one knee and asked her to be his wife.

It had been perfect. The proposal fit exactly who he was, who they were together. She'd cried and said 'yes' and then the Fischer's had brought out refreshments of cookies and hot apple cider. It filled her heart to know that this was the first of many celebrations yet to come with this man, her Atticus.

Their first official act as a newly engaged couple had been to answer an ad by the animal shelter pleading with the public to help them find homes for a number of abandoned kittens. When Eve spied the orange fur and blue eyes of this little guy peeking out from the sea of grey and black kittens, she'd known immediately that he was supposed to be theirs. He looked just like Atticus! And when she picked him up and showed him to Atticus, the man was completely smitten.

Atticus loved cats. He also loved tradition and family and children and Eve thought she was probably the luckiest girl in the world to have him as her future husband. Another thing he loved, she had found out, was decorating for holidays. Determined to help her change her house's reputation as being haunted, Atticus spent hundreds of dollars and they had both dedicated several hours to decorating the house and yard. There were countless strings of purple and orange lights, funny scarecrows, jack-o-lanterns with wide, happy smiles and cartoon witches and ghosts all over the house. Nothing too scary. Everything fun.

The doorbell rang and Atticus jumped up from the couch. "I'll get it!"

Eve heard a chorus of little voices shouting "Trick or treat!" Then Atticus exclaiming appreciatively over their costumes as he passed out candy bars. Apparently all of their efforts had worked. The little kids were definitely not afraid to approach the house this Halloween.

Eve sighed pleasantly, looking around at the warm, cozy living room. So much joy had been in this room for so many years. All of the holidays and plain old evenings she'd spent here with her father flashed through her heart. And now there was new joy and a new life laid out in front of her, one that was more full than she'd ever imagined it could be. She wished her Dad was here, and her Mom. They would have liked Atticus, she was certain.

The sister cats gazed at her thoughtfully with their large, yellow eyes and Eve swore they looked like they were giving her knowing smiles. Merlin mewed and stretched his neck high in the air, bobbing his little head back and forth, trying to look her in the eye. She leaned her face down and touched her nose to his. He mewed at her again. Eve smiled.

"You're right, Merlin," she said to him, "and ladies," to the sister cats, "I do believe you are correct. Mom and Dad are here with us now. Beautiful memories are what make this house enchanted and we will all be very happy here together for a long, long time."

The End

LOVE IS at the

THANKSGIVING ROMANCE

Table

DARCI BALOGH

To Dad.
For your love of ping pong and horseshoes, for sharing your knowledge of birds, for the music, the art, and the fun you always bring to the table.
And for bringing the unforgettable production of 'The Pirates and the Pilgrims' to life!

Thank you, Dad, for all of the Thanksgivings, holidays and regular days you've made so special throughout my life. And thank you for teaching me to be creative, to love knowledge and to laugh.

Chapter One

"Love is a noun or a verb, it's something you do." Jenny scowled out the windshield as she drove and complained to her brother. "Love is not a name, okay? Nobody is called *Love*. That's stupid. Like being called Excitement or Hate."

"What about Joy? There are people named Joy," Jimmy responded. "I worked with a Joy once. She was nice."

Jenny rolled her eyes for the hundredth time since she'd picked him up at his condo. The four hour drive to their parent's vacation home in Iowa was nearing its end.

During the drive they had covered many topics of conversation; the fact that she'd chosen to wear her work slacks instead of something more comfy, his new haircut, pop music, his marital status—newly separated, and her love life—currently stagnant, but Jenny had focused most of her talking points on the woman their widower father had married a few months ago, Love Hathaway. A woman neither she nor Jimmy had met. A woman who would be playing hostess over Thanksgiving with their Dad at their family's beloved Lake House retreat.

Jenny had reluctantly agreed to spend one whole week with this Love person at the place her mother had made into their home away from home. Now that the week was about to begin she was having a hard time accepting the whole situation.

"It just...it just sticks in my craw," Jenny said.

Jimmy laughed out loud, "Why are you talking like a farmhouse grandma?"

"I don't know," she answered. His amusement made her smile, revealing the small gap in her front teeth, the one she'd inherited from her Mom. "I get this way when I leave the city."

"Well, I don't care what her name is as long as she's a good fit for Dad," Jimmy said, always the level headed one. "And don't roll your eyes at that. Don't you want him to be happy?"

"Yes," Jenny admitted with an exasperated growl. "But how can he possibly know her well enough to be happy?"

Their Dad had married Love only 18 months after their mother passed away. Not even two years! In Jenny's opinion, that was not long enough to get over a 42 year marriage.

Jimmy gave her a one shouldered shrug and took a sip out of his travel mug. "I guess we'll find out this week."

"I don't understand how you're so blasé about it."

"He's a grown man, Jen, you can't stop him from getting remarried."

She glowered at his comment and they drove in silence for a few minutes. It was early afternoon and not a cloud in the sky. The landscape had changed drastically from downtown Chicago. Her sedan cruised through rolling hills dotted with quaint farmhouses and giant bales of hay, all surrounded by trees and shrubs in full fall foliage. The colors were brilliant.

"What if she's after his money?" she asked.

"I don't think Dad has the kind of money that inspires that kind of behavior," Jimmy quipped.

"She looks like a hippie in her picture," Jenny continued. "She's got to be with a name like that. And she's from Denver. She probably smokes weed!"

Jimmy made a fake shocked face and placed his hand on his heart as if he was having a heart attack. She reached over and punched his shoulder in protest. He pretended to fall into the passenger side door in great pain.

"Stop it, I'm being serious," she said.

"You're being insane," Jimmy replied as he straightened in his seat.

"This whole thing is insane. I don't know why I agreed to come. It's bad enough that Mom is gone, but now we have to be nice to Love," she said the name with a slight sneer. "And Dad said she invited some neighbor of hers or something?"

Jimmy nodded, "Yeah, Erin I think he said. Must be some hippie friend of hers. They're probably gonna smoke weed then eat all of the pies."

Jenny chuckled at the thought.

Jimmy patted her knee. "I know it's insane, little sister, but any Thanksgiving without Mom is always going to suck. We'll just have to do our best to get through it for Dad's sake."

Jenny nodded. He was right. He was usually right, a fact she'd refused to admit when they were younger.

"Now," Jimmy continued, "Can we get back to talking about my problems?"

"Yes." It was Jenny's turn to pat his knee.

Her heart hurt for her big brother. He and his husband, Paul, had only been separated for six weeks. Their 5-year old daughter, Penelope, was spending Thanksgiving with Paul and his family in Chicago. She'd seen the strain on Jimmy's face the moment he'd opened the door to her this morning.

Her brother had a slight build, average round facial features, fair skin that freckled easily, and reddish brown hair.

As siblings, they looked very much alike except her hair was a bit darker, even more so since she'd started coloring it a deeper auburn. His eyes were hazel and hers were brown. He was about 5'8" and she was 5'5". Those were the biggest differences between them, besides being different genders.

When she'd seen him this morning she noticed he was paler than usual, his eyes had the rimmed look of someone who had been crying. He was shaved and dressed nicely, which was normal, but she could tell he wasn't feeling himself. Who could be in his circumstances? A separation right before the holidays? Spending Thanksgiving without his little girl? He was probably in shock. She knew she was. The news of his and Paul's marital difficulties had come as a huge surprise to her. They'd always been the most solid couple she'd known, except for her parents of course.

"How are you doing?" Jenny asked, giving her brother a sympathetic look.

Jimmy sighed heavily. "The same as I was an hour ago."

"Aw, honey." Jenny patted his knee in empathy.

"It's all kind of surreal, you know?" Jimmy looked out over the picturesque landscape, his voice cracking a little as he spoke. "I mean it's so beautiful out here and it's going to be beautiful at the Lake House, and the holiday is happening even though Penny isn't here, and Paul isn't here...it just doesn't feel real."

Jenny watched her brother out of the corner of her eye as she maneuvered the car along the winding section of the road that took them into the wooded lake area, that much closer to their destination. Jimmy put his hands over his face, covering the fact that he was crying.

"Oh, honey," Jenny didn't know what else to say. She was no relationship expert and hadn't even known there was a problem between Jimmy and Paul until they separated. Her advice was next to useless.

"I just miss them so much." Jimmy wiped his eyes with a napkin from the pile they'd collected at the drive through getting their road trip breakfast.

"I know," Jenny replied. "Is there any way Paul would meet up with you the day after Thanksgiving? At least let Penny come for part of the holiday?" She thought having his daughter with him for a few days this week might help.

Jimmy shook his head 'no'. "We agreed that might be a lot of disruption for her, especially after all of the mayhem of him moving out."

Jenny nodded, "I can see that." She smiled at him encouragingly. "Well, we'll be there soon. You gonna call Penny when we get there?"

Jimmy nodded and they drifted into silence again, mesmerized by the scenery.

They had entered the woods and a myriad of brilliant fall colors blanketed the sky above the narrowing road. The ground under the trees was covered with crimson red, bright orange and deep golden leaves. All of them presumably fell from the branches above, but those branches looked dense with the same vibrant foliage. It seemed to Jenny that the trees couldn't possibly hold that many leaves. Yet there they were. Some of them were even falling lightly from the branches overhanging the road, floating downward on the breeze until her car drove through them scattering them in all directions.

"God it's gorgeous," Jimmy said out loud, echoing her sentiments.

Jenny pushed the button on her door so her window lowered and the cool autumn breeze filled the car. The air was damp with the scent of decomposing leaves, wood, and the rivers and lakes nearby.

The road curved and brought them to a new amazing view around each corner. Memories flooded her mind. Her parents had brought them here several times a year since she was small, five-years old to be exact. The drive was part of the experience and their Mom had always loved to see the fall colors.

"The bridge is next, right?" Jenny asked, pretty sure she knew where they were on the road.

Jimmy fumbled with his cell phone. "Slow down, I want to take a picture and send it to Paul...or Penny, I guess."

"Sure, we'll pull over."

As they came around the next curve the trees opened up, revealing a narrow river that snaked through the woods complete with an antique covered bridge to take them to the other side. There was a small shoulder right after the bend that allowed Jenny to pull her car over and park. They both got out, breathing in the wonderful smell of fall, enrapt with the scene.

"I can't get over the colors this year." Jimmy walked onto the blacktop, getting into a better position to take the picture.

Jenny could not have agreed more. She had always thought of the covered bridge as a kind of portal into the Lake House, which sat nestled in a grove of trees just five minutes up the road near a small lake.

She had crossed the covered bridge countless times over the years, beams of sunlight piercing through the narrow openings between the ancient wood planks, the bridge creaking under the weight of their car, the water tumbling over rocks below them in the river. Each time she made it to the other side Jenny always felt like she was transformed into something more, someone who belonged in the woods, was one with nature, a friend of the forest, maybe a magical fairy or woodland gnome. Silly, of course, but she still felt that way, even as a full grown woman who would be turning 33 in a few months.

Jenny felt a pang of grief as she realized, once again, that her mother wasn't waiting for her on the other side of the bridge. It didn't seem possible. Just like Jimmy said about Paul and Penny. The whole situation was surreal.

For a moment she let herself believe in the magic of the woods beyond the bridge. She wished as hard as she could that her mother would somehow still be alive on the other side, waiting for her with a huge smile and a warm hug, like always.

"Ready?" Jimmy asked. He'd finished taking pictures and rejoined her by the car.

She breathed in deep through her nose and exhaled through her mouth, then asked him, "Are you?"

Jimmy threw his arm over her shoulders and took in his own deep breath, then he wiggled her shoulders and gave her a big grin. "As ready as I'll ever be."

Chapter Two

The first thing that jarred her was the sight of her father standing with his arm around the waist of a total stranger. Like a paper doll cut out had been slipped into place next to him where her mother would normally be standing—should be standing.

She had seen what his new wife looked like in the images he had emailed. They'd even managed to film a short video on his cell phone of their wedding, elopement really, that he'd sent to her and Jimmy. Her Dad had remarried on a fast informal trip to Vegas followed by a honeymoon in the Caribbean. Neither she nor Jimmy or anyone else had been invited. Not that Jenny would have gone.

The second thing Jenny noticed was the state of the woman standing next to her father. She was small, thin, and wearing a bright blue, high necked, shapeless dress that brushed against her ankles. The bright blue had a floral print of red poppies and pink roses, a garish contrast to the deep reds, golds and browns in the surrounding landscape.

Her hair was long, grey and soaking wet, sticking in messy strands against her cheeks and neck. Her feet were bare and must have been freezing as she stood with their father on the front porch, watching them get out of the car. The pictures and video could not have prepared Jenny for meeting the woman in the flesh. Nothing could have.

"Button!" Her Dad called from the porch as she shut the car door. "Jim Boy," he smiled widely at both of his children, his expression full of joyful anticipation.

Unable to wait for them to approach, their Dad, Rudy Combes, stepped down and walked towards them with open arms, leaving the woman behind, stranded on the porch by her bare feet.

Rudy was a small man, not much taller than Jenny and just a little shorter than his grown son. He had blue eyes, thinning white hair that had gotten thinner during their mother's long illness, and a strong round body. He was a retired electrician, a member of the United Methodist Church, a teller of lame jokes and a capable provider. He had worked hard his whole life, but never at the expense of his family. Her Dad had been home for dinner every night when they were growing up. He had been at every recital, school play, graduation, and wedding celebration. Well, Jimmy's wedding, not hers of course.

When her mother was diagnosed with cancer, her Dad took early retirement to care for her without complaint. And when she succumbed to that cancer two years later her Dad decided to donate his electrician talents to nonprofits and churches instead of returning to full time work. That's where he met his new wife, Love.

Love ran a nonprofit organization out of Denver that promoted art therapy for people, women mostly, who were healing from abusive relationships. All of this sounded great on paper, but it didn't keep Jenny from being full of uncertainty about the woman.

"Dad!" Jimmy reached him first and gave him a long hug.

Rudy gave him a few hard, emotional pats on the back. Jenny understood that her Dad was deeply concerned over his son's marital troubles and the gesture somehow conveyed that concern, making Jimmy tear up again.

"Jim Boy." Rudy pushed his son away and held him at arm's length, looking at him with worry and pain etched on his face. Then he pulled him in again for another bear hug. Jimmy laughed.

"Dad, you're choking me," Jimmy said, pulling away.

"How are you holding up?" Rudy asked, not letting him go until he got another good look at him.

"I'm all right." Jimmy gave a quick nod to his father, but his red rimmed eyes and strained expression didn't go unnoticed.

"Yes." Rudy nodded gruffly and squeezed Jimmy's shoulders. "You're gonna be fine, son. I'm glad you're here."

Jenny had positioned herself behind them, hiding from the smiling stranger marooned on the porch, wanting to greet her Dad before she was forced to meet his new wife. Rudy turned his attention to her, his face lighting up.

"Hi, Dad," Jenny said, stepping into his outstretched arms.

"Button," he said quietly into her ear as he squeezed her tight. The nickname settled in comfortably on her, making her feel safe and warm. When he was done with her big hug, he wrapped his arms around both her and Jimmy's waists and propelled them towards the porch. "Jenny, Jimmy, this is Love," he said.

Jenny could tell by his tone that her Dad was nothing but proud of Love. If he understood that she was anything but delighted to meet the woman who was now her stepmother, he didn't show it. He practically glowed with delight as he walked with them to where she stood. And Love, for her part, beamed back at him.

Love had a wide smile. Jenny was reminded of Julia Roberts, that kind of plain pretty face that didn't seem overly attractive until she lit up with a smile. Love was in her sixties at least and definitely not a movie star, but Jenny could see how she may have been quite beautiful when she was young. The blue dress, it turned out, was a vintage bathrobe and Love's bare feet were calloused along the sides of her big toes, suggesting she went barefoot a lot.

"It's so wonderful to finally meet you both," Love gushed a little, unable to contain her excitement.

Jenny leaned in when Love reached for her, allowing a short stiff hug. Love smelled like cinnamon, her wet hair giving off the aroma of a natural foods store. She was shorter than Jenny, making her the smallest among them.

Jenny stepped back awkwardly to allow Love a chance to hug Jimmy as well. Her cheeks hurt from smiling, but she didn't stop. She knew her Dad was watching.

"Let's go inside." Rudy said and opened the front door, ushering them all inside.

The warm smells of the Lake House surrounded her. Wide planked oak floors and high rough wood beamed ceilings welcomed her, making her feel like she had stepped back in time. Comfortable, worn furniture and handwoven rugs her parents had furnished the house with were the same as always. Even her mother's black and white checkered throw was tossed on the chair in the corner of the sitting room, as if she'd just gotten up to greet them when they arrived and left it there.

Jenny had not been back to the Lake House since her mother passed away. They hadn't had the heart as a family to do much over the holidays after her death. Jimmy and Paul had hosted Thanksgiving that year and they had all gone to spend Christmas at their parent's home in the suburbs with their Dad instead of making the trip to the lake country.

Jenny had always known returning would be difficult. She'd just never expected to be returning with a stepmother in the mix.

"Did you enjoy your drive?" Love asked as she motioned them past the front sitting room towards the kitchen, that faint smell of cinnamon, herbs and candles trailing behind her. "Aren't the trees absolutely beautiful? We've got some coffee on," Love kept chattering, perhaps from nerves, as she led them into the kitchen where the rough wooden beams and plank floors continued from the living room. Rudy followed them from the rear, herding them all into what had always been the best part of the Lake House.

The kitchen and dining room were one large space, full of light from rows of windows and a set of French doors on the outside wall. The large room had been remodeled years before in a traditional style.

The cabinets were off white, the counter tops were black as were the iron hinges, drawer and cabinet handles, and light fixtures. The inside wall was exposed brick with built in cubby holes to hold a variety of items including firewood for the large fireplace that sat at the end of the long room. The view out of the windows was remarkable. A brick patio just outside of the French doors ended at a short grass yard that led up to a thick grove of trees, gracing them today with the full range of fall colors.

"Sit down," Rudy told them as he and Love gathered mugs and small plates.

The smell of fresh coffee warmed the air and something else, a yeasty, cinnamon scent that got stronger as Love set a plate of fresh baked cinnamon rolls on the table. Rudy placed one mug in front of each of them and then fetched the pot of hot coffee and began pouring. Jenny looked across the long dining room table at Jimmy and wondered if he was thinking the same thing she was, their Dad had never served them coffee, ever. Jimmy caught her gaze and read the confusion in it, giving her an almost imperceptible shrug to let her know he noticed and he was going with the flow.

"I was hoping you would get here before your Dad ate all of the treats," Love said with a wide smile at Rudy.

"I just had to taste one to make sure it was baked through," Rudy answered, chuckling as he said it, his eyes twinkling.

Jenny cringed. Were they going to be flirting like this the whole week?

"They smell delicious." Jimmy took one of the gooey treats and plopped it onto the plate Rudy had set in front of him. He handed Jenny the serving spatula with a 'be nice' look.

"Yes, thank you," she managed to say.

She took a cinnamon roll even though she knew she wasn't going to be able to eat it. Her stomach was tight. She felt like a stranger in their Lake House, in her Mom's kitchen. Love playing hostess was too much. Jenny realized that she may not be able to eat anything for the entire Thanksgiving holiday.

"I'll just have one more," Rudy announced. Love shook her head and smiled at him. "They're too good!" He declared as he pulled a corner off and popped it in his mouth. "Besides, I burned up the first one in the hot tub."

Jimmy swallowed what was in his mouth and asked, "Hot tub?"

"Oh, honey," Love said to Rudy. "You let the cat out of the bag!"

"There goes the surprise!" Rudy threw up his hands in mock despair.

"What hot tub?" Jenny asked stiffly.

"It's an early Christmas present," Rudy explained. "I'll show you."

Sure enough, just outside the French doors and to the right, out of sight of the kitchen windows, sat an oversized, bubbling, completely gaudy hot tub.

"Did you bring a suit?" Rudy asked. Both Jenny and Jimmy shook their heads 'no'.

"Oh no, we should have told you to bring one." Love's face fell.

"Naw," Rudy waved his hand dismissively. "They both have so many suits packed away in this house. You'll find one that fits, don't you think?" He looked at them hopefully.

Jenny was still speechless. She was just trying to keep her mouth from dropping open. She looked to Jimmy to answer.

"Yeah, there are probably a few bathing suits here," Jimmy answered, but was a little distracted, still surprised at the appearance of such a modern, opulent amenity in their back yard. "Dad, what made you decide to do this?"

Rudy put his arm around Love's waist and looked at her happily. "I decided there's no time like the present."

Jenny cringed again. This was going to be a very long week.

❧

LATER, in her room, Jenny was glad to be alone. The sun had set, Jimmy was in his room talking to Penny on the phone and, she hoped, Paul. Her Dad and Love were putting away dinner dishes. Jenny hadn't eaten much and excused herself to her room fairly early feigning fatigue. That wasn't a total lie.

She flopped onto her double bed that still had the rosebud patterned comforter she and her Mom had picked out. They had redecorated the room together when Jenny graduated from high school. At the time the rosebud pattern had seemed quite grown up.

She was tired. Getting up early, the long drive, her heart

aching for Jimmy and his separation, the newness of Love being here, the look of joy on her Dad's face, everything was too much. Hot tears filled Jenny's eyes and her heart sank.

She wished her Mom was here. That was the real drain, the real sorrow.

Jenny pushed the palms of her hands onto her eyes and pressed the tears out, wiping them away and sniffing hard. She had cried so much already. The air in her room hung around her, empty, joyless.

She rolled over so that she was on her side, the soft rosebud covered pillow under her head. Facing the window, more memories flooded her mind. She and her Mom had bought the white lace material for her curtains in town. Then her Mom had sewn them on her portable sewing machine, the one she kept in the basement laundry room. It had taken her less than an hour.

More tears rolled down Jenny's cheeks. She didn't try to stop them this time.

After a while the tears subsided and she sat up, wiping her face with the cuffs of her shirt. May as well get into her pajamas and go to bed. She couldn't make herself go downstairs and spend time with the newlyweds.

After all of her clothes were unpacked, she changed into her navy blue flannel jammies with the large, white polka dots. Pajamas were the one place where Jenny allowed her tight control of fashion to loosen up a little. She sat on the edge of her bed, wondering if she should just turn off the lamp and go to sleep or read a little bit first, when a stack of books on the small writing desk at her window caught her attention.

Jenny went to the desk and turned on the reading lamp that sat on its corner. A card lay on top of the stack. The image on the front of the card was a beautiful drawing of a peacock, its colors vibrant, the magnificent feathers on its tail embellished with swirls of gold, silver and purple glitter. Jenny picked up the card and flipped it open, recognizing the tilted flourish of her mother's cursive handwriting immediately.

Her hands trembled slightly. Jenny sat down at the small desk chair to read the message. It took her five tries before she could read through to the end without being blinded by tears.

My Dearest Girl,

My Jennifer. I just watched you drive away, heading back to your life once again, looking so grown up and beautiful. It was wonderful to spend time with you this long weekend. Your father and I love it when you kids can make it out to see us. It can get a little quiet without you all around, and we didn't buy the Lake House to be quiet!

I remembered after you left that I forgot to tell you I found these old journals of yours when I was cleaning out some boxes. I am leaving them here on your desk so you'll be sure to see them when you come back next time.

I have to confess that I read through some of them. They're not diary journals, but story journals. So I thought maybe that wasn't too nosy of me.

You know what, Jenny? These stories are really, really good! You have always had a real talent for writing. I know you write a lot for your work, but can I be a pushy kind of Mom for a moment and suggest that maybe you should do more creative writing? It's just a thought. I would love to read more of your stories.

Well, I'm running out of room on this card. Isn't it pretty? I got it at that new little boutique by the sandwich shop. I'll take you there sometime when we're all here again. Won't that be fun?

Love you,
Mom

When was this written? She flipped the card over and looked for a date. There was none. She thought back, trying to remember the last time she'd been to the Lake House. It was after her Mom got sick, she knew that for sure. But it must have been before they all realized how sick she really was.

Jenny ran her thumb over the handwriting and took in a shuddering breath. She should have come to see her parents every weekend. She shouldn't have assumed her Mom would be there forever.

Jenny closed the card and placed it carefully on the desk. She ran her hand over the pile of journals and spiral note-books. The whole stack fit neatly on her nightstand and she had just enough room to set the peacock card up where she could see it from her pillow. She was about to pick up the top journal when she was interrupted by a soft knock on her door.

"Yes?" Jenny said.

The door swung open partway and Jimmy stuck his head in. "Are you still up?"

Jenny scooted over on her bed so there was enough room for him and patted the space next to her. He closed the door behind him and hopped onto her bed, stretching out next to her under the comforter and angling himself so their bodies were separate, but their heads slightly touched.

"How'd your phone call go?" she asked.

"Pretty awful." He sounded tired.

"I'm sorry." She reached for his hand and squeezed it. He squeezed back.

"It is what it is, you know?" he responded.

"Mmhmm," Jenny mumbled.

They were quiet for a few minutes, just staring at the light fixture above them, thinking. Jimmy finally broke the silence with a question, "So, what do you think of Love?"

Jenny didn't answer. She had already fallen asleep.

Chapter Three

Warm smells of coffee brewing and bacon frying drifted upstairs, drawing Jenny out of bed and down the old staircase towards the kitchen. The ancient wooden steps creaked under her pink fuzzy slippers and she pulled the matching pink robe more snugly around her in the chilly morning air.

The Lake House had been built in the early 1800's. A Cape Cod style, solid and dependable, but definitely prone to uneven temperatures throughout. The upstairs hall and bathroom, the stairway and the front sitting room were almost always colder than the rest of the house. Jenny didn't mind. It made her feel like she was on vacation. She followed her nose into the toasty kitchen where she found her Dad cooking breakfast with Love.

"Good morning, Button!" He smiled at her and lifted an empty mug in the air. "Do you want some coffee? We just made a fresh pot."

"Yes, thank you," she mumbled, still groggy as she perched on one of the tall kitchen stools

"Cream and sugar, right?" Love asked, setting the small

cream pitcher and sugar bowl in front of Jenny, anticipating a 'yes' response.

Jenny nodded. "Thanks."

Love looked decidedly more put together this morning. She was fully dressed, wearing jeans that were worn, but not full of holes or anything. She had a lavender Henley shirt on under a long pastel striped sweater whose sleeves reached all the way over the palms of her hands. When Love's hair was dry, Jenny noted, it was a pretty silver color and naturally wavy. It fell past her shoulders which didn't quite make her look like a witch, as Jenny might have thought it would, but more like an old wise woman from a fantasy story.

Classical music played on the small CD/Radio combo that sat on the counter. Jenny watched as her father tended to the bacon that popped and sizzled in a large cast iron skillet and Love slid a casserole dish full of what looked like French toast into the oven.

"Did you sleep well?" he asked as he repositioned himself so Love could place another skillet on the burner next to the one occupied by bacon. Love kept her hand on her Dad's back just a few moments longer than necessary as she moved behind him to go to the refrigerator.

"Yes, I did," she managed to answer.

"Is that bacon or am I still dreaming?" Jimmy announced his arrival with the question. He staggered into the kitchen in a kind of fake sleepwalk routine, bundled in his own warm robe, but without the fuzzy slippers.

"Coffee, son?" Rudy held up another empty mug. Jimmy nodded and sat on the stool next to Jenny.

They sipped their coffee and observed their Dad in the kitchen with Love. With sideways glances, Jenny watched as Jimmy emerged from his sleepy cocoon and the strangeness of their Dad's behavior registered with him. When Rudy pulled a bag of oranges out of the refrigerator and started slicing them in half in order to juice them with a small, hand held juicer, Jenny and Jimmy shared a look of disbelief.

"Dad, I've never seen you cook before," Jenny said.

"I like to cook," he answered, happily grinding the pulpy juice from an innocent orange rind. "I guess I never had time when you were growing up. I was working all the time."

"We're making a big breakfast today. My friend, Aaron, is coming this morning," Love interjected.

Right. The little old lady who smokes weed.

"Where do you know Erin from?" Jimmy asked.

"Oh, wow." Love stopped what she was doing, which was apparently hand whipping sugared cream cheese with some blueberries. "We've been neighbors in Denver for more than 30 years now."

"How nice," Jenny said, imagining Love and another quirky free spirited little old lady in their back yard full of rose bushes and bird baths, smoking a joint. She gave Jimmy an amused look and knew by his quick nod that he was thinking something similar.

"I'm excited for you both to meet Aaron," Love continued. "I think you'll all get along wonderfully." She flashed her brilliant smile at them, which was a little overwhelming first thing this morning.

"I'm sure we will," Jenny answered politely. Internally she sighed, another stranger she had to be nice to over Thanksgiving.

"Can we help you with anything?" Jimmy asked, always congenial.

The siblings were given the task of setting the dining room table. They used the casual off-white stoneware with the embossed edges and plain off-white cloth napkins. Love suggested they set a place for her soon to arrive buddy, so they put two places on what had always been Jenny's side of the table.

Once everything was ready the kitchen seemed even more warm and inviting and Jenny decided she could probably make small talk if necessary, as long as she had plenty of coffee. She thought briefly about going upstairs to change out of her polka dot pajamas, but decided there was no need. How important was it to look good for Love's little old lady friend?

All of the delicious food filled the center of the table, smelling wonderful. They pulled their chairs out and sat down at their places to dig in. The sound of crunching gravel in the driveway sent Love into a flurry of activity.

"Aaron's here!" She exclaimed, popping out of her chair and flying by them on her way to the front door. "This is going to be such fun!"

Rudy watched her excitement with much pleasure. Jenny saw the gleam of satisfaction in his eyes as his new wife hurried to meet her friend and she felt a sense of betrayal. It didn't seem right that he could look at another woman that way. Rudy's gaze turned to Jenny and she dropped hers to the floor, hoping she didn't have a scowl on her face.

"Have you met Erin?" Jimmy asked.

Rudy nodded. "He's very nice."

He?

Jimmy and Jenny barely had a moment to exchange surprised looks before a tall, handsome, young man entered the kitchen followed by Love. They all stood up to greet him.

"Aaron, nice to see you again." Rudy stuck out his hand.

"You too, Rudy." Aaron took his hand and shook it firmly. "Thanks again for inviting me." He turned his attention towards the siblings and Jenny, for one, was at a loss for words.

Aaron was tall, at least 6'1", ruggedly built, with long, wavy blonde hair loosely pulled into a man bun. His features were strong and sharp like a Viking's, and his eyes were such a bright, frosty blue they almost glowed. He had a lengthy rough beard of blonde and red whiskers that Jenny at once hated and found attractive. His skin was tanned with that reddish tone that the fair skinned are cursed. He wore a navy blue, long sleeved T-shirt, worn jeans and a pair of broke in brown hiking boots.

He looked like he knew how to build a wooden boat from scratch. He looked like he had just cross country skied into a snowed in village to deliver medicine to sick children. He looked like he could brew his own pale ale while gutting a fish and playing the fiddle. He definitely did not look like a little old lady.

Aaron locked his eyes onto hers and a flutter of nerves burst through her stomach. She couldn't think of one thing to say to this man. His icy blue eyes seemed to be holding her in a trance.

Time froze for a moment as they connected, albeit silently. His eyes searched hers until he found something, what was it? Pain? Loneliness? Attraction? Jenny's feelings were in a free fall. She couldn't put her finger on what was happening between them, but she could tell the moment Aaron found what he was seeking, because she was suddenly exposed, vulnerable, and had the insane desire to flee out the French doors.

Then it was gone. The bright light of his searching gaze dimmed. He toned it down. She understood immediately that he had seen into her for the briefest second, felt her discomfort, and pulled back. Like a horse whisperer or a psychiatrist working with frightened children, he knew when to back off, but her heart had quickened nevertheless. It still beat loudly in her chest.

"Hello." Aaron's face broke into a smile that crinkled the corners of his eyes. Eyes that twinkled so brightly it was difficult for Jenny to maintain her gaze. She fought the urge to look away.

"Hello," Jimmy answered, thankfully one of them could speak. "I'm Jimmy."

Aaron stepped towards him and they shook hands, Jimmy smiling just a smidge too hard. Jenny stifled a giggle. She knew Aaron's intense good looks were not lost on her brother.

Aaron turned towards her, causing nervous butterflies in her stomach again. The urge to giggle grew stronger. Jimmy slipped behind Aaron and peered at her over the taller man's shoulder, his eyes wide with an 'Oh My God He's Gorgeous' look. Jenny had to completely ignore him and focus hard on greeting Love's friend appropriately. That didn't work.

"I thought you were a woman," she said, startled at the words as soon as they left her mouth. Aaron's smile went from welcoming to politely confused. Jimmy disappeared behind Aaron's back, she was getting no help from him. She tried to explain, "I mean, my middle name's Erin with an 'e' and, you know..." she fanned her hand back and forth between them, "Aaron...Erin...I thought Aaron was a girl's name." Without thinking, she allowed her fingertips to touch his chest and felt the muscles underneath his shirt for a brief, enticing moment. "So I thought you were a girl!" A nervous laugh escaped her lips.

She wrapped her arms around her waist in a self-hug and was immediately reminded that she had on her polka dot pajamas and pink robe, and still had a head full of bed hair. Oh my God, had she really just touched his chest?

The whole room was silent. Aaron hadn't looked away from her since she started her awkward ramble. Jenny heard Jimmy clear his throat from somewhere on the other side of this rather marvelous looking man. She knew her brother was fighting not to laugh. Her own desire to giggle abandoned her completely and heat rose in her cheeks. Aaron's brilliant, icy eyes searched hers again, this time they were full of humor. He cocked his head towards hers in a charming nod.

"Sorry to disappoint," he grinned, expertly converting this awkward interaction into a playful moment. Their first private joke.

She blushed even harder, ducking her head and smiling at the floor in an uncontrollable coy reaction. As she lifted her gaze she saw her Dad and Love watching them with blatant knowing smiles plastered across their faces. The soft, squishiness she'd been feeling suddenly hardened. Why were they looking at her like that? Were they trying to set her up with this man bunned hipster? Was Love playing matchmaker?

Jenny stiffened. She dropped her gaze to the table and sat back down in her chair, shrugging nonchalantly to indicate she was not disappointed. Why would she care either way? If he was a man or a woman or an orangutan, it didn't matter to her. He was just another stranger in her mother's house for Thanksgiving and that's how she would treat him.

Chapter Four

The first item on the agenda after cleaning up breakfast dishes was horseshoes. At least, that was the first item on Rudy's agenda. Jenny had helped clear the table, taken the cloth napkins downstairs to the laundry and upon returning found that Love and Aaron had taken over washing and drying dishes.

"Your Dad and Jimmy went out to play horseshoes," Love told her. "We've got the rest of this I think, don't we?" She looked up at Aaron, because everyone in the house had to look up when speaking to him, they were a tiny lot and he was like a great, blonde lumberjack among them.

"Absolutely," he responded. "We can catch up on old times." Aaron nudged Love with his elbow and it was all Jenny could do to keep from rolling her eyes. She managed not to, excusing herself to go get dressed instead.

She took a quick shower in the small upstairs bath and spent another half hour drying her hair and putting on a little makeup. She didn't want to get too fixed up, but after this morning she felt like putting her best face forward, so to speak.

Once back in her room she sat down at her desk. She could see her Dad and Jimmy in the back yard playing horseshoes. They were chatting and laughing with each other and she watched them for a while. She was lucky to have both of them in her life. They were good men, she knew that for sure. Other men in her life had not turned out to be quite as supportive or loyal or even as much fun as her Dad and brother. Sometimes she wondered if they'd spoiled her for any kind of romantic relationship. She hadn't found a man that lived up to her expectations yet. Maybe she never would.

"You'll find the right man one day," her mother used to tell her when Jenny was having one of her lonely breakdowns. "Don't settle for the wrong one. You deserve to find real love." Jenny remembered those talks fondly. They would have cake and hot tea with honey if it was cold outside, or cookies and iced tea if it was hot. Their conversations about boys and romance were never contained to only one part of the year.

Jenny sighed. She looked at the journals and card resting on her nightstand and decided she would spend some quiet time in her room reading her old stories. She brought everything back to her desk and turned on the little lamp. After reading through the peacock card again, she propped it up on the corner of the small desk where she could see it, then picked up one of the oldest journals and flipped it open.

The first story was about a circus elephant who escapes during a show and rampages through the streets, ultimately being trapped and killed for rebelling against its captors. The last chapter was particularly gory, the elephant dying in a huge pool of blood still wearing its gaudy circus hat. Dark. That was from her middle school years. The writing was juvenile, but really not too bad for a 13 or 14-year old girl, she thought.

She picked up the next journal and skimmed through it, looking for something she'd written in high school. She found one with the title scrawled in her wide, optimistic teenage cursive across the top, "Once I Loved You". Reading through the story, Jenny recalled the boy it was based on, a beautiful dark haired quiet boy who'd been one of the nice popular kids. He was a star on the baseball team and Jenny had developed a real interest in baseball while suffering under that crush. The main character in the book was named after him, Gabe. She smiled at the memory. The interest in Gabe had faded after she wrote this story, as had her interest in baseball.

She looked through each of the journals. As a child she'd always wanted to be a writer. She'd never told anyone, but she was pretty sure her mother had guessed. Intimidated by the brilliant literary writers she admired, Jenny had chosen to pursue a degree in Communications rather than English. She'd worked in the Communications department of a healthcare company for the last six years. They operated several hospitals and it was her responsibility to keep up the internal communication between management and staff, mostly through informational emails, newsletters and presentations at large meetings. The job suited her and provided her the opportunity to use some of her writing skills, but it was nothing like writing fiction.

The last journal in the pile was different than the others. Instead of the used look and the general teenage girl designs of the previous covers, lots of pinks and purples and bubble letters, this one was a sleek deep green with gold script lettering on the front that read 'Dream Big, Be Brave.' And it was brand new. Jenny opened it to find that it was empty save for an inscription on the inside front cover from her Mom.

Jenny, For all of your new stories! Love, Mom

She didn't want to cry again, but she did. Just a little. Just enough to mess up her makeup.

"Jenny." A knock sounded at the same time Jimmy opened the door and popped his head into her room. His expression fell when he saw her. "You're still in your robe?"

"Do you mind?" Jenny pulled her robe tighter around her.

"Dad wants to have a ping pong tournament. Love's making snacks."

"Snacks? We just ate."

"It's been, you know, an hour since then." Jimmy grinned at her. "I guess Aaron brought some stuff. Apparently he works at a natural food company and is some kind of foodie." He paused, then wiggled his eyebrows up and down at her. "In addition to being the hottest human being I've seen in a very, very long time!"

"Shut up," Jenny said, trying not to laugh.

Jimmy did a silly swing walk over to where she sat and grabbed her by the arms, standing her up as he did. He made a pleading face, "Come on! You can't just mope up here in your room forever. Put on something fabulous and get downstairs to play some highly competitive ping pong with that gorgeous man."

Jenny laughed, "He's not that gorgeous."

"Right, Miss Melt Into a Puddle of Goo when you met him." Jimmy let go of her in mock disgust. "If I was single and he was gay there would be no holding me back."

"You're sure he's not gay?" She asked.

"I'm sure," Jimmy sighed, a sound of resignation. "Besides, I'm still officially married, so even if he was..." He let the rest of his sentence trail off into sadness.

"Oh, honey." Jenny reached out to give him a comforting hug.

"Nope." He held her at arm's length. "I'm not doing sad today. We've got horseshoes, we've got ping pong, we've got a hunk waiting for us in the basement, and enough food to choke an elephant. Today is going to be fun, dammit!"

Jenny agreed to join the ping pong tournament and sent Jimmy out of the room so she could get dressed. She chose a pair of jeans and a dark grey blouse with a crisscross V-neck that hung nicely around her shape without being too clingy. She slipped on socks and a pair of flat tennis shoes, more to keep her feet warm than anything, and made her way down to the basement.

The merriment could be heard before she even reached the main floor, which was empty because everyone had already moved to the basement. The house smelled delicious, she assumed from whatever snacks had been prepared. Jenny walked quickly by the empty sitting room where her Mom used to sit in the chair in the corner, reading. She knew that if her Mom was alive she would probably have spent the morning visiting with her in that room, but she didn't want to think about that too much right now.

The basement was a fun recreation space. It was all one great room except for a storage area, a bathroom and the laundry room. A giant sectional sofa with a big screen TV took up one side of the room. They had spent countless hours watching movies on that TV as kids. Right now it was tuned to a football game, it looked like college teams. The other side of the room had a small bar with a short counter, which currently held three trays of hors devours and a pitcher full of sliced citrus fruit floating in a dark red liquid. That side of the room also held a juke box, a fuzball table and, Rudy's all-time favorite, a ping pong table, where he now dominated one side of what appeared to be a heated volley with Aaron.

Love and Jimmy were perched on two of the three barstools that bumped up against the bar. Love gave Jenny a happy little wave when she entered the room. Jenny returned it with a conservative smile.

"This looks serious," Jenny said as she approached the table.

"You're up next," Jimmy told her.

"I've already lost," Love said brightly, scooting out the empty barstool next to her so Jenny could sit down. With no other options, Jenny took the seat. She positioned herself so her back was towards the bar so she could watch the action.

"Sangria?" Love asked, moving the pitcher towards her.

Jenny sipped Sangria and took in the sight of her elderly father whipping a much younger man in ping pong. It wasn't that Aaron was bad at the game. It's just that her Dad was so good at it. Her vantage point made it easy for her to appreciate Aaron's physical attributes while not appearing to stare. She liked how he talked and laughed with her Dad, and she even liked how his hair got a little tussled from the exertion, long pieces of it falling down into his angular features. She wondered how long his hair actually was and what he looked like when it was down. Once or twice, he glanced in her direction and she sucked in her breath. The piercing, cold blue of his eyes riveted her attention in those moments and she couldn't look away.

"You're up, Button," Rudy exclaimed the instant Aaron missed the final point. He turned and pointed at her with his paddle, his face alight with the thrill of victory. Aaron placed his hands on the table and feigned exhaustion. Jenny popped a mini mushroom quiche into her mouth and hopped off of the barstool to take his place.

"This is a mean game," Aaron said as he handed her the paddle. Their hands brushed against each other in the exchange and once again Jenny felt the warmth of him tingle through her fingertips.

"Only with my Dad," she said, trying not to smile too much at him, and failing.

"Have you seen the Bruce Lee video when he plays ping pong with nunchucks?" Jimmy piped up from the bar.

"Yes!" Aaron exclaimed. He mimed nunchuck moves as he approached the bar and he and Jimmy entered into a lively conversation about Bruce Lee and Kung Fu movies.

"Ready?" Rudy asked Jenny. She nodded and the game was on.

Jenny wasn't as good at ping pong as her Dad, but she was close. Countless ping pong tournaments had occurred in this basement since she was a little girl. Both she and Jimmy had learned early that their Dad wasn't going to just let them win. They had practiced with each other and eventually become real competition for their table tennis obsessed father.

Her Dad delighted in her expertise as they served and volleyed and teased each other good naturedly. Despite her best efforts, Jenny finally succumbed to his lightening reflexes and lost the game, allowing Jimmy to take his place as the next challenger.

Jenny took a seat at the empty bar stool between Aaron and Love, the latter immediately offered her a raspberry filled doughnut hole.

"No, thanks," Jenny said. "They look delicious, though. Did you make them?"

"Aaron brought them," Love replied.

"Did you make them?" Jenny asked Aaron, glad to have even the tiniest subject to build a polite conversation with both of them.

Aaron shook his head 'no'. "I brought them from a little store near my house."

"Barnaby's?" Love asked with delight.

"Yep," he answered as he took the tray Love offered him and ate one of the doughnut holes.

"So, you two lived next to each other?" Jenny thought she should at least try to put the pieces together.

"Yes," Love answered. "Aaron's parents moved next door when you were, what, two or three?" She looked at Aaron for confirmation.

Aaron nodded as he took a drink of his Sangria. Jenny tried not to notice the way his neck muscles flexed when he swallowed.

"That's what I'm told," he answered.

"We, my husband and I, had a dog named Pewter. A little silver haired terrier," Love explained. "And that dog loved Aaron from the moment they met. They were like best friends growing up together." She gave Aaron a sweet smile, which he returned.

"Love was my second Mom when I was a kid," Aaron said. "Still is."

Jenny had a sudden urge to leave the room. She stayed seated, however, she didn't want to seem bothered. She wanted to remain cool and aloof and unruffled.

Aaron leaned in towards her, his eyes smiling at the corners. "You are an excellent ping pong player."

A small, almost imperceptible, shiver ran down her spine. She could feel her heart beating a little faster than normal. Was she really that affected by his physical presence? Ridiculous. It was probably the alcohol in the drink. Sangria was always stronger than you thought it was going to be. She took in a deep breath to calm herself and realized he was so close she could smell him. He smelled like soap and fresh cut wood and leather. Jenny inhaled again without thinking, liking his smell, then realized he was waiting for her to respond.

"Oh, yeah, Dad insisted we play with him. It's a tradition at the Lake House."

Aaron nodded with appreciation. "That's nice. This is a beautiful house, too."

"Isn't it?" Love chimed in, looking around the basement recreation space with admiration. "I've been in love with it since we got here."

"Yes," Jenny said quickly, not hearing the spite until it was out of her mouth. "Mom and Dad did a really great job fixing it up."

The air around the three of them grew quiet, even as Rudy and Jimmy continued with their raucous game a few feet away. Jenny's throat felt tight and she stared into her glass of Sangria without looking up. She didn't need to look up to feel the tension from her remark. The hurt. Inwardly she was defiant, stamping her feet at Love and all that her presence at the Lake House represented, like a little girl who wasn't getting her way. She was also ashamed. Sorry that she couldn't reciprocate the kindness Love seemed to be trying to show her and guilty for resenting her Dad's newfound happiness. The Sangria in her glass blurred and Jenny was mortified to realize she was about to cry.

"Excuse me," she muttered, taking her drink and hurrying away from the bar and up the stairs.

Chapter Five

The next day was Sunday. Jenny got up before sunrise, dressed in warm layers including her favorite oversized navy blue sweater, slipped the green journal and a pen into her sweater pocket and went carefully down the old stairs to try and keep them from creaking. At the bottom of the stairs she quietly opened the closet and retrieved her coat and hat. Aaron was sleeping on an air mattress set up in the front sitting room, since all three bedrooms were already occupied. Jenny couldn't see him, but she could hear him breathing deeply like a sleeping bear. She snuck down the hallway and slipped out the French doors off the kitchen, just in time to see the first rays of morning light sparking through the trees.

It was cold. Really cold. Jenny half wished she'd brought gloves on top of her hat and coat, but didn't want to go back inside and risk running into anyone. She wanted this day to start off clear, no botched conversations, no coming upon Love somewhere she expected to see her mother, nothing but her and the trees and the crisp, cold autumn air.

She strolled past the giant Oak tree in the side yard, where their tire swing still hung invitingly. She considered it for a moment. No, too cold. Jenny shoved her bare hands in her coat pockets and followed a small path into the woods that led to the clearing. By the time she got there the sun was halfway up. Dawn painted the trees and leaves with a golden glow and Jenny heard geese honking as they flew overhead.

She paused for a moment at the edge of the clearing and took in its pure beauty. The clearing was just that, about an acre of cleared area hidden in the dense woods on their property. It was covered in a carpet of thick grass with various flowers and shrubs, both wild and perennials that she and her mother had planted over the years, growing around the edges, some reaching into the grassy areas. There were two benches in the clearing. One on the east side facing west and one on the west side facing east. They'd placed them this way so they could come in the morning and watch the sun rise over the trees or the evening and watch it set on the other side.

Jenny sat down in the east facing bench. The wood was so cold it almost felt wet through her clothes, but there had been neither rain nor frost overnight. She took in a deep breath of the sharp morning air, the scent of ancient trees and rich soil filling her lungs. She wished she had a thermos of coffee or, better yet, hot chocolate. Her Mom had always brought hot chocolate in their huge thermos with the red plaid print on the outside when it was cold. She had decided to skip making coffee before coming out this morning, she figured just the smell could wake someone up, especially Aaron since he was sleeping in the room right next to the kitchen.

The geese sounded again, followed by the chirping of other birds that Jenny didn't know well enough to name. Soon they would be flitting through the trees and in and out of the shrubbery looking for bright red berries or seeds to eat. The clearing was secluded enough that there was usually no noise from any of their nearest neighbors and literally none from any cars driving on the nearest roads. Jenny relished the silence. She spread her arms across the back of the bench and kicked her booted feet out in front of her, crossing them at the heels. The rays of the sun were bright enough now that she could feel them warming her cheeks. She gave a contented sigh. She would sit here and let the sun do its work until the air lost its bite, then she would do what she came here for, she would write.

Reading through her old stories had sparked something inside of her, something that had been sleeping for a long time. The message from her Mom had brought it all to the surface and Jenny felt like she at least owed her Mom the respect to consider her suggestion to do more creative writing. So she sat in the chilly morning until it wasn't so chilly anymore, then she pulled the green journal and pen from her sweater pocket and positioned herself sideways on the bench so she could write comfortably.

She read the inscription again and smiled, then turned to the first, perfectly blank, empty page and stared. She hadn't given one thought yet towards what she actually wanted to write, and the blank page wasn't giving her any great ideas. She wrote the date on the top right hand side of the page and the pen wimped out halfway through the year. She shook it and tried again. She stuck the tip of the pen just inside her open mouth and breathed on it, maybe it was too cold for the ink to run. That worked and she was able to scribble the rest of the date, but then the pen just hung there over the starting point on the top left of the page. Nothing.

A heavy crunching sound echoed through the clearing and Jenny forgot all about her writing. The crunching was definitely steps of someone, or something, approaching. Her mind whirled with stories of bears in the woods and she cursed herself silently for not bringing her mace. She stood up to face where she thought the sound was coming from, the opening of the path into the clearing, which was less than ten feet from the bench. Whatever it was, it wasn't crashing through the trees but staying on the path and heading right towards her. Even if it was a deer, rutting season could still be affecting the bucks in the area and they might be dangerous. For an instant she thought she might duck into the trees behind the bench and hide, but that thought came too late, the culprit emerged from the path into the clearing at a full run.

It was Aaron.

Jenny yelped when she saw him, a visceral reaction that she couldn't control. Her hands flew to her mouth to cover it, making her drop the pen and journal on the ground.

Aaron's forward momentum was disrupted by the sight and sound of her. He did a cartoonish scrambling that propelled him backwards a few steps before his mind registered who she was and he stopped. He put his right hand over his heart and let out a surprised laugh.

"Jeez, Jenny!" He laughed again. His breathing was hard not only from the shock, but because he was out for what looked like a morning run. He wore dark grey sweat pants, a loose T-shirt and a faded red hooded sweatshirt. "You scared the hell out of me!"

Jenny dropped her hands from her mouth. "You, too!"

Aaron noticed the journal and pen on the ground and walked towards her. "I'm sorry, let me help you get these." She started to refuse, but he was already down on one knee in front of her picking up her items. He stood up and brushed a few stray leaves off of the journal before handing it and the pen back to her. "I didn't know anyone was out here."

"I came out here to..." she paused, not certain how to explain.

Aaron's eyes flicked to the journal in her hand then back up. "To write?"

Jenny nodded mutely. The morning glow tumbled through his hair, making it even more golden blonde. His beard looked lustrous with its red and gold highlights.

"Do you come out here to write every morning?" He asked.

"Yes, well, starting this morning."

"I'll have to take my run another way. I don't want to disturb you." He smiled at her. It was a gentle smile. Maybe it was because the morning was so beautiful, maybe being in the clearing made her feel calm and centered, she wasn't really sure what came over her, but what she blurted out next came as a surprise to both of them.

"Oh, no, it's no problem. Come here any time you want. My Mom and I used to come here all the time...with hot chocolate." She smiled a little nervously, unsure why she had shared that last bit with him.

Aaron shifted his weight from one foot to the other and considered her for a moment. Jenny felt exposed as he looked at her, but tried to return his gaze with equal calm. Once again she was under the spell of his crystal blue eyes, but she was able to let him look into her without panicking this time. He took his time, searching her eyes for what, she wasn't sure. The truth? Just when it was about to get uncomfortable, his face lit up with a big grin.

"That's very nice of you. I might do that when I'm done with my run."

"Good" She nodded, silently recognizing that she was disappointed he wasn't going to join her on the bench right now.

"I'll let you get back to your writing," he said as he took a few steps back towards the opening in the trees.

She gave him a little wave, then thought of something. "There's a path that starts near the mailbox in the driveway.

It goes all the way down to the covered bridge. If, you know, you're interested."

"Great! Thanks," he answered. He nodded at her then turned, his walk turning into a jog as he disappeared into the woods.

When Jenny got back to the house breakfast preparations were in full swing again. It wasn't quite as strange to see Love and her Dad cooking together this morning as it was yesterday. Maybe it was something that would grow on her over time. Aaron arrived, freshly showered after his run and smelling good.

"Good morning, again," he said, giving her a quick wink. A flurry of butterflies shimmered through her stomach. She shook them off.

"Again?" Rudy asked. She wondered if his Dad radar was turning on.

"We ran into each other outside this morning, in the clearing," she explained.

"Are you ready to make your world famous crepes?" Love asked Aaron, holding up a nonstick frying pan.

"Absolument!" Aaron answered in pretty good French. He took the pan from Love then stopped uncertainly, realizing that he was in a strange kitchen and didn't know where anything was kept.

"Jenny, would you mind showing him around the kitchen?" Love asked her. "We'll set the table." With that, Love led her Dad into the dining room.

Jenny was a little taken aback. It was the first time Love had spoken to her like that, like they were more than strangers, like they might be part of the same family. She didn't have much time to think about how strange it made her feel, because Aaron was still standing in the middle of the kitchen holding his frying pan.

Jenny showed him where the mixing bowls and utensils

were. Then she opened the fridge and pulled out the ingredients he requested. He didn't consult a list, but told her from memory. Soon she was leaning against the counter watching him mix the crepe batter with a wire whisk. Again, a few strands of blonde, wavy hair had come loose from his man-bun and fell lightly against his cheek, getting hung up with the whiskers of his beard. It took everything in Jenny not to reach out and tuck the stray pieces behind his ear. What was the matter with her? She should try and think of something to say instead.

"You speak French?" She asked.

"Yes," Aaron dipped his head in a half nod. "Well, je parle un peu français." He held his finger and thumb together indicating a tiny amount.

Jenny laughed and answered with a rusty accent, "Moi aussi, un peu."

"Excellent!" He exclaimed with the French pronunciation. "Did you learn in France?"

"Oh, no," Jenny shook her head, pooh-poohing the idea with a chuckle. "I took some in high school and one semester in college."

"You have a good accent," Aaron complimented as he threw a pat of butter in the pan that was heating on the stove. When the butter hit, it sizzled and slid around the surface. He tilted the pan until the butter had coated it, then poured a dipper full of the thin, yellow batter into the center. Immediately he moved the pan in a slow, swirling motion until the batter filled the bottom. He obviously had some skill in the kitchen.

"Did you learn to speak French in France?" She asked, curious.

"Yes, mostly." He picked up a flat spatula from the counter and talked as he watched the edges of the crepe turn dry and brown. "My parents and I spent a lot of time there when I was growing up. They're there now, in fact. With my father's family."

"Too bad you couldn't be with your parents on the holiday," Jenny offered.

Aaron lifted his shoulder and let it drop in an almost imperceptible shrug. "I didn't want to spend the whole week flying and getting jet lag. Besides," he looked into the dining area where Love was showing her Dad how to fold the cloth napkins properly, "It's great to spend some time with Love."

"Yeah," Jenny said, though she was looking at the floor. "That's great."

"So far, I've had a really good time," Aaron continued. When Jenny looked up he was grinning at her, his eyes twinkling. Her butterflies came back, but before she had a moment to squash them, Aaron turned his attention to the frying pan. He lifted the pan off of the flame, jiggled it forward and back a few times to loosen the crepe from the bottom, then flicked his wrist so the crepe let go, flew in the air, turned half over and landed back in the pan on its uncooked side. Jenny's eyes flew open with delight. Aaron gave her another wink. Show off.

"Did you learn to cook in France, too?" She asked with a laugh.

"Oui, mademoiselle." He placed the pan on the burner, let go of the handle and turned his palms upward, as if he'd just done a magic trick. "Voila!"

Despite her best efforts, Jenny's butterflies returned with a vengeance.

Chapter Six

Jimmy finally made it downstairs when they were halfway through breakfast. He was dressed and chipper, but Jenny thought he looked like he hadn't slept much. During breakfast, he leaned into her ear and told her he'd been on the phone with Paul since five in the morning.

"Is that a good thing?" Jenny was hopeful.

"Maybe," he answered.

After breakfast was cleaned up, Rudy made an announcement.

"All right," he started, reaching his arm around Love's shoulders as he spoke. "This year is the first Thanksgiving we're hosting as a married couple." Love smiled up at him and the sight of it wrung Jenny's heart. "It's also the first big Thanksgiving plans we've had since your Mom passed away." He looked meaningfully at Jimmy and Jenny. "And, the first time most of us have had the pleasure of Aaron at our Thanksgiving table." He smiled at Aaron as he spoke. "Love and I were talking and we would like all of us to come together as a group, as a family, and create the Thanksgiving menu."

Jenny looked at Jimmy, confused. What was there to think about a Thanksgiving menu? It was turkey, stuffing, mashed potatoes, gravy and pumpkin pie. Boom, you're done.

"A menu?" Jimmy voiced the question for both of them.

"We want everyone to come up with two dishes. So one side dish and either an appetizer or a dessert. Then we're going to go to town together tomorrow and shop for ingredients so we can get cooking on Wednesday!" Rudy beamed at them, his arm still draped around Love. Her serene expression made it obvious she agreed with this plan, maybe she'd been the orchestrator of it from the beginning. "I understand Aaron is quite a cook, and we got a taste of that this morning with those crepes." Rudy rubbed his rounded belly, like he was a cartoon mayor of a cartoon town who'd just eaten a big meal.

"Rudy and I will manage the turkey, so you don't have to worry about that," Love spoke up.

Jenny scowled. This wasn't how they had ever done Thanksgiving.

"Those were good crepes," Jimmy said to Aaron, giving her a sideways glance. If nobody else could tell that she disliked this plan, she knew her brother could. Her Dad probably could, too, but he seemed to be perfectly comfortable telling her how it was going to be despite how it might make her feel.

"Sound good?" Rudy asked, making eye contact with Aaron, then Jimmy, then her. Both of the guys nodded in agreement, Aaron with more enthusiasm than she would have expected. When her Dad looked at her and waited for a response, Jenny couldn't get herself to say 'yes' or indicate her compliance in any manner whatsoever. A memory played on a loop in her mind. It was her Mom pulling the perfectly browned turkey out of the oven, moving it to its special platter and placing that platter on the table for carving. It had been the same year after year after year. She hadn't been expecting anything else. She didn't want anything else.

"Does that sound good, Button?"

Tears filled her eyes without warning. Her throat tightened, first with sorrow then with shame. She looked hard at the floor where her shoes blurred. She blinked and two fat tears fell towards the floor, splashing on top of each of her shoes. She shook her head up and down for 'yes'.

"Oh, sweetie." Love's voice sounded, kind and sympathetic.

"It's fine," Jenny blurted out. "I'm sorry. I'm fine and the menu thing is fine." That was all she could say. She turned and hurried up to her room without looking at any of them.

Once she'd cried out all of her tears, she still didn't feel like facing anyone. She laid on her bed for a while, thinking. She made a move to turn on her side and felt the uncomfortable lump of the green journal that was still stuck deep inside her sweater pocket. She sat up and took it out along with the pen and in a sudden flash of insight knew exactly what she wanted to write as her first entry. Sitting down at her desk, Jenny got busy putting down on paper all of her memories of her Mom cooking Thanksgiving dinner.

At about noon, Jimmy came to fetch her and convinced her to come down for lunch.

"We're going to play board games!" He said enticingly through the door. He knew this would get her, she had a naturally competitive spirit.

The dining room table was set up with a Monopoly board, the same one they'd been playing with for decades. When she entered the room, her Dad came to her and gave her a bear hug and a big smooch on the cheek.

"C'mon, Button, you can have the horse," he said as he led her to her seat. Nobody said anything to her about her earlier breakdown. It wasn't because they didn't support her, it was more because they were simply accepting her emotions. That was the nice thing about her family, and Love and Aaron seemed to be taking it all in stride as well.

The chairs were set up the same as they had been since their first breakfast together, with Aaron next to her. So she had Aaron on one side of her and Love on the other, with Jimmy across the table. She had to admit she liked being seated next to Aaron, she could smell his woodsy scent and every time their hands came close to each other when they were moving pieces or counting money, there was a delicious tingle on her skin.

Jenny had the horse, Jimmy had the race care, Rudy took the ship, Aaron chose the dog, and Love chose the wheelbarrow, which Jenny found funny for some reason. She tried to think of a time when anyone in their family had chosen the wheelbarrow and couldn't think of one. She and Jimmy usually argued between the horse and the race car. Rudy usually took the ship or the top hat, sometimes the cannon. Her Mom had always, always, always chosen the thimble. The wheelbarrow had remained untouched for over 20 years in its little compartment inside the Monopoly box. Until today.

Board games were a good way to pass the time on a cold afternoon. They were also a good way to see into someone's personality. Almost two hours later, Rudy was on top of the game, fiercely going after whatever properties he could and putting as many hotels on them as possible. Jimmy and Jenny were scrapping for second place. Love had dropped out of the game fairly early, lacking the hardened emotions necessary to annihilate her opponent. Aaron had lasted longer, but eventually went bankrupt after landing on Park Place and having an especially brutal dealing with its landlord, Rudy.

When it was finally over, Rudy got out pads of paper and pens for everyone, Love piled the cookbooks in the middle of the table, and they set about deciding on what dishes they were all going to focus on. The cookbooks were a combination of her Mom's, which had always lived in this kitchen, and some new ones that Jenny had never seen before, including one called "Eat Your Avocado", that apparently belonged to Aaron.

"Have you made many of these?" Jimmy asked Aaron as he thumbed through the listings of Mango Avocado salad and Avocado pasta sauce.

"Yeah," Aaron looked sheepish. "I'm kind of a food nut."

"Jenny," Love pushed two well used cookbooks towards her, "These must have been a few of your Mom's favorites." She smiled kindly at both Jenny and Jimmy. "Maybe you'll treat us to something you've always loved."

It was becoming increasingly difficult for Jenny to dislike this woman.

"Thank you," was all she said.

"Oh, Jen!" Jimmy had already flipped one of the cookbooks open. "Remember Angel Food Cakes?!" He laughed and turned it around so everyone else could see the picture. "Remember she made one every year and it never looked like this picture?"

Rudy smiled and nodded, a poignant sparkle in his eyes. Jenny laughed, too. She could picture exactly what Jimmy was describing. How they had teased her every year, and they'd all laughed, their Mom laughing the hardest. Jenny made a mental note to include the Angel Food disaster stories in her journal.

"Well, I have no choice but to put Angel Food Cake down as one of mine," Jimmy said, a quiver of emotion betraying his jovial expression.

"That's a great choice, son," Rudy told him.

"And pies! I love making the pies." Jimmy completed his recipe choices by shutting the cookbook in front of him.

"I'm thinking about yeast rolls," Jenny said, actually

looking forward to making them from scratch. "And maybe the green bean casserole?"

"Oh," Love responded, "That sounds delicious. I'll do the sweet potatoes, and how does brussel sprouts and goat cheese salad sound?"

Jenny screwed up her face at the suggestion. You couldn't have that on Thanksgiving, could you?

"That might be nice with Avocado pie," Aaron piped up from the seat next to her. Jenny's scowl increased as she looked at him.

"Avocado pie? On Thanksgiving?" She asked.

"Yes," Aaron stumbled a little bit on his response. "We've had it a few times, everyone always liked it." He hesitated while writing it on the list, looking around at the others for confirmation that it was okay to do so.

Rudy cleared his throat so loud it caught Jenny's attention and she turned her scowl on him. He gave her a meaningful look before speaking, "Jenny, let's be sure to consider some new traditions from other families as well as our own, please."

It wasn't a request, really. Jenny felt heat crawl up her cheeks. She felt like a little girl getting scolded at the dinner table in front of company. They were all looking at her, again.

"Sure," her voice was monotone. She could say the words, but she couldn't fake the emotion. "I'm sure it will be delicious."

She knew, of course, that it wouldn't.

THE COLD DAY finally turned into an even colder night. Jenny had spent the afternoon alternating between having a mediocre time with the new 'family' to sulking in her bedroom. Nothing seemed to cheer her up and even though she knew she was acting like a teenager, she couldn't stop moping about

Thanksgiving dinner. It was silly, really. She couldn't remember ever caring this much about Thanksgiving dinner before now.

Jimmy called to speak with Penny to find out how her day had gone and wasn't able to get through. Paul texted him after a few missed calls to tell him they were heading into the movie theater and would let him know when they were done. This sent Jimmy into his own funk, and her brother's reaction to being in a funk was often to act the exact opposite.

"Who wants to try out the hot tub?" Jimmy asked the room as they were cleaning dinner dishes. He held up two bottles of wine, one in each hand.

"Sounds good," Aaron answered.

"Jenny?" Jimmy pointed at her with one of the bottles. "I think you need a little mellowing out, don't you?"

"Sure." Jenny glanced at the piles of dirty dishes still stacked on the counter next to the kitchen sink.

"Don't you worry about this," Love said to her, "Your Dad and I will take care of it. You kids go have some fun."

And so Jenny was off to her room, searching through drawers for a swimsuit that she may have left behind and that still fit. She finally found one in a plastic tub full of shorts, tank tops and flip flops on the shelf in her small closet. The swimsuit was a tankini, bright aqua with a giant bow positioned right in the middle under her bust. She hadn't worn this suit for over ten years and she barely fit in it, luckily it was a forgiving cut and even though the bow was a little juvenile looking, she wasn't completely disappointed when she checked her reflection in the mirror. The aqua didn't wash her out and was a nice contrast to her nearly auburn hair. Though the fit was tight, it worked to push her not so large bust up, making it appear a little bigger, and when she checked out her backside in the mirror, it looked pretty good.

Lots of walking and trips to the gym helped her out in that arena.

"I'll be in the hot tub most of the time anyway," she said to her reflection, then grabbed a towel and headed downstairs.

Jimmy was already in the hot tub with a half drank glass of red wine in his hand. Steam lifted off the surface of the bubbling water and a green light from somewhere near the bottom illuminated his legs and swim trunks. The night air was bitter cold and though the hot tub was only steps away from the house, the trip in her tankini seemed long. Jenny hurried across the patio and climbed carefully up the steps, her exposed skin shivering.

"Wine?" Jimmy asked, pouring into a second glass before she had a chance to answer.

"Yes, please." Jenny slid into the deliciously warm water and floated down until she found a comfortable indentation on the bench to sit. She took the glass of wine Jimmy offered and leaned into the jet stream that pulsed against her back.

"Cheers?" Jimmy raised his glass and she clinked hers against it.

"Cheers," she answered, taking a sip and turning her head at the sound of the French doors opening. The wine glass never reached her lips, because the instant Aaron walked out of the house wearing only his swim trunks Jenny froze in place.

His hair was down, flowing in wavy glory over his shoulders, a few stray strands tickling at his collar bones. His chest and shoulders were wide, with lean, athletic muscles that flexed slightly as he moved. His abs were strong, with the vague outline of a six pack and a small line of blonde-red hair dropping from his belly button and disappearing under the front of his black swim trunks.

Jenny sucked in her breath as he approached the hot tub.

The litheness of his body reminded her of a thoroughbred racehorse being led to the gates. Jimmy, too, was distracted by Aaron and he let out a very low whistle that only she could hear over the frenzied sound of bubbles.

"It is cold!" Aaron said as he climbed the stairs and lowered himself into the water, his arms and chest rippling slightly with the effort. Jenny realized she was staring and took a quick gulp of her wine.

"It's pretty warm in here," Jimmy quipped, giving her a sideways glance full of amusement. Jenny did her best to ignore him and took another mouthful of wine. What she couldn't ignore was the closeness of Aaron's bare body to her own, the way the water splashed against his chest, how his strong hand carefully held his wine glass, how the tips of his hair got wet and stuck against his shoulders and biceps as if all they wanted to do was touch his skin. That's all she wanted to do. She wanted to reach out and trace her finger up his arm, put her hand under his lush hair and push it back over his shoulder. She wanted to run her fingers through his hair then brush them across his lips and over his beard to see if it was rough or soft. She looked down and realized her wine glass was empty. She was feeling quite warm and tingly.

Aaron and Jimmy were talking, but she had lost track of the conversation. Something about Paul and the struggles of relationships. Aaron was admitting that he'd never been married, never found the right girl. Jimmy was confessing that he couldn't imagine living without Paul for the rest of his life, that he'd thought his marriage was going to last forever.

"Maybe you can work things out," Aaron offered. He grabbed the second bottle of wine and gave Jenny a questioning look, did she want more? She nodded, enjoying the pleasant tingling she was feeling. Aaron moved closer to her, their legs sliding next to each other secretly under the water. He looked at her mischievously as he poured the wine and let his ankle wrap around hers, sending mini shock waves through her body. She didn't look away. "When you find someone you really connect to, you've got to give it your best shot," Aaron said, not taking his eyes off of hers. Those icy blue eyes cut through something inside of her and a shiver started in her belly and moved through her whole body. "Are you cold?" He asked, so close to her, speaking low, his brow furrowed in concern.

"No," she managed to shake her head. "I'm not cold." Her voice was almost a whisper. She felt him move his body closer to hers under the water so their sides were still touching even as he put the wine bottle down. They stayed that way, pressed next to each other in secret, Jenny trying to act as if her heart wasn't leaping out of her chest.

They had polished off both bottles of wine and hashed out Jimmy and Paul's relationship problems when Aaron excused himself to go to bed. Jenny knew she needed to go to bed soon, too. Something in her was afraid to leave at the same time he did, afraid of what might happen once inside the dark house. She and Jimmy watched as Aaron put his hands on the edges of the hot tub and lifted himself out, his glistening wet skin and flexing muscles were almost more than she could handle. He thanked them both and said good night, smiling at her before hurrying back into the heated house. Jenny stared after him, her senses still overwhelmed at the sight and touch of him. Jimmy, who had drank more wine than the other two, propped his arms up on either side of the hot tub. His head dropped back and he closed his eyes, letting out a great sigh.

Then, without looking at Jenny, he spoke up, "Definitely not a little old lady."

Jenny smiled and chuckled at her brother's astute observation. "No, definitely not."

Chapter Seven

The next morning in the clearing, Jenny knew exactly what to write about. As soon as the coldest air had given in to the sun's rays and she could write without making her fingers numb, she put down everything she could remember about being in the hot tub with Aaron. The physical sensations, the way the wine softened her, the fluttery way she had felt, was still feeling. Geese flew high overhead, their sounds of their honking were gentle and soothing from so far away. Jenny filled five pages without having to pause and think once. The flow of writing description and emotion took over her senses. So involved in her task, she lost track of how long she had been sitting there and she didn't hear any footsteps until he was practically upon her.

"Jenny?"

She jumped, startled by the noise and Aaron's sudden presence.

"I'm sorry," he said. "I didn't mean to scare you." He was not dressed in running clothes today, but his normal jeans, boots and a dark grey flannel jacket with a blue and green scarf wrapped around his neck. He held the large red plaid thermos in one hand and two thermal mugs in the other. He lifted them up, his eyes dancing. "I brought you something."

Jenny quickly, and hopefully nonchalantly, flipped the green journal closed and smiled at him. "What is it?"

"Hot chocolate, of course. May I?"

Jenny nodded and he sat down next to her, their legs touching, as if the closeness of the hot tub the night before made it normal for their bodies to touch. Somehow, though, it did feel normal and Jenny didn't move or put any distance between them.

"That sounds delicious," she said, placing her journal and pen on the empty bench on her other side. "Thank you."

Aaron carefully unscrewed the lid and poured the steaming hot beverage into one of the cups, which she took gratefully.

"This smells amazing," she told him.

"I made it from an old family recipe," he answered.

"You did?" Jenny looked down at the frothy, chocolaty goodness, impressed.

"How is your writing going?" He asked as he poured a cup for himself.

Jenny shrugged nonchalantly, trying not to look guilty about writing her intimate feelings about him. "Oh, it's fine. I'm really out of practice."

"Don't you write for work?"

"Yes, but this is different." She hesitated for a moment. He waited patiently, watching her over his cup as he blew on the hot chocolate to cool it down. "I've decided to try writing fiction," she added.

Aaron lifted his eyebrows and nodded as he took a sip. "Sounds fun."

"Yeah," she smiled at him, her nerves on high alert, not only because he was so physically close to her, but also because she wasn't sure about sharing her writing plans with anyone.

"What made you decide to do that?" He asked.

Jenny wasn't sure what came over her, perhaps it was the beautiful surroundings of the clearing, or the butterflies in her stomach, or maybe it was the way he leaned back so comfortably next to her, watching and listening with such interest. Whatever the reason, she told him the whole story. She told him about finding the stack of journals with the card from her Mom and then reading through the stories she'd written when she was young. She told him how much she missed creative writing and how she had chosen something more practical for her career.

Aaron listened attentively, his eyes fixed on her, looking into her as she spoke and pulling more and more of the truth out of her. When she stopped talking there was a pause when neither of them said anything. Then Aaron's face broke into a huge smile and he nudged her gently with his shoulder.

"Good for you!"

She blushed and smiled at her hot chocolate. "Thank you."

"That's really cool," he continued. "Have you already started a story?"

She blushed harder, thinking about what she'd just written about him in her journal. "Not exactly. I've just started with some writing exercises."

"Well I think it's great you want to go after something like that, you know? Following a dream."

Something in his tone made her wonder. "Do you have any dreams you wish you would have gone after?"

He thought about it for a moment then nodded. "I do."

Jenny nudged him with her shoulder. "Yeah? What are they?"

He laughed and shook his head 'no'. "Nothing important."

"Come on," she said. "I told you mine."

Aaron looked out across the clearing and thought for a second, then he cocked his head at her and gave her a grin. "I always wanted to be a chef."

"Really?" She was surprised and not surprised. "A French chef?"

"No teasing," he warned with a comical shake of his finger.

She laughed, "I'm not teasing. A chef, huh?" She looked him up and down. "I can see it."

"You can?"

"Sure, you obviously like to cook." She held up her cup as evidence then took a sip. "And this is so good!"

He laughed, "You're definitely teasing me now."

"No I'm not," she smiled. "Love said you worked in finance?" He nodded in response and she continued, "How did you get there from wanting to be a chef?"

"Well, I've always been good with numbers, so that's what my parents, mostly my Dad, wanted me to study. I'm finance director for a natural foods company. So it has all of the stability that my parents drilled into my head and a little something to do with good food."

She understood the connection, but still found it a little sad that he had ended up so far away from what he loved. They sat together quietly, sipping their hot chocolate and looking out over the clearing.

"I guess you'll get a chance to cook up a storm tomorrow," Jenny told him.

"I will." He grinned again. "Oh, by the way, Love said we are all going food shopping together as soon as you and I get back."

DECIDING who would drive into town turned out, to Jenny's embarrassment, to be a thinly veiled attempt at matchmaking. Since Aaron didn't know the way, they all agreed he would be a passenger. Since not everyone could fit into just one car, it was agreed they needed two drivers. Jenny assumed Jimmy would come with her, and Love and Aaron would go in her Dad's car. To her surprise, that is not what happened.

"Son, why don't you ride with us?" Rudy suggested after receiving a barely concealed whisper of instruction by Love.

Jimmy, who had already started towards Jenny's car, paused mid-step.

"Yes," Love chimed in. "And Aaron, why don't you ride with Jenny?" She tried to give it a light hearted spin, like it was just a meaningless idea that had popped into her head with no forethought.

Jenny didn't buy it.

Love nudged Rudy and he spoke up again, "That'll work. Give us a chance to catch up with you, Jim Boy." He reached out his arm towards Jimmy and motioned for him to come over to his car. Jimmy and Aaron exchanged a look. Jimmy shrugged and turned to Jenny, wiggling his eyebrows up and down at her and sideways glancing towards Aaron.

"I'll go with Dad and Love," Jimmy announced.

And that was that. Jimmy climbed into their car leaving Aaron standing on the passenger side of hers.

"Do you mind?" Aaron asked.

"No," Jenny said politely, though she was mortified at the blatant attempt to get her and Aaron alone in a car. "Not at all."

Aaron was much taller than Jimmy and had to adjust the seat all the way back to fit comfortably. It had been a few years since Jenny had had a man in her car and being so close to him she could smell his fresh soapy, leathery scent. She fumbled with her keys a little as he clicked on his seatbelt.

"That wasn't too subtle was it?" Aaron asked.

Jenny laughed, "So it's not my imagination?"

Aaron shook his head in an exaggerated 'no'. "I definitely think they're playing matchmaker."

Rudy, Love and Jimmy pulled past them, Rudy honking and waving at her to follow, as if she didn't know her way to town. Love leaned over and smiled excitedly at them. They could see Jimmy from the back seat giving them a grin and, Jenny thought, a rather sarcastic thumbs up.

"Oh my God, this is so embarrassing," Jenny groaned.

"I think they mean well," Aaron chuckled, then leaned in towards her as if he was going to tell her a secret. "I don't mind if you don't."

Her heart picked up a pace. He was very close, their shoulders touching. She waved her hand as if the whole thing was nothing, meant nothing.

"I don't mind, it's harmless I suppose," she answered.

Aaron settled back into his seat and smiled to himself as she finally found the right key and started the car.

The scenery on the ride to town was magnificent. A lot of the time both Jenny and Aaron were silent as they drove through the brilliant fall foliage. They did manage to spark one significant conversation about Aaron's family when Jenny asked him how long his parents were staying in France.

"Who knows," he answered, a twinge of bitterness in his tone.

Jenny glanced at him. "Do they travel a lot?"

He nodded. "Yes, my parents have never been the type to stay still or even nearby for very long." He didn't look at her as he spoke, but focused on the scenery outside the passenger window. "We never had holidays like this, playing games together, cooking together. They're not the warm, fuzzy types."

"Is that why you spent time at Love's when you were a kid?"

He nodded, "Yep. She's a sweet woman. And her husband was a good man. It was really sad when he passed away."

Jenny understood and felt a pang of guilt over her resentment of Love. She hadn't thought much about Love's past and whether or not she'd suffered loss and pain.

"It's too bad she never had children of her own," Aaron continued, still watching out his window. "She would have been a great Mom."

Apparently everyone in the surrounding area was shopping today. When they reached the town it took much longer than normal to drive through because people filled the sidewalks and flowed in front of their car at the crosswalks. The parking lot of the only grocery store was packed full as was all of the parking on Main Street. Jenny drove around in an ever widening circle until she finally found a space on a side residential street about ten blocks from the grocery store.

Just as she put the car in park, her phone buzzed. It was Jimmy.

"Hey," Jenny answered.

"Where are you?" He asked, "We had to park five miles away because of the crowds!"

"Us too," Jenny informed him as they climbed out of her car. "I guess we'll just meet you at the grocery store?"

"Sounds good," Jimmy agreed before ending the call.

"We're going to meet them there," Jenny informed Aaron, who had joined her on her side of the car.

"Great," he flashed her a smile as he swooped his arm gallantly towards the bustle of Main Street. "Shall we?"

She blushed a little at his invitation and his Nordic blue eyes twinkled.

The day was brisk and cold, but still sunny, a beautiful fall day. Aaron fell into step next to her and Jenny enjoyed how normal it felt, how comfortable, to have him stroll with her down Main Street. He was very much a gentleman, always putting himself between her and the street and even moving in close and lightly touching her back to guide her through large crowds. His height and strikingly attractive Viking look drew stares from more than one woman. Jenny felt a hot spike of jealousy whenever it happened, but noticed that he didn't pay attention to any of them, just continued chatting and laughing with her as they walked. They came across a small, gourmet cooking shop and Jenny saw Aaron's eyes light up.

"Would you like to look around in here?" She asked.

"I'd love to," Aaron said. "Do we have time?"

"Of course." She was happy at the idea of taking a little diversion with him and they popped into the store.

A heavy scent of spices and rich coffee filled the little shop. Though it was small, the room was stuffed from top to bottom with shining pots and pans, ceramic cookware and dishes in bright colors, crisp tea towels, napkins, aprons and oven mitts in vivid patterns, and small, intricate gadgets stored in earthy crocks on tables that groaned under the weight of the merchandise. Jenny and Aaron both paused after entering, enjoying the warmth on their cheeks and the enchanting displays.

"Would you like some mulled wine?" A round faced elderly woman asked them from behind an old fashioned looking cash register.

Aaron looked at Jenny before answering. She gave him a 'why not' face and he stepped towards the cashier, pulling his wallet out of his back pocket.

"Oh, no charge, dear," the lady said, her round cheeks squishing into a smile.

"Thank you," Aaron said. As he waited for the cashier to fill two paper cups with mulled wine out of a silver coffee dispenser, his eyes wandered happily over the items for sale on the counter. He picked up a fat ceramic cup shaped like a chick with a hole in its beak and showed it to Jenny.

"What is that?" She asked, giggling.

"It's to separate egg whites," he explained. "You crack the egg in the top and pour the whites out of its mouth."

"Those are one of my best sellers," the cashier told him as she handed him the mulled wine. Aaron took the cups and handed one to Jenny.

"Thank you," she said, smiling.

The cashier took a second look at her and smiled in recognition. "Oh, hello, aren't you the Combes girl?"

"Yes," Jenny smiled back.

"Aren't you grown up and beautiful, just like your Mom," the cashier continued. Jenny's face stiffened, though she was able to hold onto her smile for the elderly lady's sake. "I remember when your Mom would bring you and your brother in here when you were just little bitty things," the cashier reminisced. Caught up in her own thoughts, she didn't notice how Jenny's good mood had slipped away or how her gaze had dropped so that she stared hard at the red mulled wine in her cup. Aaron looked quickly at Jenny then back at the cashier.

"Do you own this shop?" He asked.

"Yes," the cashier answered proudly.

"How long have you been here?" Aaron asked, stepping a little forward so his body partially blocked Jenny from the cashier's view.

He was trying to shield her, she realized, and was suddenly grateful.

She turned halfway away as if she was looking at a pile of nearby tea towels while Aaron distracted the cashier with small talk. Her stomach roiled slightly and she knew there was no way she was going to be able to finish her drink. The fun excursion with Aaron had turned sour, the warmth of the little store now seemed overwhelming and all she could think about was getting away.

Thankfully, Aaron kept up his distracting conversation long enough to gulp down his drink. When the cashier was busy with another customer, he discreetly took Jenny's still full cup and disposed of it at a trash can near the front then steered her out the front door.

Out in the cool air again, Jenny took a deep breath.

"Are you okay?" Aaron asked, his brow furrowed with concern.

"Yeah," Jenny said, although she wasn't sure it was true. "I'm sorry, it's silly, I just kind of froze," she tried to explain.

"It's not silly and don't be sorry," he told her.

She sighed. She had a real talent for ruining the mood.

"I suppose we should get to the store," she said.

"Lead the way," he answered.

Even though he was being as upbeat as ever, for Jenny, the spell of their walk had been irreparably broken.

Chapter Eight

Wednesday morning was warm for the season and the day promised to get even warmer. There was colder weather moving in later in the evening and the next day, Thanksgiving, was supposed to be very cold so Jenny was determined to take advantage of this beautiful weather while it lasted. She headed to the clearing earlier than normal and didn't even have to wear a hat or warm up the tip of her ball point pen by putting it in her mouth before she wrote. She sat down in the bench with the sunrise view and waited for it to be light enough to write. She had a list of stories about her Mom that she wanted to write about today, Thanksgiving stories, holiday stories.

The problem was thoughts of Aaron kept popping into her mind and not going away. The way his eyes twinkled when he flipped crepes, how they'd shared a cart while shopping for food, how he looked when he laughed in the car, how he'd chatted up the overly friendly cashier to try to save her from being sad, the feel of his skin next to hers in the bubbling warm water of the hot tub. Aaron consumed her thoughts and try as she might, she couldn't focus her writing on childhood holiday memories. Her mind had other ideas.

Frustrated, Jenny shoved her pen into the center of the green journal and forced it closed before pushing it all awkwardly back into her jacket pocket. She refused to write about Aaron. That wasn't what this holiday was about. Her sole focus during her time here at the Lake House was supposed to be about her Mom and keeping her memory alive, not having the hots for some guy Love invited here. Besides, Jenny knew that Love wanted her and Aaron to hit it off, and she was having none of it.

Feeling restless and not in the mood to write, she thought maybe she could clear her mind with a walk. She made her way back to the house from the clearing and to the end of the drive, turning at the mailbox onto the path that led all the way to the covered bridge. Going to the bridge might give her new inspiration.

She walked briskly, working off some of her irritation as she moved through the woods. Along the way she saw a few fat squirrels hurrying from tree to tree, one of them chattered angrily at her from the branches. There was a rabbit hiding just underneath the deep rusty red leaves of a chokeberry bush, sitting as still as possible in the hopes that she wouldn't notice him. She kept a wide birth around him, not wanting to scare him out of his hiding place.

By the time she was almost to the covered bridge she had once again found the delight she always enjoyed in these woods. Surrounded by the stunning colors of fall, the magical way the rays of sun shone through the tree canopy, the narrow path carpeted with fallen leaves and the woodland creatures all around, Jenny had always felt a little like a fairy tale character in this place. Even though she was no longer a little girl or a whimsical teenager, a piece of her still believed that wonderful things were possible in this fanciful forest.

The rhythmic sound of footsteps coming from behind her were at once familiar and surprising. She knew before she turned around who it was, and her face brightened with an expectant smile. Aaron, on the other hand, didn't expect to see her standing in the middle of the path where he was jogging.

"Woah!" He exclaimed as he stopped short, breathing hard from the exertion of his run.

"Hi," she gave him a little wave.

"Jenny," Aaron said, letting out a startled laugh as he spoke. "You're here." He tried to catch his breath as he let his eyes slip over her from head to toe, "Not writing today?"

"I thought I'd take a little walk," she answered.

"I see that," he said.

Aaron approached her and stood close, very close. His breath was still rapid, but Jenny was suddenly not sure if it was only because he'd been jogging. He was so near she could breathe in his scent. He looked down into her face, his eyes capturing hers like a magnet. Her heart melted in his gaze. He reached up towards her ear and a thrill filled her body. She leaned towards him, expecting his fingertips to brush her temple then push into her hair and draw her into a kiss. She closed her eyes and held her breath, waiting to feel his lips on hers, the tickle of his beard on her skin. Instead, she felt a tickle on her scalp and opened her eyes. Aaron was still there smiling at her holding up a small, orange oak leaf he had plucked from her hair.

"You're becoming one with the forest," he said, his amusement at her misunderstanding obvious.

Jenny blushed furiously. He must think she was a pathetic, lovesick soul. He probably thought she purposely came down this path to see him on his run. Had she? The thought made her flustered. She'd been so caught up in thinking about him it never crossed her mind that he might not be interested in her. Had she misread everything? Of course she had, that much was clear. It was entirely possible that Aaron had only been being polite towards her the last few days, nothing more.

"Thanks," Jenny smoothed her hair self-consciously. She turned back towards the covered bridge to try to hide her embarrassment. "I just thought, you know, I thought I'd take a walk, go down to the bridge. It's so nice today, nice day for a walk..." Why couldn't she stop talking? She took a few steps to prove that she was, indeed, going to the covered bridge.

"Mind if I come along?" He asked, falling in step next to her.

She shrugged so hard nobody for miles around could have misinterpreted the fact that she didn't care one bit if Aaron joined her on her walk. She pursed her lips together so she wouldn't keep rambling on and on about nothing as they walked. She decided to concentrate mainly on not allowing their arms or hands to brush up against each other.

They made their way silently around the last turn in the path and down a small incline that led to the edge of the river and the covered bridge. There was a dead tree laying over the last section of path, blocking any normal passing. Aaron stepped on top of the most horizontal section of the trunk and balanced, then offered his hand to her.

"Let me help you," he said.

Jenny hesitated, her humiliation of the non-existent kiss still fresh. Aaron beckoned her up with a quick motion of his hand.

"We don't have to go all the way there," Jenny said.

"Come on," Aaron coaxed. "It's clear on this side."

She gave in and reached her hand towards his. He took it in a firm grip and pulled her up on the log in one quick swoop so she was facing him and they were standing just inches away from each other. The log wiggled from their movement and

Aaron held her hand even more tightly, bracing her from falling by putting his other hand on her waist.

"Oh!" Jenny was off center from the moving log under her feet as well as the feeling of being in Aaron's arms, even innocently.

"I've got you," Aaron said, his voice was low and calming. Still, the butterflies in her stomach would not stop fluttering. He held her there for a long moment, warming her with his touch, looking down into her face with an expression Jenny couldn't quite read. Try as she might, she couldn't keep her heart from beating wildly at the closeness of him. Then, without a word, Aaron guided her with his hands and helped her off the other side of the tree, hopping down next to her as soon as she was safely placed on the path.

"Thank you," Jenny said quietly.

"My pleasure."

The old covered bridge was as enchanting as ever. The rays of the morning sun shone through the spaces between the planks, creating an elaborate light and dark pattern inside. Jenny walked in the entrance, wanting to look at the river and trees through the slatted sides. Aaron followed her and something about being together in the quiet shadowed protection of the bridge felt intimate, almost sensual. When he spoke, it was in the same low tone he'd used when he held her close on the log.

"Beautiful," he said. He was standing close at her side as she peered out through the planks at the river, but when she glanced at him he was looking at her, not the river.

"I used to think this bridge was magic," she confessed, not sure why she was telling him. Something about Aaron made her say things she would normally keep inside. She looked back at the river, embarrassed at her secret.

"Magic?" He asked, looking around at the dust particles

dancing in the rays of light. "I can see that. Did you ever have a wish come true here?"

She shook her head 'no. She never had.

They looked at each other for a long moment. His eyes were even more intense in the slatted shadow and light of the bridge. Aaron started to say something to her when the sound of a car coming down the road interrupted them and they stepped out of the covered bridge and off the road. When the car passed and they were safely out of the way Aaron turned to speak, but Jenny was already walking up the path back towards the Lake House.

LATER, when they were gathered back in the house, Love asked Jenny to help her pick out the china to use the next day for Thanksgiving.

They stood together with the doors to the china cabinet open so the different patterns were easier to view. Jenny was struck again at how small and light Love seemed. The older woman was very tiny, not frail really, just a small, thin woman.

"What pattern do you think we should use?" Love asked. Her grey hair was down, long and wavy with little stray pieces floating out of place. Even her hair was lighter than air. She wore jeans and an untucked long sleeve rose colored blouse with pearl buttons. She didn't have on any jewelry except for her wedding ring, a plain platinum band. She also wore no makeup. Jenny had not seen her wear one drop of makeup since they arrived.

"I like these two." Jenny motioned towards the off white pattern with red and gold ribbons on the edges and the hunting pattern, which featured different wild game birds on each size plate as well as a tumbling black and brown leaf patter on the edges.

Love picked up a salad plate with a pheasant on the front, running her finger along the pattern. She flashed an approving smile. "I was hoping you would say this one. I think it's beautiful."

Jenny nodded, her Mom had excellent taste in china, as well as in decor and clothes and everything else.

"We could mix them," Jenny suggested, taking out a larger dinner plate from the plainer pattern and adding another pheasant salad plate to the top.

"Oh, what a wonderful idea!" Love was delighted, she touched Jenny's arm in her excitement. To her surprise, Jenny didn't have to fight the urge to pull away. It felt nice to be part of these decisions and she knew Love was making a concerted effort to include her. She couldn't fault the woman for being kind.

"Hey, are we going to use the little turkeys?" Jimmy joined them. He picked up the small sterling silver individual salt and pepper shakers shaped like wild turkeys that lived inside the china cabinet with all of the finer table dressings.

"Of course!" Love answered, pleased with his interest.

"Shouldn't you be making your pies?" Jenny teased her brother.

"Aaron's gonna help me, we're doing a baking marathon," Jimmy said over his shoulder as he carried five pairs of the tiny turkeys to the table.

"Shall we get everything out and wash it?" Jenny asked. Love nodded in approval.

Soon they were standing at the sink full of hot soapy water, carefully washing, rinsing and drying the china by hand. Jimmy and Aaron had begun their pie marathon, which resembled more of a pie assembly line on the large dining room table as Aaron mixed pastry dough and rolled out pie crust after pie crust and Jimmy carefully shaped each crust into its pie pan then filled them and popped them into one of the double ovens. They made pumpkin, pecan, apple strudel and, last but not least, Aaron's avocado pie, which turned out to look more like key lime. He held it proudly up for Jenny to see it.

"It doesn't look that bad, does it?" He asked.

"It looks great," Jenny quipped. "I just don't know if I want to taste it." She made a face as if a bad flavor was already in her mouth.

"Just wait and see," he said happily, placing the pie in the refrigerator to chill overnight.

"Who's up for ping pong?" Rudy appeared at the top of the basement stairs looking for some opponents to challenge.

"I'm game," Aaron said. He looked at Jimmy, "We're done here, right?"

"Yep," Jimmy said. "Let's do it."

"You coming, Button?" Rudy called to Jenny.

"Yes, we're almost done. I'll be down in a minute," she answered.

When the men had all disappeared downstairs Jenny and Love could hear the distinctive sound of a ping pong ball bouncing back and forth combined with the guy's hooting and hollering.

Jenny shook her head and chuckled, "Boys."

"Yes," Love agreed. She sloshed the dishwater looking for the last few items in the bottom of the sink as she asked, "How do you like Aaron?"

Jenny was a little taken aback. "Aaron?" She thought about him holding her tightly while they stood on the log, then remembered when she'd closed her eyes thinking he was going to kiss her, and her cheeks flushed. "Oh, he seems like a nice guy." Best to be as nonchalant as possible.

"He is, he is a very nice guy."

They were quiet for a few more moments, Jenny focused on not dropping the Thanksgiving china. She hadn't been truly alone with Love since they'd met and it was making her uncomfortable. The air between them seemed to be heavy with an unknown thought, a conversation that wanted to be had. Finally, Love spoke it out loud.

"So, I have a confession to make," she began. Jenny cringed at the statement, not knowing or wanting to know what Love could possibly be ready to confess. She looked at the plate she was drying carefully, avoiding eye contact with her father's wife. Instead of answering Jenny just made a light grunting noise, hoping this would put Love off. It didn't.

"I have known Aaron since he was a tiny little thing, barely potty trained..."

Probably too much information, Jenny thought.

"He was always a really wonderful little boy and now he's a truly wonderful man," Love continued.

"Mmhmm," Jenny agreed, hoping that would end whatever this was. It didn't.

"Of course, I've never met you before this week, but your father has told me so much about you," Love gushed and Jenny was a little terrified of what she was about to say. "Well, because of everything your father told me about you, which he was right I can tell after meeting you," Love tried to butter her up, "I convinced Aaron to come to Thanksgiving so that you two would meet." Love looked at her with eyes wide, like she couldn't believe she'd just admitted to doing this deed. "Is that horrible of me?"

Horrible? That was a strong word, Jenny thought. Presumptuous, meddling, pushy, these were all better descriptors in her opinion. She considered which of these words she should use to correct Love's statement, but then realized she wasn't surprised at her stepmother's confession and, even more shocking, she wasn't upset about it either. Taking her silence as disapproval, Love started talking again.

"I know it was horrible and pushy. And I wasn't being

calculated about it or anything," she tried to explain. "I wanted him to spend Thanksgiving here with us regardless, I just thought it was beneficial that you are both currently unattached and maybe it would all work out into a really romantic love story."

Love stopped talking and smiled hopefully at her. Jenny, despite herself, smiled back.

"Are you upset?" Love asked.

"Not upset, exactly..." She didn't know what else to say. The thought that she and Aaron might be well matched was not an abhorrent idea to her. The fact that Love thought so too was actually a little encouraging. Then another possibility entered her mind and her stomach sank. She looked at Love with growing dismay, hoping against hope that what she was thinking wasn't true. "Love..." she started.

"Yes?" Love answered, open, kind, waiting expectantly for Jenny's next words.

"Does Aaron know you did this?"

Chapter Nine

"I still don't understand why you're upset," Jimmy said, his words thinning as he lifted into the air away from her. He was swinging on the tire swing with Jenny pushing him. He'd insisted, citing many moments in their shared childhood when he'd pushed her even when he was suffering from heartbreak or romantic anxiety.

"I don't like people meddling in my life," she answered. Jimmy swung back towards her, twirling a little as he did so she had to step to the side in order to get her hands on his backside to push him again.

"But I thought she said he didn't know she was playing matchmaker," Jimmy asked, his words once again floating high in the air above them.

"Can you keep your voice down?" Jenny requested, worried that Aaron might overhear them.

"Do you think he's gonna pop out of the shrubbery?" Jimmy teased, laughing as he tilted back in the tire swing and pumped his legs. Jenny abandoned her post and sat down cross legged on the picnic blanket they'd brought out and laid at the base of the huge oak tree.

"I don't know where he is," she answered crossly. This was true. Jenny hadn't seen Aaron since the morning. She'd been in the kitchen kneading her yeast rolls when he came to find her, apparently he'd gone looking for her in the clearing.

"Not writing this morning?" He'd asked cheerfully, setting the thermos of hot chocolate down on the counter.

"No, I wanted to get my rolls ready to rise." If he was disappointed she didn't see it, she was laser focused on kneading the ball of dough on the counter top.

She'd pretended that seeing him each morning wasn't any big deal, that she'd forgotten about the last few days, that she had other things to do besides wonder where he was going to be and put herself there. In reality, Jenny had hidden out in her bedroom trying to write, but failing. Instead she'd watched out the window and seen Aaron leave for his run before the sun came up. She then watched him return to the house and leave about 20 minutes later walking towards the clearing, thermos in hand. That's when she'd hurried downstairs to start her rolls, so she would look busy.

"Earth to Jen," Jimmy said. He'd stopped swinging and was hanging almost upside down from the tire waiting for her to answer his question.

"What?" She asked.

"I said," he pulled himself upright and kicked the ground so the tire swing spun slowly, "Do you like him?"

"Aaron?"

"No, Leonardo DiCaprio." Jimmy rolled his eyes in mock frustration. "Aaron, Jen, do you like Aaron?"

Jenny looked at her brother, but didn't say a word. She clamped her lips together to keep from blurting out an answer. Heat rose in her cheeks and she tried to look angry.

"You do!" Jimmy declared, pointing an accusing finger at her as he kicked the tire swing into a faster twirl.

"It doesn't matter," Jenny retorted. "That's not the point!"

"That is exactly the point," Jimmy argued. He scraped his feet in the dirt, stopping the twirling tire so he could look her straight in the eyes. "If you like him and he likes you, what does it matter how you met or who introduced you or even why they did?"

Jenny opened her mouth to answer, but Jimmy was on a roll.

"Jen, you're always doing this. You're always pushing good things away, like you think you don't deserve them or don't want to be happy or something." His eyes teared up as he continued, "It's not every day you come across someone who you could fall in love with, and when you do, you shouldn't throw it all away on a...on a technicality."

Jenny could see that they were no longer talking about her situation alone.

"Is that what I do?" She asked him meekly.

He nodded then sighed. "We both do."

They sat quietly for a while, Jenny hugging her knees at the base of the oak tree and Jimmy dangling from the same tree, scuffing his feet in the dirt.

"Sucks to be us," Jenny said. Jimmy laughed so suddenly he snorted, which made her laugh.

"Think of it this way, at least she didn't try to fix you up with some horrible, ugly, jerk of a guy," Jimmy said. "I mean, he's got a good job, he's nice, he can cook, and he's gorgeous...truly gorgeous!!"

Jenny laughed again and stretched her leg out to push the tire swing away with her foot.

"Help me! Help me!" Jimmy continued, keeping the swing just out of her reach and flailing his arms around as if he was in great peril. "I've been set up with an Adonis!"

"Daddy! Daddy!" A little girl's voice rose above their laughter and they both turned to see Penny running around the house into the back yard.

"Penny?" Jimmy's face went from confusion to sheer joy at the sight of his daughter. He scrambled to climb out of the tire swing and made it just as she reached the tree. She raised her hands towards him and he swept her into his arms.

"Daddy!" She said into his neck.

"Penny, Pumpkin, how...?" The answer to his question came before he could finish forming it as Paul made his way around the house and into the back yard.

Paul was tall and lanky, with dark hair, eyes and a complexion that he always said came from his mish-mashed ancestry that had all melted together when they fell in love and had babies in America.

Jenny's heart leapt with joy at the look on Paul's face. He didn't look like a man on the brink of divorce, he looked like a man long separated from the one he loved and now within sight of that person once again. He walked purposefully towards his husband and daughter. Jenny could see that Jimmy was openly crying as he held Penny tightly to his chest and Paul approached. She stood up, intending to go and leave them some privacy. Paul gave her a quick nod and a teary smile as she did. She beamed back at him, so happy to see him, so happy he had come for Jimmy's sake.

Her Dad and Love stood in the open French doors off the dining room, watching with joy filled expressions. Jenny could see Aaron standing behind them. Paul wrapped his long arms around Jimmy and their daughter and they stood there together for a few minutes, Jenny and the others stayed still, afraid if they moved they would break the spell that surrounded the reunited family. Jenny couldn't make out what Jimmy and Paul were saying to each other, but she could hear the low tones of their voices punctuated with Penny's soprano tones every now and then. Finally, she did hear Paul's voice bellow out from their hug circle.

"It's freezing out here!"

Everyone laughed and the three of them broke slightly away from each other so they could see the rest of their family.

"Hi Aunt Jenny!" Penny exclaimed, giving her a little wave.

"Hi, honey!" Jenny stepped forward and gave Penny a kiss on her round little cheek, then kissed Paul's cheek as well. He gave her shoulders a squeeze. "I'm so glad you're both here!"

"So are we," Paul answered.

"Where's Grandpa?" Jenny craned her neck to see past the adults around her, looking for Rudy.

"Why don't you all come inside where it's warm?" Rudy called from the patio. "We've got breakfast almost ready."

"We?" Paul looked at Jimmy and Jenny curiously.

"Dad cooks now," Jimmy explained with a 'who knew' shoulder shrug. They all started towards the house when Jenny remembered the blanket. She went back to get it, still smiling at the joy she'd seen on Jimmy's face. She picked up the blanket and shook it, but the dry leaves from the ground were holding fast to the fuzzy material and barely any of them came loose.

"Need some help with that?"

Jenny's stomach did a back flip at the sound of his voice. She turned just as Aaron stooped over and picked up the opposite end of the blanket.

"Thanks," she said, trying to remain calm.

They spent a few moments using one hand to hold up the blanket and the other to brush off dried leaves. The sounds of the family reunion inside the kitchen drifted over the back yard and made her smile.

"It's great your brother's family made it," Aaron suggested, smiling at her. The look on his face made her a little weak at the knees.

"Yes, I'm so happy for him."

"I can see," Aaron said. He glanced at the tire swing hanging still nearby. "I also noticed that you didn't get a chance to swing."

"Oh," Jenny shook her head with a laugh. "Jimmy was hogging the swing. Story of my life." Aaron chuckled.

They brushed most of the debris off the blanket. The next step came naturally, almost like a dance that they both knew. Taking a corner in each hand, they stepped away from each other so the blanket was a large rectangle between them, then they folded it once over, and once over again, before walking towards each other joining their folded corners. Their hands touched at that point sending a jolt of electricity through her. Aaron's eyes smiled at the corners and he tilted his head in that way he did when he thought something was funny.

"Hop on." He took her corners from her and completed the folding of the blanket on his own. "I'll push you."

"Oh, no, you don't have to do that."

"I'm not doing it because I have to," he answered as he placed the folded blanket carefully on the grass in the lawn. He stepped to the tire swing and held it as if he was a chauffeur opening the door to a limousine. "C'mon, it'll be fun!"

"It's getting colder every minute. It's supposed to start snowing!"

"All the more reason to do it now. It could be your last chance." He cocked his head at her, eyes twinkling.

Jenny couldn't think of any more reasons why she shouldn't. So she did.

Soon she was sitting in the center of the tire, her hands gripping the rope. Aaron bent behind her, his hands placed on either side of the tire, his chest brushing against her shoulders, his mouth close to her ear.

"High or low?" He asked, his breath tickling her neck.

"High," she answered, "as high as you can go."

"You sure?"

She nodded, a thrill building in her stomach, "I'm sure."

Aaron pulled her backwards so she hung in the air facing almost straight down and she had a moment to consider how high Aaron could actually go. Then he was running forward, moving her in front of him and over him as he lifted her above his head and ran his full height underneath, sending her whooshing in a great swoop towards the branches of the tree.

Jenny squealed with delight as the cold air rushed past her, biting her cheeks and ears as she held tight to the rope. The tire turned as it flew, so one moment she was facing the tree, then the sky, then the ground. She reached the peak of the swing and relished the feeling of floating high in the air with nothing around her for an instant before gravity did its duty and pulled her back towards the ground. She squealed again. As she swung to and fro snow started falling in light flurries.

"It's snowing!" She exclaimed.

"Are you done?" Aaron asked, "Or do you want to go again?"

"Again!" Jenny laughed. Snowflakes tickled her face and hands, wet and cold, as she felt Aaron's powerful body take hold of her, his strength pushing her up and up until she was flying through the air once more.

Soon it was too cold to continue. Her hands were like ice and she wasn't sure if she could hang on to the rope any longer. She swung slower and slower, passing back and forth in front of Aaron until he was able to grab the tire and bring her to a stop in front of him.

"I think my hands are frozen," she laughed.

"Here," Aaron wrapped his hands around hers on the rope. Jenny was surprised that despite the fact that it was snowing, his strong hands were still incredibly warm. He helped her extricate herself from the tire and before she knew what was happening, they were standing just inches from each other with his hands holding hers. Snowflakes had collected on his shoulders and in his hair. The blue of his eyes was even more pronounced against the grey snowy skies than it was normally, or maybe it was because he had been laughing.

Even with the snow falling harder around them, Jenny felt like she was in a bubble of light. He pulled her closer to him, holding her hands to his chest. His eyes held her in place and Jenny couldn't stop looking into them. He was warm and strong and she wanted to lean into him, let him wrap his arms around her and make her warm and safe.

"You look..." Aaron's voice cracked as if his throat was dry. He stopped what he was saying and cleared his throat, never letting go of her hands. "You're beautiful," he said. Jenny felt a piece of her heart melt into his.

Snow swirled around them, silencing anything else, as if they were the only two people in the world.

Chapter Ten

Thanksgiving Day was full of fun and preparation. Love invited Penny to help her stuff the turkey and everyone else talked and laughed as they worked on their assigned dishes and helped set the magnificent table. Places were rearranged and extra china prepared to accommodate Paul and Penny's arrival. Instead of Jenny and Jimmy sitting on one side with Aaron on the other, it was now Jimmy, Penny and Paul on one side and Jenny seated next to Aaron on the opposite side. Dad and Love kept their places at the ends of the large dining table.

Having Penny around was a treat for everyone. She was such a smart and fun loving little girl, always interested in helping, which was adorable. Jenny saw how enchanted Love was with her and it warmed her heart towards the newest member of their family. She could not have accepted a woman who didn't like children, even if she was married to her father.

Penny took an interest in Aaron right away. Maybe it was because of his Viking looks, his long hair, his easy manner, or just that Penny, having two Dads, had grown up very comfortable around men. Whatever the reason she warmed up to him quickly when he let her help him get the wood ready in the fireplace. With the snow picking up outside, it was a perfect day to have a fire. Jenny overheard their conversation as they sat on the hearth.

"You have long hair," Penny told Aaron as she handed him a piece of newspaper.

"Yes, so do you," Aaron answered, crumpling up the newspaper to fill the bottom of the fireplace.

"Mine is this long." Penny pulled her dark hair forward so it laid over her chest. "How long is yours?"

"I'm not sure." Aaron reached up and let down his man-bun, shaking his head so his hair fell down in a wavy mass. "Is it as long as yours?" Penny pulled a piece of his hair forward over his shoulder to compare. "Yours is longer, you win!" Aaron said. Penny giggled.

Throughout the day the turkey cooked and they all munched on veggies and dip and delicious slices of salami and cheese that Paul had brought as his contribution to the meal. There was football playing on the basement TV as well as an endless rotation of ping pong games. While upstairs a fire roared and some old R&B played in the sitting room. The whole house was full of the smell of food cooking and the sound of laughter.

And no matter where she went, Jenny found Aaron at her side.

He brought her drinks from the kitchen, sat next to her to watch the fire and visit with Love and her Dad. He challenged her to a ping pong game and offered her and Penny his spot on the sectional sofa to watch football on TV when they carried in the popcorn.

"You girls can have my place," he said, moving to stand up and make room for them.

"No," Jenny smiled at him, ignoring the fact that Jimmy

and Paul were observing from their position on the couch and, no doubt, coming to their own conclusions about her and Aaron's relationship, "We can fit." She sat down very close to Aaron, so close their legs couldn't help but touch and he had to lift his arm over the back of the couch so their shoulders weren't rubbing. She patted the space next to her for Penny to climb up, which snuggled the little girl nicely between Jenny one side and Paul on the other.

Jimmy and Paul gave each other a look. Jenny pretended not to notice. She enjoyed being this close to Aaron. With his arm up behind her it felt like she could nestle into him and let him keep her warm and protected. He smelled so good and as they shared a bowl of popcorn she thought she could get used to this feeling.

Soon it was time to get dressed for Thanksgiving dinner. Jenny had always loved this ritual. Silly as it may seem, it made her feel like a princess or a fine lady who lived in a great house and had servants. Getting dressed for the evening meal made the holiday all the more special.

Up in her room, she brushed out her hair and pulled it up into a loose bun, which it was barely long enough to accomplish, but she got it done and liked the result. She slipped into a wine colored mid-thigh length dress with a halter neckline that fit well and showed off her shoulders. She touched up her makeup adding an extra dab of deep red lipstick for drama then put on a pair of crystal teardrop earrings she saved for special occasions. She had only brought a pair of black ballet slipper shoes, as she hadn't planned on having to look too impressive. Nevertheless, Jenny was pleased when she studied her reflection in the mirror.

As she made her way down the stairs into the front sitting room, Jenny had no doubts that Aaron was pleased as well. From his position on the sitting room couch he could see her descending the stairs and his eyes lit up when she appeared.

He stood up as if he'd been waiting for her, as if they were going on a date. She smiled at him, unable to contain her reaction.

If she was being honest, she was impressed with his clothing choice for the evening. He wore a pair of black slacks, nicely fitted, black leather shoes, a crisp long sleeved white shirt buttoned at the cuffs and unbuttoned at the neck, and a pair of black suspenders. His beard was lustrous and his hair tumbled over his shoulders, loose and blonde and amazing. As she watched him watch her, a delectable shiver went down her spine.

The table looked amazing. All of the china and silver shimmered under the dozen orange, red and deep brown tapered candles set down the center. A huge flower arrangement of sunflowers, red daisies and orange roses that Love had ordered sat in the very middle. As a final touch, Rudy and Love had folded each deep red cloth napkin into the shape of a turkey.

They all oohed and awed over the beautiful table, taking pictures of one another using it as the backdrop and getting one picture of everyone by using Paul's timer on his camera. Then it was time to get everything on the table. In a kind of water bucket brigade fashion, they passed dish after dish after dish to the table until it was packed full. Then everyone but Rudy and Love sat down and waited for their hosts to carry the golden brown turkey to the table for carving.

As they sat waiting, Aaron leaned over to Jenny putting his hand on her knee to get her attention. His eyes glittered in the candlelight and his long hair brushed against her bare shoulder. His hand was warm, almost hot on her skin and her heart fluttered as she tipped her head to hear what he had to say.

"You look fantastic, Jenny."

She smiled coyly at him and turned slightly so her mouth

was close to his ear. "You do too." He squeezed her knee and left his hand resting there, as if that was where it belonged.

"This bird is heavy!" Rudy declared as he carried the turkey to the table. He looked dapper in his blue shirt and grey sport coat and Love shimmered in a charcoal grey lace dress next to him. Before they said grace, Love read a poem from a slim, blue book. The words were lovely, but complicated, and Jenny forgot them almost as soon as Love read them, but she got the gist of the poem. Love conquers all was the basic message.

"Let's say grace," Rudy said and they all held hands and bowed their heads.

Jenny's hand rested comfortably in Aaron's and she thought again how much she enjoyed his touch.

"Lord," Rudy began, "We thank you for this glorious bounty you've given us today and all the blessings you give us every day. We thank you for this beautiful place to gather together, the time you've allowed us all to be here and both the old and the new friends and family that are gathered around this table."

A terrible thought struck her as she listened. Jenny's heart lurched.

"We have all lost loved ones, my dear Suzanne and Love's husband Carl to name a few of our most precious. We have also known the joy of finding spouses and having children and are grateful to you for the millions of ways you take care of us through the love of others."

Overwhelmed with shame, Jenny could no longer bow her head. As her father spoke she looked around at the bowed heads of everyone at the Thanksgiving table and felt the horrible stab of grief over the one who was missing, her mother, Suzanne Combes.

She was a terrible daughter. How could she sit down at this table on this day in her mother's own house with her mother's own china in front of her and not think about her one time? Not once had the memory of her mother crossed her mind since they'd come in to eat, since Aaron had swung her on the tire swing, since yesterday. Had it truly been that long? She couldn't even remember!

Her father continued saying grace, but Jenny was no longer listening. Aaron continued holding her hand, but Jenny's heart was far away from him, from everyone. Her heart was back with her mother. Where it should be. Though the Thanksgiving meal would take place, Jenny would not enjoy it. The guilt of forgetting stewed inside of her and she resolved that she would not forsake her mother's memory again. Not for anything or anyone, especially not for a trifling flirtation with a man she barely knew.

Chapter Eleven

Her pen flew over the pages of her green journal, recounting not only Thanksgiving memories, but memories of other holidays, of Christmas Eves and Easter mornings, of Halloween costumes and fireworks on the Fourth of July. The storm had moved on and the morning sun was brilliant on the day after Thanksgiving, bouncing its rays off of the thin blanket of newly fallen snow. Jenny had bundled up, brought a dark blue wool blanket and the big brush she used to scrape snow off of her car to the clearing so she could clean off the bench and enjoy this gorgeous, crisp morning with her writing.

She was wasting no time describing all of the most precious thoughts she wanted to remember about her Mom. She'd actually started her writing streak after Thanksgiving dinner as soon as she'd been able to get away from the others. Feigning sleepiness, Jenny had excused herself to her room. With the journal in front of her on her desk by the window in the room her Mom had decorated with her, she'd begun putting her thoughts into sentences and forming the sentences into stories. Sometimes funny, often poignant, she stayed up until after midnight writing then rose early to continue.

Maybe it was because of the soft snow covering the ground, or maybe it was because she was so engrossed in crafting a description of the dollhouse she'd gotten for her eighth birthday, either way she didn't hear any footsteps until he was right there beside her.

"Mind if I join you?"

Jenny looked up to see Aaron wearing his favorite grey flannel with his blue and green scarf and an addition of a matching blue and green hat. The knit hat was the long, slouchy style she'd seen snowboarders wear and came complete with a pom-pom that flopped at the back. Despite the interruption and her resolution to focus on writing about her Mom, Jenny smiled. With the hat and his beard and the snow covered surroundings she couldn't help but think of him as some kind of gnome or elf. A tall, strikingly handsome elf.

Jenny reasoned that she couldn't very well send him away, even if he was interrupting her writing. So she motioned towards the wool blanket she'd spread over the bench to help keep her warm. Aaron sat down.

"I brought a special treat." He lifted the familiar plaid printed thermos and two thermal mugs.

"Oh? What is it?"

Aaron twisted off the lid of the thermos and lifted it up to her nose. The enticing smell of rich coffee with Bailey's Irish Creme drifted with the steam out of the top. She raised her eyebrows in surprise.

"I thought it might be nice with the snow," he grinned. "Would you like some?"

"Please."

Aaron handed her a thermal cup and moved close so he could carefully pour the hot liquid into it. "It looks like your writing is going well," he said.

She nodded, taming the butterflies in her stomach at having him so close. "It is."

"What are you working on?" He finished pouring hers and started on his, then added, "If you don't mind sharing."

"I don't mind." She took a sip of her coffee, burning her lip a little. "I'm writing about my Mom, mostly. Memories of her during the holidays and when I was a kid."

"Oh, wow," Aaron said. "That must be challenging. Although I could see you were really into it." A thought came to him and he looked into her eyes, "Would you like me to go? I don't want to interrupt you."

She shook her head 'no' and took another sip. "I don't mind the break. I've been at it since last night anyway, gotten a lot done."

"Have you? Anything you want to share?"

Jenny felt suddenly shy as she laid her hand on the journal she'd put down on the bench. "Oh, you don't want to hear any of this."

"Sure I do," he said. "I would love to hear something you've written."

"Really?"

"Really."

She knew she shouldn't do it. What she was supposed to be doing was forgetting about him. The urge to shrug him off and tell him 'no' was strong, but something in her wanted to share this with him more than it wanted to hide.

"Okay, I'll need a little liquid courage first." She took a big gulp of her Bailey's coffee making Aaron laugh, then placed it on the bench. She flipped through the pages of her journal, being careful not to look at anything towards the front which she knew held page after page of her impressions of him half naked in the hot tub. Fingers trembling, not from the cold, and cheeks growing hot, not from the spiked coffee, Jenny found a suitable passage. It was a short memory about when she was twelve and they'd been snowed in on Christmas Eve during a blizzard. "Here we go," she said, clearing her throat before starting to read.

"Snow, snow and more snow fell to the ground that day. Not fell, exactly, plummeted was more like it. Big, fat, heavy flakes, sometimes bending to the wind that blew mercilessly, but mostly dropping from the sky in great quantity and building a deep, quiet blanket on everything and everyone who happened to be outside."

Jenny looked up, wondering what Aaron thought so far, not sure about continuing if he didn't like it.

"That's good," he said, smiling at her with his twinkly eyes. "Is there more?"

She nodded. "Do you want to hear more?"

"Yes." Aaron raised his cup to her in an encouraging gesture. Jenny continued.

She read to him about her Dad announcing they were not driving anywhere in the blizzard, her Mom insisting they all get dressed up in the church clothes they would have worn to the Christmas Eve candlelight service. She read to him about her Mom getting out all of their extra candles and finding a couple of Christmas Carol music sheets so Jimmy could play them on his keyboard and they could have their own private candlelight service. She read to him about singing Silent Night and lighting their candles and afterwards, how her Dad had put an Elvis Christmas album on and pulled her Mom into the middle of the living room to dance. She read about how fun and magical it was, how perfect.

When she was done she looked at Aaron, who was concentrating on the snow covered ground in front of them as he listened. He lifted his gaze to hers, his icy blue eyes glistening.

"So, what do you think?" She asked.

"That was wonderful, Jenny," he said. A little thrill shimmered through her when he said her name. "It was sad and sweet...and, man...you're really, really good!" She smiled, blushing hard at the compliment as she closed the journal and put it down on the bench. "I just...I don't know what to say," Aaron continued. She giggled a little at his reaction. He seemed overcome. "Can I...can we...actually, I do know what I want to say." He turned towards her with surprising intensity. "I have something I want to say to you and I hope it's not too...I hope I'm not assuming too much."

"Okay," Jenny answered slowly, not sure what to expect.

Aaron dropped his head and looked at his lap, searching for the right words. When he looked up again she was taken aback by his expression, it was happy and hopeful and full of intention.

"I have something to confess. Three times in the past few days I have wanted to kiss you." Jenny's heart jumped into her throat. "Three times I've had to stop myself from doing the thing that seems like the most natural thing in the world when I look at you, to take you in my arms and kiss you." He reached forward and put his hand on hers, its warmth spreading through her hand and into the rest of her body. "I don't know if you feel the same, and I know maybe this is fast." He shook his head as if he couldn't believe what he was saying either. "But I have to tell you that I have never felt this way about anyone before. You're intelligent and funny and amazing and I want to kiss you right now. I want to have a thousand more chances to kiss you."

Jenny was lightheaded, her breathing shallow and fast. Aaron's eyes were locked on hers, looking into her, pleading with her for what he most desired. Her gaze dropped momentarily to his lips and a powerful surge of attraction pulled them closer to each other. She knew his lips would be warm, insistent, powerful, and they were only inches away. She looked up at him through her lashes, feeling his hand wrap completely around hers. She breathed in and smelled the crisp morning air that surrounded them mixed with his warm, Irish Creme breath.

Then she uttered one, simple word, "No."

He stopped. A wall slammed down around her and she blocked the connection that had been pulling them together. She slipped her hand out of his as he loosened his grip, letting her go.

"Okay." He looked crestfallen and confused. "I'm sorry, I thought—"

"Don't be sorry," she tried to explain. "It's just, you know, I'm not sure I'm in a good place." Jenny realized she was about to start talking uncontrollably, her nerves were taking over. "And you live in Colorado, I live in Illinois, that's really far apart. And there's Love, I'm still not sure how I feel about all of that." She waved her hands in front of her, deflecting his offer, puzzled by her own excuses. She stood up quickly, not wanting to explain anymore, not wanting to look into his beautiful eyes again and face what she'd just rejected. "Excuse me," she muttered, and left the clearing as fast as she could without running.

Chapter Twelve

Great deals at the day after Thanksgiving sales beckoned and Jenny was afraid she would be doomed to drive Aaron in her car again. Luckily, Penny didn't want to go shopping and both of her Dads didn't really want to take a reluctant five-year-old with them, so Jenny volunteered to babysit. She led Penny downstairs to pick out fun movies to watch for the day while the adults got ready to leave. She heard Aaron return from the clearing and fought the urge to eavesdrop from the bottom of the basement staircase.

In the end, Jenny didn't know who drove which car and what people rode along. All she knew was by the time she and Penny emerged from their first round of movie fun downstairs for a snack the house was empty. Relief tinged with sadness flooded over her, but she decided to focus on being the best Aunt Babysitter of all time and not wallow in self-pity.

She and Penny painted their toes and fingernails, played Chutes and Ladders, went for a walk outside to look at the melting snow and made a tiny 'fairy' snowman. Then they ate leftover turkey sandwiches for lunch. Afterwards, they went up to Jenny's room and she let Penny choose some of the books off of her old bookshelf to read before nap. They only made it through one and a half books before they both fell asleep.

Jenny opened her eyes to gentle shaking and found Jimmy and Paul standing over her smiling. She rubbed her eyes and looked around the room, Penny was still fast asleep in a warm little ball next to her on the bed.

"What time is it?" She mumbled.

"Don't worry, Paul already took a picture," Jimmy whispered as he sat gently at the foot of the bed.

"I did," Paul assured her, "but it was very flattering, trust me." Paul grabbed her desk chair and pulled it over to the side of the bed. "Are you awake enough for an interrogation?" He asked quietly.

"An interrogation about what?" She whispered.

"What have you done to that boy?" Paul asked, his face all seriousness, his eyes teasing.

"What?" She was still a tad groggy. She looked at Jimmy, the only other boy in the room.

"Not him," Paul dismissed Jimmy with a wave of his hand. "Aaron...what have you done to Aaron?"

Jenny carefully sat up a little, trying not to disturb her niece.

"I don't know what you're talking about."

"You should have seen him today," Jimmy explained. "Moping around like a lovesick puppy." Jimmy looked at Paul to corroborate his story.

"Oh yes, he's absolutely miserable, like a sad, gorgeous Viking, " Paul agreed. "We figured something was up since you two have been connected at the hip for the last few days, all doe eyes and giggles." Paul poked her ribs playfully.

A flicker of pleasure passed through her at the news

before she could stop it. She didn't want to feel good if Aaron was missing her. That wasn't the mature thing to do.

"I didn't do anything...really," she defended herself, but it was a weak defense and her brother and brother-in-law caught onto it immediately.

"What happened?" Jimmy grabbed her foot and shook it up and down. The bed bounced a little and Penny murmured in her sleep.

"Stop, you're going to wake her up," Jenny chastised him.

"Do tell us what magic you have used on that delicious morsel of a hipster to turn him into such a pathetic pile of emotional mush," Paul said.

"I didn't mean to hurt his feelings," Jenny admitted. "You shouldn't be happy if he is unhappy anyway."

"We're not happy, Jen," Jimmy said. "We're intrigued!"

"It probably doesn't have anything to do with me," she suggested.

"Nope, sorry, that's impossible. Every time anyone brought up your name his handsome little face would fall and he kind of slumped over and did the Charlie Brown sad walk," Jimmy informed her.

"Every time," Paul agreed.

"He did not," she argued, though secretly hoped this was true. No, that wasn't kind. She didn't want Aaron to be sad. She didn't want him to feel as bad as she did.

"What's the bump in the road?" Paul asked, his interest turning more towards concern. "You know, we're old pros at getting past romantic obstacles." He smiled lovingly at Jimmy who winked back at him. "Maybe we can help?"

She flopped her head back on the pillow and let out a groan. "No, there's nothing you can do."

"Why not?" Jimmy wanted to know. "You like him, Jen. We can all see it. Now, what's the problem? Is it that he's too handsome and thoughtful? Do you need someone more aloof with a quirky look?"

"Don't be mean," Jenny said.

"I'm not being mean," Jimmy said.

"He's not trying to be mean," Paul explained. "It's just so frustrating to watch. You two looked so happy together!"

There was a soft knock on the bedroom door and Jenny sat up. They all looked at each other like they'd been caught by their parents cussing in the tree house. She cleared the sleep out of her throat.

"Come in?"

The door clicked and pushed open revealing Aaron standing sheepishly in the hallway, her green journal in his hands. Jenny's mouth went dry.

"Sorry." Aaron took in the three of them huddled together at Jenny's bed, then noticed Penny still sleeping. He spoke quietly, "I wanted to bring this to you. You left it..." His voice trailed off and Jenny swore she saw his cheeks redden under his beard. She scrambled up from the bed, making the mattress bounce and waking up Penny.

"Daddy?" Penny said to Paul and Jimmy both.

"Hi honey, how was your nap?" Paul lifted her up in her still sleepy state and moved to carry her out of the room.

"I hope I didn't wake her," Aaron said, looking genuinely bothered at the idea.

"Oh, no," Jimmy answered as he stepped to Paul's side and they both slipped towards the door. "Come in," Jimmy waved Aaron into the room. "We were just leaving."

There was an awkward bottleneck at the doorway as Paul and Jimmy tried to give Jenny and Aaron some privacy and Jenny and Aaron tried not to look like they were about to have some privacy.

Finally, it was just Aaron remaining in her room. He looked

tall and manly next to her girlhood furniture. Even with his wide shoulders, epic mane of hair, strong cheekbones and piercing blue eyes, there was a terrible vulnerable pain in his face and Jenny couldn't help but feel bad for her part in putting it there.

"So this is your room?" He said, his cheeks definitely red this time.

"Yeah," Jenny was at a loss for words. There had never been a man in this room except for Jimmy, Paul or her Dad.

"Anyway," Aaron dipped his head, looking down at the journal before holding it out to her. "I wanted to get this back to you this morning, but we left right away and you weren't around."

Jenny took it, sensing the nearness of his hand to hers. She wondered if he'd read any more of it, if he'd seen the parts when she wrote about wanting to touch his hair or how the water splashed onto his chest in the hot tub.

"Thanks," was all she managed to say.

"Sure, well–"

"Aaron," she interrupted, clutching the journal to her stomach. "I'm sorry."

He paused, "For what?"

"For this morning, for–"

"Saying no?" This time he interrupted her, holding up his hand to stop her from saying anything else. "Don't be sorry for that, Jenny. I would never want to do anything...I mean, a woman has the right to say what she wants."

Jenny nodded, still clutching the journal. Aaron sighed and looked at the ground, then raised his eyes to hers from under his brow.

"I'm the one who should be sorry. I brought it up and now everything is awkward." He gave her a half smile. She smiled back.

"It's not awkward," she tried to deny.

"You don't find this awkward?" He looked at her disbelieving. "I do!"

She laughed at that, which made him chuckle. He shifted his weight from one foot to the other and seemed to relax as her laughter subsided.

"I guess it is a little awkward," she said.

He nodded, "Yeah, but I think maybe it will wear off." He turned sideways as if he was about to leave, then looked back at her once more, a genuine smile crinkling the corners of his eyes. "You think we can be friends?"

She let the question hang in the air for a moment, believing that once they agreed to it there was no turning back. Her fingers held tight to her journal as she felt herself drawn into his eyes one last time, letting him look into her and hoping that what he saw would help him understand.

"Yes, of course," she said, and as soon as she said it she felt him withdraw from her, respectfully.

When he was gone, Jenny sat down on the side of her bed still holding tight to her green journal, her palms sweaty and her heart beating slow and heavy in her chest. She'd made the right decision, surely she had. What she didn't understand was why making the right decision made her feel like the world had just been ripped out from under her feet.

Chapter Thirteen

On her last morning walk to the clearing, Jenny lingered, taking in the feel of the earth under her boots, still heavy with the weight of melted snow. Many leaves had fallen in the storm and now lay in a thick, squishy layer along the path. Some of fall's colors were still present in the limbs above her, but the snow had been cold enough to turn much of the brilliance to brown and it was only a matter of time before all of the leaves would fall and turn into mulch on the ground.

She was sorry to see the wonder of autumn go. Perhaps it would make leaving tomorrow to return home to her condo and her job more tolerable. Perhaps not. She took in a deep breath and smelled wet woods and damp leaves. The glow of dawn was getting stronger, illuminating the path and the detailed texture of the bark on the trees as she moved towards the clearing.

Settling into her bench to watch the morning break, Jenny tried to think about anything but Aaron. Since their discussion in her bedroom they had managed to be civil and even friendly towards each other at dinner and the game of cards that followed. Jenny didn't accept Jimmy's invitation to join him and Paul in the hot tub, saying she had a headache and was going to bed. She noticed that Aaron didn't join them either and wondered if he'd refused for the same reasons she had.

Today was the last day of Thanksgiving vacation. She was leaving tomorrow morning, a blessing and a curse. On one hand, she wouldn't have to go through any more encounters with Aaron, which was a relief. On the other hand, the knowledge she wouldn't see him again after today left her with a deep sense of longing.

The same problem faced her this morning. She knew that Aaron knew where she was. Would he come to see her? Or not? Both options were wholly unsatisfactory. She took in a deep breath and let out a heavy sigh.

"That's why it's a good thing that everything is over tomorrow," she said out loud, her voice drifting into the calm morning air.

"Talking to yourself?"

Jenny turned quickly in her seat, startled by the voice even though she recognized it immediately.

"Dad?"

Rudy appeared from the woodland path, and walked over, joining her on the bench.

"It's a little cold out here this morning, isn't it?" He lifted his shoulders up and down as if trying to warm his muscles and shoved his hands into his pockets.

"A little," she agreed. "What are you doing out here so early?"

"Oh, I don't mind getting up early every now and then." He looked around the clearing, the sunrise had officially begun and the golden hour of light made everything around them shimmer. "Sure is pretty."

"Yeah," she answered.

They sat together silently for a few minutes enjoying the sunshine as it grew stronger and warmed their faces.

"Your Mom loved watching the sunrise out here, you know," he said. He looked at her with a grin. "You look just like her sitting here."

Tears filled Jenny's eyes and she smiled back at him without answering. Her Dad took one hand out of his jacket pocket and patted her knee.

"How are you doing, Button?" He asked.

Jenny swallowed hard before answering, "I'm fine."

"You are?" He gave her a skeptical look.

"Why do you ask?"

"Well, this is the thing, everyone is worried about you. Love told me she thinks something is the matter. Jimmy and Paul said so, too. Jimmy told me he was gonna come out here this morning and talk to you. I told everyone to just hold on, it's a Dad's job to check in on his little girl when something's the matter." Here he paused and gave her another quizzical look. "So tell me, Button, what's the matter?"

Big, fat tears welled up in her eyes and her throat tightened as she tried to keep from crying. Her Dad put his arm around her shoulder and pulled her to him.

"Oh, Dad," Jenny said and burst into tears. He held her gently as she let out her grief and frustration. Soon her tears had turned to sniffles and he pulled a freshly ironed handkerchief out of his jacket pocket and gave it to her.

"Now, now," he said softly, "what's all this about?"

"It's everything," Jenny shrugged and let her hands flop into her lap.

"Everything?" He raised his eyebrows in mock surprise. "Now that is something to get upset over. Everything is a lot."

She smiled despite herself and shook her head 'no'. "Not everything."

"Let me take a few guesses and you tell me if I'm right," he said. She blew her nose into his handkerchief and nodded in agreement. "Does it have anything to do with that long haired fella?"

Jenny laughed a little then nodded, "A little."

"Okay, that's a piece of it." He squinted across the clearing, pondering what he was going to say next. "Does it have anything to do with Love?"

"Your Love?" Jenny sniffed as she clarified.

He nodded 'yes'.

"A little," Jenny said shyly. She didn't want to hurt her Dad's feelings.

"Okay, that's something I expected you to have trouble with," he admitted. Jenny was surprised that he wasn't surprised. He looked at her keenly, waiting. When she didn't say anything else he asked, "And what else, Button? What else is bothering you?"

Jenny's face crumpled as her grief took over. She lifted the handkerchief to her mouth trying to control her break down and succeeded only long enough to say, "And I miss Mom." Then she broke down, bawling like a baby into her Dad's shoulder. They stayed like that for a while, long enough for her sobs to mellow into sniffles. When she finally lifted her head to wipe her eyes and nose, her Dad had tears in his eyes too. He wiped them away with the back of his hand.

"I do too." He looked down at his hands then up at the sunshine filtering through the trees across the clearing. "You know, I think about your Mom every day, all day long really."

Jenny sniffed. She hadn't known that.

"It's one of the things that connected Love and I, we can talk to each other about our spouses. She lost her Carl and I lost my Suzanne and there's something nice about being able to talk about them when you think of them."

Jenny let that sink in before answering.

"I can see that," she said.

"I think I would have liked Carl if I'd known him," he acknowledged with a grin. "I'm sure Love and your Mom would have liked each other."

Jenny smiled at the thought of Love and her Mom picking out china for Thanksgiving dinner together and had to admit it seemed plausible. She sniffed again before conceding.

"She is nice."

"Yes, she sure is," he agreed. He smacked her knee warmly. "You know who else is nice?

"Who?"

"That long haired kid, what's his name?" He winked at Jenny and she felt fourteen again.

"Da-ad!"

"I'm gonna tell you something, Jenny, something I think you should know."

"Okay," she waited.

"Losing someone you love doesn't mean you have to feel sad forever. It's not a life sentence of mourning." He watched her as he spoke, making sure she was listening. "Your Mom wanted you to be over the moon happy when she was alive and she wants the same thing for you now that she has passed. It's fine to have memories and to cry when you need to." He squeezed her shoulder so she was squished into him. "And it's also fine to laugh and have fun, to make plans and even, if the right guy comes along, to fall in love."

A deep sense of comfort flooded through her body. She suddenly realized her shoulders had been tight and heavy, but now felt relaxed and light, as if she was ready to dance. Relief took over and what must have been pent up guilt simply slipped away.

They walked together back to the house. Jenny found herself looking for Aaron. She didn't see him anywhere outside or in the house when they went in to make breakfast.

Love was there, creating some kind of quiche she had found in one of the old cookbooks. She gave them one of her wide smiles when they came in the French doors.

"Was the sunrise beautiful?" She asked.

A happy glow took over Jenny's face and she gave Love a genuine smile, "It really was."

"There's coffee if you want some," Love offered.

She truly is a nice lady, Jenny thought as she poured a cup of coffee. Then, because she couldn't ignore his absence, she wondered where Aaron was.

Chapter Fourteen

A aron didn't appear during breakfast and even though the table was full with Jimmy and his family, and Love and her Dad, it seemed to Jenny like there was a gaping hole in the room.

As they were clearing the dishes from the table Jenny posed the nonchalant, she thought, question, "Has Aaron already eaten?"

Love responded with an apologetic look then replied quickly, "He left really early, said he wanted to get a look at the big lakes north of here."

Jenny's stomach tightened with such force it made her feel sick. For a second she was afraid she might lose her breakfast. Love watched her with an empathetic smile. Jenny simply nodded and put the dirty dishes she was holding down on the counter. They landed with a clatter.

"Sorry," Jenny said, trying to hide her shaking hands by wrapping her arms around her stomach.

Love placed her hand lightly on Jenny's back and said quietly, "He'll be back later today." Jenny tried to act like his return meant nothing to her, but she wasn't fooling anybody.

"Aunt Jenny," Penny asked from the table, "Do you want to color with me?"

"Sure," she smiled at her niece as the little girl hurried out of the room to get her coloring supplies. She was thankful for the distraction.

It turned out Jenny needed to fill her entire day with distractions. Aaron didn't return until just before dinner was on the table, but he came bearing gifts. Everyone was full of smiles as he passed them each something out of a large paper tote bag. First up was Penny.

"Now, this is for you to share with your Dads," Aaron told her, his hand still hidden inside the bag where she couldn't see.

"Okay!" She agreed, her cheeks pink with excitement.

Aaron pulled out three sheep hand puppets. Two had ram horns, one with white wool and one with black. Then there was an adorable baby lamb puppet with soft grey wool and big doe eyes.

"Aww," Paul said, "It's our family!" He and Jimmy grinned at each other as Penny delighted putting the puppets on each of them and then herself.

"Thank you!" Penny told Aaron, always the sweet one.

"You're welcome," Aaron's face glowed, happy in his role as the giver of presents, like Santa come early. He was, by far, the handsomest Santa Jenny had ever seen. He dug in the bag again.

"Rudy," Aaron said, handing her Dad a beautiful wood handled chef's knife. "For your kitchen. And Love," he pulled a heavy cookbook out of the bag handing it to her. When she read the front she laughed out loud and turned it around for everyone else to see, 'Love is at the Table' was the title. "I couldn't pass that up!" He said as she gave him a hug and kiss on the cheek.

"Thank you, sweetie," Love said.

"You're welcome," he told her, then to both of them, "I really appreciate you inviting me here for the holiday."

"You're welcome anytime," Rudy told him.

There was a beat, a minuscule glitch in the casual fun vibe of the room. Then Aaron turned to Jenny. A hush fell over the room, or maybe it was her imagination, either way she couldn't tear her eyes away from him. His eyes shone as he stepped closer to her. They held her fast in their grip, so much so that she didn't look away to see what he held in his hands until he pressed it into hers. She blinked and looked down at a deep blue leather bound book. No, not a book, a journal, with script on the front that read 'Fill your paper with the breathings of your heart'.

"Oh," she said, a sweet sadness rushing through her.

Aaron tipped his head towards her, pieces of his blonde wavy hair tumbling down around their faces when he did. "It seemed to me you might fill up your other one pretty soon."

She beamed at him, the intimacy of his gift and the expression on his face made her a little faint. No words came to her, but she managed a quiet, "Thank you."

He leaned closer to her and she thought for a split second that he might kiss her cheek, like Love had kissed his. He didn't.

"You're welcome," he said quietly, and that was all.

The evening carried on and Jenny did not recover her voice. The urge to talk to Aaron came often. All night she wanted to pull him aside and sit with him in a quiet place to tell him that she thought she'd made a mistake, that maybe they could have a romantic relationship maybe even fall in love, that she really, really wanted him to kiss her. Even though the desire was there she couldn't find the right time or the right words. Every moment seemed frozen, untouchable, yet they went by so fast it was time to go to bed before she knew what had happened.

Her Dad and Love excused themselves first, worn out after a week of company. Paul and Jimmy said their hushed goodnights as Jimmy carried a sleeping Penny up the stairs towards their room. That left Jenny alone with Aaron in the front sitting room, watching the fire die down to embers. They were silent for a while. He was sprawled comfortably on the couch while she sat curled up in her mother's favorite chair. She didn't know what to say to him, but couldn't bring herself to leave. Finally she had a thought.

"Thank you again for the journal. I really love it."

He shifted his gaze from the fireplace to her, taking a moment before answering, "I'm glad." His smile was soft and tired. It occurred to her that he must be exhausted after driving up north and back today. She was keeping him up and probably making him uncomfortable. This was his makeshift bedroom after all. He couldn't go to sleep with her sitting there watching him. Embarrassment flooded over her.

"I should get to bed," she said, unfolding herself from the chair.

He sat up, too, then stood when she stood. For some reason this action infuriated her. They weren't at a formal dinner, why was he acting like such a gentleman?

"Sure, it's late," was all he said.

"Yeah," Jenny snapped, "it is." She walked to the stairs and started to climb.

"Jenny," he said. Her stomach flipped at the sound of his voice speaking her name. So ridiculous, but she stopped anyway.

"Yes?"

"I'm glad we're going to be friends."

Hot disappointment shot through her heart, but all she could manage was a polite, "Me too."

Chapter Fifteen

The next morning was a bustle of activity as the whole house woke up and got ready for their long drives home. Breakfast was minimal, coffee was in abundance. This was a good thing, because Jenny hadn't slept a wink. Every moment she and Aaron had spent together over this past week kept running like a movie through her mind, keeping her awake through the night. Nevertheless, it was time to leave this vacation behind and move on with life. She was glad she'd had some time to get to know Love and be with her Dad and brother and his family...and she was glad to have met Aaron even if they weren't meant to be together.

That's what people did, right? Be glad about the experience no matter if it ended with their heart crushed into a million pieces.

Jenny packed, adding her stack of journals on top of her folded clothes. She placed her Mom's peacock card carefully sandwiched carefully between her green journal and the blue one Aaron had bought her as a sign of their friendship. She sighed, resigned to leaving. There was nothing more to do here. She'd already ruined her best chance at love, may as well go home.

Downstairs Penny was running wild as Jimmy and Paul hauled luggage to their car. Jimmy would be riding home with them instead of with Jenny as he and Paul and their daughter were now a reunited family. She would be driving home alone, of course.

Aaron was still in his pajamas deflating the air mattress. No doubt he would wait until they all left so he could pack and leave in peace. Though she was irritable at not having any sleep, she still found herself watching him, appreciating the way he looked, the way he moved. He wore a pair of flannel Pj's that hung dangerously low on his hips and a very faded orange Broncos T-shirt. Yet, somehow, with his hair tumbled on top of his head in a mop, he still managed to look good. She didn't know if she could forgive him for that.

They found themselves alone for a moment in the kitchen while she was filling her thermal mug with coffee to go. He sat on the opposite side of the kitchen island watching her, his eyes rimmed red as if he, too, had not gotten a good night's sleep. Jenny clicked the lid on her cup and looked around the kitchen. It was time for her to go.

"Well, I guess this is it," she said.

He nodded and yawned his response, "I hope you have a good trip home."

Then he stood up and jogged around the island to where she was, opening his arms to her for a goodbye hug. After a tiny hesitation she let him wrap her up in a comfy pajama embrace. Her cheek pressed against the muscles in his chest and his strong arms were warm and safe as he held her for a long moment.

As the pulse of his heartbeat fluttered against her cheek and the ends of his beard tickled her forehead her mood softened. Suddenly sleepy, she wished she could crawl back into her bed upstairs, taking the hug with her. Instead, she said the first thing that came into her mind.

"I'm sorry I said no."

Her voice was muffled against his T-shirt.

He pulled away from her. "What did you say?"

Jenny looked up into his face. Even bloodshot his eyes were beautiful.

"I said I'm sorry I said no. I think I would have liked to kiss you," she answered.

Aaron stared at her for a moment, not saying anything. Then he opened his mouth as if to speak only to shut it again.

Jenny pulled away and grabbed her coffee cup. It was obvious this was not a conversation he wanted to have and now she just wanted to get away.

"Goodbye, Aaron," she said, and walked out of the kitchen.

Once outside, her Dad helped her get her suitcase into her trunk and she busied herself with saying goodbye to Penny. She had to promise her niece that she would come to see them for Christmas and her birthday, which was right after Christmas. Jenny promised. Then she hugged Paul and Jimmy goodbye, happy they were getting back together, feeling melancholy taking over at the same time.

She looked for Aaron, but he was nowhere to be seen. He must be packing and thanking his lucky stars he avoided any kind of connection to her, a crazy person who doesn't know what she wants. He was probably thrilled he'd dodged that bullet. She felt tears pressing at the back of her throat and eyes, but swallowed hard and held them back long enough to say goodbye to her Dad and to Love.

She hugged them both and managed to smile and wave at them as she pulled away from the house. Paul and Jimmy had already gone. Aaron was still hiding from her. She was all alone.

The tears came once she started down the winding road. Flowing hot and heavy down her cheeks, they were the tears of a broken heart. The scenery was grim. Most of the trees in the surrounding woods had lost their leaves, leaving mostly gnarled branches spreading for as far as she could see. They looked like she felt...empty. She didn't know how she was going to get through the next few hours driving and crying at the same time. She didn't know how she was going to get through the rest of her life knowing that she'd pushed Aaron away.

Ahead she saw the covered bridge, one of the places Aaron had wanted to kiss her, one of the moments that was forever lost to her. She was crying so hard now she had to slow the car down as she entered. Moving slowly through the bridge, she wiped the tears from her eyes with the back of one hand in an attempt to keep from crashing her car into the ancient wooden walls.

Suddenly she saw a flash of orange move in front of her car and a loud thump sounded on the hood. She screamed and slammed on her brakes. In an instant her fear turned to surprise when she saw Aaron standing in the middle of the road in front of her leaning against her hood as if he had stopped her car by force. She stared at him, shocked. He said something that she couldn't hear. She put the car in park and stepped out.

"I have a question for you," Aaron said, he was breathing hard. He must have run all the way from the house to catch her here.

"What are you doing? I could have killed you!"

Aaron shrugged, unconcerned. Jenny looked him up and down. He was still in his Pj's, but had added a pair of boots pulled hastily on, his flannel pajama bottoms crumpled at the top of them. Jenny was speechless. Aaron was a little out of breath, but he had something to say.

"I have a question for you," he said again.

She half-laughed, half-snorted. This was ridiculous. Her car was idling in the middle of the covered bridge with its nose sticking out one end and this wild haired barely dressed Viking looking man blocking her path demanding to ask her a question.

He raised his eyebrows at her, waiting for a response.

"What?" She asked, because she basically had no other choice.

He lifted his hands off of her car and straightened to his full height. Locking his eyes on hers, he took the few steps between them and was almost instantly standing directly in front of her, so close she could feel the warmth of his skin emanating through his T-shirt.

He reached up and touched her cheek, pushing her hair back behind her ear, exactly like she had wanted to do to him for so long.

"Jenny," he said softly. He let his gaze wander from her eyes to her lips and drop to her chest that was lifting up and down rapidly with shallow, excited breaths. He smiled and raised his icy blue eyes to look into hers again. "Jenny," it was almost a whisper.

She tried to answer, but her voice caught in her throat. He let his hand move from her hair, running his fingers along the side of her neck, over her shoulder and down her arm until he had her hand in his. Electric shocks shimmered through her body at his touch. She waited.

"I have a question," he said again, his voice cracked as he said it. His own feelings overtaking him.

"What?" She asked, her own voice matching his in a whisper.

"Can I kiss you?"

She sucked in her breath as a shiver went down her back.

Placing her hand on his chest to steady herself, she answered, "Yes."

The corners of his eyes crinkled into a smile. His hands moved to her waist, wrapping around her, steady and firm. Then, finally, he dipped his head down and his lips were on hers. Softly, so softly, he kissed her, holding her tightly to him as he did.

His beard and mustache tickled her cheeks and chin. She moved her hands up his chest and around his neck, pushing her fingers into his thick, wavy hair. Still, he kissed her, drinking her in. Sunshine filled all of the dark places in her heart. Her sadness and loneliness dissolved and trembled deep inside her core before drifting outward through her skin and the tips of her fingers, floating away. What remained was pure joy and passion.

He pulled his mouth away from hers and looked down into her face, his eyes shining, "That's one."

"One?"

"I told you, I want to kiss you a thousand times."

Her brow wrinkled into a frown. "A thousand?"

He nodded, a questioning look on his face.

She traced her finger along his temple and cheek, smoothing over his mustache and finally letting it rest on his lips, those fantastic, insistent lips. Then she grinned, her eyes mischievous, and said, "At least!"

Aaron threw his head back and laughed. Then he kissed her on her mouth, on her nose, on her cheeks, finally burying his face into her neck. He lifted her up, twirling her around in a joyful hug. She laughed and held tight to him. Her Viking, her wild haired man with the piercing blue eyes, her gift from Love.

THANK you for reading Love is at the Table! If you enjoyed this book you may enjoy the other books in the series...

Enchanting Eve - Halloween Romance

Mistletoe Madness - Christmas Romance

New Year in Paradise - New Year's Eve Romance

❧

YOU MIGHT ENJOY Darci's Dream Come True series. The first book, Her Scottish Keep is a fun and flirty romance set in the Scottish Highlands...a clean and wholesome contemporary Scottish love story :)

Epilogue

Jenny stood in front of the mirror in her bedroom at the Lake House, taking a minute to herself before one of the biggest events of her life began.

Her dress was pure white. A beautiful, lace bodice fit smoothly over her curves and an off the shoulder cut made her shoulders look especially graceful. The lace turned to French tulle at the waist, which fell softly and elegantly to the floor. She did not wear a veil. She had decided that would be too much for the small ceremony they had planned, but her hair was swept up into a loose bun held in place with crystal encrusted hair combs and hair pins decorated with tiny crystal rosebuds.

Jenny touched the simple pearl necklace at her throat and smiled. Her mother had worn this necklace when she married her Dad, and he had proudly gifted it to her when she and Aaron arrived at the Lake House last week for Thanksgiving and to begin their final wedding preparations. Then Aaron had surprised her with matching drop pearl earrings he bought for her to match. So sweet, the two of them working in cahoots together to make her wedding day that much more meaningful. She was so lucky to be so loved.

She checked off the list quickly in her mind. Something old, her necklace, something new, her earrings, something borrowed, her crystal rosebud hair pins were actually Love's, which she'd offered happily for the occasion. And something blue, she lifted her skirt slightly to reveal a slim, aquamarine anklet that Jimmy and Paul had found on one of their weekend getaways. She was covered from head to toe with love, of that she was certain.

There was a soft knock on the door announcing Jimmy and Paul's arrival.

"Come in," she said, turning towards the door. Her brother and his husband stepped into her room, looking sharp in their matching red and black checked waistcoats with white rose boutonnieres.

"We have your flowers," Jimmy said as he carried a tasteful bouquet of orange lilies mixed artfully with red and white roses to her. "Jen," he looked her up and down, smiling the whole time, "You look beautiful!"

"You're gorgeous, darling!" Paul added, giving her a kiss on the cheek. "This is going to be a wedding of epic beauty."

Jimmy nodded as he handed her the bouquet, "You should see that boy of yours." He gave one of his low whistles and Jenny giggled.

"He looks grand, darling, like a Viking who won the lottery!"

"Or a fur trader who has become a prince!" Jimmy added.

"Aunt Jenny," Penny called as she came through the door. Six-years old now, Penny wore an adorable deep orange flower girl dress and carried her own mini version of Jenny's bouquet. "Grandpa says we're ready!" Her eyes shone with excitement, reflecting Jenny's feelings perfectly.

A cello played as Aaron's father escorted his mother down

the stairs into the sitting room that had been emptied of furniture, filled with folding chairs and decked out in white lights, candles and so many flower garlands the smell of roses hung sweetly in the air. They were followed by Paul escorting Penny down the stairs, then Jimmy escorting Love, who looked radiant in a deep rose colored dress.

Finally, Jenny's Dad took her arm at the top of the stairs. He kissed her on the cheek and patted her arm saying, "You are a vision, Button. You're Mom is so proud of you right now, I can feel it."

"I love you, Dad," she said, as she kissed him on his cheek. She blinked back tears.

"Ready?" He asked. She nodded and he walked proudly with her down the stairs to the small group of friends and family that were already seated, and to the man she was going to marry who stood waiting for her.

Aaron's eyes were always brilliant, always bright when he looked at her, and always full of love. But Jenny had never seen them quite as shining and intense as they were on this day, their wedding day. He stood tall and masculine in narrow black slacks, crisp white shirt and his own waistcoat of pure black. His boutonnière had red and orange roses, as he was the groom. And an impressive groom he was.

His wavy mane of blonde hair was loose except for the very top that was pulled back off of his face. He had trimmed his beard to the length she liked the best, and she thought he had never looked more handsome than he did in this moment.

Her walk down the aisle was not long, but it seemed like forever before she was finally standing next to him. Her father ceremoniously gave her hand to Aaron then sat down with Love. Aaron's warm, strong hand held hers and did not let go throughout their vows.

When he placed the shining wedding band on her finger,

slipping it up to nestle next to the princess cut diamond engagement ring he'd given her just a few months before, Jenny's heart swelled with love and joy.

When it was time for them to kiss as husband and wife, Aaron took her by the waist and turned her to him, drinking her up with his eyes before he leaned down and kissed her sweetly on the mouth. The small crowd clapped and cheered and Aaron leaned back, looking at her with a brilliant smile.

"That's one! Our first married kiss," he said. Jenny laughed, her happiness overflowing.

"We're going to lose count!" She exclaimed.

"I hope so," Aaron replied and took her in his arms again.

She was his, utterly and completely, and he was hers just the same.

THE END

IF YOU'RE in the mood for a Christmas romance, get your copy of Charlotte's Christmas Charade the first book in A Sugar Plum Romance series – antics of chefs who get in over their heads at Christmas time and end up in charming holiday love stories!

MISTLETOE
Madness
CHRISTMAS ROMANCE

DARCI BALOGH

For my sister, Robin.
Thank you for your enthusiasm for life, for projects, for building forts,
and especially your enthusiasm for Christmas.
Your spirit has always been an inspiration to me and your skill at
creating an ambience and a sense of fun wherever you go and
whatever the circumstances is nothing short of miraculous. I love
Christmas, and you are a big reason why. May we share countless
more holidays and every days together, and may your Christmas
always be merry and bright!

Chapter One

Abigail spent the first day in tears. The second day she wallowed in self-pity and frustration. The third, fourth, fifth, and sixth day she toiled away, desperately searching for freelance gigs online. And on the seventh day, December 1st, Abigail started packing up her apartment.

Getting fired had come as a shock. Getting fired immediately after Thanksgiving had ended a year that started off tentatively bad and was wrapping up bang on horrible.

She began the year with a break up from her on-again, off-again, never committing boyfriend. If you could really call him that.

Then she'd been demoted to part-time in her position as a contract graphic designer for a mid-level, sometimes sleazy, marketing firm.

In the middle of the summer her unofficial roommate had moved out to get married to an attractive and successful engineer she'd met online. Leaving Abigail to shoulder rent and utility payments by herself on her part-time salary.

In an attempt to do something positive, Abigail had planned a two week trip home to see her parents and brother for the Christmas season. Graphic design work was notoriously slow around that time of year. Companies were usually focusing on getting through the holidays before they started big new projects at the beginning of the year. But when she brought up her upcoming time off during a video meeting the weekend after Thanksgiving break, her supervisor, Jennifer, surprised her with an out of the blue announcement.

"Actually, Abby, I have some unfortunate news."

Abigail hated to be called 'Abby', but nobody at this virtual job had ever gotten that memo.

"Oh, what's the news?" Abigail asked, blissfully ignorant for a few more moments that her life was about to be completely dismantled.

"I'm sorry to have to tell you this, but we don't need your services anymore," Jennifer's two dimensional face said, looking at Abigail with a mixture of authority and sympathy from the computer screen.

A few beats went by as Abigail's brain processed the information. Then her mouth dropped open and her already long and thin nose pinched together at the top with what could only be described as an expression of anguish. Blotches of red climbed from her pale neck to her pale cheeks. She looked like one of the angry birds from that game, the red one, except with an out of control curly mop of dark hair that bordered on frizzy. Her mouth opened and closed several times as she tried to think of a response, giving her the appearance of a dying, blotchy, outraged fish.

Abigail knew without doubt that's what she looked like, because she could see her face in the small square at the bottom right of her computer screen. Courtesy of Zoom.

"I'm sorry to be the bearer of bad news," Jennifer said, alarmed at Abigail's reaction. "The company is moving in a different direction and we just can't justify the expense of another graphic designer."

In retrospect, Abigail wished she'd had the wherewithal to click her computer camera to the off position. That would at least have prevented Jennifer from watching her cry.

"Abby?" Jennifer's natural style and grace was having a hard time not reacting to Abigail's crumpled, tragic image, which was full screen on her end, Abigail remembered later with much embarrassment. "Are you all right?"

"No," Abigail managed. "I'm not!"

That's when she dropped her face into her hands and wept, rather uncontrollably. She tried to stop crying so she could leave with at least a shred of dignity, or at least give Jennifer a piece of her mind with some scathing exit commentary.

Neither of those things happened, however. Abigail just kept bawling into her hands, her face getting redder and her nose filling with snot until she reached out blindly and found the mouse on her desk. Abigail glanced up briefly to make sure she clicked on the End Call button. She saw Jennifer's shocked and uncomfortable face for one horrible moment before it disappeared from her computer monitor forever.

She was out. Fired. Done.

The humiliation turned to fear turned to shock turned to anger, then back to humiliation, and the whole process started again.

She'd never been fired before. It was not something she knew how to deal with or something she was prepared to handle. Emotionally or financially.

Her meager savings had burned up covering full rent since her roommate left. She'd been considering asking her parents for a small loan to help out until she could either pick up more work or find a new roommate. That wasn't the main reason she was going home for the holiday, but it had been on her mind.

She couldn't ask them to cover her expenses completely,

though. That was too much. She was a grown woman, after all. Fully capable of paying her own way in life, usually.

Then there was the unfortunate timing of her lease ending on December 5th. There was no way her dusty old landlord was going to renew a lease with her if she didn't have a job. He wasn't that kind of landlord. The nice kind. He'd never liked her much, anyway, but he was fastidious about doing a full review of all tenant's financial circumstances before signing any paperwork. Even tenants who had lived there for six years.

For several days following her virtual dismissal Abigail experienced bouts of anger. She would rail at the empty room around her the way she wished she would have railed at Jennifer when she let her go, or Tom when they broke up. She found that it didn't matter how recent the wrong, she was angry at anyone and everyone who she harbored any resentment towards. Nobody was immune from becoming the unknowing victim of her verbal outrage.

"Moving in a new direction? Could that new direction possibly be overseas where you can hire a graphic designer for $5 an hour instead of $30? Would that be the direction this company is moving, Jennifer?" Abigail practically shouted at her kitchen cupboards as she was looking for potato chips or cookies or any kind of junk food she could use to assuage her disappointment.

Then, when she ran out of groceries, "Can't take time off work to go out, Tom? Really? I saw you out two nights ago on Instagram. Who was that red head you were with, Tom? Would it really be that difficult to call or text and invite me to go with you? And on that note, when was the last time you called or texted me first? When, Tom?" Abigail whispered intensely to herself as she walked through the grocery store buying Ramen soup and eggs to get by for the next few days on next to no cash.

Being a contract worker meant she billed on Saturday for all of the work she'd done that week and was paid the following Wednesday. With Thanksgiving being a slow week, Abigail barely had enough money in her last paycheck to pay for gas to drive to her parent's house, let alone groceries.

In retrospect, it really had been a horrible job. No benefits, no vacation or sick time, high expectations for less and less billable hours. She wasn't even sure she liked doing graphic design anymore. Dealing with clients was always stressful and often infuriating.

"Honey, why don't you just come home for Christmas and stay with us for a while?" Her Mom had asked when Abigail called with the news.

"I don't want to impose," she answered miserably.

"What, impose?" Her Mother scoffed at the idea, "Zeke only moved out three years ago. Do you think him living here all that time was an imposition?"

Yes, that's exactly what Abigail thought, but she didn't dare say it to her mother.

"What's going on?" She heard her father's distant voice over the phone. He was asking her mother to explain their conversation. When she called her parent's house, she never only spoke to one of them. They conversed as a team.

"It's Abigail, she's coming home to live with us for a while," her mother explained to her father, her voice a little dimmer because she had loosely covered the mouthpiece with her hand.

"Leaving the big city?" he asked, surprised.

"She lost her job," her mother's voice had become a hissing whisper, yet Abigail could still make out every word.

"Oh, that's a shame," her Dad answered. "Tell her to come on home. Zeke's apartment is empty."

Zeke was short for Ezekiel, her older brother by just one year. Zeke had dropped out of college midway and ended up living back at home until he figured out what he wanted to do when he grew up, which was apparently own a used book store.

Three years ago he bought a run down old building in the run down old part of their home town and opened a used book store and coffee shop called The Thinking Bean. Then he moved into the tiny upstairs apartment above this fine establishment and left his basement apartment their parents had remodeled for him empty.

"Did you hear that, honey?" her Mom asked. "Come home. Zeke's apartment is empty."

"Yes, I heard," Abigail answered. Despite her best efforts, she could tell she was going to cry.

LEAVING MOST of her furniture behind wasn't too difficult. Much of it had been thrift store purchases or left behind by her roommate who'd moved on to a posher existence when she married her engineer.

Abigail packed only her most precious possessions, which included many, many books, into her modest hatchback. Once she included her dishes, her clothes, her bedding, a couple plants she'd managed to keep alive over the years, her computer, and the few pieces of artwork that she actually liked, her car was loaded top to bottom. She couldn't even see out of her rear view mirror.

As torn up as she'd been about losing her job and not being able to find a new one fast enough to stay in her apartment, she had to admit she felt a little relieved when she pulled out of her assigned parking space and dropped the keys into the landlord's mailbox. She couldn't comfortably afford this place by herself, even at a full time salary. And she'd learned a few things.

She'd learned that she wasn't really cut out for roommates. She was a loner. She also knew that she needed to find a better job, a company job maybe, someplace that would value her creativity and pay her accordingly.

Abigail pulled onto the highway and headed southwest. It would take her 17 hours to drive to Pitkin Point, home of her family and all of her teenage angst. A place she swore she would never return to live unless she could build the biggest house in town and ride around in a limousine all day. This wasn't quite the homecoming she'd fantasized about. Without enough money to even spend on a hotel to break up the drive, she was planning on stopping occasionally in busy parking lots and napping in her car if she got tired. Asking her parents for help with money right now seemed like too much. They were already going to put her up.

She had that much to be thankful for and she refused to worry over the dissatisfaction and unpopularity of her youth. So she wasn't coming home as some rich man's wife or a famous artist or movie star. She was lucky to have a welcoming place to go in order to regroup and get her life in order. There was no way it was going to take longer than a few months before she was gone again. She could handle that.

Realizing that she'd forgotten her phone in the bottom of her purse, which was nestled safe and completely out of reach behind her seat, she turned on the radio. Christmas music.

She'd all but forgotten about Christmas after everything she'd just went through. A new wave of irritation rippled through her at the cold and inconsiderate way she'd been let go right before Christmas. Was she really surprised? That place had never treated her with much respect, they used her and threw her away on a whim, without ever truly offering her anything substantial.

Suddenly, Tom's face flashed through her mind. Abigail had to chuckle at a realization that came to her just as she was passing the highway sign telling her it was 46 miles to Springfield.

The parallels between her ex-boyfriend, Tom, and the horrible job she'd just lost were eerie. Each of them kept her around just enough to restrict her ability to look for something better, in boyfriends and in jobs. She remained in a continual holding pattern around both of them, waiting, watching, and never allowed to either land and be safe on the ground or fly away to greener pastures.

"Good riddance," Abigail said out loud.

She decided right there and then that this would mark a new moment in her life, one free of settling for anything less than what she truly wanted and deserved. In work or in love.

Happy with her decision, she turned up the radio. 'Jingle Bell Rock' was playing and Abigail sang along, only 16 hours and 40 minutes left until she was home for Christmas.

Chapter Two

D riving through Pitkin Point at 2:00 am was like driving through a ghost town. Nobody, absolutely nobody, was awake. There were no lights on anywhere, except the street lamps, which were thick on Main Street, but grew sparse in the residential areas.

Abigail weaved the hatchback down the short quaint streets of her childhood, taking in some of the differences that stood out against her memories.

Some of the familiar houses had changed their faces with different color schemes, new landscaping or remodeling. The Schmidts had built a new garage next to their house. The Petersons had added a second story. All of the trees were much bigger, while the houses all looked smaller. Maybe they appeared so because of the growth of the trees, or maybe it was because Abigail viewed them through her grown up eyes. It was difficult to say.

She automatically turned down the music in her car as she approached her parent's home and pulled slowly and quietly into the driveway, if it was possible to actually drive quietly. The brick ranch home was the only one on the street with lights still spilling from its windows. Abigail knew it was unlikely her parents had stayed up this late, but they were welcoming her home with light. Abigail smiled at the idea that they had left lamps on in order to make it easier for her to find her way around when she could easily walk through this house blindfolded.

They had also left the Christmas lights on in the front yard. She assumed other houses in the neighborhoods had decorated their yards as well, but turned them off when they went to sleep for the night.

Not her parents.

Her parents were a little over the top with their yard ornamentation. They collected outdoor Christmas decorations and their display had grown over the years.

Her father was Jewish, although he didn't practice the religion of his youth. He had always embraced the Christian holidays to make his wife happy, but his tastes in Christmas decorations leaned towards the secular. As did her mother's, who was not the type to attach to a particular religion or church. For that reason their yard was full of Christmas polar bears, penguins, dogs, cats, one large moose, a tiny llama, and a whole herd of deer.

The wire framed animals made of tiny white or colored lights were grouped together geographically, making it look like the herd of deer were migrating across the front of the lawn towards the driveway, the penguins were tightly packed together for warmth in the corner flower bed, the polar bears were lurking in the shrubs waiting to pounce on the penguins, the moose lumbered along the lilac bushes, the llama was up on a raised bed as if on the side of a mountain, and the dogs and cats were all near the front steps waiting to be let into the house. Abigail's gaze drifted over the bright and happy, if a little goofy, scene. It was good to be home.

She stepped out of the car, grabbed her purse and

overnight bag, and went to the front door. She tried the door-knob and found it unlocked, not surprising. Pitkin Point was very small. Everyone knew everyone else. This made it a safe place to live, although Abigail, after living in the city, had convinced her parents to at least lock their doors when they went to bed at night. They agreed and to her knowledge kept up that practice, except tonight. Tonight they were expecting her to arrive late.

When she stepped into the well lit entryway the smells of home hit her first.

What did home smell like, exactly? Abigail didn't really know. Maybe it was her mother's cooking, or the lemon spray she used when she dusted the wood, or her father's wool hat and coat hanging on the coat rack right behind the door. She couldn't say for certain. The combination of all of the scents in the house created the singular smell that made her feel safe and loved. She took in a deep breath.

"Sweetie," her father's voice, deep and sleepy, came from the adjoining living room. Abigail jumped a little, startled to find anyone awake.

"Dad?"

By habit, she peeked around the partial wall towards his reclining chair. She could just see his legs stuck out on the extended leg rest, his feet wiggling inside thick black socks.

"I wanted to make sure you got in," he mumbled a little as he put the recliner into sitting position and stood up. His glasses and the book he'd been reading slid off of his lap and landed softly on the carpet by his feet.

"You didn't have to wait up for me." She made her way to his chair and gave him a warm hug.

"Your mother was worried about you driving all that way," he said into her hair.

"It wasn't bad."

Abigail stooped down and picked up his glasses and book

while her Dad, Marty Ackerman, rubbed the sleep out of his eyes. He was a tall man, slumped now a little with age, but still broad and masculine, with a large nose to match his other strong facial features, and kind brown eyes. His hair was almost completely grey, but still thick and unruly, with a few remnants of the deep black it once had been.

"Thank you," he said as she gave him his items and kissed him on the cheek. Fully awake now he slipped on his glasses and gazed at her face carefully. Then he put his large hand on the side of her head and stroked her hair. "It's good to see you, sweetie." He leaned down so he could reach her fore-head, and kissed it.

"You, too, Dad," she smiled.

"You tired?" he asked. She nodded. "Come on, your mother fixed up Zeke's old room for you. It's a lot more...feminine than it was." He moved towards the stairway that led to the basement, picking up her overnight bag she'd left in the entryway as he did.

WAKING up the next morning in Zeke's room instead of the room she had grown up in was both familiar and disorienting. Her old bedroom, located next to her parent's room on the main floor, had long ago been converted to a sewing room for her mother. Zeke's basement bedroom was a little bit bigger than hers, had but one full sized window, which, though it let in light, still only offered a view of the window well.

There was a new quilt on the dark wood four poster bed and a matching valance on the window. The quilt was in a flower pattern, using dark greens, light greens, white and a wide range of different shades of pink and red swatches. This, Abigail assumed, was her mother's feminization of Zeke's old space. Her Mom was a self proclaimed textile artist and quilting was her passion. Abigail liked this one, the pattern and colors almost made it look like a field of poppies.

Her eyes had fluttered open just as the morning light made its first attempts to penetrate the window well. The plants she and her Dad had brought in from her car the night before to prevent from freezing sat neatly on a white bookshelf just under the window. As Abigail rolled onto her back and stretched, she noticed that the walls were bare and was glad she would have a place to hang her artwork. Sometimes her mother decorated to the point nothing could be added without going into sensory overload, but she hadn't done that this time.

She was up early. Her body clock was still running on Eastern time, which meant she was two hours ahead of everyone else here. Her Dad had waited up late, plus her Mom was never one to get up too early in the morning. It would be a while before they were awake.

Abigail had a thought to do something nice and go pick up pastries for breakfast. She had a few dollars left in her bank account, she could splurge on her parents.

Plus, it would give her a chance to drop by Zeke's and wake him up early. She hadn't seen her brother in over two years. It would be fun to bug him a little bit and get a look at his new digs, now that she was taking over his old ones.

Driving through the freezing, empty streets of Pitkin Point at dawn was almost as desolate as driving through them at 2:00 am. There were a few more people up and around, a handful of cars rolled down the streets. The two stop lights on Main, however, were still set to blinking red and would stay that way until 7:00 am when the town officially woke up.

At this hour of the day, two places were open; the gas station and the bakery. The latter was owned and operated by John and Judy Halina.

Judy was probably what everyone in Pitkin Point considered Abigail's closest childhood friend. Abigail would agree with that statement, although 'closest friend' was a relative concept. Still, as she pulled into one of the several empty parking spaces in front of the bakery, Take the Cake, Abigail was both nervous and excited to see Judy.

"Well look what the cat drug in," Judy exclaimed from behind an orange and cream striped counter that almost completely hid her from view. Judy was a tiny woman. She'd been so small as a child that, if she folded her legs together properly, she could fit comfortably inside Abigail's backpack with just her head sticking out of the top. Taller now, but only just, Judy had gorgeous smooth skin and shining black hair that hung down to her hips. Her natural beauty was only slightly diminished by the ridiculous orange and cream striped paper hat and matching apron she wore.

"Hi, Judy, got any doughnuts?" Abigail tried this as a light-hearted greeting and it seemed to work. Judy hurried around the counter and gave her a hug, asking what she was doing here and if she had time for a cup of coffee. "Not today," Abigail answered. "But I am here until after Christmas. We should get together," she added, and she meant it, even if her introverted habits balked at this kind of socializing. She left out the part of being jobless and homeless at the moment. That information would be readily available to everyone in town soon enough.

"Sure, absolutely," Judy responded, beaming at Abigail with small, perfect teeth. "Where are you off to this morning?"

"I'm going to wake Zeke up and surprise him," Abigail didn't have to say much about Zeke to Judy. She had often been a victim of his obnoxious big brother pranks when they hung out as kids.

"Oh, Zeke," Judy rolled her eyes jokingly. "He's practically certifiable, you know that, don't you?"

"Oh, I know," Abigail answered.

Judy showed her their doughnut inventory and Abigail chose a dozen, taking half cake and half raised, all with chocolate frosting. With a promise to schedule a time for coffee as soon as possible, Abigail said her goodbyes and took her paper box of doughnuts into the biting cold, anxious to get to Zeke's.

The building Zeke had purchased for the site of his brilliant used book store career was not too far from Take the Cake, but might as well have been a world away. Main Street gave way to Central, a quick right onto 2nd, follow 2nd for three blocks and there it was. Teetering on the corner of 2nd and Cherry stood the two story brick building that housed The Thinking Bean, the avant-garde used and rare bookstore combo coffee shop that nobody in this town ever wanted, or at least never knew they wanted.

The building was on the far end of a row of connected industrial type buildings built in the late 1800's. Most of these buildings had been out of use as far back as she could remember. Although she recalled one of them used to be some kind of storage place for animal feed or something of that nature.

If Pitkin Point had a bad area of town, this was it. Empty and abandoned, it reminded Abigail of some of the trendier places near her apartment–old apartment–where funky casual people sat on rickety wooden chairs and sucked down expensive drinks. All of those places had been forged out of similar unused old buildings like this one.

Balancing her doughnut box in one hand, Abigail took a chance on the front door and found it unlocked, big surprise. She shook her head, it was unbelievable that a business could leave their door open all night and not get robbed. Yet, here she was, wandering through The Thinking Bean looking for the stairway she knew was there somewhere that would lead her to the upstairs apartment while the owner slept.

The air inside the little bookstore was barely warmer than the low 20's outside. She wondered if Zeke kept it cold on purpose or if this was just an unfortunate aspect of an aged building.

"He probably keeps it this cold," she muttered to herself.

As she sought the stairs, Abigail took in all of the renovations Zeke had done. The entire first story of the building was floor to ceiling windows in the front. The windows were framed out in sections with black frames, giving them the look of an all glass garage door that could be opened up completely if desired.

The inside was split into two narrow sections that reached much farther back than expected. The first section, the one she entered through the front door, was the coffee shop section. The floor was painted concrete, the walls were exposed brick, and the ceiling had been painted in a black and white checkerboard pattern. There were eight tiny square tables with four bistro chairs each set up in the dining area. A used sofa, upholstered in plush dark red fabric, sat against one section of wall flanked by two equally used, and equally comfortable looking, reading chairs.

A polished wood counter provided a border to the coffee preparation area, which looked well equipped with a shining stainless steel commercial size espresso machine and open wooden shelves lined with white coffee cups of all shapes and sizes. An old fashioned looking cash register sat proudly on one end of the counter. Beside it was a large glass jar with a handwritten sign reading "Tips" taped to the side. There were a handful of bills and some change in the tip jar. Again, Abigail shook her head. It had been a long time since she'd been in such a trusting atmosphere.

An open doorway led from the coffee section of the shop

to the book section, which was equally long and narrow, but seemed even more so because every square inch of space of the walls were lined with books. Wood shelves, painted black, covered every wall from floor to ceiling and every shelf was stuffed with books. Handmade tags stuck out of the shelves at varying intervals with fat lettered writing that said things like "Fiction - Mystery - Aa" or "Non-fiction - Travel - Rr".

The narrow book section was separated into three sections by walls made of bookshelves which spanned the narrow space. A clever arched doorway led from section to section. Two fat chairs were shoved into the front up against the window, a modest end table on spindly legs between them.

Abigail was impressed despite her desire to be cynical. She ran her free hand along the spines of a line of paperbacks labeled, "Fiction - Fantasy, Dark - Ee", losing herself just a little bit in the presence of so many books.

She loved books. As did Zeke. Bookstores and libraries had always felt like places of refuge to her and her brother. An escape from the confusing demands of society. A place they could feel at home.

A heavy thump sounded upstairs, drawing her out of her thoughts. Excited to surprise her brother with doughnuts and, mostly, with her presence, Abigail located the cramped staircase at the back of the last section of books and made her way upstairs. At the top of the stairs was a small landing where she could look down over a banister and see the floor of the bookshop below.

She deduced that the one and only door on the opposite side of the landing must lead into Zeke's apartment. Hesitating for just a moment to wonder if she should knock first, she quickly decided 'no', and turned the knob, shoving the door open as fast as she could for effect.

The room was empty. Very anti-climactic.

"Hey, it's me," she shouted into the air. "Put some pants on, I brought breakfast."

Footsteps sounded from a dim hallway at the other end of the room. Abigail held the doughnuts up for display like she was on the Home Shopping Channel selling them to millions of viewers.

Zeke entered the room, a faded, dusty blue bath towel wrapped casually around his waist and another one flopped over his face as he rubbed it vigorously on his wet mop of hair. It appeared he had just gotten out of the shower.

"What?" A muffled voice came from under the towel.

Abigail's eyes widened as she instantly realized two shocking facts. First, this man was virtually naked. Second, this man was not her brother.

Chapter Three

Abigail stood frozen in place, her mouth hanging open in surprise, the doughnuts still poised at an attractive angle towards the stranger. A momentary irrational fear that if she moved, his towel might fall to the ground crossed her mind.

Without thinking, she looked the nearly naked body of the man in front of her up and down, taking in his wide shoulders, the muscles in them flexing as he rubbed his hair dry. He had a pleasingly muscular frame, not too pumped up like a body builder, but well formed and naturally masculine. A patch of dark chest hair, still damp from his shower, narrowed at the top of his abs, turning into a dark line that crept all the way down to his belly button and below, disappearing under the towel.

"What?" He said again, annoyance in his tone.

The stranger dropped his towel. The one that covered his head, thankfully, not the shabby blue one that hung loosely on his hips. Still, Abigail felt heat flash across her cheeks as her presence was revealed. She lifted the doughnut box higher, a feeble shield from his state of undress.

"Oh!" An involuntary yelp escaped her lips.

His eyes flew open, astonished at the sight of her. A few seconds passed when neither of them moved, not one muscle. Then surprise softened his shocked expression and turned it to recognition. He tilted his head an said, "Abby?"

Abigail was turned sideways, hiding behind the doughnut box and squinting as if looking at him through narrowed eyelids would reduce the amount of naked flesh she could see and make her intrusion a little less personal. She didn't notice the use of the despised nickname as much as she noticed the voice. She straightened up and stopped squinting.

"Jamie?"

His face transformed into a big, goofy smile. His wet, dark hair stuck out in all directions and he hadn't shaved yet, leaving him with a grown up manly stubble look than she'd ever seen on him before. But the sloped nose, the dopey grin, the way he was kind of bobbing his head up and down like a pigeon showing he was happy to see her, it was Jamie all right. No doubt about it.

"Abby, how are you?"

This time she heard the nickname and a wave of irritation came over her. What was Jamie Turner doing in Zeke's apartment?

Her gaze dropped to his towel, then lifted back to his face. Suddenly, Jamie remembered that he wasn't dressed. His shoulders hunched forward and he reached to secure the towel around his waist, accidentally loosening it in the process. Because of his bumbling, the towel slipped off his hips, dropping to his feet with a soft thud. The instant the towel slid out of reach, Jamie remembered he held a towel in his other hand. He quickly held that towel up against himself, saving her too much of a peep show.

"Jeez, Jamie!" Abigail exclaimed, squeezing her eyes shut

and holding the doughnut box directly in front of her face to add another visual blocker.

"Sorry, sorry," Jamie said.

She waited for his rustling to stop, then risked the slightest opening of one eye to see if he was decent. He was now safely wrapped, but still flustered.

"What are you doing here?" They asked each other at the same time.

Abigail scoffed, then opened her eyes just wide enough to glare at him as she demanded, "Where is Zeke?"

As if on cue, the sound of someone running up the stairs two at a time came to them. Jamie clenched the towel around his waist, checking that it was secure. Abigail knew him well enough to know that he wouldn't want Zeke to find him in a compromising position with her. She sniffed at him with thinly veiled distaste, then turned towards the door as her brother breezed into the room. His voice preceded him by a few moments, bellowing into the small apartment.

"Jamie, have you seen my sis–" Zeke stopped short when he saw her, his long face and wide mouth breaking into one of his amazing smiles. "Abbah Dabbah!" He opened his arms wide and wrapped her up into an infamous monkey hug. It took all of her concentration to keep hold of the doughnuts while he held her tight and rocked her side to side. "I saw your car out front," Zeke said, practically lifting her off the ground with the rocking.

Abigail wasn't short. She stood just under six feet tall, so it was unusual for her to feel dwarfed by anyone, even a man. However, Zeke was 6'6", and though he wasn't broad, his lean frame with its long, stretched limbs, was still formidable. She always felt small and dainty when she was with him. He pushed her away and held her at arm's length.

"You're squishing the doughnuts," she complained, not really upset.

"You look good for someone that just got fired," Zeke joked, his dark brown eyes laughing.

"You look hairy," she quipped. He did. He'd grown a substantial beard since she saw him last. His dark hair was thick and wavy, long enough to reach his ears, yet sticking out in all directions like he was a crazy professor who constantly ran his hands through his hair. "You look like a young Moses," she said, grinning at him.

"Very young," he answered, stroking his beard with one hand mimicking a wise old man. He finally noticed Jamie, who was still standing in his towel taking in the sibling reunion with a silly grin on his face. "Get some clothes on, man," Zeke commanded.

"Oh, right," Jamie snatched the escaped towel off the floor and retreated down the hallway.

Abigail leaned towards Zeke and whispered, "What is he doing here?"

"Jamie?" Zeke glanced at the hallway where Jamie had just disappeared, "He's crashing here for a while."

"Really?" Abigail scowled.

Zeke nudged her with his elbow. "He's single now, you know."

"Oh, God." Abigail made like she was gagging.

Zeke laughed his deep, contagious laugh, then added, "No, seriously, he got laid off a while ago. So he's staying here. He helps me fix up the place for cheap rent."

"Oh." Abigail still didn't like it. Jamie had been horrible to her when they were growing up. Always teasing, always playing stupid jokes. Her senior year she hadn't had a date to prom and he made fun of her for it, putting on an elaborate stunt just to embarrass her in front of her friends.

"What do you think?" Zeke asked.

"Well, I know you've always been friends, but he can be kind of a jerk," she told him.

Zeke look confused, then her words registered. "Jamie? Nah, he's all right," he dismissed her comment with a quick shake of his head. "I meant the place. What do you think of the place?"

She shrugged, not sure if she wanted to commit to an answer. Her reaction only encouraged Zeke. He grabbed her hand and drug her downstairs, giving her a tour of every inch of the bookshop and cafe area. She ended up sitting at one of the small cafe tables munching on a doughnut while Zeke prepared cappuccinos on the elaborate equipment behind the counter. About 7-ish, he went through his routine of opening the store.

First, he turned on all of the overhanging lights. Their warm glow lit up the corners of the room and brought out the texture of the exposed brick. The light made it possible to better see the paintings that hung along the walls by the tables. He'd told her that local artists brought their work to show and, hopefully, sell. She took her cappuccino as she got up to stand in front of the paintings, peering at each small, white tag with the name of the painting, name of the artist and price written in Zeke's scrawling hand.

"This is cool," she said, nodding towards the mini-art gallery.

"Yeah, I change them out every few months." He was at the thermostat, nudging the little red lever up to a higher temperature. "Sometimes we even sell one!" He added brightly.

"Why do you keep it so cold in here?" Abigail had not yet removed her coat and she held her cappuccino partly because she wanted to drink it, but also to keep her fingers warm.

"Because he's a Scrooge," Jamie answered her question. He'd slipped in when she wasn't looking and stood at the coffee machine behind the counter.

"Man up, Turner. Go get your blanky if you're cold," Zeke

called over his shoulder as he went to the front door and flipped the small open/closed sign over so the word 'Open' was facing out.

Jamie chuckled as he noisily prepared his drink. He was dressed, thank goodness, wearing jeans, tennis shoes and a long sleeve, olive green Henley shirt with the sleeves pushed up around his elbows. His hair was still damp, dark brown and not too short, but not as long as Zeke's. He had shaved and looked a little more like the Jamie she remembered, although not completely.

Since the last time she'd seen him, Jamie had grown into a man. He'd had that mid to late 20's growth spurt guys went through that took them from thin bodied and baby-faced into stronger, more angular, and hardened male specimens. As she watched him go through the elaborate motions necessary to fix a cappuccino, the long muscles in his forearms flexing, she had to admit that Jamie had grown into a pretty good looking man. Her mind wandered to the very recent memory of him in his towel, the dark trail of hair down the center of his stomach.

Jamie glanced her way and caught her staring. One side of his mouth lifted into a half-smile, almost a smirk. Abigail scowled and turned away, taking a sip of her drink, pretending she hadn't been looking at him at all.

"Maybe you'll paint something to put up?" Jamie suggested, carrying his drink to the table with the doughnut box and sitting down.

"Me?" She gave him a cursory glance over her shoulder before stepping further away to look at the next painting.

"Yeah, you," Jamie answered. "You still paint, don't you?"

Abigail didn't like having to talk with Jamie. She felt on edge, waiting for him to be sarcastic, "A little, I guess."

"You were always good," Jamie said before taking a sip of his drink.

Like he would know. Abigail rolled her eyes at the brick wall. Jerk.

"No, no, no, no, no!" Zeke took her by the arm and led her back to the table. "No time for making art. I've got bigger plans."

"Here we go." Jamie shook his head and took another sip.

Zeke sat her down next to Jamie before taking the chair on the other side. "I need your full attention and focus for something else, something bigger!"

He flipped open the top of the doughnut box and grabbed one of the raised doughnuts before spinning the open side of the box towards Jamie and nodding to him to take one as well. Jamie looked at Abigail, not sure if he was the intended recipient of the treats. She could hardly say 'no'. She gave him an almost imperceptible nod and he reached for a cake doughnut.

"I have big plans for this place. Do you realize we have entered the money making time of the year? December is the month that can make or break a small business. And I intend to put The Thinking Bean on the map this year. No more screwing around!" He lifted his doughnut into the air like he was talking to an audience, then bit into it with relish.

Zeke had a history of rash and unusual activity. There was no doubt he was smart, Abigail thought he was smarter than both her and their Mom, and probably even smarter than their Dad, which was saying something. He'd been accepted to every college and university he'd applied to, and received scholarship offers from all of them. When he chose Dartmouth, she alone had wondered how he would do so far from home. When he dropped out in his second year, everyone else had wondered why. It was never a huge mystery to Abigail.

Her brother liked learning, loved books, lived for discussion and debate, but was the biggest softie. She'd always known his heart was with his family and the people he loved. He wasn't really cut out for the pressure of high academia. In that way he was very much like their father, who had carved out a nice life as a high school counselor even though his intellect could have taken him much farther in the field of psychology. Their Dad was happier in a close community helping people. She wasn't surprised Zeke had chosen, similarly, to stay in their home town.

"What are you planning?" She asked. Jamie gave a little laugh that sounded more like a snort and Abigail shot him a look.

"Mistletoe Madness," Zeke announced into the air above their heads, holding his hand up, palm out, and sweeping it slowly from left to right as if he saw the words written on a giant sign high on the opposite wall. He paused for effect, then looked at them both with a gleam in his eye.

Jamie groaned. Abigail waited for some further explanation from Zeke. He took an aggressive bite of his doughnut, making his hair flop crazily into his eyes. He flipped his head back dramatically to put it back in place and chewed at her with a confident grin on his face. She shifted her gaze to Jamie who gave her a weak, apologetic smile.

Turning her attention back to her big brother, she asked, "What, exactly, is Mistletoe Madness?"

Chapter Four

"Mistletoe Madness is a genius marketing plan I have devised that will entice customers into this place, bring the community together, create the biggest and best holiday celebrations this town has ever experienced, and make me a ton of cash!" Zeke stood as he spoke, stretching his long arms wider and wider, and raising his voice with each word. When he didn't receive a response, he looked down at Abigail and Jamie, waving his hands up and down like he was trying to get them to applaud.

Abigail and Jamie looked at each other. Jamie gave her a half-shrug as if to say, "See what I have to live with?"

"Music!" Zeke's eyes flew open and he dashed to the counter, putting one hand on the shining surface and throwing his feet and legs over, landing on the other side with a flourish. He ducked down so only the top of his head was visible and must have pushed an unseen button, because acoustic guitar music suddenly filled the room.

A car pulled up in front.

"Customers!" Zeke announced happily. "Talk amongst

yourselves. I've got this," he told them and began pulling cups down from the shelves in preparation.

Abigail and Jamie looked at each other again. She was confused, but she sincerely doubted she would get any clarification from Jamie. She took a sip of her cappuccino and watched as a middle aged couple she vaguely recognized entered the coffee shop.

"Randy, Jill!" Zeke greeted them warmly. The couple smiled at him and went to the counter to place their order.

As Zeke chatted with the couple and the soothing acoustic guitar filled in the quiet, Abigail stared at her drink. Jamie shifted uncomfortably in his chair. She hoped he would just quietly eat doughnuts until Zeke was back. The thought of walking in on him mostly naked was more embarrassing when her brother wasn't there as a distraction. Jamie cleared his throat and she knew he wasn't going to remain silent. He had always done the opposite of what she wanted him to do.

"You glad to be home for Christmas?" Jamie asked.

Great. Now she had to talk to him.

"Yes, of course," she answered. She barely looked at him as she responded, then went back to staring at her cup. A new humiliation came to her mind. Jamie must know that she'd been fired. Zeke knew, he'd even said so when he greeted her upstairs. She scowled. Discretion was impossible in this little town.

"So, um, sorry about earlier. I didn't know—" he started to say.

"Let's not talk about it, okay?" She interrupted crossly.

"Sure, right," he bobbed his head up and down.

Zeke was still chatting up his customers at the counter. Abigail wondered if Jamie would leave soon, maybe go to work? But then she remembered Zeke said he'd been laid off. She glanced at him sideways. He was tapping the handle of his coffee cup, looking awkward. Abigail felt a little bad for snapping at him. It wasn't his fault she'd barged into Zeke's apartment unannounced.

"So..." she started.

He perked up and looked at her, leaning forward.

"You're living with Zeke?" She asked.

"Yeah, yeah," he head bob nodded again.

"How's that going?"

"Oh, you know..." He glanced at Zeke who was talking animatedly behind the counter, keeping Randy and Jill laughing. "It's always exciting." He switched his gaze to her and grinned.

She chuckled a little. Zeke was nothing if he wasn't exciting.

"You're not working?" She ventured the question.

"Well, I've been staying pretty busy helping him with some projects around here. Shelves and lighting, that kind of thing. And I've been doing a few handyman jobs around town," he explained.

"That's nice."

There was a short pause, then he continued, "I got laid off last year. Zeke really helped me out letting me stay with him."

She could sense a humbleness in his tone. He'd stopped tapping his cup. His hand, now still, lay quietly on the table.

"I just got laid off...or let go, I guess," she said, a little surprised at her own confession. A surge of emotion moved through her and she was mortified to realize that her eyes were wet with tears.

Jamie watched her, concern on his face, "That sucks, Abby." He had such an empathetic look on his face, she couldn't bring herself to reprimand him for calling her 'Abby'.

"Well, what can you do?" She brushed the tears away with the back of her fingers.

"Yep, you just gotta keep going," he said. They sat

awkwardly for a moment, then Jamie moved the doughnut box towards her, offering her another one.

"No, thanks."

"You want another drink?" He made like he was going to stand up and make her another cappuccino.

"No, thank you," she gave him a small smile so he would know she was okay.

He smiled back. His big, crooked, dopey Jamie smile, but Abigail found it almost comforting this time. Familiar.

"Are you helping with Mistletoe Madness?" She asked, hoping to change the subject.

Jamie leaned back in his chair, his shoulder's slumping in defeat, "Yes."

"He's Santa," Zeke informed her as he joined them back at the table. Randy and Jill waved to all of them as they left with their coffees.

"Santa?" Her mouth pulled into a smirk. She looked at Jamie for verification. He wouldn't look up, just sighed and nodded in agreement.

"I can't be Santa, because I'll be too busy," Zeke explained. "I need someone who can focus on the role while I take care of everything else."

"I see," she said. Although she didn't, not really.

"I'm going to be a Snowman," Zeke declared.

"I don't understand what's happening," Abigail cracked up a little as she spoke.

"I told you, Mistletoe Madness! We're going to host weeks of events and parties and special decorations leading up to the big day," Zeke explained. "I've got a band lined up and all kinds of stuff. Oh!" He grabbed her arm, "You can paint the windows."

"What?"

"You know, with that white snow looking paint. Make something really festive, something totally unique." He was so excited, it was difficult not to fall into his enthusiasm a little bit.

Abigail turned her attention to the floor to ceiling windows in the front of the store. It would be fun to create something beautiful on them. She'd never really thought about painting on glass.

"I guess..." she answered.

"See? You getting fired is a blessing in disguise. You can work for me!"

Abigail squirmed a little bit at the 'fired' comment. Although, if painting was involved in this little adventure maybe it wouldn't be so bad. She could earn some money while she was searching for the next big move in her career. She took in a deep breath, the smell of coffee mixed with books was a good smell. Since he'd turned the heat on, it was starting to warm up a bit. Her eyes wandered across the funky little space Zeke had created. An elaborate version of Jingle Bells played on acoustic guitar filled the room.

"What do you say?" Zeke waited, his eyes hopeful.

"Sure," she answered. "Why not?"

"Great!" Zeke moved his big hand to her shoulder and pushed her back and forth, making her sway in her chair. "Mom's working on the costumes."

"Is she?"

"Santa," Zeke pointed at Jamie, who resigned himself to the role with a brief nod. "Snowman," he pointed at his own chest. "Elf," he turned his long finger towards Abigail.

"Elf? What?"

"It's too late, you already took the job!" Zeke stood up and started stacking their used cups in one hand to carry to the sink.

"You didn't say anything about wearing an Elf costume," she argued.

"You have to wear a costume," Zeke told her.

"Why?"

"Tell her," Zeke said to Jamie as he stepped away from the table.

Jamie let his head flop back and sighed in the way of the long-suffering soul who carries a heavy burden.

"Tell her," Zeke commanded as he walked away.

Jamie let his head loll to the side to look at Abigail. When he spoke, he kept his face slack, like a zombie. Speaking in monotone, he told her, "Because it's Mistletoe Madness."

&

"COME ON, SWEETIE," her Mom waved to her from the other side of a wall of elderly women, motioning her to hurry up.

They were in Needle Point, the Pitkin Point craft store that was stuffed full of bolts of material suitable for Elf costumes as well as Christmas craft supplies. Today was a 50% off sale. They had come to pick up some sewing supplies to finish the Santa, Snowman and Elf costumes that Abigail's Mom was making. Abigail had agreed to help her mother, but she had not expected the madness that a 50% off sale could inject into a geriatric craft crazy crowd.

Luckily, her Mom was brutal in these situations. She hurried and leaned and pressed her way past even the most aggressive little old ladies in order to get the material she wanted. Abigail was too afraid of stepping on someone's toes or, heaven forbid, knocking a fragile grandmother over and having her break a hip. So she hung back, letting her Mom get what she needed while she waited. Apparently her Mom was now done and wanted Abigail to get to the other side of the crowd where the cash registers were busily ringing up half-off purchases.

Abigail made a face at her mother. She was not good at

crowds. She certainly wasn't good at pressing her way through crowds.

"Go around," her Mom instructed as she made wide circular motions over her head like she was twirling a lasso. "I'll get in line for the cashier," she said before turning her back on Abigail's situation and joining the long line of crafters waiting on the cashiers.

Abigail looked for a way around. Up until now, she'd stayed relatively out of the way by backing up against the wall of 75% off Thanksgiving supplies, which were not in high demand, plus the wall was mostly empty of any products. She stood on her toes and spied a path along the Thanksgiving wall, through the wedding section, which she assumed would be in low use at this time of year, then to the front door.

Within a few minutes she was waiting for her Mom outside in the parking lot. It was freezing cold, but she preferred that to being in the crowded store.

The door of the pizza place next door opened. She knew this because someone had attached sleigh bells to the door so they jingled every time it opened and shut. It had opened and shut a half dozen times since she'd escaped the craft store. Often enough that she'd stopped paying attention.

"Hey, Abby," a familiar voice called.

She turned to see Jamie walking towards her with a sullen teenage boy trailing behind him. Jamie wore a brown Carhart jacket and a black hat pulled down over his ears. She was struck again by how much more manly he looked these days. He had never been small, he was at least a few inches taller than her, not quite as tall as Zeke, but he'd never looked quite this strong. It wasn't just his size, though. Something else was different about Jamie Turner. He looked...competent.

"Hi." She smiled thinly at him.

"Are you all right?" Jamie looked around, presumably for a car with a flat tire or dead battery. Why else would someone stand around in a parking lot in sub-freezing temperatures as night was falling?

"I'm fine. I'm waiting for my Mom, she's in there," Abigail jerked her head towards the craft store.

"Oh," Jamie noticed the stream of little old ladies leaving the store with multiple bags. "Wow, they're really busy," he said.

The boy, maybe 13 or 14-years old, was shuffling behind Jamie, his head bent over the glowing screen of a cell phone. Jamie stepped aside and put his hand behind the boy, presenting him to Abigail.

"This is my son, Dillon," Jamie said with more than a little pride in his voice.

Son? Abigail searched her mind for any information about Jamie having a son. She supposed she had heard something about it at some point. He had married Raegan Faller after high school. Zeke had been his best man. She remembered Zeke telling her about it when she was away at college. And she remembered they had divorced some time ago. Yes, she had heard about him having a son. But that was a baby boy. This was an almost adult human standing in front of her.

"Dillon." Jamie waited for the boy to respond. He didn't. He just kept thumb typing into his phone. Jamie looked at her, "Sorry." Then he took his palm and lightly bopped the boy on the back of his head. Dillon looked at him angrily. "Dillon, this is Abby, Zeke's sister," Jamie said. Then he glanced furtively at Abigail before continuing, "And my friend."

The introduction took Abigail a little by surprise. So much so, she decided not to correct Jamie about her name. Not in front of this surly young man who obviously didn't care who she was. Not when he'd just called her his friend.

"Nice to meet you, Dillon," Abigail said.

"Nice to meet you," Dillon mumbled, giving her the

briefest look before staring at the ground in front of him. He remained off of his phone, but didn't attempt any further engagement.

"He looks so much like you," she said without thinking. Jamie smiled and ducked his head, taking it as a compliment, which it was.

It was also true. Seeing Dillon standing in front of her kicking at the asphalt brought back memories of Jamie when they were kids. Besides his hair being a little lighter in color than Jamie's had been, Dillon was the spitting image of his Dad. The skinny, gawky, uncomfortable Jamie she had grown up with. Dillon's attitude seemed to be about the same, too.

"Here I am," announced her Mom in a sing-song voice.

They turned to see her mother approaching them, laden down with several bags stuffed with everything she would need to finish their costumes. Abigail's Mom was almost as tall as her daughter. Slender, with dark, straight hair she kept cut in layers, and swooped up in the latest fashionable look. She had a thin nose, high cheekbones, full lips and wide set, narrow eyes. Abigail had received almost all of her mother's features, but she'd always felt like they settled better on her Mom's face than on her own. Her mother's face was open and confident where Abigail's always looked pinched and morose.

"Hello, Jamie," she said warmly.

"Hello, Mrs. Ackerman," Jamie said. He reached out for her bags, "Let me help you with those."

"Thank you," she said, letting Jamie take them. Then, seeing Dillon, her eyes lit up, "Dillon! My goodness you've grown! You're turning into quite the handsome young man."

What might have been a smile flickered across Dillon's grim expression. He nodded and said something unintelligible.

"You two need to come over for dinner soon," her mother said as she popped the trunk for Jamie to deposit the bags.

"Thank you, that would be very nice," Jamie answered, glancing at Abigail as he said it, as if the invitation had been her idea.

Driving home in the car, Abigail watched out the window as they passed yards full of Christmas decorations, her Mom chattering on and on.

"He's had such a rough time, that Jamie. Such a nice boy. And his son! Could you believe how big he was? He's going to be taller than his Dad soon I bet," she paused to take a breath.

Abigail continued staring out the window. She, too, was having a hard time thinking about Jamie having a child so near to being grown up. It was strange, seeing him act like a Dad. Like her own Dad acted.

Her Mom glanced at her sideways, "He's handsome, too. Wouldn't you say?"

"Dillon?" Abigail asked, confused.

"No, Jamie," her Mom responded, giving Abigail a meaningful look.

"No, I don't know, I guess," Abigail turned to her Mom. What was she trying to say?

"Well, I think he's handsome. And he's the nicest boy."

Abigail scoffed, "He's not a boy and he's not as nice as you think he is."

"What do you mean?"

"He's, you know..." Abigail searched for the words and couldn't find them.

"He's always polite and such a hard worker," her Mom offered evidence for her opinion.

Abigail scoffed again, "He's not always polite, Mom."

"Oh? When has he not been polite?"

"When we were kids! He and Zeke were always playing jokes on me, being mean."

"Oh, well, honey, that's just kid stuff." She carefully

steered the car around the last corner before their house. "Besides, it was mostly Zeke playing jokes. Jamie was always falling all over himself trying to get your attention." She made a 'tsk-tsk' sound. "He was such an awkward boy, and so in love with you."

Abigail heard the words, but couldn't exactly process the information. She stared at her mother, her mouth agape. What a ridiculous thing to say.

A burst of laughter came out of her so hard it turned into a snort. "Jamie Turner is not, and has never been, in love with me, Mom."

Sarah Ackerman gave her only daughter an amused nod and a knowing smile. "Whatever you say, sweetie, whatever you say."

Chapter Five

Abigail balanced on a plank of wood placed across two eight foot ladders, a cup of white paint in one hand and a paintbrush in the other. The ends of the plank were stuck through both ladders right above the fifth rung, adding over five feet to her height and allowing her to reach the upper most regions of the coffee shop windows.

She wore a large, white apron over her Elf costume, which consisted of red tights and a bright green belted tunic with a red and white long sleeve shirt underneath. She also had bright green and white striped Elf shoes and a green Elf hat with a fat, red tassel, but she'd left those on one of the tables to avoid getting paint on them. She felt ridiculous enough wearing this costume. Besides, her hair was having an unfortunately frizzy day and she worried that the Elf hat just exacerbated that look.

The sounds of Zeke and Jamie having a loud discussion behind the coffee counter filtered through the Christmas jazz music Zeke had chosen for this morning's ambience. Abigail glanced back at them and found a silver lining in this whole

Mistletoe Madness experience. She may look ridiculous in her costume, but they looked even more ridiculous in theirs.

Jamie wore the classic Santa Claus suit, complete with pillows stuffed under his jacket and cinched with a wide, black belt, to make him look plump and jolly. His red Santa hat had a white Santa wig sewn to the bottom so when he took the hat off, the Santa hair left with it. He also had a huge, white curly beard that fixed over his ears, which he wasn't wearing at the moment. It was tucked into his black belt for safe keeping and easy access.

Zeke's costume, however, took the cake. Abigail had to give her Mom kudos for the ingenious way she'd built his Snowman suit. With wire forms, she'd made what was once just a long, white triangle of material with giant black pom-poms affixed to the front for buttons into a Snowman looking body that puffed out from Zeke in all directions. He had a white hood that he pulled up over his head and a black top hat that fit over the hood. He wore black tights on his legs and a long sleeve black shirt, giving the Snowman stick like arms and legs. He also had a bright red and green striped scarf wrapped around his neck.

He was identifiable as a Snowman. However, his extremely long limbs seemed even longer sticking out of his puffed up body. And his beard added too much hair to the look. Plus, with the added girth to his normally lean frame he had already had a few accidents. His Snowman butt had pushed a bag of sugar off of the counter, spilling it all over the floor. And already one cup had been lost to the same fate, making an even bigger mess.

"I can't eat with the beard," Jamie was arguing.

"Santa doesn't eat," Zeke told him.

Jamie scoffed at the stupidity of that statement, "Well, this Santa eats. I'll put it on as soon as I'm done with this." Jamie held up a half a bagel smeared with cream cheese,

"Anyway, how do you think Santa got his jolly look?" He pushed his rounded belly towards Zeke who gave him a scowl.

Zeke was tense. They were one day into decorations for Mistletoe Madness and he was a man under pressure. He'd put so much thought and energy into this idea, he was going a little crazy, like Zeke had a tendency to do.

The day before they had all been fitted for their costumes. Then they strung little white lights in every nook and cranny of the bookstore. There were houseplants with long, delicate vines that hung all throughout the narrow reading areas. They twisted white lights carefully through the vines, giving the cramped areas a festive, almost fairy like appearance.

"When did you get all these?" Abigail had asked, letting her eyes drift across all of the plants. Zeke didn't' have a green thumb to her knowledge.

"They're Jamie's," Zeke, whose hands were busy holding on to an extra long vine while Abigail fixed lights on it, used his forehead to point at Jamie.

"Yours?" She asked Jamie.

"Yeah, I have a little plant addiction," he answered. "I had to bring them with me when I moved in. We thought they looked good here."

Abigail nodded in agreement, "Nice."

Jamie took the compliment with an embarrassed head bob. For a moment she thought about what her Mom had said in the car and wondered if it could be remotely true. Was this goofy awkward head bob thing Jamie always did a residual effect of some long ago crush he had on her when they were kids? She thought about all of the stupid pranks he and Zeke had played on her, the way he'd always laughed when she got mad and yelled at them, and the way he'd barged into her 18th birthday party and mocked her for not having a date to her senior prom. No, she decided, her Mom was mistaken.

Abigail had drawn up a design for the window painting which included snowflakes and elaborate curlicues across the top, turning into elves and presents and sparkly books down the edges. Then a sweeping snow scape across the bottom that included all kinds of adorable woodland creatures wearing hats and scarves, and reading books. She left the large center section empty of design, because Zeke wanted to build a Christmas tree by stacking old books into a cone shape and then decorate it with lights. He'd insisted that he wanted the book tree visible through the glass.

He'd also insisted she wear her Elf costume while painting.

"It will look like we're actually in Santa's workshop!" He had told her, delighted with the idea.

So now she was a real, living, breathing Elf on a Shelf in the window of The Thinking Bean, painting snowflakes and listening to her brother and Jamie bicker. She couldn't help but smile at the oddness of it all.

"Abigail," Zeke called to her.

"What?"

Zeke pushed his Snowman body past Jamie's Santa body and squeezed out from behind the counter. He headed towards the front window. Jamie followed him, grinning at his view of the Snowman outfit from behind, and chewing his bagel.

"I scheduled a meeting in the morning at the library," Zeke informed them.

"What meeting?" She asked.

"To organize Mistletoe Madness," he answered, exasperated with her ignorance. He let his stick arms droop to his sides like someone fighting a losing battle.

Abigail looked at him, "Why the library? Why don't we just have the meeting here?"

Zeke chuckled as if she was a foolish child. Abigail caught

a flash of humor cross Jamie's face as he watched the back of Zeke's head. She crinkled her brow at him, what was the joke?

"We need to meet somewhere else, so we can focus," Zeke explained.

"Tell her the real reason," Jamie nudged the middle of Zeke's back.

Zeke shook him off, "That is the reason."

"That's not the reason," Jamie responded, taking another bite of his bagel and moving to one of her ladders, leaning lightly against it as he chewed. He was facing Zeke now, and he looked up at her, his eyes twinkling with merriment at making Zeke uncomfortable.

Abigail turned around, placed her paint can and brush on the wood plank, and sat down so she was facing them. Her red Elf legs were hanging off the edge of the plank. She swung them like a little kid.

"What's the real reason?" She asked.

Zeke tried to stare them down, which was impossible when he looked like an angry, bearded marshmallow.

Jamie swallowed and said again, "Go on, tell her."

"There's nothing to tell," Zeke argued, but his voice had lost its commanding tone.

"Tell me what?" Abigail wanted to know.

"Want me to tell her?" Jamie teased.

Zeke threw his long stick arms into the air in defeat, "Fine, tell her."

Jamie turned his attention to Abigail. When she looked down into his face his eyes were dancing, ready to share a joke, and she felt a small tingle of excitement.

"One word," he said, "Fern."

Apparently the new librarian at their small county branch was named Fern. And apparently Fern was younger than the previous librarian, much younger, with short, stylish blonde hair, a pretty face, and a perky, fun attitude. And apparently she was wicked smart and well read, and Zeke had something of a wild crush on her, and was always coming up with reasons to go to the library these days. All of this was according to Jamie, but none of it was denied by her brother, who paced uncomfortably around the room in his Snowman costume while Jamie told Abigail all about it.

"So I like her? What's wrong with that?" Zeke defended himself as he rearranged the bagged coffee bean display with agitation, his top hat slightly askew.

Abigail, amused at the idea of her wildly confident and outgoing brother having a sweet, old fashioned crush on a librarian, shrugged and smiled, "Nothing's wrong with that." She looked down at Jamie for confirmation who was chuckling as he took a sip of his coffee.

"No, nothing wrong with that at all," he agreed. Then he winked at her, and Abigail felt another little thrill.

She stopped thinking about Zeke for a moment and considered her reaction to Jamie. He looked more than a little ridiculous in his Santa outfit, especially without the beard. But as she watched him pop the last bite of bagel into his mouth and chew while eyeing Zeke with a highly amused expression, she realized that she felt attracted to him. Physically.

How was that possible?

Her mother's comment had gotten under her skin and now she was having a major overreaction to Jamie Turner. That's how. Sheesh.

"Customers!" Zeke called out, happy for the distraction.

Jamie turned to see who was coming as he reached to his belt for his Santa beard. Suddenly, his amused expression fell and he looked tense, guarded. He didn't take the beard out of his belt, but he did glance quickly up at Abigail as if he was expecting something to happen. What, she didn't know.

The door opened, jingling the sleigh bells they had affixed

to it yesterday while decorating. Abigail turned just in time to recognize Dillon stepping in the door.

"Dillon," Jamie moved towards his son, who was gawking at his father. The boy looked like he was halfway between cracking up laughing and wishing he could leave.

Behind Dillon, a tall woman with curly, blonde hair cut just above her shoulders, and a slightly shorter man, who was nonetheless wide shouldered and fit, followed close behind. They almost ran into Dillon because he had stopped short upon seeing Jamie's Santa outfit and not left them enough room to enter.

"No dilly dallying...Dillon," the man said, laughing at his alliteration. At the sound of his voice, Abigail immediately knew who he was, though she hadn't recognized him by look alone. Blake Thompson.

"Mom," Dillon stepped away from the woman when she gently placed her hands on his shoulders. An attempt to move him out of her and Blake's way.

Mom. Abigail's mind clicked everything into place. This was Raegan. Tall, gorgeous Raegan who used to be a brunette, and was now a blonde. Who used to be married to Jamie, and now was not. Mother to Dillon and...married to Blake Thompson? Abigail suddenly recollected that she had heard that bit of gossip during some distant conversation in the past. Blake Thompson. She thought again what she had thought then, who in their right mind would marry Blake Thompson?

"Dad, what are you doing?" Dillon was still staring at Jamie with that special blend of humiliation and contempt that teenagers have down to an art form.

"I'm Santa," Jamie said, lifting his arms out to his sides as if showing off more of the costume would help his son understand, or forgive, him. It didn't do either.

"Dillon, come here and get your drink," Zeke called to the

boy over the sounds of the espresso machine. Dillon made for the counter, bypassing Jamie.

"Really, Jamie? Santa Claus?" Raegan said, the snide tone impossible to ignore.

Abigail felt the hackles on her neck rise. She'd never liked Raegan, and she really didn't like the way she was looking down her nose at Jamie in his costume and, by association, Zeke.

"Abby?" Blake had spotted her on her perch and moved towards the makeshift scaffolding, smiling his car salesman smile.

She was surprised to be seen, but then realized that was silly. Did she think she was invisible just because her feet weren't touching the floor?

Raegan turned her attention to Abigail and let her gaze slide up and down her huge apron with the Elf tunic underneath. Abigail wished she was having a better hair day. She wished she was wearing something a little more intelligent. She wished she was doing something more...big city. One side of Raegan's upper lip twitched into something that was not quite a smile, "Abby, wow, I didn't know you were back in town."

That was a lie, Abigail was almost positive.

"Abigail, I go by Abigail," Abigail corrected them.

Raegan and Blake exchanged a look.

"Of course, Abigail" Blake said, smiling at her with gleaming teeth.

Raegan's eyes wandered down Abigail's costume to her shoeless, red tight covered, feet. She opened her mouth to say something.

"I'll drop him off tonight, then?" Jamie interrupted. He had returned to the ladder just next to Abigail, closer in fact. The presence of him in his bright red jacket was oddly comforting. Abigail trained her eyes on him and didn't look back at the other two. Maybe she could avoid a conversation by denying them any eye contact.

It worked.

Jamie conversed with Raegan about when Dillon needed to be taken home and what their schedule was for sharing custody over the next week. It seemed congenial, but Abigail sensed it wasn't. Not completely.

Blake had lost interest. Because she wasn't allowing him to catch her eye, he meandered over to the counter and ordered two lattes. When she was sure everyone was engaged and not paying any attention to her at all, Abigail allowed herself one furtive look. Blake stood next to Dillon with his arm around the boy's shoulders. She noticed that Dillon was equally averse to Blake being chummy with him as he had been with Jamie. She was happy that Jamie wasn't the sole recipient of Dillon's ill mood. Blake had taken off his winter hat and Abigail noticed that he was completely bald. Another win for Jamie.

She looked away, down past her feet dangling off of the wooden plank and to the floor. What did it matter to her if Jamie was getting along with his son, or competing in any way with Blake Thompson? She had no interest in his personal life. Not really.

Abigail peered at Raegan, careful to keep her head down and look as if she was still staring at the floor. Jamie's ex-wife was still beautiful. Raegan had a strong, firm body. She'd played volleyball and basketball in high school and was always very good. Her medium length blonde hair was curled loosely and complimented her heavy jaw. She was dressed like someone with money. She'd always dressed that way, probably because she came from a family with lots of money. She was, however, not a kind person in Abigail's opinion. There were countless incidents she could remember of Raegan, and Blake for that matter, being awful to her or someone else in school.

Bullies. And now they were married and probably bullied the world together.

Abigail's gaze slipped back to Jamie standing near her feet. He looked tall and strong from this perspective. She could see the muscle in his jaw flexing as he listened to Raegan complain about something and deduced he was gritting his teeth. His hair was messy from when he'd taken off his Santa hat, but it was thick and wavy. Again, she felt a small victory for him in that fact.

She curled her toes a little inside the red tights, they were getting cold. The voices of everyone else blended into the background as Abigail withdrew into her thoughts. They weren't thoughts, really, more like emotional memories of her childhood.

She remembered how excited she would get when Zeke and Jamie invited her to go with them somewhere, anywhere. How her friends, few that they were, would swoon over her brother and his friend when they were at her house. How, when things were good, the boys had made her laugh harder and longer than anyone else ever could.

She glanced up and took in the scene of Jamie having a tense conversation with his ex-wife while dressed like Santa. And Zeke, his Snowman outfit causing him fits while making coffee and serving from behind the counter, politely and confidently holding his own against one of their town's notoriously obnoxious men. And her, she looked down at her red and white striped arms and thought about how silly this all must look to someone like Raegan. And she didn't care.

A sense of pride and camaraderie swelled in her chest and Abigail decided that she was glad to be working here, helping her brother, on the same team with Jamie, and doing her part in the gloriously over the top festivity of Mistletoe Madness.

Chapter Six

The next morning, while their mother watched the shop, Zeke, Jamie and Abigail convened at the library meeting room to focus on the details of Mistletoe Madness. Zeke did not dress like a Snowman. In fact, he dressed pretty snazzy for someone who was merely going to the library. He smelled extra good, too.

When Abigail saw Fern she understood why.

Fern was petite, but had an air of smart and sassy. She dressed pretty hip for Pitkin Point wearing loud, floral tights and a black skirt with layer upon layer of shirts, sweaters and scarves, all in varying shades of teal. She had a short, funky blonde hairdo, which Abigail suspected might be dyed pink or blue if the locals were less conservative. She was naturally pretty and didn't wear much makeup, if any, underneath her dark purple rimmed glasses. Her blue eyes sparkled when she saw Zeke, so much so that Abigail shared a look with Jamie, who gave her an I Told You So eyebrow raise.

"Did you close down the shop?" She asked, her voice pleasant and perky.

"My Mom's watching it for us," Zeke answered. Abigail

detected a slight crack in his baritone and had to contain her smile. Her brother had it bad.

"This is my sister, Abigail," Zeke said.

Fern's face broke into a perfectly lovely smile, "Well, hello, Abigail. I've heard a lot about you."

"Have you? Anything good?" Abigail took Fern's offered hand warmly. She liked her.

"You've been recruited for Mistletoe Madness?" Fern asked.

"No getting around it, I'm afraid," Abigail answered. She wondered just how much time Zeke spent with Fern. She seemed to know a lot about his life for a mere crush. "Have you been? Recruited, I mean."

Fern motioned to them to follow her. "Of course," she laughed and the sound of it mixed with the jingling of a bunch of keys that hung from a lanyard around her neck, making her movement seem like it was accompanied by bells.

"Fern's going to help with Christmas poetry reading night," Zeke said excitedly.

Abigail heard a sigh escape from Jamie.

"Not into poetry?" She asked him.

"Some of it. But I have a feeling poetry night might be a long night for ol' Santa," he answered.

Fern showed them to the meeting room and left them to their planning. Zeke had come equipped with an oversized calendar and colored markers. Until the moment she saw him plotting out a Christmas cupcake decorating party with an orange marker, Abigail hadn't completely understood how seriously he was taking this whole Mistletoe Madness thing.

Not only was the cupcake party planned for tomorrow, with flyers having gone out to the local schools and churches as well as the YMCA, but he had ideas for a bookstore scavenger hunt date night, a children's book reading of selections like How the Grinch Stole Christmas and Bear Stays Up for

Christmas for which he'd hired a few actors from the local theatre company, poetry night, of course, and he was trying to find a horse and wagon for some old fashioned hay rides around town. All of this was going to culminate with the Christmas Eve dance that Pitkin Point always held outside at the gazebo in the park, rain or snow—or freezing ice storms. Abigail was impressed.

"Fern suggested a Dicken's night, where we read parts of A Christmas Carol and maybe get some of the church choir to come as carolers," Zeke told them, his excitement building.

"When did Fern tell you this idea?" Abigail was curious.

"Oh, when we were out the other night," Zeke answered.

Abigail raised her eyebrows, "Are you and Fern a thing, Zekey?"

Zeke's face turned red under his beard and he completely ignored her, which told her everything she needed to know.

"He's afraid to jinx it," Jamie informed her.

"Don't talk about it," Zeke said, still staring at his colorfully marked up calendar.

"This is so cute," Abigail said. "Does Mom know?"

"No!" Zeke looked at her now, "Don't tell Mom, not yet. I'll tell her when it's time."

"Okay, okay." Abigail grinned, pleased to see him this way. It would be nice for Zeke to find someone, and judging from her first impression, Fern seemed like a good fit.

"I really think that we can pull people in and get them to finally branch off from the town square for once," Zeke said, changing the subject.

The citizens of Pitkin Point were notorious for staying within what was referred to as The Town Square, a two block area that included Main Street, and basically ignored businesses outside of that area. All of the town's best restaurants and retail shops were inside The Town Square. Main Street was lined with old fashioned lamp posts that were hung with lights and Christmas wreaths, giving it an extra special appeal during the holidays. Even though The Thinking Bean was only a few blocks outside of The Town Square radius, it may as well have been on the other side of the world.

"I think you have a shot," Jamie said.

"A shot at Mistletoe Madness working or a shot with Fern?" Abigail asked. Zeke glared at her.

Jamie grinned, "Both."

"Enough! Let's get organized. We can't leave Mom manning the shop forever," Zeke said. To keep him from having a melt down, Abigail and Jamie turned their attention towards event planning instead of matchmaking.

THE CHRISTMAS CUPCAKE Decorating Extravaganza was a big hit. Kids, young and old, came to decorate twelve dozen cupcakes that Take the Cake provided at cost. Zeke and Jake put up a long lunch table that they borrowed from the school down the center of the coffee shop section to hold the cupcakes and all of the frosting supplies. Judy had delivered the plain cupcakes and stayed to give advice on how to decorate them with panache.

The coffee shop was packed with children and their parents, and the book sections were abuzz as they browsed and picked out Christmas gifts. Their Mom manned the cash register, while their Dad helped customers find books. Jamie's Santa chair was set up in the front corner of the coffee shop. Abigail stuck to her Elf job and assisted him by keeping the line of children waiting to see Santa as orderly as possible, and by wiping their hands and faces with wet wipes to avoid getting frosting in his Santa beard. He was wonderful with the kids, patient and kind, Ho-Ho-Ho-ing like a pro.

Zeke was in his element. As a host he was marvelous, welcoming everyone, directing them towards what they were looking for, encouraging them to decorate a cupcake, happily making espresso drinks for the grown-ups. As a Snowman, he was a little less impressive.

He still hadn't mastered total control over his puffy rear end and Abigail witnessed several incidents where it came into contact with the head of a small child or the cupcake they were holding. Once he turned to greet someone at the door and bumped two cupcakes off of the center table onto the floor. As a result, Zeke's Snowman behind was blotted here and there with brightly colored frosting. She hoped their Mom had some killer ideas on how to clean his costume.

Dillon was there to help as well. Raegan had dropped him off after school and he'd ended up helping Abigail's Dad in the book section. There was an old fashioned wooden rolling ladder that could be used to reach the top most shelves, and Dillon had taken charge of it. He was the official climber, fetching books for people and monitoring the little kids who were drawn to the ladder like it was a toy. When he wasn't getting books, he gave the kids careful, slow rides on the ladder back and forth between the cupcake table and the book sections.

Old fashioned Christmas carols by Dean Martin, Bing Crosby and a few by Elvis set the mood. As Abigail watched the semi-chaotic festivities, the children laughing, the parents happily buying books as gifts, the smell of sweets and rich coffee and mocha drinks filling the air, she thought it really did seem like...well, like Christmas.

"Your Dad is really good with Dillon," Jamie said to her. There was a lull in their Santa line and Jamie was sitting back, observing, like her.

Abigail glanced to where her Dad was talking to Dillon by the ladder and, surprisingly, Dillon was laughing and talking back to him. His face had lost its teenage angsty look and he seemed bright and happy. She looked back to Jamie who was watching the scene with a smile in his eyes, which was all she could see because of his beard.

"Dillon does look like he's in a better mood, today," she said.

"Oh, he's usually in a good mood...with everyone but me and his Mom," Jamie said with a small sigh.

"I guess that's a teenager thing, isn't it?"

"Yeah, I suppose it is. Probably a divorced parents thing, too."

There was a pause as they both watched Dillon. When he was light hearted and chatty, he was quite a good looking young man. He really did remind her of Jamie when he was young. A question popped into her head, but she wasn't sure Jamie would want to answer it.

"It's none of my business," she began, "and you don't have to answer, but do you and Raegan get along? Or was it a nasty divorce?"

Jamie looked at her then thought for a moment before he answered, "It wasn't pretty, that's for sure. It was such a long time ago, though. Dillon was only two. So it's better now. I've just never lived up to what she wanted me to be, and she's not shy about letting me know how she feels about it."

"What did she want you to be?"

"Rich," he laughed a little, as did Abigail. Then he got more serious, "I worked construction out of high school, which is good money...when there's work. And we were so young, we probably should have never gotten married to begin with, we were very different."

Abigail nodded, but remained quiet. Her eyes drifted between watching Dillon and watching Jamie as he talked.

"I got hurt at work right after Dillon was born. Things just went downhill after that." He lifted one shoulder in a half-hearted shrug. "Things weren't too bad, though. I couldn't go back to construction, not like I did before I was hurt. So I worked at the hardware store and concentrated on being a good Dad."

She smiled at that. Putting aside the fact that he liked to tease when he was a teenager, it seemed like he'd mellowed out quite a bit now that he was grown. It wasn't difficult for her to think of him as a good Dad.

"I'm sure you're a good Dad. What are you going to do now that the hardware store is closed?"

He dropped his gaze. "I don't know, exactly, besides doing odd jobs. Fixed up the gazebo for the town council." He watched her and there was weighted meaning in his eyes. "Do you remember when we used to go to the gazebo?"

Memories of them at the gazebo in the early morning, before the park was officially open, and watching the sunrise came to her. Then more memories of being there late at night. She recalled that the goal was to be at the gazebo when nobody else was there, when they weren't supposed to be there either. She didn't remember Zeke, just her and Jamie. For some reason the thought of it made her feel shy.

"I remember going there a few times," she answered, looking down at the floor.

Jamie watched her, his eyes focused and still holding an emotion that she couldn't quite read. The space between them filled with something almost electric. After a few moments he glanced away and released her from his gaze. When he looked back he was normal old Jamie again.

"What about you?" He asked.

"Me?"

He leaned forward in his chair, pulling his Santa beard down so it hooked underneath his chin. "Yeah, do you think you're gonna stay here? Do you like being a graphic designer?"

It was Abigail's turn to do a half-hearted shrug. "I don't

know what I'm going to do. I'm not sure I want to stay in graphic design. It's interesting, but dealing with clients is awful."

Jamie nodded in understanding.

"I do know one thing, though," Abigail continued. "I'm not staying here."

Jamie's eyebrows lifted under his Santa hat. "No?"

She shook her head to bring the point home. "No, I'm not into the whole small town thing."

"Oh." He looked around at the mellowing cupcake party. His head bobbed up and down slightly as he considered her comment. When his eyes moved to the windows that she'd painted, he paused. He tilted his head at the window and asked, "What about painting? You've always been an incredible painter."

Abigail followed his gaze to the window decorations and scoffed a little. "That? That's just messing around. It's not real painting."

Judy, whose cupcake table had finally emptied, approached them with a great sigh of relief.

"That was crazy fun wasn't it?" She asked.

"Yes, it was," Jamie answered.

"Zeke said you did this," Judy was talking to Abigail, but pointing at the window decorations.

"Yes," Abigail nodded.

"Do you think you could do it for the bakery?" Judy asked.

Abigail didn't know what to say. Jamie's eyebrows lifted again as he looked first at Judy then at Abigail.

"I'd pay you," Judy added.

Jamie smiled and nudged Abigail, giving her his I Told You So face. Abigail still didn't know what to say.

"It's just so beautiful, and I was thinking maybe you could make something sort of similar, but with little elves baking?

That would be cute for a bakery, don't you think?" Judy continued.

"That would be real nice," Jamie said, smiling at them both.

Abigail was flattered, and flustered, but Judy waited patiently for an answer. Finally, Abigail gave her a small nod.

"Sure, I could do that," she said.

"See?" Jamie said happily after Judy left, "I'm not the only one who thinks you're talented!"

Chapter Seven

After the wild success of the sugar-filled, child-focused, Christmas Cupcake Decorating Extravaganza, Zeke was unstoppable. His plans for the Holiday Poetry Reading expanded to include hiring a local teenage girl who was one of the best cellists in the state as extra entertainment. In addition to selling coffee and snacks, he decided to offer free wine to the adults, figuring this would loosen them up to read poetry as well as make purchases.

"As long as you don't let them leave with it," Charlie, one of the two deputies Pitkin Point paid to patrol their quiet town, instructed him.

Charlie was just a few years older than Zeke and Jamie. They'd all gone to school together. Abigail had gone to school with Diego, the other deputy. He'd been a few years behind her.

The two deputies perfectly complimented each other. Where Charlie was broad and fair, Diego was lean and dark. Where Charlie was a stickler for the rules, Diego was more likely to let you off with a warning.

"Of course," Zeke readily agreed to Charlie's conditions.

Since The Thinking Bean didn't have a liquor license, technically they couldn't serve wine. But Charlie was willing to let it slide since it was a special occasion and Christmas, but he explained to Zeke that anyone receiving wine would have to be over 21-years old, and they couldn't leave the premises with the alcohol.

"I'm serious about this, Zeke," Charlie's ruddy cheeks darkened as he warned her brother. He wasn't a fan of Zeke's over the top personality, though they had always been decent to one another. Charlie was thick and heavy with a wide face made even wider by his blonde buzz cut. He was old fashioned in his thinking, but a solid cop. He just wasn't necessarily in for all of the shenanigans that Zeke had always been prone to creating.

"I know you're serious, Charlie," Zeke gave the deputy an agreeable yet sternly competent face.

"We'll keep an eye on it," Jamie added, putting his hand on Charlie's shoulder. Charlie looked at Jamie's hand then at Jamie, but didn't crack a smile.

"See that you do," he said. Taking his coffee to go, Charlie left the scene, shaking his head in vague disapproval as he did.

With that begrudging go ahead, Holiday Poetry Reading Night at The Thinking Bean was on.

Since this was more of an adult, evening type affair, Zeke agreed to ditch their costumes for the night.

"As long as you dress up," he instructed as Jamie and Abigail high-fived each other. Abigail was happy to gussy up a bit after wearing her Elf costume for days.

She spent the afternoon at Take the Cake, visiting with Judy and painting their window with some Christmas fun. After they came up with the initial design, the painting only took her a few hours. Judy gave her a crisp $100 bill and a lemon meringue pie. Not bad for an afternoon's work.

Abigail ate a pleasant early dinner with her parents with the pie for dessert. Then she headed down to Zeke's old room to change. She took a quick shower, avoiding getting her hair wet so she wouldn't have to blow it dry. Blow drying really brought out the frizz in her hair. Letting it get steamed up in the shower, however, gave it extra curly bounce.

She dressed in jeans, black suede boots, and a black, form fitting, off-the-shoulder sweater. She found a silver and rhinestone snowflake necklace that her Mom had given her years ago that she'd hardly worn. Along with the matching snowflake earrings, the necklace added just the right amount of Christmas to her casual, beatnik look.

The Thinking Bean was abuzz with activity when she arrived. She counted at least a dozen people in addition to her parents. Zeke was there, and Fern, who looked lovely in black tailored slacks and a tight fitting jacket with a V-neck that was trimmed in faux black fur. Jamie was nowhere to be seen.

"Lookin' good, sis," Zeke beamed at her from behind the counter.

"You're just used to seeing me in an Elf costume," she quipped. "Where's Jamie?"

"He went to pick up Dillon," Zeke answered. He lifted up two bottles of wine for her to choose, "Red or white?"

"I'll have white," Fern said, stepping up to the counter next to Abigail.

"I love your sweater," Abigail told her. Fern's smile lit up her brilliant blue eyes as she thanked her.

"One white," Zeke handed Fern a glass of wine with what Abigail noticed was a flirty and extended look. "What'll you have, Abbah Dabbah?"

"Red, please," she answered.

"Make that two," Jamie's voice came out of nowhere from just behind her shoulder.

Abigail turned around to tell him he'd scared her, but as soon as she laid eyes on him, she struggled to remember what she was about to say.

Maybe it was because of the little white lights that decorated the coffee shop. Maybe it was because he was standing so close to her, close enough she could smell his cologne, and it smelled good. Or maybe it was because she'd been looking at him in his overstuffed Santa outfit for the past few days, but Abigail was shocked into silence when she saw him.

He had that just shaved look that made her want to reach out and touch his cheek. He wore a burgundy corduroy long sleeve shirt with the top few buttons undone, and a pair of jeans with boots. His hair had a messy, just got out of bed for a photo shoot kind of vibe, and there was a glimmer in his blue eyes. Eyes that seemed particularly blue tonight.

"Hi," she said, because she realized her mouth was hanging open.

He smiled and she noticed something that she'd never really noticed before, Jamie Turner had dimples. He ducked his head before looking up at her, a little bashful, "You look beautiful, Abby."

The tiniest thrill tumbled through her stomach at the sound of him saying her nickname. That, combined with the look in his eyes and the fact that he smelled so good, made her decide not to correct him. Just inches away from each other, a memory of him in his towel flashed through her mind and she blushed.

"Two reds," Zeke said.

Jamie moved to take both drinks. As he did, there was a silent exchange between the two men that Abigail couldn't put her finger on. Of course, her hormones were reeling from Jamie's body skimming past hers to grab the wine, the closeness of him overtook all of her senses. She started to say something to Zeke, wanting him to explain, break up these feelings, offer her some protection. But Zeke kept his eyes trained on Jamie and vice versa until Zeke gave his friend an almost imperceptible nod. It was that man nod that men do to one another when they are acknowledging something from the secret man club. It was a move she'd seen men do countless times but never really understood the social cues surrounding it. Understanding or not, Abigail knew something was different now that it was done, and that it had to with her. As if Zeke was giving permission to Jamie to...what, exactly?

The moment was gone in an instant and her brother turned to help another customer, leaving her with Jamie. And even though the small room was full, when he shifted his attention back to her she felt as if they were completely alone.

"Your wine," he said, offering her one of the glasses. When she lifted her hand to take it, her arm brushed against his. He didn't move, just watched her, his eyes smiling. Abigail wrapped her hand around the wine glass and, without meaning to, covered his fingers with hers as she did. He didn't pull his hand away, probably waiting until she had a good grip on the wine glass. Probably.

"Thanks," she managed to say. Her mouth felt dry and it made her voice sound hoarse.

He lifted his glass to hers and clinked it, leaning towards her so she could hear him over the cello music and chatting customers. He was so close she could have easily turned her face and kissed his cheek.

"Cheers," he said. His voice was low and deep, rippling across her shoulders and neck.

Abigail couldn't speak, she just lifted her glass and took a sip. Jamie did the same, keeping his eyes locked on hers. Try as she might she couldn't look away from him. He was literally attracting her, holding her attention. And for reasons she could not understand, she liked it.

"This is pretty," he dropped his eyes to her throat where the snowflake necklace sparkled. He lifted his hand and put his finger under the pendant, balancing it on his fingertip to see it better. His touch was light, but enough for her to feel the warmth of his skin on hers. So gentle. Abigail felt her breath quicken and the heat rising in her neck and cheeks.

"Ladies and gentleman, can I have your attention please," Fern's lilting voice rose above the murmur of conversations, breaking whatever moment was happening between her and Jamie. Abigail turned to face the front corner of the room, which had been Santa's area and was now the poetry reading corner. Even with her back to him, Abigail could still feel Jamie's presence. He wasn't touching her, but for some insane reason she kept thinking about him touching her. She took a sip of her wine and absently fingered her snowflake pendant, the warmth of his touch on her throat still distracting.

Thankfully, Fern was in full control of Holiday Poetry Reading Night. As a librarian, lover of poetry and literature, and one of the most open minded and lyrical people in their midst, she was a perfect choice to MC the event. With nearly 30 people now sitting in the cafe area or wandering through the book sections, there was an air of nervousness when she invited anyone in the room to kick off the event by volunteering to go first.

There was no way Abigail was going to get up in front of an audience of any size and recite poetry. It just wasn't in her. Apparently nobody in the room was feeling any braver, because Fern's invitation was met with an uncomfortable silence.

"I'll go," Zeke spoke up from behind the counter. He glanced at Abigail and gestured towards the cash register, a silent request for her to run the counter for him. She changed places with him and he made his way to the corner. Though he must have been at least a full foot taller than Fern, somehow they looked really good next to each other. Like a team.

Zeke pulled a sheet of paper out of his pocket. He'd come prepared.

"Since this evening is a holiday themed event, I've chosen to read Good King Wenceslas by John Mason Neale. I'm not going to sing, so you can all relax," he said. A few chuckles broke the silence.

Reading the lyrics turned out to be quite beautiful, especially with Zeke's deep voice and spirited interpretation. The crowd broke into applause when he was done and he swept his long arm behind him as he bowed low.

"Now," he stood up, beaming at his audience. "Who's next?"

A number of people got up to read Christmas or holiday poems. Abigail kept busy behind the counter, refilling wine glasses or selling goodies, even making drinks, though she tried to do that in between readings since the noise was distracting. She was able to enjoy her mother's recitation of Christmas Eve: My Mother Dressing, and Miss Pearl, a retired school teacher who was probably the oldest person in town, reading The Oxen by Thomas Hardy.

During one break, Dillon approached the counter with a five dollar bill in his hand. His shyness was palpable and she wondered if he would bolt out the front door if she said the wrong thing.

"What would you like?" She asked with a smile.

"Um, a chocolate chip cookie...please," he managed, holding the money out to her.

"Oh, don't worry about it," Abigail waved the bill away. "It's only fair that Santa's son gets a free snack every now and then."

Dillon kind of laughed and she figured a half laugh was better than nothing. Abigail reached into the back of the glass counter and grabbed the biggest chocolate chip cookie they had with a thin tissue. Bent over, she thought she heard Jamie's voice from the far corner of the room. She stood up and caught Dillon looking at her with surprise, then they both turned to see Jamie taking his place at the poetry reading corner.

"I don't have a Christmas poem," he began, Zeke and a few of the others booed, only teasing. "But," Jamie held his palm up towards the hecklers, "I do know one poem by heart. So I figure that's the one I should do."

"You know a poem by heart?" Zeke called out to him, still joshing.

"I do." Jamie scanned the room. He looked nervous until his eyes fell on Dillon and he relaxed a little bit, smiling. "I memorized this poem in high school." His gaze moved past Dillon to Abigail, where it held for a few beats, long enough for Abigail to feel that tingling excitement she'd had earlier return. "It's called 'She Walks in Beauty'," his face broke into a huge, goofy Jamie smile, then he looked back to the crowd, "and it's by Lord Byron."

For the next few minutes nobody asked for a refill or a snack, which was good, because Abigail was captivated by Jamie's recitation. The whole room was, in fact. Not having to read while he spoke, Jamie made eye contact with the audience. A hush fell over the room as he recited the beautiful words, a starry eyed tenderness on his face.

On the last line, he caught her eye again and she was held hostage to his look, unable to think or move or even breathe for a few moments. His voice ended and a lovely silence filled the space, as if everyone was afraid to move or speak. Then several people turned to see what Jamie was gazing at with such adoration. Their attention broke whatever was connecting Abigail to him and she quickly averted her eyes, staring at the floor at her feet, blushing furiously.

Dillon turned back, really looking at her for the first time, his face full of curiosity. Before anyone could say anything, Abigail shoved the chocolate chip cookie at him, blurting out a hushed, "Here you go. Excuse me." Then she fled to the book section and out the back door into the alley.

The night air was cold, below freezing, and her breath plumed in front of her face as she paced up and down the alley. She was too angry and embarrassed to be cold. The back door clicked open and Jamie leaned into the alley, lit by a triangle of light.

"You okay?" He asked.

Abigail stopped pacing and turned on him. "What was that about?"

Jamie glanced back inside the bookstore then stepped all the way into the alley and let the door shut behind him. They were now bathed only in the blue light of the moon and the washed out glow of a distant streetlamp.

"What was what about?" He asked.

"That!" Abigail waved her hand wildly at the door. "What were you doing in there?"

Again, Jamie looked to the bookstore, then back to her. He shoved his hands into his pockets, bewildered at her anger yet sensing he was supposed to feel guilty. "A poetry reading?"

Abigail scoffed, "What's with all the...googley eyes and 'You look beautiful, Abby' baloney?"

Jamie was stunned at her jabs. In truth, she was too. She wasn't sure why his poem had brought on such wrath, but she didn't want to figure it out. She wanted him to take it all back and stop acting like such a buffoon.

"I didn't mean to make you mad," he began.

"Well, you did," she snapped at him, crossing her arms tightly across her chest.

"I—it's just—" he fumbled for words, which annoyed her even more.

"You what?" She asked impatiently.

"That poem always reminded me of you," he confessed. He looked down at his feet, shuffling them like he used to when they were young, like his son did now. "I wasn't trying to make a big deal about it. I thought I was being nice," he said.

"Like when you made a joke about asking me to prom? That same kind of nice?" Abigail spat the words at him before she even knew they were coming out of her mouth.

He stopped shuffling and looked at her with surprise. She couldn't blame him. She was surprised herself.

"What?" He looked puzzled.

"When you barged in and made fun of me for not having a date for prom at my birthday party," she said, the memory of it flooding back. Her 18th birthday party. The pink and purple balloons festooning the table her parents had reserved for her and her few friends at the fanciest Italian restaurant in town. How grown up she'd felt. How special. Then Jamie bursting into the room wearing a ridiculous black wig and fake mustache, singing Happy Birthday to her like an opera star, asking if she had a date to prom in a stupid Italian accent. The whole restaurant had watched him, laughing at him, at her, at them. She'd been mortified.

For a few moments he didn't say anything, just looked into her eyes, his breath like chugs of steam that floated past his face and up into the moonlit night.

"It wasn't a joke," he said.

It was Abigail's turn to be stunned. Finally, she managed, "What?"

"It wasn't a joke," he said once more.

"It wasn't a joke?" She asked. Her mouth was getting dry again.

"No," Jamie let his eyes follow the curves of her face, lost in some memory. "I wasn't making fun of you. I wanted to take you to your prom." He ducked his head for a long time. Then came back to the present and lifted his eyes to her. "Apparently I wasn't very good at asking." He broke his gaze away from her face and looked around the alley, letting out a frustrated sigh. "Apparently I'm not good at any of this."

"Any of what?" Her heart was pounding, anger and confusion mixing together inside of her chest.

He shook his head, "It doesn't matter." He shoved his hands deeper into his pockets and raised his shoulders up towards his ears. "It's freezing out here. You should get inside."

A shiver went through Abigail's stomach, but she didn't know for sure that it was caused by the cold.

Chapter Eight

They were called Fivedust and their equipment barely fit into the front half of the cafe section of The Thinking Bean. A local indie rock band, the only decent local indie rock band according to Zeke, Fivedust had agreed to do a gig two Saturdays before Christmas and include as many Christmas songs as possible on their song list. They also offered to lead the audience in Christmas carols as a finale to their performance. Zeke was in seventh heaven.

After the resounding success of the Cupcake Extravaganza and Poetry Reading, word had spread through Pitkin Point and beyond about the fun and festive events at The Thinking Bean. If the line forming at the counter and winding its way all the way out the front door this Saturday night was any indication, it seemed Mistletoe Madness was working its magic.

"Where are we going to fit everyone?" Zeke wondered, his eyes alight with excitement.

"Dillon and I can get those extra chairs out of the basement," Jamie said.

"If we took out some of the tables we could fit more chairs in here," Abigail suggested.

Zeke snapped and pointed first at Jamie, "Do it!" Then he did the same to Abigail, "Great idea!" Though her brother had once again relaxed the staff costume requirement for this evening's event, Zeke had taken a liking to his Snowman top hat and wore it now with his street clothes. Abigail thought he looked like a mix of Abraham Lincoln and a character straight out of a Charles Dickens story, but he still managed to come across as kind of cool and fairly intelligent. She had to hand it to him, despite his sometimes zany ideas, her big brother was kind of an impressive guy.

The big table and chair move began. Zeke took care of the line of customers while Jamie and Dillon retrieved chairs from the basement and took the tables that Abigail moved out of the cafe area.

Unfortunately, the close quarters and number of customers in the room made it impossible for her to ignore Jamie, which she'd been successfully doing since their conversation in the alley. Not ignore exactly. More like keep things professional or pretend that nothing intimate or embarrassing or hurtful had taken place between them.

"Sorry," Jamie said. Their shoulders had bumped accidentally when he was carrying a stack of chairs past her just as she straightened up from pushing a table towards the back.

"It's okay," she said politely. Her voice sounded calm, but she wanted to scream at him to not apologize, to stop being so kind, to man up and be offended or irritated or aloof. That would have been preferable. It would have been a normal reaction after how she'd treated him in the alley. But not Jamie. He lived his life, apparently, to be a thorn in her side.

At first he'd been a reminder of the embarrassment she'd felt when they were young. Now the sight of him made her rethink everything she'd ever believed about him, every assumption she'd ever made about his behavior. And it made her wonder if her reactions over the years had been justified or cruel. When she looked at him Abigail felt like she'd just kicked a puppy. And that was not a good feeling.

"Dad," Dillon stuck his head into the cafe from the book section of the store. "There's just a few more down there, I'll get them." He disappeared, leaving Jamie standing next to the stack of chairs he'd just put down. Uncomfortably close.

"Need some help?" Abigail asked.

"No, I got it," he answered as he grabbed a chair from the top and set it on the floor. "Thanks," he added. Unrelentingly polite. Infuriating.

Fivedust started their gig at 6:00 pm, which was early for a band, but not so early for people who frequented coffee shops. The music was good and really loud in the small space. People were crammed wall to wall, sitting and standing, sipping their hand made refreshments. Zeke had not been able to convince Deputy Charlie that free wine at this event was acceptable. A poetry reading was one thing, but a "rock concert" with alcohol that might find its way into the gentle, quiet streets of their small town was too much of a risk.

It turned out that this was a good call on Charlie's part, given how the evening turned out.

As Fivedust performed to The Thinking Bean's packed audience, the temperature in the shop became unbearably warm. Zeke asked Jamie to prop open the front door and the back door that led to the alley in order to let in some of the arctic air from the mid-December night. This action had two unforeseen results.

First, people who were a little late to the concert weren't dissuaded from entering the shop because they could easily hear the loud music outside on the red brick sidewalk. They ducked in and got a hot drink, then enjoyed the music happily from outside. Second, the customers who got tired of sitting in the too warm building wandered out the front door to mingle with others on the sidewalk, or out the back door to take cigarette breaks in the alley. All the while Fivedust's music carried from the coffee shop out into the quiet night.

Fern had joined Zeke behind the counter and there wasn't a lot of room for anyone else to assist. Besides, Zeke seemed happier when Fern was around and Abigail didn't want to invade on their space.

The growing crowd on the front sidewalk drifted across the street to the park. The Southeast corner of Pitkin Point's beloved City Park was nicely situated near The Thinking Bean. It looked charming, too, with a number of park benches, old fashioned street lamps festooned with giant Christmas wreaths, and the quaint gazebo that had been dressed up for the season with pine boughs, huge red velvet bows and white lights of its own.

Given there wasn't a lot she could do to help at the moment and she didn't want to take up room inside where a paying customer could sit, plus the fact that she felt the need to avoid Jamie if possible, Abigail decided to go to the park. She discreetly retrieved her black wool coat from the coat rack near the door, pulled it on outside and wandered over to the gazebo.

It was beautiful. She hadn't spent much time at the park since coming home. She'd been too busy with Mistletoe Madness. But it had been one of her favorite places when she was a kid. One of their favorite places, her and Zeke...and Jamie.

The music floated through the clear night air and added to the mood. Fivedust was currently playing a beautiful version of Have Yourself a Merry Little Christmas that they'd dressed up with their own style. She took in a breath of the fresh, cold air and let out a sigh as she walked. It was the first time she'd had a few minutes with nothing else to do in a while. This was exactly what she needed, some time by herself enjoying the night and forgetting her problems.

The last snow had come just after Thanksgiving and remnants of it were still scattered in the shadiest parts of the park. There had been talk of a big snowstorm possibly heading their way soon and Abigail hoped it would. If she was going to be in Pitkin Point for Christmas, at least it could be a white Christmas.

She smiled at a few people who had made themselves comfortable on one of the benches while they listened to Fivedust. It was remarkable how clearly their music traveled on this clear night.

Abigail noticed that nobody was in the gazebo, so she decided she'd pop inside and get the full effect of the Christmas decorations from its higher vantage point. As she gripped the handrail and trotted up the stairs, she was startled to find Jamie sitting on the bench seat opposite her. She hadn't seen him from the path as she approached.

"Oh!" She put her hand on her heart.

Jamie stood up, holding his palm out to her like she was an animal he didn't want to frighten, "Sorry."

She took a few deep breaths. "It's okay."

"I thought I'd take a break. It's hot in there."

She nodded. "Me too. It is, isn't it?" She laughed, out of nerves more than humor.

Jamie nodded. He glanced around at the empty benches along every wall of the gazebo. He took a step forwards, then backwards, then did a half turn and stopped again, never once looking her in the eye.

"Well, I'll leave you to it," he said and sort of lunged towards the top of the stairs where she was standing, trying to make a quick exit.

"You don't have to leave," Abigail blurted out.

He stopped a few feet in front of her and lifted his gaze.

When she looked into his eyes it felt as if someone was squeezing her heart. There was sadness in his eyes and longing, and worst of all a loneliness that she recognized. She'd seen the same look in her own reflection. Abigail reached out and touched his chest, as if her hand alone could keep him from pushing past and leaving.

"Please don't go because of me," she said, so quietly she wasn't sure she'd even spoken the words out loud. Except she was sure, because she saw him relax. Felt him relax.

He had a question, she could read this much on his face, but he didn't ask it. A group of concert goers walked by, talking and laughing. Jamie glanced at them, let his eyes follow them as they passed, then looked back at her.

"Okay, I'll stay," he said.

She pulled her hand back and pushed both of her hands into her coat pockets.

"Do you want to sit down?" Jamie gestured towards the bench seating. She shook her head 'no'. He nodded, his head bobbing up and down like it did when he was nervous. A smile pulled at the corners of her mouth.

"It's beautiful isn't it?" She said, moving to the edge of the gazebo and looking out over the park. The moon was high in the sky, and the tiny white lights hung all around them on the gazebo, as well as on each wreathed street lamp. They looked like sparkling gems placed by magical Christmas elves.

"Yes, it is," he answered, stepping next to her, but leaving a more than comfortable distance between them. Those few extra inches squeezed her heart again. What she'd said to him, what she'd thought about him all these years, had put an invisible wedge between them. And that made her sad. For the briefest of moments Abigail thought she might tear up, but she blinked hard and managed to keep her cool.

"Do you remember the Christmas Dance when Zeke and I were seniors?" Jamie asked. He was looking into the middle distance, focusing on a memory, his hands in the pockets of his dark brown jacket.

Her mind clicked back through several memories of the Christmas Dance here in the park. It was a wonderful yearly celebration with a bonfire, fresh kettle corn made in a giant cast iron kettle, hot chocolate and hot apple cider, music, everyone dressed up and wrapped in their warmest and finest. It had only been snowed out twice as she was growing up. The people of Pitkin Point welcomed snow at the Christmas Dance and only shut it down when it veered towards blizzard conditions. She tried to remember Zeke and Jamie's last year in high school.

"I think so," she said, recalling some specifics. "It was kind of warm that year, wasn't it?" She remembered that detail because she could picture the dress she had worn. A midnight blue dress with long sleeves and crystals sewn into the bodice. She remembered she'd found blue sparkly tights that matched and had been thrilled she didn't have to cover up the dress with her coat during the whole dance.

Jamie nodded, glancing at her, "You had on a blue dress."

She looked at him in shock, "You remember my dress?"

He nodded again and chuckled, "I had it bad for you, Abby."

"You did?" Again, shock.

"I bought boxes of mistletoe and hung it all over inside this gazebo." Jamie pointed up and down the eight beams that stretched out from the center of the gazebo to the edges. "I was trying to make sure to get you under the mistletoe." He shook his head and chuckled again at his youthful determination. He looked at her sideways, his eyes crinkling at the corners with humor. "Not that I would have known how to go about kissing you under the mistletoe if it had worked."

Abigail's mouth hung open with surprise at this story. A story she'd never heard, "Jamie, I had no idea!"

"I know," he answered.

She took a few moments to think about what he'd said. Then her brow wrinkled with confusion. "Why didn't it work?"

"Well, a lot of guys noticed you that year, I guess. You spent the whole night on the dance floor. You never came up here."

She did remember dancing a lot that year. She'd always attributed it to the fact that it was so warm and everyone was dancing.

"I didn't come up here once?"

"Not once. I waited."

She pondered his answer, then asked, "Why didn't you ask me to dance?"

Jamie sucked air through his teeth, "Dancing? That wasn't a thing when I was that age." She laughed at his reaction and he smiled at her again. "I guess I lost my nerve."

"Oh." Abigail travelled back to that night and thought about Jamie waiting for her in the gazebo, too afraid to ask her to dance. It was so sweet and sad. She tried to read his expression as his eyes drifted across the moonlit park and the happy couples enjoying their impromptu outdoor concert.

"That was the night I decided to ask you to prom. Of course, I chickened out that year. But I finally got up the guts the next year for your senior prom..." he chuckled again, but there wasn't much humor in it this time. "And we both know how that turned out." He shook his head and looked away from her.

"Jamie, I—" she began.

"No, I'm not telling you all this so you can feel sorry for me," he interrupted, turning back to her and raising his palm up as if warding off her pity. "I just want you to know that there was zero chance I was trying to make fun of you or embarrass you in any way when I did that. I just wanted us to be square on that point."

She didn't say what she'd been about to say, which was that she was sorry she'd fled in embarrassment from him at that Italian restaurant, left him without an answer. She'd only done it because she really didn't know he was asking her to prom. She would have said 'yes' and they would have gone and had a great time. If she'd only known.

Abigail stood mute, looking into his eyes, and realized that he wanted to end it this way, on sure footing. There was no reason to dive into all of their teenage angst and misunderstandings. It's not like they were a couple or going to be one.

"Okay, we're square," she said.

He waited for something more. When it didn't come, he nodded curtly, finalizing the deal. "Okay, good."

A few moments went by, the space between them filled with unspoken words. Her heart squeezed again, but Abigail didn't pay it any attention. This wasn't high school and there was no row of mistletoe hanging over their heads. This was reality.

"Friends?" She asked, or rather, demanded.

He didn't look away from her, just stared right into her eyes. The muscle on his jaw flexed as if he was biting his tongue, then he started to answer, but his voice caught. He cleared his throat, "Okay, friends."

And that was that.

Chapter Nine

"What do you mean I have to be his date?" Abigail asked. Zeke, wearing his tophat, towered over her in their parent's living room.

"He also has to be your date. It's mutual," Zeke explained, sort of.

"I don't see why I need a date or why he needs a date at all," Abigail argued.

"It's the Mistletoe Madness Bookstore Scavenger Hunt Date Night," Zeke said, raising his arms so they were even with his shoulders, like he was a ringmaster in a circus.

"Why don't you want to go with Jamie?" Her mother asked. She was sitting on the couch, knitting a sweater from a large ball of bumpy, olive green yarn.

Abigail didn't want to get into a discussion about Jamie with her mother. She glared at Zeke, who was blissfully ignorant of how touchy this situation was for his two top, only, staff members.

"It's not that I don't want to go with him, I just don't understand why Zeke thinks we should go together," she tried to explain.

"You're the only two people who know how the scavenger hunt is supposed to work, besides Fern and I. You need to be each other's dates so you can lead by example," Zeke told her.

"Do you have someone else to go with?" Her mother asked.

"No, Mom, I don't," Abigail felt her resistance crumbling. She sighed, then asked, "Did you already tell Jamie?"

"Yeah, he's down with it. No problem," Zeke answered.

"I like Jamie," her Mom interjected.

Abigail had a headache.

"His son's a good kid, too," their Dad got in on the conversation, speaking out from his chair where he'd been reading a book. Being the high school counselor gave him final word on the goodness or badness of any given teenager in town.

"You know, sweetie, it wouldn't kill you to go out with him on a real date," her mother said.

"Mom!" Abigail felt like she was 13-years old.

"Not Dillon, of course, but Jamie," her mother said.

"I knew you didn't mean Dillon," Abigail said. "Can we talk about something else, please?"

"All right, you don't have to get upset," her mother turned to Zeke, who had sat down in one of the wing chairs with his long legs stuck out in front of him, crossed at the ankles. "So you and Fern are getting pretty serious, aren't you?"

THE SCAVENGER HUNT Date Night was the most complicated of the Mistletoe Madness events. It had taken all four of them, Abigail, Zeke, Jamie and Fern, several hours each afternoon for three days to come up with the scavenger hunt list, create the printouts and rules, and decide on the prizes.

Basically, a couple would arrive at the bookstore and mark the time they started the scavenger hunt on their printout. They would be allowed 90 minutes to find as many things as possible on the list. Then they would turn in their printout with the time they finished written on it. At 8:00 pm the printout would be reviewed for accuracy and the winners chosen.

First prize was a dinner for two at Ming's Golden Palace, the best Chinese restaurant within 50 miles. Second place was dinner for two at the pizza place. Third place was two tickets to the movie theater. Five runner ups got a $10.00 gift card to The Thinking Bean, and everyone else who entered got a $5.00 off $10.00 purchase at The Thinking Bean. The questions ran the gamut from 'Find a book about what you wanted to be when you grew up' to 'Find a book with the word Rock in the title' to 'Find a book about a robot', and so on.

Any other time, Abigail would be happy to take part in this kind of scavenger hunt. It was intellectual and light-hearted all at the same time, and something she would normally enjoy. But now that she and Jamie had been paired together as the example date for other patrons to emulate, she felt nothing but nervous.

To make matters worse, stupid Zeke refused to lift the costume requirement for this event. He was in his full Snowman gear and she and Jamie were stuck as Santa and his Elf. At least, she thought, that might make it seem less like a real date and more like work. Fern had agreed to be Zeke's date and, in the name of getting into the spirit of things, was dressed as a Penguin.

"What about this one?" Jamie held up a sci-fi book with a robot on the cover.

"What's it about?" Abigail asked, moving closer to him so she could see the description on the back of the book.

They had begun the scavenger hunt, choosing to go first and get it over with while Zeke and Fern ran the counter. Then they would switch places.

"It's not about a robot," Jamie said, sliding the book back into place. "Which begs the question, why is there a robot on the cover?" Sarcasm was thick tonight.

One thing none of them had thought about was that The Thinking Bean was a rare and used bookstore, so the titles were often obscure and little known. Even when you could think of a book that fit the scavenger hunt question, it was not always a book that was in the store. So far, Abigail and Jamie had been hunting for 30 minutes and had only filled in two of their questions.

Jamie made a frustrated growling sound, "This is hard." He skimmed over the printout in his hand and pointed to one of the questions, incredulous, "Find an author who has the same name as your middle name? Find a book with 394 pages?!? Who came up with these questions?"

"We did," Abigail said, laughing a little at his outburst, which was made all the more amusing because he was dressed like Santa.

"Right." He slumped comically against the wall. "I would rather face a line of little kids who want to give me their Christmas lists," he whispered just loud enough for her to hear.

She laughed again, "I thought this sounded fun, but it is a bit tedious, isn't it?"

He nodded at her, his Santa beard askew. Without thinking, she reached out and tugged on one side so it was even. A look flickered across his eyes, but it was so fast Abigail couldn't be sure she'd actually seen it. She dropped her hand and he cleared his throat.

"Quite a few people came," he said, looking away from her and towards the other couples in the book section.

John and Judy were there. Nannette and Pete, who owned the pizza place, were also there. Deputy Diego had brought his wife, Marissa. He was in street clothes. In fact, all of the couples were in street clothes. Except her and Jamie.

When their 90 minutes were up, they had only managed to answer five of the 30 questions on their printout, and they were exhausted. As they took over the counter from Zeke and Fern, Jamie gave Zeke a hard time.

"If anyone can answer all of those questions in 90 minutes we should give them more than a Chinese dinner."

"Let's see how many we can do," Zeke said to Fern.

"Right on," she answered, giggling.

They turned and strolled arm and arm towards the books. One tall, spindly limbed Snowman and a short, beautiful Penguin. They offset each other and created a perfect match. Abigail was happy for her brother, she truly liked Fern. But watching them saunter off so content, so in tune with each other, just made her feel depressed.

"You good?" Jamie asked from his position at the espresso machine.

"I'm fine," Abigail said, turning towards the next customer.

Maria Cortez, Abigail's high school Spanish teacher, was waiting with her elderly mother at the cash register to place their order.

"Oh, Abigail, you look adorable in that costume. I heard you had moved back to town," Maria, or Mrs. Cortez as Abigail had always called her, exclaimed warmly.

"Hi, thank you. I'm just back for the holidays. Not staying forever," Abigail said. She felt the need to clarify her plans to anyone and everyone. Especially herself.

"Oh, that's a shame. It would be nice to have you around again," Maria smiled so kindly when she spoke. She had always been kind.

"It's good to be home for Christmas," Abigail admitted.

"Can my mother and I play this game?" Maria asked, noticing the scavenger hunt printouts on the counter.

"Of course," Abigail responded.

She and Jamie continued to work close together behind the counter, often bumping lightly into each other, especially with his extra large Santa body in the way. They were good at reading what the other person needed and getting orders out fast, even though they did it with very little conversation. Inside, Abigail felt tight, like her neck and shoulders were binding up and her stomach was pulling together in knots.

With all of the customers, the little shop got very warm again. She was hot in her long, striped sleeves and tights. She glanced at Jamie, who still sported his Santa hat and beard. He must be boiling. He didn't complain, however. He kept working.

When the scavenger hunt was over and the printouts were being reviewed, Jamie excused himself.

"I've got to get out of this suit," he told Zeke. "I'm cooking in here."

Zeke nodded, "Sure, man, go ahead."

And he was gone.

Abigail spent some time helping look over the printouts, but after a while Zeke and Fern seemed to have a system going and she felt like a third wheel. She looked at the clock and realized Jamie had been upstairs for almost 45 minutes. She had assumed he would return, and as each minute passed and he didn't appear, Abigail was more and more distracted. Was he okay? Had he gone into Santa costume induced heat stroke?

As soon as the winners were decided, she told Zeke she was going to take a break and he nodded his approval. A minute later Abigail was climbing the narrow, antique stairway up towards the apartment. She hadn't been up there since the first day she'd surprised Jamie getting out of the shower. This time it was dark. Very dark. There was no light on in the stairway or on the landing and she didn't know where the switch was to turn it on.

As she moved up the stairs her stomach fluttered with...something. Nerves? Excitement? Was she actually worried she might find him having a seizure on the floor?

At the landing she felt her way to the door and hesitated. Maybe he didn't want company. Maybe he specifically didn't want her company. She almost turned around, insecure about how he would respond to seeing her at his door. Then she stopped. They were friends, right? That's what they'd agreed. A friend could check up on a friend, couldn't they?

She took a deep breath to stay the terrible shiver of nerves in her stomach and knocked on the door. Not too soft, not too hard. The knock of a friend.

The deep tones of his voice muffled through the door, "Hang on." She heard movement, then the door handle turning, the door pulling open, dim light from inside the apartment spilled into the hallway onto her Elf costume. "It's not locked—"

He stopped. He was expecting Zeke, of course. Not her.

"Hey," Abigail gave him an awkward little wave.

"Abby," he said, as if he needed to say her name to make her real. She felt relief at the sound of her nickname. It meant he didn't hate her.

He was out of his Santa costume, his hair going in all directions as if he'd pulled the wig/hat off quickly mand left it at that. He wore a green T-shirt and casual black workout pants. He looked tousled and casual jand extremely sexy.

"I...um, I wanted to—" she fumbled for words, unable to explain her presence there in his personal space.

"Do you need me?" He asked. She knew he meant downstairs in the shop, not literally. But she felt her heart thumping in response.

"No, no, it's not that. I was just checking on you."

There was a long pause as he studied her face. Her vision adjusted to the low light and she could see the outline of his jaw, his biceps and shoulders, his hand holding the top of the door. Suddenly, unbidden images of Jamie wearing only a towel flitted through her mind and her heart thumped hard again.

He pulled the door open and stepped to the side. "Want to come in?"

Yes. She did.

He closed the door behind her and motioned to the couch, "Have a seat."

Abigail sat down on one side of the worn, comfortable couch. There was a lamp on in the corner of the room. It gave off a low, warm glow. Jamie went to a second lamp and reached for the switch, intending to turn it on.

"Don't," Abigail said. He stopped. "You don't need to. It's nice in here. Relaxing."

He sat down on the other side of the couch and turned towards her. Abigail let her head move back and rest against the cushion. Enveloped in the quiet of the room with Jamie's presence so close by, she wanted to sink into the cushions and stay there.

"Rough day, wasn't it?" He asked.

"Mm-hmm," she murmured.

"I don't know why tonight was so hard," he wondered out loud.

Abigail thought she knew, but she didn't want to say. Her eyelids felt heavy and she fought the urge to close them. She turned her head on the cushion so she could look at Jamie, so solid and calm.

"I'm sleepy," she admitted, letting her eyes close before opening them slowly again.

"Then sleep," he said. Abigail felt a warmth move through her body and she relaxed. Remarkably, without thinking any more about it, she drifted off to sleep.

When she woke, minutes or hours later, she couldn't be sure, she was in the exact same position. Jamie had moved. He was facing forward, his feet on the coffee table, the back of his head resting on the couch as he looked thoughtfully at the ceiling. He must have heard her stirring, because he turned his head and grinned at her.

"I'm sorry," she said, the fog of sleep lifting slowly from her brain.

"It's okay, you must have been tired."

Abigail stretched her shoulders and arms, waking up, but not yet wanting to leave the warm comfortable couch.

"How long was I asleep?"

"I don't know, half hour?" He watched as she rubbed her eyes and sat forward a little. "Do you want to go back to sleep?"

She shook her head 'no', "I'm fine." That 30 minutes had refreshed her completely and she was once again very aware of Jamie sitting so near her, looking homey and adorable.

"You're awake?" He asked.

"Yes, completely," she nodded.

His grin turned into a smile and his eyes twinkled with fun. "Want to see something cool?"

Chapter Ten

The roof of The Thinking Bean was a flat industrial space. A huge square air conditioning unit covered in sheets of plastic tarp jutted up out of the roof near the back. Various pipes and vents stuck up in small groups at different degrees of height, billowing steam into the night. Weather beaten wood planks were built into a shoddy looking shed structure whose exact role was a mystery. A hip high brick wall bordered the edge of the entire roof, which discouraged anyone from stepping off and dropping to the sidewalk below. The top of the fire escape they had used to climb up was still visible on the other side of that brick wall from where they now stood, but just barely.

All of the charm and character of the old building that was present inside was non-existent on the roof. In fact, the roof of The Thinking Bean was one of the ugliest places Abigail had ever been. Still, she stood silently next to Jamie, enrapt with what he'd brought her to see.

Not the roof, but the view from the roof.

City Park stretched out over several blocks. The gazebo on the closest corner and the pond surrounded by trees on the far end, all sparkled with Christmas lights. The meandering pathways that ran throughout the park were lit by street lamps hung with shining Christmas wreaths. The two streets that lined the park opposite them were lit up in their own festive decorations. The windows of the little shops and restaurants along the streets were decorated by each owner, the street lamps on those streets were hung with wreaths and lights as well. A canopy of lights had been hung over Main Street, which was just past their view, but they could still see the canopy. Some of the more heavily decorated houses lit up the far distance.

From their vantage point, they could see every bit of Christmas joy on display all over Pitkin Point. It was breathtaking.

"This is amazing," she said.

He looked at her with one of his goofy smiles. "And that's not even the best part." Jamie took her by the elbow and turned her around so she was facing the old, crooked shed, "Stay there."

She watched and waited. Her feet were cold from being outside this long in her Elf shoes. It seemed like the temperature was even lower up here on the roof. But Jamie had draped one of his winter coats over her before they climbed out the window onto the fire escape and she snuggled comfortably into its spacious warmth now.

Jamie disappeared around the back of the dilapidated structure. She heard fumbling and a muffled curse word then, suddenly, the dark space he'd ducked into lit up. He stepped back into her view, backlit so she couldn't see his face, but she knew without a doubt that he wore a dorky smile.

"Ta-da!" He said, stretching his arm towards the light like a magician.

"What is it?"

"Come here," he reached a hand towards her and she went

to him, letting him take her hand and lead her around the corner.

What she found on the other side made her gasp with delight, "Oh, Jamie!"

Colored Christmas lights, the type with the big, round bulbs, were strung back and forth like a shining roof across a charming sitting space. A futon style outdoor seat with fat striped patio pillows placed along the back provided a comfortable place to sit. Two other patio chairs faced the large seat, each with their own all weather cushions, and a low iron table with a glass top served as a type of coffee table in the center. Everything rested on a deck that lifted the seating high enough to see over the roof wall. Positioned as near to the edge of the roof as possible while still being safe, with the shed acting as a wall on one side and, she guessed, a nice windbreak, the sitting area provided a wonderful view of the town below and the city beyond.

With the night sky above, the magical glow of the Christmas lights, and the stunning view, Abigail thought it might be one of the prettiest places she'd ever seen.

"Do you like it?" Jamie asked. He was watching her reaction.

"Like it?" Abigail stepped to the futon and sat down with a flourish, looking out across the Christmas-scape below them. "I love it!"

Jamie beamed, rocking back and forth on his heels like an excited kid.

"Come and sit." She patted the open space next to her.

Jamie tilted his head in her direction and took three quick strides that carried him to the low stairs, up the low stairs, past the chairs and to the futon seat in a matter of seconds. He turned his body and did a small jump like he was pole vaulting over an invisible barrier and landed heavily next to her. Abigail laughed.

"Did you build this?" She asked.

He nodded, "Yep."

"Does Zeke know it's here?"

He shook his head, "Nope."

She laughed again, "Really?"

He nodded. "Dillon and I built it right after I moved in here. I thought it would be good for us to have a place that was just ours, you know, father-son time."

"That's sweet," she said, and she meant it.

Jamie leaned back in the seat and put his feet up on the table, taking in the view. She did the same. The futon seat wasn't as wide as the couch inside, which meant their shoulders and arms were comfortably touching. Abigail didn't mind.

After a few minutes of quiet contemplation, Jamie turned to her, looking her up and down, her red and white striped tights and Elf shoes sticking out from underneath his giant winter coat.

"Are you warm enough?"

Abigail shrugged, "My feet are a little cold."

He sat up and she started to follow suit. But before she could, Jamie put his hand on her knee to stop her. "Stay here, I'll be right back."

He disappeared down the fire escape for a few minutes and she was alone on the roof. She listened to the occasional car driving past or sound of voices somewhere far below.

When Jamie returned, she heard him before she saw him. The metal rattling of the fire escape cut through the quiet around her and she watched as his head, backlit from the lights beyond, appeared at the edge of the building. He had carefully carried a bottle of wine in one hand with a wine opener already screwed partially into the cork as he made his way up the fire escape, which was really just a glorified ladder hanging on the outside of the building. He had a down sleeping bag hung over his shoulder and two wine glasses, one in each coat pocket.

Soon they were cuddled under the downy warmth of the sleeping bag. Jamie had unzipped it completely so it lay like a puffy square over them. He'd been sure to tuck the ends completely around her feet before snuggling in next to her and covering himself.

The warmth of the wine spread through her pretty quickly, seeing as she hadn't eaten any dinner. And the sleeping bag captured their body heat, making it nice and cozy for her Elf feet. Nice and cozy for her whole body.

They talked about a lot of things, and laughed about even more. Common memories of friends and family, of each other, growing up. By the time Jamie emptied the last of the wine into their glasses Abigail's sides hurt she'd laughed so hard.

"So, you really don't want to stay here?" Jamie asked, indicating Pitkin Point below with a nod of his head.

She shook her head a little too hard, the wine taking effect, "No!" Her voice carried far into the empty space around them.

"Why not?"

"I'm an artist, Jamie," she said it like he should already know the answer to his question. "Artists don't live in their tiny little home towns and marry their high school sweethearts and have babies," her words slurred a little as they came out, but the flow had already started and she couldn't stop it. "They go out into the big, bad world and make a name for themselves. They live in loft apartments and throw amazing parties. They don't cave to society. They stay up all night creating and scramble every month just to pay their electric bill and buy food. They meet brooding strangers and have anonymous sex..."

Jamie's eyebrows lifted. Abigail didn't know how to continue after that last comment, so she took a gulp of wine.

"Hmm, I didn't know that," he said, laughter in his eyes. He pretended to ponder the idea. "Is that what you've been doing since you moved away?"

She smacked his shoulder with her free hand and he exaggerated the power behind it, falling away from her in slow motion.

"Shut up," she giggled.

He sat up, pleased with himself as he took another drink of wine. After a few moments of calm, he continued the conversation.

"I guess I just don't understand. I mean, everybody's from somewhere. There's no shame in liking where you're from, even loving it. Is there?"

The words resonated with Abigail and she peered at him, taking in his roughed up hair, his kind, blue eyes, the squareness of his jaw, the shape of his mouth. Her gaze moved to the beautiful and, she had to admit, romantic little space he'd created here to look out over Pitkin Point. He appreciated the little things. That was nice. Whoever ended up with Jamie Turner would be a lucky woman.

The sound of metal rattling came to both of them at the same time and they looked first at the fire escape, then at each other, then back at the fire escape. The rattling got louder and before either of them could react, the silhouette of a head wearing a flat brimmed Deputy's hat appeared on the edge of the building.

"Charlie?" Jamie asked.

The figure kept climbing until its broad neck and shoulders appeared. It was breathing a little hard having just climbed up over two stories of fire escape ladder.

"Jamie is that you?" It was Charlie.

"Yeah, it's me," Jamie answered. He gave Abigail an

awkward glance before standing.

Charlie huffed and puffed his way over the top of the ladder and onto the roof. As soon as he got sure footing he turned on his high beamed flashlight and shone it on Jamie's face.

"Jeez, Charlie," Jamie lifted his hand to shield the blinding light.

The light switched to Abigail and she clenched her eyes closed against its brightness.

"Abigail?" Charlie asked.

"Yes, it's me," she answered, her eyes still squeezed shut.

"Stop shining that thing in our faces," Jamie said.

Abigail opened her eyes a peep and the light was no longer aimed at their faces.

"Are you guys drinking up here?" Charlie's voice conveyed that betrayal felt by an authority figure when they discover someone they like breaking the rules.

Abigail would have said 'no', except the light was shining directly on her hand holding her wine. She fought the sudden urge to laugh, and lost. Although, the laugh came out more like a snort.

"I brought the wine," Jamie volunteered.

"You can't have alcohol up here," Charlie informed them, all seriousness. Always seriousness.

"Are you kidding?" Jamie asked.

He wasn't.

Soon Abigail was climbing carefully down the fire escape using just one hand to hold on, while the other hand tried to keep her wine glass steady. She had insisted on taking her wine down with her. The glass was almost full after all. Charlie was below her on the fire escape and Jamie was above. It was slow going and, try as she may to steady it, the wine in her glass sloshed terribly, sometimes over the edges and down, she presumed, on top of Charlie's hat.

"Abby," Jamie said to her from somewhere above.

"Yeah?"

"Go into the apartment. I'll talk to Charlie," Jamie told her. She liked that he was going to manage this situation, because she was probably a little too tipsy to talk to Charlie with a straight face.

As she clambered into the apartment from the fire escape, a surprised Zeke and Fern watched her from where they sat on the couch.

"What are you doing?" Zeke asked.

"Coming in!" She said, laughing.

"Where's Jamie?"

"I think he might be getting a ticket," she answered, just as Jamie's figure climbed by the window on his way down to the ground.

Zeke stood up and came to the window, looking down at the alley below.

"Is that Charlie?" He asked. Abigail nodded then lifted her now half empty wine glass to Fern in greeting and took a sip.

"Were you on the roof?" Fern asked, obviously amused at the situation.

Abigail nodded.

"Charlie really is on a roll tonight," Zeke complained, still watching the two men in the alley.

"What do you mean?" Abigail asked, trying not to slur the phrase into 'whadya mean'.

"He gave me a ticket, too."

"What? Why?" Abigail was flabbergasted. "Were you drinking on the roof?"

"For noise pollution," Fern explained, rolling her sparkling blue eyes. She could even make an obnoxious teenager expression like the eye roll seem spunky and hip.

"Oh, wow," Abigail said. She thought about it for a few

more seconds then started giggling.

"It's not funny," Zeke said, turning from the window.

Abigail tried to contain her laughter, which only made it burst out more merrily.

Just then Jamie came through the door.

"That guy is too much," he said. His cheeks looked red, maybe from drinking wine or maybe from the exertion of climbing ladders and running up the stairs. But probably from getting a bogus ticket.

"Did he give you a ticket?" Zeke wanted to know.

"No, but he wanted to," Jamie answered. He looked at Abigail, who was still giggling in short little spurts. "I talked him out of it." He gave her a quick, reassuring wink, which was not lost on her brother.

Zeke switched his gaze to Abigail, who tried very hard to look serious. Then he looked at Jamie, then back to Abigail, "What were you guys doing up there?"

Jamie opened his mouth to say something, but Abigail beat him to it, "We were looking at the lights." Zeke's eyes dropped to the wine glass in her hand. She tipped it at him as if he held a glass and she was clinking his glass with hers. Then she said pointedly, "Relaxing."

Zeke didn't say anything, though she could tell he was itching to. He looked back and forth between her and Jamie again, then he looked to Fern. She held his gaze for a moment before expertly quieting his angst by tilting her head the tiniest bit and lifting one side of her mouth in a sweet smile.

Zeke closed his eyes, gathering his thoughts. When he opened them Abigail could tell he had decided not to get involved with whatever had happened, or was still happening, between her and Jamie.

"I hope you got all of your relaxing out of your system," Zeke stressed the word 'relaxing' with more than a little bit of sarcasm. "Because we have big plans for tomorrow."

Chapter Eleven

The following morning brought two big surprises.

First, the largest snowstorm the region had seen in a while was suddenly on the near horizon. The trajectory of an oncoming cold front had switched directions unexpectedly and Pitkin Point found itself in the path of a major winter wonderland producing storm one week before Christmas.

Second, parked outside The Thinking Bean was the next big event of Mistletoe Madness, a two horse team pulling a wagon full of hay or, as Zeke had dubbed it, The Jingle Bell Hay Ride.

The wooden wagon was charming, decked out with real pine boughs and big red bows draped along the sides. Inside the wagon were bales of hay set up like benches around the edges, so several people could sit and enjoy the slow moving scenery. Several thick horse blankets were thrown over the tops of the hay bales to make the seats more comfortable, and softer, plaid woolen blankets were folded in neat piles, ready to cover cold laps or shoulders if necessary.

A pair of white draft horses were hitched to the wagon, their necks draped with brass sleigh bells and small red bows were tied into their flowing, white manes. A local rancher and friend of the family, Willard Gustaf, had brought the wagon and team for The Jingle Bell Hay Ride. In exchange for a small fee and a month's worth of free drinks at The Thinking Bean for himself and his wife, Emma, Willard would drive the team.

The Mistletoe Madness deal of the day was a free hay ride for anyone who purchased a drink in a to-go cup. Combine the availability of Santa Claus inside the coffee shop with the fact that it was the Saturday before Christmas and everyone was in town shopping anyway, made The Jingle Bell Hay Ride another huge success for Abigail's marketing genius big brother.

The place was packed and Abigail stayed busy all morning managing the ever growing line of little children who wanted to sit on Santa Claus' lap. She'd grown so accustomed to seeing Jamie in his Santa suit, as well as wearing her own costume, that she wondered what it would be like when they returned to wearing street clothes after Mistletoe Madness was over. In fact, she had started wondering what it would be like to find a job and move away after Christmas. Starting over once more in a faraway city. No longer seeing her parents and Zeke every day...or Jamie. Alone.

"Come on," Jamie said, reaching his hand towards her. She took it without knowing where they were going. She had been tucked into the farthest back corner of the book section, curled into one of the reading chairs that was shoved into a small nook there, sipping some hot tea and taking a little break. Jamie led her out towards the front of the store.

"Where are we going?" She asked.

He looked back at her, his smile hidden under the Santa beard, but visible in his eyes. "On a hay ride!"

Zeke had asked Jamie to go for a turn in the wagon and wave like a friendly Santa at anyone and everyone he saw.

Jamie told him he needed to take his Elf along. And now they were seated on one side of the wagon, sharing a hay bale and a blanket over their knees.

The day was definitely more cloudy and colder than it had been lately. The smell of snow was in the air and this seemed to have pulled more people into the main shopping streets of Pitkin Point. Christmas was almost here and snow was on the way. People needed to shop while the shopping was good.

The horse's hooves clopped on the pavement and their brass bells jingled merrily. A young family that Abigail didn't know sat opposite her and Jamie. The three little kids gawked at Jamie as he kept in character, ho-ho-ho-ing and waving at everyone they passed. Every now and then he would look sideways at one of the kids and give them a twinkly eyed smile or a wink.

The horses moved so slowly that it was possible to have conversations with people on the street as they passed. Abigail saw Judy outside Take the Cake and waved at her.

"Hi!" Judy exclaimed.

"Happy Holidays!" Abigail said.

Jamie gave Judy an official Santa Claus wave and she shook her head, laughing again.

"Your brother's got you guys hooked into his crazy stunts doesn't he?" She teased Abigail.

It was Abigail's turn to laugh, "He does!"

As the wagon inched away, Judy gestured towards her window and called out one more time to Abigail, "Everybody loves the window, by the way."

Abigail gave her a thumbs up.

"Dad!" A familiar voice came from further up the street. Jamie turned immediately and Abigail leaned out over the edge of the wagon past Jamie to see Dillon on the sidewalk in front of one of the town's best cafes. Raegan and Blake were with him. All three of them were watching the slow approach of Santa in the hay wagon with varying degrees of surprise on their faces.

Jamie beckoned Dillon over. "Come on, jump in!"

It warmed Abigail's heart to see the look on Dillon's face. Because teenagers are often stuck pretending to be grown up when, deep down, they still have a child's heart, she was afraid he was going to scowl and turn away. But instead, Dillon's face lit up at the chance to jump on the hay wagon, even if his Dad was dressed in a Santa Claus suit.

He started to run to the wagon then stopped at something Blake said. Dillon turned back to his mother and step-father and Abigail held her breath. She could see Raegan talking, but couldn't hear them, of course. After a few tense moments, she saw Raegan dip her head in a reluctant 'yes' and Dillon ran to the wagon.

Dillon used one hand to grab the box of the wagon as Jamie took the other hand firmly in his. With a big lift and pull effort, Dillon was up over the side and sitting on a hay bale. The three little kids riding with them watched in awe as Santa Claus performed this stunt. Dillon, being a nice kid, didn't give away that Santa was his Dad during the whole ride.

"No reindeer today, Santa?" Dillon asked Jamie with a twinkle in his eyes that was familiar to Abigail. She'd seen it in Jamie's eyes a thousand times.

"Ho-ho-ho, not today little boy. The reindeers are resting, getting ready for Christmas Eve," Jamie answered, staying in character. He nudged Abigail with his elbow, "Isn't that right, Elf?"

"Yes, Santa, they need their rest," Abigail agreed.

Dillon grinned at her, still in a teasing mood, "Do you have a name, Elf?"

Abigail hesitated. Did she have an Elf name? She'd never thought about it. She had just been Elf. Their three young passengers watched her with curiosity.

"Uh–sure, of course I do," Abigail said.

"Why, this is Abbah Dabbah Elf," Jamie chimed in, throwing in a ho-ho-ho for good measure.

"Abbah Dabbah Elf?" Dillon asked with playful skepticism.

"Yes, I'm Abbah Dabbah Elf," Abigail stuck her hand out to him as if they were meeting formally. Dillon took her hand and tipped an imaginary hat.

"Nice to meet you."

Somewhere along their route it started to snow. At first it was just a few flakes here and there that went unnoticed. But as the flakes became more regular they were tossed around on the chilling breeze that was picking up. The youngest of their fellow passengers, a little girl about three-years old, clapped her mittened hands together in front of her face and shouted, "It's snowing! It's snowing!"

Willard pulled the wagon up in front of The Thinking Bean a few minutes later. He climbed off of his seat at the front of the wagon and went to the back to help the young family get their little ones safely to the sidewalk. Jamie, Abigail and Dillon stood near the front end of the wagon box patiently waiting their turn. The great, white draft horse's ears flicked around, listening to all of the different sounds. Just as the last of the other family hopped to the ground, Zeke came out the front door to greet them.

As he stepped into the snow, he threw his arms up in his ringmaster move and declared, "It's snowing!"

Later, when they went over the details, they couldn't be sure why the horses spooked at the sight of Zeke's tall, spindly limbed Snowman costume, but spook they did.

The great beasts leaped in unison away from Zeke, heading sideways into the road with a clash of brass bells. As they forced the hitch into an unnatural position there was a horrible sound of crunching wood and metal added to the clamor of sleigh bells, and the horses bolted. Lurching forward, the wagon went out from under Abigail's feet and she started to tumble over the edge. Jamie grabbed her arm and pulled her back to the center of the wagon box where she sat down so hard her teeth smashed together.

Dillon, too, almost fell over the edge and was pulled back by his Dad. He fell on his hands and knees next to Abigail. The sound of men shouting faded away behind them as Jamie managed to grab hold of the front of the wagon box and stay on his feet. Because the reins were now dragging on the ground and whipping around the horse's back legs, they were even more spooked. The powerful draft horses were picking up speed and running away with the three of them stuck in back. Dillon started to get up.

"Stay down," Jamie shouted at him. He pulled his Santa hat, wig and beard off and dropped them into the wagon.

Dillon sat down next to Abigail. The horrible lurching and rumbling of the wagon rolled them back and forth and they bumped into each other repeatedly. She reached over and took his hand in hers, which he gripped tightly.

She could tell they were heading away from Main Street, which was good. With all of the people and cars out today a runaway team of horses would certainly cause chaos. Even though she was scared and being tossed around like a rag doll, Abigail tried to think about what they were approaching since they were heading away from Main Street. When the answer came, her stomach dropped with fear.

The train tracks.

She looked at Jamie as he was trying to keep his balance and they locked eyes. She knew that he knew exactly what she was thinking, because he was thinking it too.

It wasn't as if there were always trains on the train tracks, but there could be. Owen Jones had been killed crossing those train tracks when they were kids and Abigail had always been terrified of getting stuck on them. Jamie used to give her a hard time about her irrational fear of them.

"Do NOT get up," Jamie yelled at them again. Then he turned and started climbing up to the driver's seat.

Abigail didn't know if they were going faster than before, but it felt like they were. How long could horses run before they slowed down? What if they veered off the road or through a ditch? Wouldn't that roll the wagon? They could be thrown out, crushed, or trampled under the hooves of the huge draft horses.

Dillon looked at her, his eyes wide. She squeezed his hand and pulled him closer to her. She didn't want her fear to transfer to him. They both watched with growing panic as Jamie, the reins unreachable to him from the driver's seat, got ready to jump onto the horse's back.

With disbelief at what they were seeing, Abigail and Dillon sat mute and terrified in the back of the wagon. They watched as Jamie, looking like a young Santa surrounded by the swirling snowflakes of the oncoming storm, made a wild leap off of the driver's seat toward the broad backs of the draft horses. Without getting up, they couldn't see what happened after that. Abigail's heart was beating out of her chest. Where was Jamie? Why weren't they slowing down yet?

"Dad!" Dillon shouted, the same fear she had in her heart coming out in his voice.

"I've got 'em!" They heard Jamie's voice from somewhere on the other side of the driver's seat. Abigail thought she was going to cry she was so relieved. She did, actually, start to cry. She wrapped her arm around Dillon and they hugged in shared relief.

The horses began to slow down and within a few minutes had stopped completely. A full quarter mile to the train track.

The sound of a train whistle floated eerily through the light snow.

She and Dillon hopped off the back of the wagon as soon as it stopped. Abigail's knees wobbled a little as she landed on the ground and her stomach felt queasy.

"You okay?" Dillon asked her, a glimpse of the man he would eventually be coming through in his concern.

She nodded. "Yes, I'm fine."

They ran to the front of the wagon where Jamie was holding both of the horses gently by their bridles, talking low to them.

"Move slowly, they're still a little spooked," he said quietly. They did. As they approached, Jamie checked both of them with sideways glances, keeping most of his attention on the horses. "You both okay?"

"I think we're fine. What was that?" Abigail asked, trying to keep her voice calm.

"Yeah, Dad, what are you a stuntman or something?" Dillon added.

Jamie chuckled.

A few minutes later they were surrounded by people. Some had ran after them, some had driven their cars. Willard got there and took over caring for the horses. Deputy Diego pulled up in the sheriff's car. Abigail said a little prayer of thanks that Charlie wasn't on duty today. He would have probably locked them all up for several violations under obscure runaway horse laws.

Jamie looked after Dillon until Raegan showed up in a flurry of concern. Before leaving with her, Dillon gave his Dad a bear hug. Then he turned to Abigail and gave her one, too.

"Thank you, Dillon," she said.

"Thank you, Abby," he said and a little piece of her heart melted.

"See ya, Stuntman Santa." Dillon pointed at Jamie as he walked backwards towards his mother. Jamie waved his comment off, but Abigail could tell it meant something to him that his teenage son obviously thought he was cool.

Zeke showed up, stripped of his Snowman costume, wearing a pair of jeans he'd hastily pulled over his black leggings.

"Holy cow!" He said as he walked up to them both and grabbed them in his long, lanky arms. "Are you all right? Where's Dillon?"

"He's fine," Jamie said.

"We're fine," Abigail said. As she did her arm slipped easily around Jamie's waist in a show of solidarity. He grinned at her and put his arm, still wrapped in his Santa suit, around her shoulders.

"What are you doin' Snowman? Scaring the horses!" Jamie pushed Zeke's shoulder in jest.

"I am so sorry," Zeke said. His long face was full of guilt. Mistletoe Madness had gotten away from him and he knew it. "We're trimming the tree at Mom and Dad's tonight. Having dinner and eggnog and such. You and Dillon should come. My Mom is worried sick about you both," Zeke said.

Jamie looked at Abigail. "Is it okay with you if we come over?"

She nodded. Yes, that was perfectly okay with her.

Chapter Twelve

Zeke sent Abigail and Jamie home after their ordeal. Willard hauled the overly excited draft horses back to his place and Fern stepped in to help Zeke out for the rest of the afternoon at The Thinking Bean.

Even though she went straight home and didn't think she'd been too affected, Abigail couldn't shake the shivering sensation in her stomach. Adrenaline, she guessed.

Her Mom insisted that she take a hot bath right away, which she did. She put on some fuzzy fleece pants and a sweater while her hair dried into its curly mop. Her Mom was in the kitchen cooking goodies for their evening party, but she wouldn't hear of Abigail helping her or exerting herself in any way.

"You've been through a shocking experience, sweetie. You need to rest," she told her daughter.

Her Dad was in the living room going through lights for the tree. Abigail sat with him, sipping hot tea and watching the snow as it continued to fall outside.

Phantoms of the event came upon her every few minutes. The jolt of the wagon under her feet when it almost threw her out. Jamie's hand yanking her to safety. The look on Dillon's face as Jamie climbed up onto the driver's seat. The terrifying moment Jamie leaped out of their sight and they didn't know if he had made it or fallen under the wagon.

As the hours ticked away she began to wonder if the shiver in her stomach had to do completely with the runaway wagon or if it was also because Jamie was coming over. The thought of seeing him again kept slipping into her mind and filling her whole body with a fluttering anticipation. Distracted by the feeling, she had to ask her Dad to repeat himself whenever he said anything.

"Are you feeling okay, Abigail?" He finally asked. He was sitting in his corner chair, piles of tangled Christmas lights in his lap as well as to his right and left on the floor. His sharp eyes looked at her over the top of his glasses.

"I'm just a little shaky," she answered.

"Because of the wagon incident?"

She shrugged, taking a sip of her tea. Her fingers trembled on the warm mug. Her father watched her evenly over his glasses. His psychology brain patiently waiting for the truth to come to the surface.

"Is that all that's bothering you?" He asked.

Well, maybe not 100% patient.

"What else would it be?" She deflected.

He leaned back in his chair, "Well, now, let me see. You did recently lose your job, you packed up and left your apartment and the life you'd built and came home..." Again he peered over his glasses.

"Oh, that," she said.

"Yes, that."

She shrugged again.

"And there's Jamie," he said.

Abigail's stomach did a flip flop, "What? What about Jamie?"

"Your mother told me there's some possibility of a...a bit of a romance between you two?"

"She said what?"

He seemed surprised at her surprise. "Is she wrong?"

"What? No! I don't know!" Abigail was flustered.

"Any one of these situations can cause feelings of uncertainty or anxiety. Although, as your father, I would hope that a romance would make you happy, not anxious."

"There's no romance, Dad," Abigail said.

Her father seemed disappointed. "That's too bad, I've always liked Jamie."

She paused, curiosity overcoming exasperation. "You have?"

"Yes," he nodded slowly as he spoke. "He was a good friend to Zeke, and you. A nice, steady character, even when he was young." Again he peered over his glasses at her, this time with a smile in his eyes. "He doted over you when you were kids, that's for sure. A father likes a young man who dotes over his daughter."

"He did not dote over me." She waved her hand in the air as if erasing what her Dad had just said. Even as her stomach burst into butterflies.

"Well, you never wanted him to, but he did. It was painful to watch sometimes."

"Dad, stop."

He smiled at her, "Okay, okay, no more talk about romance."

He was true to his word and didn't say anything more about Jamie, but that didn't mean Abigail wasn't thinking about him. She excused herself to her room to get ready and spent the next few hours agonizing over what to wear for the tree trimming. Then chastising herself for fretting. She didn't want to look shaky or uncertain about anything. She also didn't want to look too fixed up, like she was trying too hard.

Yet, she did want Jamie to like what she wore. She liked the way his eyes lit up when he saw her dressed up. Then she felt guilty and ridiculous for feeling that way.

She was completely out of sorts about all of it.

Finally, she decided on a pair of jeans, a simple off-white V-neck sweater with flared sleeves and a pearl pendant necklace.

When she was finally ready, she took a long look in the mirror. Her jeans were her most flattering pair, the sweater was soft and hung nicely over her curves, her hair had extra shine and bounce because she'd let it air dry all afternoon. Abigail determined she looked fine, as good as she was going to look at least. It's not like this was a date or anything.

She went upstairs and found Zeke and Fern already arrived. Fern was becoming a regular fixture in Zeke's world. Their parents, Mom especially, couldn't have been more thrilled.

Abigail made conversation with Fern over the spinach dip, although she didn't eat any. Her stomach still felt fluttery.

The snow was really coming down now. What if Jamie decided not to come, choosing instead to ride out the storm and spend some quality time with Dillon on his own at the empty apartment? An irrational glumness fell over her. Zeke offered her some eggnog and she refused.

A firm knock on the door lifted her spirits and she almost ran to answer it. Managing to keep her cool, Abigail moved towards the door, but Zeke got to it first.

"There they are!" Zeke exclaimed.

And there they were. Jamie and Dillon came in the front door, brushing snow off their shoulders and stamping it from their boots. They both looked taller in her parent's house. Jamie especially.

"Thanks for inviting us," Jamie said as their Dad came to greet them.

"It's the least we could do after Zeke tried to kill you!"

Everyone laughed. Zeke groaned and took their coats to hang up. Jamie pulled his hat off, handing it to Zeke, leaving his hair in its signature out of control style. He ran one hand through it in an attempt to tame it and that's when he saw her. He paused, their eyes locking from across the room and everyone else fell away into the background. The fluttering in her stomach expanded and reached her heart, making it skip a beat. Even from across the room she could see the glimmer in his eyes.

Jamie's hand dropped and he smoothed the fabric of his black dress shirt. She couldn't look away from him. The side of his mouth lifted into a crooked, sexy smile.

"Jamie!" Her mother crowded past the others and gave him a hug. Then she turned to Dillon. "Dillon, Merry Christmas!" She hugged him, too. This kicked off a hugging fiesta between all of them, peppered with holiday greetings. Jamie hugged his way to her. First her Mom, then her Dad, then Fern, then he stood in front of Abigail, looking down at her, his body pressed against hers in the crowded, small space.

"Merry Christmas, Abby," he said softly, and wrapped his arms around her waist, pulling her into him for a hug. She let her arms circle his neck, pressing her cheek against his. His face was still a little cold from being outside, but his body was warm and strong, and he smelled amazing.

"Merry Christmas, Jamie," she whispered into his ear. His arms tightened around her, making her heart beat even faster. For a few moments Abigail was utterly lost in his embrace. She didn't want him to let go.

But let go he must. There was dinner to serve and eggnog to drink and, of course, a tree that needed trimming.

They had prime rib, which was delicious, and garlic mashed potatoes, and a wilted salad made with greens, bacon and a hot dressing. Abigail, Jamie and Dillon sat on one side of the long dining room table. Zeke and Fern sat on the other. Mom and Dad sat on each end.

Abigail was glad to be sitting next to Jamie. She knew she was having exaggerated feelings because of their earlier ordeal, but she felt safe next to him. It was a nice feeling, especially when her parents asked for details of the runaway wagon.

Dillon chimed in and told the story of how Jamie, in full Santa regalia, saved the day. It was good to hear him so animated and open. He told the story with a lot of funny details that made all of them laugh.

"How did you know what to do?" Her father asked Jamie.

Jamie shrugged. "I've seen a lot of westerns."

"You're crazy," Zeke said, laughing into his wine glass before taking a sip.

Abigail laughed along with everyone else, but she felt the shivering in her stomach again and she had to press her hands into her lap to hide the fact that they were trembling.

Jamie noticed and gave her a quiet, questioning look. She smiled weakly at him then had to look at her plate. She wasn't trying to make a scene. She felt queasy and wished she hadn't eaten so much dinner.

Jamie continued talking and laughing with Zeke and her parents, while at the same time reaching under the tablecloth and finding her hands clenched in her lap, ice cold. He wrapped his hand over hers, holding them, comforting her quietly. His touch calmed her stomach and she glanced at him. He didn't look at her, but gave her hands a squeeze under the table, telling her everything was all right while never letting on to anyone else.

After dinner they all moved into the living room to trim the tree. With her parents taking on the role of surrogate grandma and grandpa to Dillon, Zeke and Fern making eyes at each other over the eggnog, and she and Jamie sewing long strings of popcorn and cranberries together on the couch, the whole scene had a very hometown family Christmas vibe. Abigail was enjoying it more than she ever thought possible.

"How do you do this?" Jamie asked her. His thick fingers weren't conducive to the fine work of pushing a needle through the fat end of a piece of popcorn with a light enough touch that it didn't break. He had shattered several pieces already.

Abigail giggled, "Here." She handed him her string that already had three pieces of popcorn strung in a row. "Let's trade. You do my cranberries and I'll do your popcorn."

"Thank you." He carefully picked a cranberry out of the bowl and pushed his needle through it lengthwise. He lowered his voice conspiratorially, "I don't want your Mom to think I'm shirking my duties."

Abigail glanced at her mother, who was in the middle of offering Dillon another cookie from a mound of Christmas cookies she had balanced on a platter.

"I think she's distracted trying to put your son into a sugar coma," Abigail said.

Jamie laughed. There were his dimples, and the corners of his eyes crinkling up, lifting her into a state of delight. She had a sudden urge to lean over and kiss him on the cheek. The idea startled her so much she stopped sewing and stared at him.

"What?" Jamie asked, noticing her focused attention. "Am I doing it wrong?" He held up his neatly sewn cranberries for inspection.

"No," Abigail said. She blinked, but didn't look away, "You're doing everything right."

Say what she would about Jamie Turner, that he was goofy and joked too much and had infuriated her all through her formative teenage years, but the man knew when a woman was thinking about kissing him. That was obvious.

His expression changed. He looked deeply into her eyes, allowing his gaze to slide down her cheek and across her lips before lifting it again. When he spoke, his voice was gruff, a bedroom voice if she'd ever heard one, "Abby..."

A crackling sensation shuddered through her. As if she'd touched a live wire. But she hadn't touched anything. Only on the truth. She wanted Jamie. She could see them being together. She trusted him. And, most earth shattering of all, she loved him.

Abigail swallowed hard. Chills shot up and down her spine then across her shoulders and down her arms, making her shiver.

"Abby, I-" he started.

"Take me to the Christmas dance," Abigail interrupted him. She pressed her knee into his, leaning towards him, wishing he could take her in his arms right now.

Abigail had never felt like this before, so certain she was right, so absolutely convinced that everything she'd ever wanted had been staring her in the face her entire life. She'd finally seen it.

"Take you to the dance?" He looked disoriented. He hadn't expected that.

She nodded with such conviction her curls bounced. "I want to go to the Christmas dance with you."

A smile slowly took over his face and when it was complete, Jamie was beaming. She basked in his happiness. As sure of his feelings as she was her own.

"That's a great idea. I kinda wanted to bring that up myself, but I didn't know if you'd be open to it," he said. "It will be nice to go with a friend. No pressure, you know?"

Chapter Thirteen

The winter storm hit in full force on the same day as The Dickens Party. That was the day before Christmas Eve, and it rang in with almost three feet of snow, white out driving conditions, and winds that reached blizzard force. Most people had the good sense to stay inside. Batten down the hatches and spend the day cooking or reading or sitting by a nice, cozy fire.

Zeke was not most people.

His dedication to the Mistletoe Madness schedule was real. Insisting that they continue with their plans for the day, he bickered with Abigail over the phone about when she was planning on coming in and what she was going to wear.

"Zeke, I'm not driving in this weather and, if I was, I would not wear that stupid Elf costume," she told him from the living room couch.

"Of course you're not wearing the Elf costume. It's the Dickens Party today. Don't worry, Fern has some extra things you can wear for this party," he said.

Why wasn't she surprised that Fern had a variety of Victorian era clothes laying around? Probably steampunk.

"Zeke, I—"

"Jamie's coming to get you so you don't have to drive," her brother said.

That was not what she wanted to hear.

"No, Zeke, that's ridiculous. Tell him not to do that," she insisted.

The last thing she wanted was to be alone with Jamie for any reason. It was humiliating enough that she'd asked him to the dance when it turned out he had no feelings for her whatsoever. On top of that she couldn't come up with a good reason to get out of it. She really, really didn't want to ride with him through a blizzard to work at The Thinking Bean.

"Too late, he already left," Zeke informed her.

Sure enough, a few minutes later there was a knock on the front door. She let her Dad answer, wanting to avoid looking Jamie in the eye for as long as possible. He'd come out in a blizzard to get her, she could hardly tell him to go away.

As he chatted with her Dad about the condition of the roads, Abigail pulled on her heaviest coat, her snow boots, and a red wool hat. Then she wrapped a long red wool scarf several times around her neck and up over her mouth. Partly to protect herself from the cold and partly to keep her emotions masked.

Outside, the wind blew the snow hard into her face as she followed Jamie down the sidewalk. His old pickup that he used to do odd handyman jobs was running and warm, waiting for them. When they got closer to the street and away from the protection of the house, Jamie took her arm in a firm grip and walked her to the passenger side of the pickup. The protective move made her heart sad.

Inside the cab Christmas music blasted along with the heater. Jamie turned the volume down.

"Nothing like a ton of snow to get you in the Christmas spirit," he said, putting on his seatbelt.

Abigail nodded, pretending that she was too cold to uncover her mouth. Maybe she could make the whole ride without any real conversation. It was only a five minute drive to The Thinking Bean from her parent's house. She failed to calculate the additional time it would take to drive through blinding snow flurries, contend with ice building up on the windshield, and huge drifts of snow blocking some of the main roads.

"We'll get there, I promise," Jamie told her at one point.

She believed him, but she remained quiet. This whole thing seemed like an exercise in futility. The Dickens Party, The Thinking Bean, the Christmas Dance, all of it was just a huge waste of time. Nobody was coming out in this kind of weather to go to a coffee shop party. She and Jamie were going to the dance as friends only. She had misread everything and he didn't have romantic feelings for her after all. Yet her feelings had only now become clear and they were making her miserable.

She was in the impossibly ridiculous situation of being in love with Jamie Turner and crushed under the realization that he didn't love her back. Probably never had.

They pulled up to The Thinking Bean, which was just a blur of bricks behind a wall of blowing snow this morning. As soon as Jamie put the pickup in park, Abigail hopped out of her side and headed straight for where she thought the door was located. Certainly she could find her way across a sidewalk in a blizzard without his help. The less she could interact with Jamie today, the better.

As expected, the shop was empty save for Zeke and Fern. The smell of fresh coffee greeted her as she pushed through the door, followed by Jamie and a harsh gust of wind carrying wet, heavy snow.

"Yuletide Greetings, sister!" Zeke called out to her. He

was decked out in a white dress shirt, red paisley vest and, of course, his now infamous top hat.

She pulled the scarf from her face and glared at him, "Bah humbug."

"Come with me." Fern helped her out of her coat. "I have some adorable things you can wear."

Without a backwards glance, Abigail followed Fern upstairs to choose from several high waisted, floor length, flouncing skirts and fitted jackets hung up in Zeke's bedroom. They were definitely steampunk, but still very doable for a modern day Dickens party.

Abigail chose a skirt in a broad red and black plaid and a black jacket that buttoned tightly around her waist and flounced out over her hips and bottom. Fern wore a black and tan striped skirt in a similar cut and a brown V-neck jacket that also had a high collar with stiff ruffles along the edge, which showed off her elegant neck and pixie blonde hair cut.

"Thank you, Fern," Abigail said, twirling in a circle. "You have beautiful clothes."

"You look gorgeous in that, especially with your hair," Fern gushed. She gave Abigail a knowing look, "Jamie is going to trip over himself when he sees you."

The words shot through Abigail's injured ego and pierced her aching heart. All of the color drained out of her face, making her even more pale than normal.

"Are you okay?" Fern asked.

Abigail couldn't answer without crying. And she absolutely did not want to cry. She avoided looking Fern in the eye and sat down on the edge of Zeke's bed, biting her lower lip.

"Abigail, what's the matter?" Fern, full of concern, sat down next to her and Abigail couldn't hold it all in anymore. She spilled the beans.

She told Fern about her and Jamie's lifelong relationship, growing up together, the wonderful times, the misunderstandings. She told her about how she'd been attracted to him ever since returning and that she'd thought he felt the same way. As she relayed the moment she realized that she was in love with him and asked him to the dance, then what he'd said in return, Abigail teared up. Her heart was hurting knowing that Jamie just wanted to be friends, but it did feel good to tell someone else the whole story.

"Oh, honey." Fern patted Abigail's back, her brow furrowed with dismay. "That's terrible." As she patted her back, Fern's dismay turned into something else. Confusion.

"What is it?" Abigail sniffed.

"It's just...I don't understand. I thought he was really into you. I mean, he can barely take his eyes off you," Fern explained. "It just doesn't make sense."

"I don't know," Abigail sighed and sniffed again.

"Maybe he's one of those weirdos that only likes you until you like them back," Fern suggested. They both chuckled at the idea.

"He is kind of weird, I guess," Abigail said. They laughed again. Somehow, this little heart-to-heart made her feel better.

By the time they went back downstairs she was able to face the situation with some grace. The stylish steampunk outfit helped.

There was still nobody in the shop. Zeke sat on the couch in the cafe area, sipping a Cappuccino. Jamie wasn't anywhere around.

"Where's Jamie?" Fern asked, glancing at Abigail.

"He won't button his vest so he is not allowed in the front where customers might see him," Zeke spoke extra loud so anyone on the first floor could hear him.

Jamie's frustrated voice came from the storage room, "I'll button the vest when another human being shows up!"

"He's pouting," Zeke told them. Fern raised her eyebrows at Abigail and they joined Zeke.

They played a game of cards to pass the time. Outside the wall to ceiling windows the snow continued to come down hard. Another foot or more of fresh snow built up on Jamie's pickup, and he still hadn't emerged into the cafe area.

Abigail excused herself to go look for a book to read to pass the time. That's when she found him. He was sitting in one of the chairs up against the window in the front book section. A pile of botany books balanced on the spindly table next to him, the lamp gave off a warm glow.

Jamie had on dark jeans and boots, a white dress shirt and a forest green vest, unbuttoned. He looked up when she walked towards him and she felt the familiar thrill move through her body when she caught his eye. She smiled at him because she couldn't help herself. He moved like he was going to stand.

"Don't get up," she said. She moved gracefully towards him, enjoying the swishing of the elaborate skirt and knowing that, if nothing else, she looked quite eye catching in her ensemble. She sat down in the other chair nestled next to his.

"You look great." He hadn't looked away from her the entire time.

She thought about what Fern had said, that Jamie couldn't take his eyes off of her. She smiled quietly at him. Not sure what to think about any of it anymore.

"Thank you, you look nice, too."

Jamie's face turned a little red and Abigail had a glimmer of hope flit across her heart. She picked up one of the books in his stack.

"Urban Botanics?" She raised an eyebrow.

The sound of the front door opening and new voices chattering interrupted them. A cold draft of air came around the corner.

"Customers!" Zeke called out so Jamie, so the whole world, could hear. Jamie lifted his gaze to the ceiling and stood up, buttoning his vest.

He offered her his hand, "My lady?"

She took his hand.

The Dickens Party had officially begun.

❧

ONCE ABIGAIL TOLD her mother that she was going to the Christmas Dance with Jamie, Sarah Ackerman went a little bonkers. Offering multiple suggestions of what she could possibly wear, only to refute each suggestion with a mumbled comment, "No, that's too casual...Too risqué, that won't do...The material is too thin, she'll freeze to death!"

"Mom, it doesn't matter. I'll just wear my black skirt," Abigail suggested.

"Oh, sweetie, you don't want to look like an old lady, do you?"

Quite honestly, Abigail had lost her enthusiasm for going to the dance the moment Jamie assumed they were going as friends. It didn't really matter what she wore. The chance of the evening turning into a romantic date were next to nil. And the weather made it impossible for them to drive to the city and go shopping for anything spectacular anyway. If she had her way the dance would disappear in a puff of smoke and she wouldn't have to think about it anymore.

For a brief time during The Dickens Party Abigail thought maybe her wish would come true. Deputy Diego had stopped by to make sure they were all right and let it slip that the town council might cancel the dance due to the weather. But that did not happen. The snow had stopped before night-fall and any rumors of Pitkin Point giving in to Mother Nature were squelched. They would dig out and persevere.

The Christmas Dance would proceed on Christmas Eve the way it had for over 50 years. Abigail was doomed to go and have her heart crushed.

"Sweetie." A knock sounded on her bedroom door. Her Mom opened the door and poked her head in. "Can I show you something?"

Abigail was relaxing in her bedroom, trying to decide if she should start looking for jobs online now or wait until the holidays were over.

"Sure, Mom, come in," she sat up and threw her legs off the bed so she was sitting on the edge.

"Look what I found!" Her Mom stepped into the room carrying a long, midnight blue dress on a hanger.

It was the dress she'd worn to the Christmas Dance in high school. The one Jamie had told her he remembered.

"Where did you find that?" Abigail stood and inspected the dress. It was still beautiful, deep blue velvet, a scalloped neckline, crystals sewn into the bodice, along the cuffs of the long sleeves, and on the hem.

"It was hanging in the closet of my sewing room...your old room." Her mother was beaming. "I think you should wear this to the dance," she said, unable to contain her excitement.

"This?" Abigail eyed the garment again. "It's so old, isn't it?"

"Oh, this kind of dress never goes out of style."

"I don't think it would fit me anymore."

"I can take it out if you need me to. It's such a beautiful color on you, Abigail. And the material, look at the material. So rich."

The dress was exquisite. She remembered feeling like a princess in that dress. Like the most beautiful girl in town. It had been the dress that inspired Jamie to ask her to prom. Was it pathetic of her to wear it now? Would he think she was trying to drum up old feelings, trick him into liking her again?

"Try it on." Her Mom pulled the dress off of its hanger.

After a moment's hesitation, Abigail thought why not?

A few small areas would need adjusting, Abigail was a bit curvier now than she had been in high school, but otherwise the dress fit. Not only that, her Mom had a long, white winter cloak and a matching white winter hat and gloves that she convinced Abigail would go perfectly with the dress. Abigail had a pair of knee high white boots to complete the look.

She had the perfect dress to wear to the dance, and she was in love with her date. Still, Abigail wished with all of her heart that she didn't have to go.

Chapter Fourteen

On the morning of Christmas Eve every person in Pitkin Point who owned a snow blower or a plow on the front of their pickup, or a hand held heavy duty snow shovel, chipped in to dig out the park. With so many hands the job of clearing the pathways, the gazebo, and the open areas where the dance floor was later laid out, was short work. Despite the bitter cold, everyone was excited. The snow that covered everything as far as the eye could see, combined with the already placed lights and decorations, made this one of the most magical backgrounds any of them had ever seen for the Christmas Dance.

Jamie was one of the people working on snow removal, so Abigail didn't see or talk to him all day on Christmas Eve. Maybe he would be too tired to go to the dance at all, she ventured to hope.

No luck there. Jamie called at 6:00 to double check that he would be picking her up at 7:00.

"Yes, that's fine," she said.

"Wait till you see it, Abby," he said with delight. "It's

really something else. You know that song 'Winter Wonderland'?"

"Yes."

"That's exactly what it looks like."

When the call ended, sadness welled up in her again and she had to let it out. A good cry into her pillow while face down on her bed helped...a little. She washed her face and did her makeup, got dressed in the blue dress that now fit perfectly thanks to her Mom, and gathered her pure white cloak, hat, and fuzzy gloves. With nothing else to do but wait, she sat down on the living room couch and looked at the Christmas tree, trying to get into the spirit of the evening.

Not even Jamie's obvious pleasure at seeing her did anything to lift her mood.

"Wow," he finally spoke after an extended pause where he simply gazed at her after being shown in the door by her Dad.

Abigail shifted uncomfortably from one foot to the other. She had originally wanted him to think she looked pretty, but she felt no joy in it now. It didn't change anything else about their relationship. A dark cloud hung over her tonight and nothing was getting through.

Jamie tilted his head and looked harder at the front of her dress where it showed through the opening of her cloak.

"Is that...is that your old blue dress?" He asked.

Abigail felt heat rising in her cheeks. What a way to start the evening.

"Mom altered it. I only wore it once," she defended herself.

"No, I didn't mean it like that. I like that dress," he said.

She flounced by him, not wanting to talk about it.

"Ready to go?" She asked.

Jamie was surprised at her reaction. He looked with confusion at her parents, who were seeing them off before getting themselves out the door and to the dance. Her Dad patted him on the shoulder in a show of solidarity or support or condolence, it wasn't clear which.

Abigail was prepared for many disappointments this evening. Jamie's description of the beautiful landscape surrounding the cleared area of the dance was not one of them. All of the extra snow did make it look enchanting, like they were going to a dance inside of a giant Christmas snow globe.

Jamie offered her his arm and watched her reaction as they entered the park, "What do you think?"

"It's just stunning," she said. Not only were they surrounded by undulating drifts of snow on all sides, but the snow had blanketed the trees, gazebo, streetlamp and wreaths as well. The Christmas decorations twinkled and winked through the frozen white.

There was a bonfire in the center of the park and gas patio heaters that looked like small fire pits were placed strategically near benches, the dance floor, and the band, keeping everyone warm. There were booths set up where you could get roasted chestnuts, hot chocolate or hot apple cider, and fresh kettle corn that was made right there in a huge cast iron kettle heating on its own fire.

What made Abigail's spirits lift most of all, however, were the people. The whole town of Pitkin Point had come out dressed in their warmest and finest clothes. They had brought the Christmas spirit with them and were talking, laughing and dancing. The feeling of celebration was everywhere and Abigail realized that she wouldn't be able to stay in her dark mood while in this place.

"You make it even more beautiful," Jamie said. His voice brought her attention back to him, to them, standing arm-in-arm at the edge of the Christmas Dance. He was gazing at her, something of a dreamy look in his eyes.

She started to say something when she was distracted by a

top hat peeking out from a group of people nearby. The top hat moved swiftly towards them.

"Merry Christmas!" Zeke greeted them happily. His black overcoat and bright green scarf wrapped several times around his neck went well with the top hat. He was grinning ear to ear and Abigail knew why. Fern was on his arm.

"Abigail," Fern exclaimed, "You look like a snow princess!"

Abigail blushed at the compliment, especially coming from Fern who looked amazing in one of her steampunk style skirts in green plaid and a Victorian style wool coat that showed off her figure.

"That's exactly what she looks like, a snow princess," Jamie agreed.

Fern's eyebrows lifted and she gave Abigail a look. The band started a new song, a waltz. Jamie turned to face Abigail and bowed. She had been so distracted with her dark mood and wanting to avoid the dance in general that she'd barely looked at him or what he was wearing...until now.

If she had to choose one word to describe Jamie's attire this evening, that word would be 'dashing'.

He wore a heavy black coat with a wide collar that was turned up against the cold. Two rows of brass buttons ran from just under the collar to his waist, pulling the coat in tight and warm, and emphasizing his masculine form. His hair was not quite as wild as it had a tendency to get, contained and shaped with some product and effort on his part, but still a rich, wavy brown. He wore a blue wool scarf knotted and tucked into the front of his coat. She hadn't noticed the scarf before, it was the same midnight blue of her dress.

He looked mature and handsome. Quietly watching her reaction. Patiently waiting for her to take notice of him. Like always.

She felt the blush on her cheek turn into something more, that impossible sparkling smile that happens when love cannot hide any longer. She couldn't help herself, even if he didn't feel the same way. Looking at Jamie Turner in this winter wonderland, the music floating around them, the lights twinkling behind him, she loved him more than ever.

"Thank you," she said.

Jamie's face broke into his crooked, goofy smile. The smile he'd given her the very first time they met in grade school. The smile she'd seen thousands of times. Countless times. The smile she now knew had lived deep in her heart her whole life.

"Would you like to dance?" He asked, offering her his black leather gloved hand.

She nodded and placed her soft, white gloved hand in his. He gripped it carefully and led her to the middle of the dance floor where he twirled her once under his arm before placing one hand on her waist and one holding her hand in proper waltz stance. She laughed with surprise at his expertise as she placed her free hand on his shoulder.

"You waltz?" She asked.

He nodded, "I learned after the last time I saw you in that dress."

With that confession Jamie Turner took her breath away. He moved her smoothly across the dance floor, turning slowly, using the lightest pressure of his hand in hers or on her waist to lead. She couldn't take her eyes off of him. She could barely breathe. They were no longer dancing, they had been lifted into the air and were floating. The cold fell away, the other dancers fell away, only the music and Jamie were here on this starry Christmas Eve.

It was truly starry, too. The storm had officially moved on and left in its wake a blanket of twinkling stars that glimmered over everyone at the Christmas Dance. But none more than Abigail and Jamie.

They danced until the band took a break and they were forced to mingle with mere mortals again. Jamie got them both hot apple cider and they strolled to the frozen pond and back. A section of the pond had been roped off and ice skaters, mostly kids and families with small children, skimmed across the top. As they walked, friends and acquaintances greeted them, everyone smiling and waving, sometimes congratulating them for surviving the runaway wagon incident. Always merry, always kind.

One such interaction was with Frank Adams, the owner of the local bowling alley and bar.

"Merry Christmas, you two," Frank said. His barrel chest even larger than normal because it was wrapped in layers for warmth.

"Merry Christmas, Frank," Jamie said.

"Merry Christmas," Abigail echoed.

"Say, I saw your work at the coffee shop, and at Judy's place," Frank said to Abigail. Her work? He must mean the window paintings. "I was wondering if I could hire you to do something like that for my place?"

"Window painting?" Abigail clarified.

"Yes, not Christmas, of course, since it's almost over. But for New Year's Eve. We're having a big party that night," Frank explained.

Abby nodded, pleased at the idea. "Sure, Frank. I'll come by the day after Christmas."

With that settled, she and Jamie continued on their stroll back, she hoped, to the dance floor. As they walked an idea popped into her head and distracted her from their surroundings.

After a minute, Jamie noticed. "What are you thinking about so hard?"

She came back to the dance, to him. "Oh, nothing really."

"It looks like more than nothing," he pressed.

"I was just thinking...I wonder how many other businesses might want their windows painted?"

Jamie raised his eyebrows, impressed at the idea, nodding in agreement, "And they could hire someone like you to paint them?"

"Yes, something like that," she said. Her mind clicked along, trying to quickly calculate how much work that would mean for someone who was needing to find a job.

Another minute passed in silence as they got closer and closer to the dance floor. Jamie cleared his throat.

"So you're thinking you might stay here? Start a business?" He asked.

His question lacked emotion, but Abigail's response was strong anyway. A sense of possibility filled her heart. Perhaps she could run her own business, paint for a living, not have to leave her family, her friends, or Jamie.

She looked at him sideways as they walked. Her arm was still linked in his. It felt right for them to be a couple at the Christmas Dance. She wondered if any of this mattered to him as much as it mattered to her.

"I think I would consider it, for sure. If I could build up a freelance kind of business and paint my own artwork on the side."

"You think you would be happy living a small town life?"

She looked around at the glittering snow covered dance and leaned into his arm, smiling, "It's growing on me."

They were at the gazebo, a few couples stood inside looking out over the park. Jamie stopped and turned to her. "Want to go in the gazebo?"

The musicians were warming up, back from their break. Abigail looked towards them, wanting to float again.

"You don't want to dance?" She asked him.

Jamie glanced at the dance floor that was beginning to fill with people. He looked back at her, into her eyes, excited about something, that much she could tell. "In a minute. Let's go up here first."

He took her hand and led her up the stairs. Back to the exact place they'd stood only days ago. The day they'd decided to just be friends.

A little of the magic drained out of Abigail as they stood there. The view was still beautiful, even more so tonight than it had been on that night. But the memory of that conversation made her sad. It made tonight seem like nothing more than wishful thinking on her part. A fantasy that would disappear like Cinderella's dress and carriage at midnight.

The other couples left the gazebo. Called by the music back to the dance floor. Yet she and Jamie stayed, like silent statues watching happiness pass in front of them, not being able to reach out and take some of their own.

Jamie started talking, his eyes still trained on the couples dancing. "It's been quite a Christmas, hasn't it?"

"Yes, it has," she answered. Miserable at the idea of their date being reduced to small talk.

"It's been good, though, working with you and...everything," he continued. He glanced at her. All of the excitement he'd had when he pulled her up the steps was gone. She didn't know why.

"Mm-hmm," she murmured. She didn't want to talk about work.

He turned to her, something on his mind. "We agreed that we were going to be friends, right?" He swept his arm towards the dance floor and band, and the festivities beyond. "All of this is just...we're just...I mean, isn't that what we agreed?" He looked at her then looked away, as if the sight of her physically hurt him.

She nodded, "It is..."

Jamie's face fell and he gave her one last pained glance before dropping his gaze to the floor at their feet.

"Right," he said.

"But that's not what I want, Jamie," she said quietly.

His eyes shot up from the floor as if he could catch her words in the air if he was fast enough.

"What?" He didn't trust what he'd heard.

"That's not what I want. I don't want to be just friends with you."

There. She'd done it. She had told him the truth. Whatever the consequences, she could hold on to that much.

Jamie stared at her. He didn't speak or move or respond in any way. Just stared. Like she was an apparition that he couldn't believe was real.

Then, ever so slowly, a smile entered his eyes. It spread to the outer corners of his eyes so they crinkled. It lifted his cheeks, pulling up the corners of his mouth unevenly into his crooked grin. While joy moved across his face, his eyes held hers, filled with tenderness, disbelief, and longing. He pulled one of his gloves off and reached up to her face, barely touching her cheek with his fingers, cupping her chin in his hand.

"I was hoping you were going to say that." His crooked grin became his goofy smile and he lifted his gaze to the rafters, lightly tipping her head back so she would see.

Mistletoe.

Mistletoe everywhere.

Mistletoe madness.

Just like he'd told her he'd done years ago when he wanted to convince her to kiss him in the gazebo. Bunches of Mistletoe dangled along each of the eight rafters, over every inch of the ceiling, side-by-side with no space between them, all of it was covered with Mistletoe lit up by white Christmas lights.

She gasped with delight. Dazzled by the sight of it and the sentiment it held. When she looked back at Jamie he was watching her. His hand still brushing her cheek. When he spoke it was with the voice of a man returning home from a long journey. A patient man who had finally reached his destination.

"I love you, Abigail Ackerman. I have loved you for so, so long."

"Jamie," she said as she pressed his hand against her cheek, wanting him to touch her, wanting him to kiss her. "I love you, too."

In an instant he had his arm around her waist, pulling her to him as he bent towards her and touched his lips to hers. Carefully at first, as if she were made of porcelain and he didn't want to break her. Then he let his hand move from her cheek to her hair. He pushed his fingers into her curls and his kiss became firmer, more possessive.

Abigail didn't know she could lose herself so completely in a kiss. She had never known such a feeling could exist. As if she no longer needed the ground below her feet or air in her lungs. All she needed was Jamie.

As first kisses go, it was possibly one of the longest build ups ever known in Pitkin Point, seeing as they'd met when Abigail was in 3rd grade and Jamie was in 4th. But it made up for the long wait by being one of the most publicly romantic first kisses in the history of the town. One that nobody who knew them was surprised to see, but one that everyone was happy had finally come to be.

When Jamie pulled away from Abigail to tell her again, as he planned to for the rest of their lives, how much he loved her, a cheer erupted from the dance floor. Led by, among a handful of others, Zeke and Fern, who were two of the loudest voices. Surprised and suddenly shy from the attention, Abigail and Jamie ducked their heads in half bows to their impromptu audience.

The band played on and the couples returned to swirling across the floor under the starlit Christmas Eve night. Jamie turned back to Abigail, his eyes shining, and took her by the hand.

"Now we dance," he said.

And never was a truer statement ever spoken.

THANK you for reading Mistletoe Madness! If you enjoyed this book you may enjoy the other books in the series...

Enchanting Eve - Halloween Romance

Love is at the Table - Thanksgiving Romance

New Year in Paradise - New Year's Eve Romance

IF YOU'RE in the mood for another Christmas romance, get your copy of Charlotte's Christmas Charade the first book in A Sugar Plum Romance series – antics of chefs who get in over their heads at Christmas time and end up in charming holiday love stories!

Epilogue

Abigail looked anxiously out the front window of The Thinking Bean. The sky was overcast and cloudy and she hoped the weather reports were right. They had been calling for snow on Christmas Eve for the past week, and if she didn't get snow on her wedding day she was afraid she would be disappointed.

Snow was the perfect weather for her and Jamie to get married in, just as Christmas Eve was the perfect day. It had been one year to the day since they shared their first kiss in front of the whole town of Pitkin Point. And today they would share their first kiss as man and wife in the very same gazebo. Snow would make the day completely perfect.

"Abbah Dabbah, you look amazing!" Zeke said as he entered the cafe from the book section of the shop.

Her dress was pure white, off the shoulder with faux fur trim. Her bodice and long sleeves shimmered like ice in the light and had an extra dab of faux fur on her cuffs. The skirt flared out at just above her hips and fell elegantly to the floor in three layers with a short train trailing for just a few feet behind her when she walked. Abigail's hair was pulled up in an elaborate mass of dark, shining curls and decorated with red and white roses.

She turned to Zeke, who looked handsome himself in a black tuxedo complete with a Christmas red vest. He was Jamie's best man and had been fussing for weeks about his responsibilities. So far, he hadn't lost the rings or anything dramatic. However, they were all a little nervous about what he had planned for his best man toast at the reception.

"Don't let Jamie in here," Fern called to her fiancé. Zeke had popped the question to Fern over Thanksgiving. Abigail liked to think that her and Jamie's wedding plans had pushed her brother over the edge into finally proposing to Fern. She was Abigail's maid of honor and now her future sister-in-law. Abigail couldn't have wished for anyone whom she would rather call her best friend and her sister.

"I'm not letting him in anywhere," Zeke defended himself. "I'm just coming in to give my sister a good luck kiss before we head over to the gazebo. Everything ready?" Zeke was talking to Dillon who had followed him into the cafe area. He was Jamie's groomsmen, looking grown up and dapper in his tuxedo and green vest.

"Yup," Dillon grinned at Abigail. It was the same lopsided grin of his father's, and whenever she saw it Abigail's heart warmed. "Abby, you look beautiful," Dillon said, a fierce blush rushing up his cheeks. Still awkward and gangly like any 14-year old boy, but she found out every day what a wonderful young man he was.

"Thank you, Dillon," she reached out to him and he came to her to give her a hug. Zeke did as well, kissing her on the cheek.

"Okay, now out. Go manage the groom. He's loose if you two aren't with him," Fern shooed them on their way.

"These are ready," Judy informed them, holding up one of the bouquets she had been checking. She was Abigail's bridesmaid. Both Judy and Fern looked brilliant in their dresses. Judy in green, Fern in red. The bouquets, made up of pine, holly and red and white roses, contrasted beautifully with their dresses and the white of Abigail's.

Nothing much was left to do. Her parents, Fern, and Judy were to escort her across the street at the designated time and the wedding would commence. They had done some extra decorating at the gazebo by putting up a fresh Scotch Pine in the center. Decorating it with thousands of white lights as well as gold, red, green, and midnight blue ribbons and shining bulbs. Jamie's vest was midnight blue, in honor of her blue dress that had captured his heart so many years ago. And, of course, she wore a midnight blue ribbon in her hair as well as one hanging from her bouquet as her "something blue".

"It's almost time, sweetie," her Dad said.

Abigail glanced into the cloudy skies and looked for any sign of snowflakes. None yet. She sighed, then smiled. She knew Jamie was doing the same thing. They had both decided months ago that snow during their ceremony would be pretty epic. She knew he was keeping one eye on the clouds.

Besides the lack of snow, everything else about their ceremony, their life really, was pretty spot on perfect. At least for them it was perfect.

Abigail had been able to build a pretty decent freelance business over the past year, painting decorative windows for small businesses in Pitkin Point and surrounding towns. It was enjoyable work that paid well and left her a lot of free time, which she used to do some more traditional paintings on canvas. Just like she'd always dreamed of doing. Zeke had featured some of her artwork on the walls of the The Thinking Bean, and she'd even sold a few.

Jamie had found his calling when he got a job over the summer at the local plant nursery. He had quickly rose in the ranks to manager. Grace and Sam Jenkins, who owned the place, were looking at retiring in the next few years, and Jamie was considering buying the business from them and being his own boss. He loved the work and was very good at it. To Abigail, it seemed like an excellent fit for him.

"It's time," her Mom announced, beaming at her only daughter as she handed her the bridal bouquet. "You look gorgeous, sweetie."

"Thank you," Abigail said as she took her father's arm and the small wedding party walked across the street to the park.

They would be married at the gazebo, go to the town hall for a luncheon and cake, then join the Christmas Eve dance. The dance would act as the end of their reception. This way they could have what they both wanted, a small, intimate ceremony and celebration combined with a huge bash that allowed everyone in town to come.

As they drew closer to the gazebo, Abigail could see their friends and family sitting on the benches that had been set up facing the ceremony. The greenery on the gazebo had been bumped up a notch for their wedding. Add that to the tree glowing in the center, and the gazebo made an extraordinary backdrop for their vows.

Their favorite cellist, who now played regularly at The Thinking Bean, had agreed to perform for their wedding. The low notes of the cello floated in the air and made Abigail feel nothing less than regal. Jamie stood with the judge at the steps of the gazebo, looking tall and handsome, and maybe a little bit nervous. Her heart was beating with the excitement. Joy filled her whole body. The anticipation of seeing him, marrying him, and being his wife was almost too much to handle. But the ceremony was underway and she only had minutes to wait. She took a deep breath and soaked in the moment.

Her mother was escorted down the aisle by both Zeke

and Dillon, one on each arm. Then Fern walked down the aisle, smiling widely, taking her place right behind where Abigail would stand. Then Judy followed suit, standing behind Fern. Finally, it was Abigail and her father's turn.

All of the guests stood as the cellist played the wedding march. For the rest of her life, Abigail always remembered the feeling she had in that moment. It was just like the feeling she'd had when Jamie swept her off her feet on the dance floor. She felt like she was floating, like she was in a dream and Jamie was at the end of it, waiting for her, loving her.

The closer she got to him the wider he smiled and she thought that nothing could make her any happier than she was on that day. As he took her hand in his and they turned towards the judge to walk up the steps and be married in front of the Christmas tree, snow started to fall. The soft, sparkling snow that made up her dreams and, now, had made her dreams come true. Abigail looked into Jamie's laughing eyes and knew that she was blessed.

THE END

NEW YEAR
in
Paradise
HOLIDAY
ROMANCE
DARCI BALOGH

For Robert
My best friend and the love of my life.
Thank you for supporting me, believing in me, and for the countless cups of coffee and words of encouragement you have given me over the years. You have taught me what true love is.
I love you always.

Chapter One

She stood waist deep in turquoise blue water. The tips of her fingers traced the surface as she moved her hands back and forth, back and forth, touching the ocean as if it were a fuzzy blanket.

The water was warmer than she expected it to be. Almost as warm as a bath, but not quite. Mellow waves, more like long bumps on the surface, pushed against her stomach rhythmically as they rolled past her towards the shore.

Without looking she knew the beach was white sand. Without looking she knew there was not another soul anywhere in sight. The gentle beauty of this place was for her and her alone, and that knowledge filled her with peace.

Flashes of bright orange, pink, and green, flitted through the water. Tropical fish, dozens of them, swam around her legs. She suddenly remembered that her feet were sunk into the ocean floor under the turquoise water. When she looked down she realized, for the first time, that she was fully clothed.

Her best business suit, her interview suit, crisp and ironed until it hit the water at her waist where the material, soaked through with salt water, floated languidly around her body.

Her heart quickened at the sight. This wasn't good. It would be ruined. She couldn't replace it in time for her interview. She would either have to go to the interview in a sopping wet business suit or go naked. Her heartbeat increased. Suddenly, she knew she was no longer alone.

Glancing to her left, then her right, just within her peripheral vision, she saw a sea of pink feathers looming. Flamingos. Hundreds of them. They made a beautiful cooing noise. Her heartbeat slowed. Calmer now. More brightly colored fish passed through the water in front of her. She knew what to do.

Bringing her hands up from her sides where they'd been tracing the surface of the ocean, she found the small business-like buttons that kept her stiff jacket closed and flicked them open until the jacket hung loose. Shrugging her shoulders, she slipped it off easily, letting it sink into the water at her back.

The cooing of the flamingos grew louder and she smiled, knowing they were encouraging her. Quickly, she unbuttoned her pale blue silk shirt that went so well with the grey of her interview suit. It, too, was taken by the ocean. Fed to the fish for all she cared.

Within a few moments, she was completely naked, standing proudly in the turquoise water, tropical fish brushing playfully against her legs, a mass of flamingos pressing her on from behind. Without another thought, she took a deep breath and dove head first into the water.

Rowan Murray woke with a start. Her eyes darted around in confusion.

Rowan, Ro for short, wasn't standing up to her waist in water. She was slumped uncomfortably in the middle seat on an airplane. Looking from side to side, she saw that she was not flanked by hoards of pink cooing flamingos. Rather by oversized tourists, stuffed first into their khaki shorts and bright colored T-shirts, then into their seats, and finally strapped tightly with their seatbelts.

On her right was a thick middle-aged man with extra wide shoulders that took up all of the room across the back of his seat as well as some of the room behind her. On her left was an even thicker middle-aged woman. The woman had the window seat. She, too, was running out of room in her assigned area and spilling over into Ro's narrow middle seat.

Ro sucked in her breath and looked down at her own form taking up the little room remaining between the larger than life couple on her left and right. Thankfully, she wasn't naked. She'd been dreaming. Ro had a twinge of disappointment when she realized that she had not been swimming with tropical fish in a turquoise ocean. At least, not yet.

"Dozed off, did ya?" the man asked with an enthusiastic smile.

Ro nodded. She pulled herself back into a sitting position, which wasn't easy given the limited amount of room.

"Well, you weren't snoring at least," he continued, laughing out loud at the thought of it.

He may not have been sleeping, but he'd certainly been drinking. Ro instinctively leaned towards the woman. She may suffocate in the pillow of her bosom, but she'd rather do that then have to fend off any clumsy advances from an overly friendly seat-mate, accidental or otherwise.

Slipping her phone out of the front pocket of her short black cotton dress, Ro checked the time. Less than an hour until they landed. Less than 24 hours until her scheduled interview.

"The captain said we're landing early," the woman told her, a smile lighting up her fleshy face. She nudged Ro, nearly knocking her into the intruding shoulder and bicep of her other neighbor, "You're anxious to get on with your vacation, aren't you?"

"Actually, I'm interviewing for a job. I'm moving here," as the words came out of her mouth, Ro still could hardly believe it was true.

"Moving to Playa del Carmen?" The woman, apparently, was blown away by the idea.

"Really?" Mr. Big Shoulders chimed in.

Ro nodded, "Really."

"You're American?" the woman asked.

Ro wasn't sure why that made a difference, but she nodded again as she answered, "Yes, I'm from Indiana."

"How did you decide to move to someplace like that?" the woman asked, still a little dumbfounded at the concept.

How indeed.

The idea had come to her only eight weeks ago, the Monday after her 31st birthday. But Ro knew the motivation behind it had begun over two years earlier.

That was when she'd broken up with her fiancé. Well, he'd broken up with her. Actually, he'd cheated on her with her friend and they'd had a huge fight where they broke up with each other. But, whatever. The end result was that they broke up and she moved on, mostly.

Theo. That was his name.

After the initial anguish of the betrayal had worn off, Theo had insisted they remain friends. And Ro, being a modern kind of girl, had agreed to stay connected on Instagram and every other social media platform they were connected.

Initially, watching Theo have fun without her was incredibly painful. She coped with it a little better when he went on what appeared to be long drinking binges full of meaningless one-night stands instead of dating one single girl. At least he wasn't marrying any of them.

That fact kept Ro sane as she created a life after Theo. Slowly their awkward friendship drifted into the realm of social media and occasional meetings at a mutual friend's party, nothing more.

All had been well and Ro thought she'd truly moved on, until just after Christmas last year.

An image of Theo with a blue-eyed blonde popped up on his Instagram. It looked like they were at a bar and it looked like they were having fun. A lot of fun. For the next few months the blonde kept showing up more and more frequently. Ro couldn't keep from watching.

That was the thing about social media. It was a great way to keep in touch and stay connected. But some things, perhaps, were better left disconnected.

Ro knew with everything in her soul that there was something different about this blonde, something more in Theo's expression when they were cheek to cheek in a selfie. Ro knew because she had experienced first hand what Theo looked like when he was falling in love. He used to look at her the way he looked at the blue eyed blonde.

Tamara was her name.

Being the modern, independent, ex-fiancé who had moved on with her life, Ro handled the situation like a pro. She online stalked Theo and Tamara relentlessly. Daily. Hourly even.

Winston, her friend from work, said she needed to delete Theo from all of her social media and her phone. Or, instead of deleting his phone number, rename him in her cell as "Jerk Who Slept With My Friend" or "Liar Who Asked Me To Marry Him Then Cheated", or something of that nature. She knew he was right, but Ro couldn't bring herself to do it. She was addicted to watching Theo and Tamara's relationship. Salaciously drinking in every perfect moment they shared.

Ro watched as they fed each other sushi in New York, as

Theo taught Tamara how to snowboard in Colorado, and when Tamara surprised Theo with the newest iPhone on his birthday. Their engagement, not even a year after meeting, threw Ro into a pity party of epic proportions. Still, she couldn't stop following their love story. The love story that was supposed to be hers.

"They're not as happy as they look," Winston had told her for the thousandth time. "Guys like that don't change. He didn't change for her, she's just willing to put up with his bullshit so she can look happy on Instagram."

He had walked into her tiny office and found her sunk in her chair staring at her phone, looking dejected. Moving some papers aside, he placed the hazelnut latte he brought her every morning on her desk.

"I know," Ro groaned.

She did know, yet her thumb kept scrolling through the images of Theo getting on one knee, of the pale blue Tiffany ring box, of the horse drawn carriage he'd arranged to carry them away, of the hundreds of congratulatory comments.

"Maybe you should take a vacation," Winston suggested. He nodded towards the phone in her hand. "From that thing for sure."

He plopped down in the chair on the other side of her desk, taking a sip of his coffee. His suit was a good cut and he wore it casually. A good looking guy, medium height, brown hair, brown eyes, Winston called himself the 'poster boy for average'. But he was cool, as accountants go anyway.

Ro put her phone face down on her desk and picked up her drink. "There. Done."

"Good, now book a cruise or something," Winston teased.

"You're one to talk," Ro answered, grinning at him. "When was the last time you took a vacation, exactly?" It was a rhetorical question. They both knew Winston had never taken a vacation.

She and Winston had started working for Strathum Inc. on the same day. They attended all of the on boarding Human Resources orientations together, and even filled out their health insurance and 401K forms while sitting next to one another.

Winston was an accountant and Ro was an administrative assistant for the accounting department. They'd been at Strathum for over five years. In that time Winston had only used two weeks of his vacation time to help his aging parents move into a condo, one week for his Grandmother's funeral, and two days to attend his brother's wedding in California.

"What can I say, I love my job," Winston said. He leaned back in his chair and put his feet up on her desk as if to show the level of his satisfaction.

Ro looked around her small office, the multiple large framed posters of flowers, a sign that read "Welcome to the Accounting Department, Where Everybody Counts" and her house plants thriving where they were perched on top of the file cabinets. Windowless, yet cheery, she'd moved into this office three years before when Cynthia had retired and Ro had taken her place.

Now it seemed to Ro that she'd been in that little office her entire life. Watching other people get what they wanted while her dreams always fell short. Always ending unsatisfactorily. She had just turned 31, and this was her life?

Ro sighed, "I need more than a vacation from this place. I need a vacation from my life."

And that's when the first nugget of an idea formed in her mind. The tiny spark of inspiration to change her life in a sweeping way started during that conversation with Winston. Every time she saw a new post from Theo where he and Tamara were taste testing wedding cakes or planning their exotic honeymoon in Bali, she was spurred on to look for a way to upgrade her own life into one that was exciting and worthy to show off on social media.

That initial spark had ended with her sandwiched between the two large tourists on her way to interview as a secretary to Cooper Rivera, owner of the Hotel Diamante in Playa del Carmen, Mexico. Just three days before New Year's Eve.

Her New Year resolution this year was to have a wild and adventurous life. Period.

Ro's phone buzzed and she looked down to see a text message from Winston.

It's quiet here without you. Let me know when you land.

She smiled. Winston had taken her to the airport to see her off. He was the only person she would miss terribly, but she had to do what she had to do. He had moped about it for weeks, but in the end Winston was a good friend and he understood.

A dinging sound rang through the cabin and the flight attendant's voice came over the speakers, asking them to turn off their electronic devices and buckle their seatbelts. The plane would be landing soon.

Ro followed the instructions. If she craned her neck just a little, she was able to look around the form of the woman at the window seat and see a sliver of bright sun and blue sky. She knew Palm trees, white sand beaches and a turquoise blue ocean were somewhere below them. Maybe even Flamingos.

Ro felt a thrill of possibility rush through her. Something she hadn't felt in a very long time.

With any luck she would impress Mr. Rivera, land the job, and be ringing in the new year with a brand new life.

Chapter Two

Ro stepped out of the cab in front of the Hotel Diamante at 8:30 am, 30 minutes before her scheduled interview. Shocked that she was on time at all after the morning she'd had, she paid the cab driver their previously agreed upon 75 Pesos, fumbling with the unfamiliar currency. The driver took the money, grunted his thanks in Spanish and made a U-turn in the narrow street to head back to the busier section of town. She watched the small, beat up cab retreat, then took a deep breath and turned her attention to the front of the Hotel Diamante.

The three-story hotel had a Spanish colonial style charm. Clay tile steps led up from the street into a courtyard. Beautiful blue and white tile work surrounded a crystal blue rectangular shaped fountain that shot water nearly as high as the third story before it fell in fat drops back into the water below. The falling water made a pleasing sound, almost like rain. Both sides of the courtyard had second and third story iron balconies, which all boasted glass French doors at the back, presumably leading to hotel suites.

Ro smoothed the front of her bright yellow sundress. She

had started off the morning in her lucky interview outfit, the sleek, grey business suit with the narrow skirt, lined jacket, and pale blue silk shirt she had worn in her dream. However, she hadn't made it out of the lobby of her hotel before realizing that the deeply unforgiving humidity was not going to allow her to wear her good luck clothes. Droplets of sweat rolled down her sides and back and she dared not take off the jacket until she was back in her room because the pale blue silk was splotched with giant patches wet from her sweat.

In a panic, Ro had gone through all of her most appropriate second choices, most of which came up unsatisfactory. She'd finally chosen the yellow sundress, even though it looked a bit too cheery for a job interview. Still, it was cotton, it went past her knees and it wasn't too low cut. Getting a job using her cleavage, as minimal as it might be compared to some, wasn't her style. She dug out her lightweight, white shell sweater that she put on to cover her shoulders. The result was passable. Not her lucky interview suit, but it would do. Maybe she needed a new kind of luck here in Playa del Carmen anyway.

Ro took a deep breath and said quietly, "No time like the present."

She walked past the crystal fountain up the three tiled steps to the front doors. Old, heavy wood frames with thick beveled glass from top to bottom, she took hold of the wide iron handle and pulled. Opening the door to her future.

A cool breeze rushed past her as she stepped into the lobby. A mixture of air-conditioning and fans, she thought, thankful for the relief from the oppressing humidity outside. The square clay tiles from the courtyard were continued into the lobby, except these tiles were twice as large. The lobby walls reached up the full three stories of the building, topped off by skillfully carved wooden beams that supported a domed, glass ceiling. A grand staircase curved up from her left, the heavy wooden banister looked antique and matched the beams in the glass ceiling. Elevator doors were on her right and located dead center underneath the glass ceiling was the front desk decorated with elegant mosaic tiles.

Behind the desk stood a man of about 30, short with the dark complexion and thick black hair of the area. He wore a crisp off white, short-sleeved shirt with gold buttons and a gold nameplate that said 'Carlos'. Behind Carlos were three double sets of French doors.

"Buenos dias, Señorita," said Carlos, smiling broadly at her with large white teeth.

"Buenos dias," Ro responded. Her nerves were tumbling through her stomach. She'd studied Spanish in high school and was pretty good at enunciation for ordering in restaurants, but that was about it. Over the past few weeks she'd gotten the most basic Spanish phrases memorized. Right now, she really hoped Carlos spoke at least a little English. "I'm Rowan Murray, I have a meeting with Mr. Rivera today."

Without missing a beat, Carlos moved into broken, but completely passible, English and Ro breathed a sigh of relief. Of course, she would learn the language if she got the job. For now, however, she silently blessed Carlos for his ability to communicate.

"Señor Rivera? Of course, you sit, please. I am getting him for you," Carlos said.

There were two Victorian style love seats placed against opposite walls under large potted palms. Ro walked to them to wait, but did not sit down. She was too nervous to sit down. She was about to meet Cooper Rivera, jet setting millionaire, owner of this hotel and, hopefully, her soon-to-be boss.

She'd Googled Cooper before accepting this interview. Her mother had insisted, though Ro would have done it without her mother's advice. Flying to another country to meet a man you'd only spoken to via emails to interview for a fantasy job could be considered a dream come true. Not double-checking his credentials, however, would have gone against Ro's cautious nature.

"What'd you find out about dream boss?" Winston had asked her after she told him about the job interview and that she was planning to do some online digging. Winston, like her mother, was anxious about her big life change. Though he was trying to be more supportive and laid back about it than her parents.

"Let's see, I found pictures and videos of him with friends, partying in Italy, on yachts, at charity balls. In those pictures he was usually with his father. I actually found out more about his Dad than him," she answered.

"What'd you find out about his Dad?" Winston sipped his coffee as he leaned back in the chair across from her desk. His daily ritual unchanged even as she was about to shift her entire existence.

"His Dad is a well known business man, millionaire type. He owns a lot of companies and is based in Arizona. He also owns a lot of property in Central and South America, plus a few interests in Europe. Big in a few charities. A few articles written about him online. He's mentioned once in a Forbes article."

Winston's eyebrows lifted in surprise at the mention of Forbes. Then he asked, "So, no prison sentences? No ugly lawsuits? No history of kidnapping beautiful women and selling them into the black market?"

Ro laughed, "No, not that I could find."

What she did find, but didn't tell Winston, was that Cooper Rivera was a very attractive man. Dark, chiseled, black hair, square jaw, full lips, and in all of the pictures she found he was wearing either a tuxedo or a swimsuit. In a few pictures he was wearing his tuxedo shirt untucked and only partly buttoned, his bow tie loose and hung around his neck. Those images popped into her mind as she waited in the lobby of his hotel and her stomach flipped with nerves.

Ro wouldn't say she was particularly beautiful. About 5'7", brown hair cut just below her chin, what one might call a cute, heart shaped face, and a nice wide smile. She did have a slim figure and was reasonably sure that she could turn a few heads on a good day.

Her eyes were probably her most arresting feature. Coming from a multi-ethnic ancestry ranging from Scottish to Italian to Indian, her great-grandmother was from India, Ro's skin had always been a uniquely golden brown. Her blue-grey eyes were that much more noticeable because of her skin tone. But she wasn't sure an astonishingly good looking and wealthy man would be terribly interested in her eyes.

She shook her head, silently admonishing herself for letting her mind slip into the fantasy that this meeting was anything more than an interview. Cooper Rivera had never seen her and, as far as he knew, she had never seen him. This whole move to create a new life for herself was not about finding a man, it was about living an exciting and adventurous life. The kind of life she had thought she was going to have with Theo.

Theo was tall, dark and handsome. She rolled her eyes at the thought. Maybe she had a weak spot for that kind of guy.

"Miss Murray?" A woman's voice came from behind.

Ro turned quickly to see an older Mexican woman. She was thick bodied and sharply dressed, with black-rimmed glasses and dark red lipstick applied expertly to her full lips.

"Yes, I'm Rowan Murray."

The older woman stuck out her manicured hand. "I'm Alicia Perez, the GM of the Hotel Diamante. You're early."

Ro couldn't tell if this was a positive or negative statement, or merely an observance of the facts. She loved how the woman said 'Hotel Diamante', as if she were announcing it over the radio on a commercial.

"Yes, I wasn't sure how long it would take to get here," Ro answered.

"You didn't stay here?" Alicia Perez scowled at this realization. Carlos had returned to his position behind the desk and he glanced nervously at Ro, as if to say 'you should have stayed here'.

"No, I didn't," Ro admitted.

She had thought it might be uncomfortable or strange to stay at this hotel if the interview didn't go well, so had booked a modest room nearby. Suddenly, she was worried that her chances of getting the job may be affected by this decision.

Alicia extended her manicured hand across the desk towards Carlos, who started slightly as if her arm was a snake lunging at him. Alicia didn't look at him as she spoke.

"12-B," she said curtly. Her palm faced up and she motioned towards Carlos with her fingers, her rings clicking against the counter top as her fingers flicked back and forth.

Carlos quickly grabbed a key card, typed something into the slim laptop that sat on the counter, swiped the card through a machine and handed it to Alicia. As Carlos worked efficiently behind her, Alicia gazed steadily at Ro, who found it impossible to return the stare. She glanced away twice, once when the French doors behind the counter opened, revealing a long hallway that ended in what looked like a luxurious swimming pool in another courtyard, and once when she simply looked at her own feet.

"Now you stay here," Alicia said with finality, handing Ro the card Carlos gave her.

"Thank you," Ro answered.

"We will send for your things," Alicia shot a look to

Carlos who nodded in agreement. "Where did you stay last night?"

"The Palma Grande," Ro answered.

Alicia grimaced and made a tsk-tsk noise with her mouth. Carlos picked up a wafer thin phone and started dialing. Alicia started towards the staircase that Ro had passed on the way in.

"Come with me, I will show you to your desk," Alicia said.

"My desk?"

Alicia continued walking and Ro followed. She gave a backwards glance to Carlos, who she felt was the only person that might understand her confusion. He was speaking Spanish so fast into the phone she couldn't even recognize any of the words, but he managed to give her an encouraging smile and a thumbs up.

Alicia's high heels clicked confidently on the clay tile as she walked. Ro hurried to catch up.

"I think there may be a mistake. I don't think I have a desk. I'm here for an interview with Mr. Rivera?" The last few words came out as a question.

"There is no mistake," Alicia said. She paused at the foot of the stairs and looked back at Ro. "You're hired."

Despite her desire to remain professional, Ro's mouth dropped open. She watched Alicia climb the stairs, her high heels silent now as she was putting all of her weight on her toes. Realizing that she was falling behind, the younger woman had to hurry again to catch up.

"I'm hired?" Ro asked at the top of the stairs, slightly out of breath from rushing.

Alicia looked at Ro sideways as they moved together along a catwalk that overlooked the lobby below, "Yes, your terms of employment are on your desk ready for you to review. If you find them satisfactory, you will sign the paperwork and begin working today." She said the words with perfect pronunciation. Still, Ro was confused.

"I don't understand, I thought I was going to *interview* today."

Alicia stopped suddenly and faced Ro. "Your references are outstanding. Your resume impeccable. Do you want to work for the Hotel Diamante as an administrative assistant?"

"Yes," Ro answered.

"Interview completed. You're hired." Alicia whisked her hand once across the front of her face like she was shooing away a fly. "Here is your desk." She turned on her heel and opened a door on the wall behind them. Ro followed her into a beautiful space.

The room was full of light. It was painted in a creamy cocoa with white trim. There were high ceilings, iron lanterns for hanging lights and several tall windows with natural wood blinds along the outside wall. The clay tiles outside the room were replaced with mosaic tiles in rich browns and blues, which had been laid so they looked like a huge rug covering the floor. The first section of the room had a loveseat and two chairs that were cousins to the Victorian love seats in the lobby. A large impressionistic style painting of an open-air market hung above the loveseat.

A wide arched doorway led into the second section of the room with the same elegant windows along the outside wall. A slender polished wood desk sat facing the windows, its back to another arched doorway that was a double door. Both doors were closed. There were floor to ceiling bookshelves along the back wall full of hardback gold embossed books and shining knickknacks.

On the surface of the desk there was only a slim laptop and phone like what she'd seen Carlos use, a thin lamp with a shade made to look like a sepia toned map, a decorative piece of white coral, and a small white vase full of pink flowers.

There was also a single piece of cream colored Hotel Diamante stationary. She assumed this was the job offer information.

"Sit here and read through the details," Alicia instructed her as she swept her hand towards the paisley upholstered rolling chair behind the desk. "I will return shortly and you may give me your decision then."

Ro went to the chair to do as she was told. Alicia turned to leave.

"Excuse me," Ro said.

Alicia turned back.

"Do you know when I will meet Mr. Rivera?" She was, after all, going to be his administrative assistant.

A flash of annoyance crossed Alicia's face and came out in her tone, "Mr. Rivera is unavailable at present." Her eyes flicked to the double doors behind Ro, then back. "When he does emerge, it will be through those doors behind you."

Ro turned to look at the heavy, closed doors. Surprised, she asked, "This is where he lives?"

"Those doors lead to his office. At the back of his office is the entry to his suite. And, yes, he does live here." Alicia gave her a sharp look. "This is his hotel, after all."

With that comment, Alicia was gone.

Ro looked around the gorgeous little office space and let out her breath. She picked up the paper and tried to read it, but her mind was spinning. She couldn't focus. She stood up and went to the window, peering through the wooden blinds at the view. This side of the building didn't face the ocean, but it did overlook the vibrant street and town beyond.

Old buildings in a similar style to the hotel were packed close together. Climbing plants stretched from the ground up and over the buildings, bursting with bright red and pink flowers. Small cars maneuvered erratically through the street and Ro thought she could see the edge of an open market that continued out of sight. She wondered if it was the same open market in the painting.

Returning to the desk she sat down with intent and picked up the paper. Scanning it quickly, it seemed like an honest and generous offer, considering her cost of living would be less here than it was in America. The nerves in her stomach became a tingling excitement that filled her whole body. She put the paper back on the desk and noticed that her fingers were trembling.

Ro knew what she was going to do. The thrill of it was difficult to contain. She rummaged through her purse and pulled out her cell phone. It wasn't yet 9:oo am. Quickly, because she wanted to read through the offer details thoroughly before signing them, Ro typed a text to Winston.

I got the job!!!

She slipped the phone back into her purse, not waiting for his reply.

Chapter Three

After reviewing the job details more carefully, Ro had no reservations about signing her name on the dotted line. It wasn't a contract, per se, simply an offer of pay, which was nominal, but it did include a room at the hotel and three meals a day at the hotel restaurant, which made up the difference. The duties listed included answering the phone, scheduling Mr. Rivera's meetings and daily affairs as well as trips, filing, reviewing his expense accounts and making necessary payments, and email duties as assigned by Mr. Rivera. Pretty basic administrative stuff. Ro signed her name with a flourish to accept the terms of employment and sat back in her new chair.

She took a few moments to enjoy her new surroundings, running her hand along the polished surface of her lovely new desk, and leaning in to gaze at the white coral. She thought it might be a good idea to familiarize herself with her new office.

Getting up she looked over the decorative items on the bookshelves then opened the small cabinets that were along the bottom of each one. Inside there was what looked like a narrow printer/scanner combination, probably operated on wi-fi. There were also paper supplies, pens, highlighters, a stapler, your standard office fare. The sight of them in this luxurious and exotic location surprised her. She'd expected something different. Something more magical than an open box of neon yellow highlighters.

A series of three thumps coming from the other side of the closed double doors startled her. She stood like a deer in headlights, not blinking, not moving. Listening.

There they were again. Muffled thumps. Three in rapid succession. Then nothing. The ambient sound of the room buzzed in Ro's ears. Her heartbeat quickened.

The front door of the office pushed open and Ro jumped at the sound. She'd been focusing all of her attention on the double doors to the mysterious Mr. Rivera's office.

Alicia stepped in the door and towards Ro's desk, eyeing the signed paper, her high heels clicking neatly on the tile floor.

"You have accepted the terms?"

Ro nodded, glancing once away from Alicia to the double doors. No more sounds emerged.

Alicia picked up the paper and skimmed over it. When her eyes came to Ro's signature, she smiled. Ro found that she was surprised to see the older woman smile and even more surprised at the warmth behind it. There were crow's feet wrinkles at the corners of Alicia's eyes.

"Good, I will send Gloria to set up your passwords and answer your questions," Alicia said. She noticed Ro wrinkling her brow and anticipated her question. "Gloria is my administrative assistant. She knows everything there is to know about this job."

"Oh, I see," Ro said. She was to be solely Mr. Rivera's assistant. Somehow, after the thumping, she was a little apprehensive about it.

"Carlos will show you your room as well. He should have your things moved there by lunch. You will join me in the restaurant for lunch?" Although it was framed as a question, Ro didn't think she actually had a choice. She nodded.

"Excellent."

And that it was.

Gloria, a grey haired, round faced woman with impeccable English, joined Ro soon after Alicia excused herself. Gloria wore a feminine below the knee floral print dress and may have been four feet tall if she stood up straight, which she no longer could because of the bending of age. Where Alicia looked high-powered corporate, Gloria looked like she could out type, out bake and out knit anyone for miles.

Not only did she speak perfect English, but to Ro's surprise, the elderly lady was wicked fast on the computer. Within half an hour Ro had been added to the hotel's operating software, which seemed to be state of the art. Ro had a moment of concern when she realized that she had no training in the software program. Gloria patted her hand kindly.

"This is for reservations and inventory, which is usually what I work on with Alicia," Gloria reassured her. "You will work mostly with Cooper using Google calendar and email...and text," here the old lady sighed quietly, "He loves text."

Gloria gave Ro basic information on the hotel. When it was first built, the 19th century. When it became a hotel, 1998. And when Cooper Rivera purchased it, just two years earlier.

"Some say he acquired it in a poker game," Gloria said. Her old, dark eyes twinkled with humor, "But I don't think he's that good at poker."

Ro laughed, then asked, "So how do you think he acquired it?"

Gloria glanced at the double doors, ensuring they were closed before answering, "I think his father bought it for him. And I think his father expects him to use it...wisely."

"I see," Ro said, although she didn't. Not exactly.

"Knock knock," Carlos said as he opened the front door and entered. Bowing slightly in their direction he lifted his gaze to Ro and she could see the smile in his eyes. "May I show you to your quarters?"

She smiled, "Of course, thank you."

Her quarters were a large bedroom with a small balcony overlooking the courtyard that contained the swimming pool. The same brown and blue mosaic tiles that graced the floors elsewhere in the hotel were lain in a rug pattern on her bedroom floor and in the gorgeous bathroom. The deep luxury bathtub and separate shower were the nicest she'd ever seen, let alone used. A large mirror framed in dark wood that matched the vanity was framed with black iron lamps covered in creamy white shades.

She had just a few minutes to put away some of her things in the antique dark wood dresser that graced the wall opposite her Queen sized bed. The bed had more pillows than Ro would need stacked three deep against a fabric headboard upholstered in a deep mustard yellow. There was a small table with two sitting chairs in the corner of the room and a flat screen TV hanging on the wall above the dresser. Ro took her toiletries into the bathroom and freshened up for her lunch with Alicia. Perhaps Mr. Rivera would finally make his appearance when they were eating together.

No such luck.

Lunch was amazing, chilled cantaloupe soup followed by spicy garlic shrimp. The dining area was even more beautiful than the lobby, if that was possible. The tables were located on a wide, covered terrace that dripped with overgrown climbing plants covered in flowers. Each table was placed to provide an unobstructed view of the beach and ocean in the near distance. As Ro entered to meet Alicia, a warm breeze carried the fresh, salty scent of the sea and mingled with the delicious smells of the kitchen.

She was almost shocked to see the glistening blue of the ocean water. Her interview and hiring had monopolized her attention since she landed yesterday. She promised herself that the first moment she had alone, she would go to the beach and soak it all in.

That moment, however, would have to wait.

"Our focus right now needs to be 100% on the New Year's Eve party," Alicia told Ro, Gloria and Carlos. Apparently they were the dream team of the Hotel Diamante. Ro was excited about this, and more than a little apprehensive.

"I have the updated list of all of the vendors who will be here between now and 3:00 pm on the 31st," Gloria pulled neatly printed sheets out of nowhere and handed them each a copy. She said something quickly to Carlos in Spanish. He smiled and nodded.

Ro scanned the sheet and her heart filled with dismay. It was in Spanish. They must have assumed she was bi-lingual when she applied. She couldn't blame them, it would have been a natural assumption. Her stomach sank knowing that she couldn't take this job after all.

"I'm sorry, I don't speak Spanish," Ro said, glancing apologetically at Alicia. "Not yet, anyway. I was planning on learning," she added quickly. "But I think, maybe, you need someone who is bi-lingual for this position?"

"Oh, my apologies," Gloria said sweetly, pulling another piece of paper from somewhere and placing it in front of Ro. The names of the vendors were still in Spanish, of course, but the categories, assignments and notes were all in English.

Relieved, but still uncertain, Ro felt heat fill her cheeks. She didn't want to be a burden. It was foolish of her to expect special treatment just because she'd never taken the time to learn more than one language.

Alicia seemed to understand the issue and leaned forward, "Mr. Rivera does not speak Spanish. It was not a requirement for your position." She peered at Ro over her reading glasses, "Although, if you chose to learn the language it would only be beneficial."

Ro was surprised at how high her heart soared at this statement. She almost laughed out loud with relief. The disappointment she'd felt at the possibility of losing this job she'd had for only a few hours was intense. She made a mental note to get the latest and best language teaching software as soon as possible. Then, gaining control of her sudden elation, she looked down and studied her schedule intently.

The New Year's Eve celebration was a huge event, Alicia explained. And it was one that the Hotel Diamante had become famous for throwing without a hitch. Since Ro was brand new, Alicia would leave her in the capable hands of Gloria to do whatever might be most helpful. Carlos would take charge of his duties on the list, and Alicia would be checking in with everyone periodically for updates.

With the business taken care of, and their plates empty, Alicia excused herself to return to her office.

"Take a full hour for your lunch," she commanded as she stood. "The next few days will be incredibly busy, you may not have another chance to relax."

Alone at last, Carlos and Gloria turned their attention towards Ro, welcoming her warmly to the hotel as their co-worker.

"How is your room?" Carlos asked gallantly, his broken English more and more charming the longer Ro listened to him.

"It's really beautiful," she said, gushing a little bit.

Carlos' smile grew wider, revealing even more of his large, white teeth, "Bien, bien!"

"Have you been to visit the beach since you arrived?" Gloria asked.

"No, I haven't. I mean to. It's been a bit of a whirlwind," Ro responded.

"No beach?" Carlos was astonished.

"I will. I just haven't had time," she tried to reassure him.

"The beach is lovely in the morning," Gloria said, her eyes dreamy.

"I'm sure," Ro said, trying to be as agreeable as possible.

After lunch Ro returned to her post in front of the still closed double doors. Gloria had given her a few small things to do for the party, but assured her that Cooper would be making an appearance soon and she would have plenty to keep her busy.

It was funny how Gloria called him Cooper when everyone else referred to him as Mr. Rivera. Ro wondered if it had something to do with age. Gloria was quite a bit older than all of them, perhaps that meant she only had to use first names. Being in a different culture left a lot of questions open. Ro didn't know the ins and outs of social niceties in the Yucatán Peninsula. Maybe they were very different than Indiana. Well, she would just have to be as polite as she knew how to be, learn the language, and hope that she didn't make any major screw ups.

She was pondering these issues with so much concentration, that she didn't hear the door handle on the double doors click and turn. Nor did she hear the swish of the large doors pulling open across the smooth, tile floor. What she did notice was a draft of cool air coming from behind her, tickling the backs of her arms.

Ro turned her head to see where the draft was coming from and cried out, "Oh my God!" She jumped up from her chair and whirled around, sending her chair shooting backwards, directly into the man standing in the open doorway.

He made an 'oof' sound as the chair hit his abdomen.

Ro's hands flew up and covered her mouth, which was still gaping open. Heart pounding, she tried to regain her composure. The man in the doorway was well over six feet tall, short, black hair, dark complexion, chiseled features, with a well built, athletic body. She knew this because he wore a pair of slim fitted swim shorts in navy blue, and that was all. It was like the swimsuit that Daniel Craig made famous in James Bond, trim, tailored, not leaving a lot to the imagination.

It was Cooper Rivera. She recognized him immediately from her online stalking. Jet setting playboy. Son of a multi-millionaire. Owner of this hotel. Her new boss.

She dropped her hands from her mouth, "I am so sorry."

"I didn't know anyone was out here," he said. Not quite an apology. It was his office after all.

"Yes, I was. I mean, I am. I'm new," she fumbled for the right words.

Cooper let his gaze drop from Ro's face and travel quickly down her whole body, taking in her dress, her shoes, her shape. His eyes were dark with heavy lids. She couldn't tell if he was tired or if this sexy, sleepy look was his permanent expression. He had a thick 5 o'clock shadow and his hair was uncombed. When he lifted his eyes to hers again she felt a tickle deep in her belly.

"Are you my new secretary?" He asked. The deep tones of his voice sent another, sharper, tickle through the center of her body.

She nodded. Then reconsidered and asked, "Are you Mr. Rivera?"

He smiled, revealing perfect teeth, perfect dimples, and a

perfect smile. He reached towards her to shake her hand, "Cooper."

"I'm Rowan Murray," she took his hand and shook it, trying to ignore how his strong, warm grip pleased her. "People usually call me 'Ro'."

"Ro," he repeated, seeming to roll the idea of her name over in his mind. Then he dropped her hand and said, "Okay, Ro. I'm going for a swim."

"All right, I'll be here."

He grinned at her, "I hope so. Oh, and people usually call me 'Coop'." Then he turned away, giving her a little wink as he did, and sauntered out the front door.

Ro watched him go. The initial shock of their meeting was over, yet it took a while for her nerves to settle.

Cooper didn't return, not that afternoon anyway.

Ro kept herself busy. Waiting for him to return from his swim with a towel hung jauntily around his neck, drops of water still clinging to his sculpted chest. But she waited in vain. When 5 o'clock rolled around she reluctantly shut down her laptop and left the office. A small but noticeable piece of her was quite disappointed.

Her first work day officially over, she joined Gloria for a light dinner in the dining room. Then, finally, Ro was alone in her room with her thoughts. And what thoughts they were.

She flopped down on her bed face up, her arms stretched out to either side. She was elated, ecstatic, exhausted. It had only been 24 hours ago that she'd landed at the airport and jostled to find a taxi to take her to Playa del Carmen. Just this morning she'd been nervously getting ready to interview, not sure she would be offered a job at all.

But now.

Now she was in her very own elegant room, working in a luxury hotel, the secretary for one of the most attractive, wealthy, mysterious men she'd ever met in person. Winston used to always tell her, "My cup runneth over." And now she knew what he meant.

Winston. She wanted to call him and tell him everything that had happened. She should probably call her mother, too, just to check in. First she'd need to fish her phone out of her purse and find her charger.

Her phone.

Ro paused.

She hadn't looked at her phone, or checked her Instagram for pictures of Theo and his fiancé, all day long.

She smiled at this realization. A happy buzzing sensation filled her head and heart. And then, before she could make herself get up and retrieve her purse from the chair in the corner of the room, Ro fell asleep.

Chapter Four

K*nock, knock, knock.*
The sound drifted into her mind, not quite registering.

Knock, knock, knock.

Again.

Ro turned her head on her pillow. The deep gentle feeling of being comfortably asleep came into her consciousness. Then it was gone.

Knock, knock, knock.

"Hello?" A man's voice from the other side of the door.

Her eyes opened. She glanced around the dimly lit room, not sure at first where she was. Then, as the fog of sleep lifted and she remembered that she was in her new room at the Hotel Diamante, the light knock and the man's voice came again.

Knock, knock, knock.

"Señorita? It's Carlos."

Her first thought was that there was an emergency. From what she could see out her windows it was not yet morning.

She couldn't think of another reason why Carlos would be knocking at her door in the middle of the night.

Ro reluctantly sat up on the edge of the bed. A murmur of voices outside her door made her even more curious. One of the voices sounded like a child.

She padded across the floor to the door and looked through the peephole. She could see Carlos standing with a woman. The tops of two children's heads were just visible. The woman was speaking to Carlos, but Ro couldn't hear what was being said. Maybe she should just ignore them and go back to bed. She wasn't due to work until 9:00 am, and it had to be before 6:00 am. The sun hadn't come up yet.

A nugget of fear sat in her stomach. She'd just met Carlos. She wasn't sure she knew him well enough to open her door to him at this hour.

Knock, knock, knock.

There it was again. Not too loud. It must not be an emergency.

"It's Carlos. We go to beach..."

The beach? This peaked her curiosity. The nugget of fear dissolved and she unlocked the door, pulling it back cautiously.

"Buenos dias, Señorita," Carlos said, beaming at her. He had one hand on the woman's back and one hand on a little boy's head, maybe seven or eight years old, who stood in front of him. A little girl, younger than the boy by a few years, held tightly to the woman's hand. "Sorry to awake you," His brow furrowed at the sight of her rumpled look.

"It's fine, is everything okay?" Ro answered, trying to sound like she hadn't just woken up.

"It's good, thank you. This is my family," his smile grew even larger, if that was possible.

Ro raised her eyebrows, surprised and pleased, "Oh, hello."

The woman nodded her head in greeting, smiled shyly, but didn't speak. The little boy smiled widely at her. He looked very much like his father, Ro noticed. The girl pressed herself into her mother's skirt, watching Ro with big eyes.

"My wife, Josefina. My son, Jorge. My daughter, Francisca," Carlos continued with the introductions despite the rather unusual circumstances.

"Nice to meet you," Ro said, smiling at all three of them.

"We go to beach each morning to walk," Carlos continued. "You come with us? Or," he looked for the right English phrase, "You like to come with us?"

"Oh!" He was inviting her to the beach with his family. How wonderful! Ro's polite smile became a full-blown look of delight, "Yes, I would like to come with you."

Carlos looked even more delighted than she felt. He said something quickly in Spanish to Josefina and the woman smiled and nodded warmly.

"You meet us in front of hotel?"

"Yes, yes," Ro glanced down at her wrinkled sundress. She'd been so tired last night she hadn't even changed into pajamas. "I'll change clothes and meet you there in...10 minutes?"

"10 minutes," Carlos annunciated the words carefully, nodding emphatically.

20 minutes later Ro was strolling onto the white sand beach of Playa del Carmen escorted by her very own tour guides.

Though warm enough to wear shorts, the absence of the sun left the temperature a comfortable cool. Ro had quickly pulled on a pair of khaki shorts, a Bob Ross T-shirt that was one of her favorites, and her red Indiana University pullover sweatshirt. With her hair up in a fast pony tail and no makeup, she felt like a little kid on an adventure.

Though the sun was not up quite yet, its presence was

obvious. Since Carlos had first knocked on her door until now, the sky had turned from deep purple to a lighter purple with a reddish glow growing on the ocean horizon. Ro had been to the oceans in California and along the East coast and Florida several times. She always loved the feeling of walking into a wide-open space with nothing but blue water stretching out for as far as the eye could see.

In this case, on the Caribbean ocean, the water was especially blue. Even with the limited light of the coming sunrise, the turquoise color shimmered across the surface. The white sand that stretched along the water's edge was muted in the pale light and broken in places by black silhouettes of scattered palm trees or the occasional pile of kelp or beach chair. A few other people were out, taking in the pre-dawn sky, but not too many. Ro thought the beach probably filled up considerably after the sun came up.

"Carlos!" A man's voice came to them from somewhere near the water.

Carlos turned and peered at the silhouetted form that jogged towards them. Then, recognition, and Carlos waved enthusiastically, "Señor Zander!"

At the mention of the newcomer's name, both children left their parent's sides and ran towards the figure, shouting happily. As the figure got closer Ro could see it was a man, medium height, wearing a pair of pink and green board shorts. He had long, bleached out hair that he wore in flopping dread locks and a curly, bleached blonde beard. He laughed and talked to the children and Ro could hear his Australian accent even though she couldn't quite make out the words.

"How're you doin', mate?" The man said warmly when he reached them, sticking out his hand to shake Carlos'.

"Good, good, Señor," Carlos said. He introduced Ro and

Zander, explaining that she was now working for Mr. Rivera, and they shook hands. Zander's hand was rough with a strong grip, but his eyes were what she noticed most. Pale blue, almost like crystals. They were what she would call piercing blue eyes even in the not-quite daylight.

"Ah, an expat are you?" Zander asked, his brilliant eyes smiling at her.

"Yes, brand new," she answered.

"You'll love it here. It's absolute paradise," he said as he gave the shoreline and rising sun a sweeping gaze.

Sunrise was growing nearer. The horizon was glowing and turning the sky above them from purple to dark pink. More light shone across the water, pulling out its bright blue and showing off the white bubbly edge of the waves as they rolled up onto the sand then retreated, leaving a shining, flat surface behind.

"It really is, isn't it?" Ro said, more to herself than anyone. She looked back at Zander who was grinning at her, and asked, "What do you do here?"

"I run a little dive shop, give scuba tours."

"That must be fun."

"It is. Do you scuba?" He asked. She shook her head 'no'. Zander's smile deepened and he nudged her arm with his elbow, "You should try it."

The thought of diving into the turquoise water and sinking far underneath, exploring the coral reefs, seeing the tropical fish and plants, swimming free under the water like she belonged there, filled her with both excitement and trepidation. She should learn how to scuba dive. She cocked her head sideways and gave Zander a bright smile.

"I might take you up on that!"

They all stood together taking in the gorgeous colors that filled the sky, the rhythmic sound of the waves swishing against the sand, and the scent of fresh salty air. Zander and Carlos chatted about a few things as Josefina kept a keen eye on her children who were racing back and forth between the adults and the waves. Without any Spanish skills there was little Ro could talk about with Josefina, but she still felt a warm camaraderie between them as the women in the group. Content to appreciate the sunrise and the laughing children together.

Ro glanced at Josefina's profile. She was a pretty woman. Dark skin, beautiful thick, black hair, and large dark eyes. Ro reminded herself that she needed to get that online Spanish tutorial software today. She didn't want to miss out on getting to know people because of her lack of language skills.

In the distance, a movement caught her eye and Ro shifted her attention to the form of a man walking towards them along the beach. Something about his movement was familiar. He was tall and lean, with wide shoulders. He was wearing a white, untucked button down shirt and what looked like knee length cargo shorts. In the muted light she couldn't exactly see his face, mostly just his form walking intently towards them.

Cooper? Her stomach did a flip-flop at the thought, and her heart rate increased slightly. In that split second Ro knew she might have a problem if she felt that kind of nervous attraction to her brand new boss. She told herself to relax and just go with the flow. He was simply a super rich, jet setting, gorgeous man who she was most likely going to get to know extremely well being his personal administrative assistant. No worries, as her new acquaintance, Zander, might say.

The man came closer and Ro could make out his face.

Not Cooper.

Her mouth dropped open. She couldn't believe what she was seeing. She gave her head a little shake, blinking her eyes. Maybe the man was a mirage or something.

But, no.

He saw her now, too, and lifted his arm in an enthusiastic wave, calling her name, "Ro!"

Her eyes were wide with surprise. And though Ro's mouth was still open, she was too astounded to return his greeting.

Chapter Five

"I found you!" Winston declared, both joy and relief on his face.

"Winston? What are you doing here?" Ro stepped away from her small group to meet him. Astonished at the sight of him.

"I'm on vacation!" He opened his arms as if embracing the entire ocean sunrise moment. He laughed at her surprised expression, put his hands on her shoulders and then pulled her into a hug.

She hugged him back. Still in shock, but happy to see him. She was always happy to see Winston.

He squeezed her closer than any of the friendly hugs they'd shared at work. Longer too.

"I don't understand," she said into his shoulder.

He pulled away and held her at arms length, "I took a month off!"

Ro was nothing short of baffled.

"But...you don't go on vacations," was all she could think to say.

He let go of her shoulders and looked down at the sand sheepishly, then lifted his gaze to hers. The first rays of the sun spread brilliant orange and pink light across his face, making his usually plain brown eyes shine. He hadn't shaved and the stubble, combined with his messy hair and wrinkled shirt, gave him a casual look. Like they'd been on a road trip together, or stayed out all night after a concert. Although, they had never done anything of the sort.

"And you normally answer your phone," he said. It wasn't a reprimand, just an explanation. She gasped and covered her mouth with her hand. She'd forgotten about calling him last night. She'd forgotten about calling anyone.

"Oh my God! I'm so sorry!"

Of course, he would have been worried about her. Everyone was probably worried about her. Her parents!

Winston half shrugged and looked out at the bright orange orb that was lifting slowly over the ocean, lighting up the water and beach and everything around them with a golden glow.

"It's not bad as rescue missions go," he said.

Ro turned away, distraught, "I need to call my Mom!"

"Here," Winston had his cell in his hand, it was dialing. The contact name read 'Margaret Ro's Mom'.

She grabbed the phone from him just in time to hear her Mom's worried voice.

For ten minutes Ro talked her Mom down. She had been worried sick and filled Ro in on how she had contacted Winston through Facebook because she knew they were close and thought maybe he had heard from Ro in Mexico. Once Winston knew that her parents hadn't heard from her either, he tried to get in touch with her, but she never answered the calls or texts. Her Dad had been packing a bag to fly to Playa del Carmen and find her when Winston stepped in. He told her parents that he had tons of vacation time and would go himself, saving them the extra expense. Ro knew that Winston was aware her parents weren't very well off. It was one of the many things she'd shared with him over the years.

"He insisted on going," her mother told her.

"He did?" She glanced at Winston who had joined her small group as she'd stepped away to speak on the phone. He was shaking hands with Carlos.

"Yes, thank goodness he found you. What a nice young man," her mother continued.

Ro paced up and down the white sand, talking to her Mom for a few more minutes and then her Dad. Meanwhile, Winston chatted with Carlos and Zander. She saw that he even managed a few short sentences of Spanish with Josefina and the two children. Ro didn't know that Winston could speak Spanish.

Satisfied that their daughter hadn't been kidnapped by a drug cartel or sold into human slavery, her Mom eventually let her hang up. Ro promised she would call her this evening after work.

Work. It was getting late in the morning. She needed to get ready for her first real day on the job. As she returned to the group, Ro heard the tail end of a conversation.

"Of course you will stay at Hotel Diamante," Carlos was saying.

"I would love to," Winston said, glancing at her as he did.

She smiled and thanked him for the use of his phone, handing it back to him. When he took it from her, his hand wrapped around hers for a moment. She found all of this touching strange. She and Winston had been work friends for years and they had never touched this much. His presence here was disconcerting, too. Like a puzzle piece that just didn't fit because it belonged to a totally different puzzle, he didn't belong here in her new life. There was no space for him.

"Everything good?" Winston asked, "You look ticked off."

He was right. She was scowling.

"No, I'm fine," she said. But she wasn't. And Winston knew she wasn't. He knew her very well.

❧

HER FIRST FULL day at her new job started much like the day before had ended. Ro sat alone in her small, beautiful office, quietly musing at what was going on behind the closed double doors. Waiting to be discovered again by her new boss. Certain she would handle it more gracefully than she had yesterday.

She tried to ignore the fact that her hair was still damp from taking a shower a little later than planned. And the fact that she still didn't have dressing for work in this hot and humid climate quite down. Ro had been forced to put aside all of the work clothes she'd brought with her because the material just wasn't suitable. Either light and silky rayon or heavier polyester blends were simply not wearable here.

Luckily, she'd brought enough cotton clothes to get her through the week. Today she wore a bohemian style ankle length skirt in a burnt orange floral print and a plain white short sleeve button up shirt. It was passible, but a little too far on the casual side for her liking. She would need to do some shopping if she was planning on staying here for good.

And stay was exactly what Ro was going to do.

If she hadn't been sure about it yesterday when Alicia showed her into this elegant, beautiful room that would be her office, she had been sure the moment she stepped onto the beach this morning. The fresh, salty smell, the cool breeze in her face, the way the sky changed into brilliant colors right in front of her eyes, the feeling of abandon, like she'd stepped into her real life after waking from a long sleep. The last time she'd felt anything like it had been when she met Theo.

"And this is all me, nothing to do with him," she said under her breath.

She stood up and went to the window to pull up the thick wooden blinds. She loved the way the light filtered through the heavy glass as well as the view. The bustling life in the street below made the scene vibrant.

The double doors clicked behind her and Ro whirled around just as Cooper stuck his head out of his office. Seeing her, he smiled, but didn't move any further into the room.

"You're here," he said happily.

"I'm here," she answered.

"Can you help me with something?"

Ro nodded and moved towards him, "Of course." Her words were choked a little with nerves, but she managed to gather herself together while she crossed the room.

When she got to the double doors, he pulled them open to reveal an exquisite office worthy of any Fortune 500 CEO or five-star hotel owner. The room was at least double the size of her office and the waiting area combined. The rich dark wood accents, prevalent throughout the hotel in every beam, in all of the trim, and in the intricately carved crown molding, was still center stage in this room. But here in Cooper's office the wood craftsmanship had been taken to another level.

The ceiling was at least ten feet high and every inch of it was covered with the deep brown shining wood. Beams of it had been carefully carved and fit together into square frames inside larger square frames three times over, creating a deep relief effect that was gorgeous. Ro had never seen a coffered ceiling quite like this, in fact she'd rarely seen one in person anywhere until now.

There were bookshelves, a large executive desk and small, ornate tables placed tastefully throughout the room. There was an imposing leather rolling chair behind the desk and comfortable looking wine colored chairs in a generous sitting area. A few large paintings with tiny canned lights trained on them from above and below graced the walls. Ro didn't know much about art, but she guessed these were expensive pieces.

Despite the fact that the room dripped with money and power, Ro struggled to take it all in or be impressed by it in any way. Her struggle stemmed from the fact that Cooper stood in front of her wearing perfectly tailored black slacks and absolutely nothing else. No shoes or socks and, most distracting of all, no shirt.

"What do you think?" He asked, holding up two hangers that held white tuxedo shirts with slightly different designs so she could see them.

"Um," Ro blinked hard, trying to tear her eyes away from Cooper's naked chest, muscled biceps and the tops of his shoulders that were flexing as he held up the shirts. "What jacket are you going to wear?" It was all she could think of to buy more time.

Cooper grinned at her, "Smart girl." He gave her the shirts to hold and stepped to a rolling clothing rack that held several different tuxedo jackets, multiple vests in different colors and what looked like a variety of cummerbunds and bow ties. He grabbed two black jackets and lifted them up as he had the shirts. Displaying them for her to see.

"For the party," Cooper said. Of course, the New Year's Eve party.

Ro liked how he spoke to her as if they'd known each other forever, as if there was no question that she knew exactly what he was talking about. She looked carefully at the two jackets. One was a classic cut with shining black satin lapels. The other was double breasted and looked like it would barely fit over his muscular chest. Both would look fantastic on him. Anything would look fantastic on him. Images from the internet of Cooper wearing his untucked, unbuttoned tuxedo shirt flashed through her mind and she lost focus again.

"This one is new," Cooper indicated the double-breasted jacket in his right hand with a quick nod.

"Hmmm," Ro nodded, pretending this new bit of information made a difference. She couldn't make a choice. Either one would be amazing. Anyway, she was having a hard time processing the fact that she was in this room giving her opinion to this beautiful man to begin with.

"Hello?" A voice carried to them from outside the double doors.

Someone was in the waiting room. She and Cooper looked toward the door then back to each other. Even though there was nothing vaguely intimate going on, Ro couldn't help but feel that they were somehow about to be caught in a risqué situation. She opened her mouth to excuse herself and take care of her reception duties when Winston poked his head into the open double doors.

"Hello," he said again, grinning.

Ro's embarrassment was just slightly outweighed by irritation. She glared at him.

Cooper looked lazily back and forth between she and Winston, his gaze finally landing on her, "Is this a friend of yours?"

Ro nodded, feeling ridiculously unprofessional, "This is Winston, he's a friend from my old job." To her surprise, Cooper smiled widely at Winston and motioned him into the room. Winston came in without hesitation and joined her. Ro refused to look at him.

"All right, my brother, what do you think?" Cooper held the two jackets up even higher so both she and Winston could see them well.

Winston considered the two jackets while Ro fumed. Why did he have to butt his head into the first real interaction she was having with her new hot, shirtless boss? Her fuming turned to mortification when Winston gave a 'meh' face and shrugged, effectively dismissing both jacket choices.

"Really?" Cooper seemed surprised and turned the jackets towards himself to look for whatever offense Winston saw in them.

"They're not bad," Winston said casually. Ro's eyebrows raised in disbelief. "But that one is gonna be too warm," Winston pointed at the double-breasted jacket. "If you're planning on wearing it around here," he added.

Cooper nodded in understanding, "True."

Winston's eyes wandered across the other options that hung on the rolling rack. Ro tried to think of something intelligent or classy or funny to say, but she was drawing a blank. All she could think about was the fact that Winston, wearing a pair of board shorts with a pink and green palm tree print, a bright yellow Corona beer T-shirt that he'd obviously just bought in the gift shop, and a pair of purple flip flops, was giving fashion advice to the man who might be the most perfect man she'd ever met.

She needed to get Winston out of here. Push him out the door so she could retrieve the moment with Cooper. She was about to say something, anything, when Winston abruptly went to the clothing rack and pulled out a gold tuxedo jacket with black lapels and cuffs.

"What about this one?"

Her initial reaction was to laugh. Who would wear a gold tuxedo? She stifled this reaction when she saw Cooper's expression. He was smiling broadly, obviously taken with Winston's idea.

"Yeah?" Cooper went to the rack and abandoned the two black jackets, taking the gold one to inspect.

Ro's vision of sipping a glass of champagne with Cooper dressed in his classy black tuxedo jacket fizzled. She could see that the gold jacket idea had peaked his interest. He took it off the hanger and put it on. With his bare chest and black slacks he looked a lot like an exotic male dancer, which wasn't necessarily a bad thing.

"What do you think?" Cooper turned towards her and posed with his arms reaching out a little, as if he was about to walk up to her and give her a hug.

She swallowed. It wasn't that he looked bad in the gold jacket. He looked amazing. But her first choice would have been the black one. Nerves filled her stomach. She felt heat rise in her cheeks and was embarrassed at being embarrassed. Why was she struggling so hard with this situation? Ro flicked her eyes to Winston who stood cool and confident behind Cooper. His presence was making her feel uncertain. It reminded her of her old life. The one she wanted to forget.

Both of the men were waiting for her response. She was overthinking. She had to say something.

"Sure," she said, nodding.

Then Ro did something that surprised her. It surprised Winston, too, she could tell by the look on his face. She moved to Cooper so that she was standing directly in front of him, looking up into his chiseled, handsome face. She put her hands on his shoulders, smoothing the material, which was softer than she had thought it would be, then let her hands run down the length of both of his arms, as if she was evaluating the cut. Cooper grinned down at her, amused. And, she could tell, a little turned on.

She smiled back at him and said, "It's nice."

"Thanks," Cooper said, his voice was deep and sensual. It reverberated through her. He smelled good, too.

Then, because apparently he was bent on interrupting her world, Winston chimed in, "Good choice. Now that that's decided, Ro, wanna have lunch with me?"

It took everything she had not to roll her eyes.

Chapter Six

"It's just that the hotel is throwing a huge New Year's Eve party tomorrow night and I won't have a lot of time," Ro explained.

She and Winston were seated at one of the corner tables in the hotel dining room. An employee and a guest eating lunch together. Ro wasn't sure if this was the kind of thing that would be deeply frowned upon by Alicia. She was pretty sure Cooper was fine with it, since he'd insisted that she make plans with Winston while they were all choosing his tuxedo in his office earlier. Her new boss had even gone so far as to send them a complimentary bottle of wine during their meal.

"Enjoy lunch, Coop," Winston had read the note that came with the bottle out loud. Then he raised one eyebrow, "Coop?"

"That's what people call him," Ro said defensively.

She'd felt defensive the entire lunch. When Winston pulled her chair out for her as they were being seated, when he asked her how her first full day was going, when he'd ordered the chicken with chili and dark chocolate sauce for them both...in Spanish. Everything he did prickled at her nerves, which was why she was trying to explain to him that she was going to be too busy to hang out with him before he went home. She was going to be working a lot on the party.

"What about after the party?" He asked, taking another bite of the creamy caramel covered flan on his plate.

"Well, I think I'm going to be pretty wiped out after the party."

Winston chuckled, "No, not right after the party. What about a day or two after the party? Will you have any time off then?"

Ro looked at him blankly.

"But you won't be here," she said.

"Of course I'll be here," Winston said, lifting his wine glass and looking appreciatively around the dining patio. "I'm on vacation!" He toasted the air and took a sip of his wine.

"But you don't take vacations," Ro continued to be stunned into making stupid comments.

"I do now," Winston said, scooping up another large spoonful of flan. "I'm not gonna fly right back after I just got here. I'm gonna look around a little, have some fun," he put the giant bite into his mouth and wiggled his eyebrows at her.

The general irritation she'd been feeling towards him escalated into full-blown anxiety. How long was he planning on staying here? Would he be constantly interrupting her new life? Did he expect her to tag along with him on this vacation fun?

"How long?" She asked the question quietly, looking down and pushing her flan around with the back side of her spoon. Her enthusiasm for dessert was dissipating.

"I took a month off from work," he said.

"You're staying a month?" She looked up at him in shock, then dropped her eyes again. Trying to hide her disappointment.

"You're upset," Winston said, dipping his head and trying to look up into her lowered gaze.

"I'm not upset."

"You are," he gave her a charming smile. Ro put down her spoon and looked away. "Don't worry, I'm not gonna hang around you like a loser," he nudged her foot under the table with the toe of his sandal.

Relieved, and a little ashamed at how relieved she was, Ro looked back at him. Winston had dressed up a little for lunch. He wore new leather all sport sandals, a white short sleeved light cotton shirt with wood buttons and a pair of olive green cargo shorts. He had been swimming and shopping for clothes while he waited for lunch to roll around, and a twinge of tropical color had taken the edge off of his normal Midwestern pallor.

"I don't mean to ignore you, Winston, I just...I just..." she couldn't explain. She didn't want to hurt his feelings. He'd come all this way to check on her, and he was her friend.

"You just want to start your new life, I got it," Winston picked up the wine bottle. There was only a little bit left and he offered it to Ro. She shook her head 'no'. This was the middle of her work day after all. Winston poured the last of the wine into his glass as he spoke, "I was talking to that Zander guy, from Australia. I think I'm gonna to take some scuba lessons. Check out the local sights. Maybe go to see some ruins!"

The image of Winston, accountant extraordinaire, making his way through the tropical beauty of the area with a map and a pair of binoculars popped into Ro's mind. She giggled.

"What? I think the ruins would be intriguing," he said.

This made her laugh again.

"Go ahead, laugh all you want. I don't get to live here forever like you do. I gotta get in some rest and relaxation type fun before I head back to the rat race."

"You should," she said, and she meant it.

"I'll find something we can do together," he started, then held up his palm to stop her from speaking, "In a few days, I know, I know. It'll take me that long to find something fun enough to pull you away from Tuxedo Man."

She laughed again, a genuine laugh.

Gloria appeared at her side just as she got over her giggle fit.

"Señorita Ro," Gloria said, giving Winston a smile and nod as she did.

"Yes?" Ro sat up straighter. Gloria may be a grey haired lady in a flowing rose print dress, but she was basically Alicia's right hand. She got, and deserved, all of Ro's most respectful attention.

"We will meet in your office at one o'clock?" Gloria asked.

"Yes, absolutely. You were going to give me all of my tasks for tomorrow's party," Ro said.

Gloria nodded, "That's good." Her fine eyebrows knit together as she let her gaze run up and down Ro's outfit. For a moment, Ro thought the older woman was going to call her out for her casual attire. Instead, Gloria asked, "Do you have a dress for the party? It is a formal event."

Ro's heart sank. She hadn't thought about what she would wear to the party. Even if more of her wardrobe was suitable to this climate, she hadn't brought anything remotely formal. Gloria read the expression on her face and placed her hand on Ro's shoulder.

"I will take you shopping tonight after work? I know the best dress shops," Gloria told her.

"Yes, thank you. That's very nice of you," Ro gushed.

"A pretty young woman should have a pretty new dress for such a big party," Gloria said. Her eyes smiled kindly at Ro, then she gave Winston a meaningful look. He lifted his eyebrows, understanding that the nice old lady must think he was Ro's date or maybe even her boyfriend. That was not the kind of rumor Ro wanted to get spread around the hotel. She started to correct her, but Gloria had already turned and was walking smoothly towards the dining area exit.

"Maybe you could get something in gold," Winston said, giving her an exaggerated wink.

This time she did roll her eyes at him.

&

BY THE TIME she and Gloria could finally step away from party preparations and go dress shopping, Ro was afraid it was too late and the best places would be closed. Though the sun hadn't gone down, it was definitely on its way. She sat in the back seat of a small taxi cab, watching the streets full of tourists and locals, bicycles, carts and more cabs, as they buzzed past. Gloria sat next to her, looking even smaller than normal because her chin barely reached the bottom of the cab window. The size of a child, she gazed out her open window, letting the breeze flow against her face.

Ro was exhausted. Their whole afternoon had been a whirlwind. There were so many details to take care of, and without knowing the language, most of Ro's duties had been of the run and fetch, or spit and polish variety. She had helped count and set up all of the silver centerpieces and candelabras so they were ready to dress the room before breakfast opened tomorrow morning, making sure they were all polished and up to snuff as she did. She had also helped decide where the floral arrangements would go and drew out a map for Carlos to have ready for the florist when they arrived.

With food deliveries tripling today and tomorrow, Carlos was overwhelmed, so Ro had also helped out at the front desk. She was the official greeter of anyone speaking English, which was fun. She didn't mind the happy chatter of tourists. In fact, it made her feel good when they were impressed that she worked there, and lived there, full time. Of course, she didn't tell any of them that she'd only been in Playa del Carmen a few days.

At first, she'd been concerned that maybe Cooper would be looking for her in her office. So she asked Gloria.

"It's okay with Coop- I mean, Mr. Rivera, that I'm away from my desk, isn't it?"

"Mr. Rivera takes little interest in business matters when a party is on the schedule," Alicia answered coldly. She was standing nearby and had overheard the question. She gave Ro a withering look. Ro didn't know if Alicia's disdain was because of Cooper's lack of interest in hotel business, or if it was the fact that she'd called him by his first name. Or both.

When everything had wrapped up for the day, Gloria had taken her by the arm and directed her out the front door past the crystal fountain in front of the hotel to a waiting cab. The cabbie, a small, wrinkled Mexican man with a huge grey mustache, straightened up when he saw Gloria approaching. Funny that she had that effect on everyone.

"Señora, Señorita," the cabbie gave them each a small bow before opening the door for them to slip in. Ro got the feeling that Gloria knew the cabbie, or at least he knew who Gloria was and held her in some esteem. When they arrived at the boutique dress shop called 'Luna Rica', that feeling was reinforced.

Not only were they greeted with a flurry of attention from three beautifully dressed mature women who spilled out the front door when their cab pulled up, but the cabbie didn't drive away in search of more patrons. Instead, he opened their doors, offered his hand to help them out of the cab, then discreetly parked up against the side of the small building and waited for them. More like a chauffeur than a cabbie.

The boutique ladies bustled Ro and Gloria inside. The air was nicely temperature controlled, several gorgeous beaded evening gowns were displayed on mannequins, which were lined up along the side walls under spotlights, making them sparkle. The back wall was covered with floor to ceiling mirrors set at angles against one another so anyone standing in front of them could get a view of every inch of their body.

The three ladies sat them down in two wingback chairs that faced the mirrors and Ro was thankful for the comfortable elegance of this place. The ladies all spoke Spanish with Gloria, murmuring quietly and taking turns leaving then returning with refreshments. They brought a white, milky, sweet drink that was cold, smooth and delicious. Gloria told Ro it was called horchata. They also brought them tiny, bitesized empanadas that were like small corn calzones full of different savory meats.

Munching her empanadas and sipping her horchata, Ro thought she had died and gone to heaven. And after a few minutes of being cooed over and fed, she was rejuvenated enough to notice more of her surroundings.

For a dress shop there were very few dresses on display. Although, those that she could see from her chair were absolutely stunning. Not really dresses, but rather gowns. Statements.

The three boutique ladies were almost exactly the same size, no variation in height or age from what Ro could tell. They were soft and feminine, curvy without being overweight. Graceful. Though their dresses were feminine and flowing, like Gloria's, they all wore black or grey or a mix thereof instead of the pretty pastels that Ro had seen in Gloria's floral prints.

Gloria noticed Ro peering around the edge of her winged

chair trying to look at the dresses, the women and their surroundings. Gloria smiled sweetly and nodded at one of the boutique ladies. Suddenly there was a flurry of activity and all three ladies disappeared behind the mirrors.

Ro wondered if she should get up and look around, perhaps take a dress into a dressing room and try it on. Before she had a chance to move, a teenage girl emerged from behind the mirrors. She was slender, not too tall, about Ro's height and size, and she was wearing a gorgeous deep green evening gown. With a princess neckline and a drop waist, the gown moved sensually as the young woman walked. Ro saw the girl looking at her and quickly looked away, not realizing, yet, that the girl was modeling the dress for her.

"You don't like this one?" Gloria asked.

"Oh," Ro shook her head and blushed a little, "I didn't know she was showing me."

"Yes, this is for you. It's less tiring this way," Gloria explained. She leaned back in her wing-backed chair and took a sip of her horchata. So, Ro followed suit, and turned a more critical eye on the green dress.

She liked the flow of it, but the color wasn't really her favorite and it wasn't as sparkly as some of the others along the wall. The girl walked back and forth in front of them, pausing and turning slowly each time she turned around. This was the first time Ro had shopped in this manner, like someone who came from wealth. She wasn't sure what the protocol was for refusing a dress. She tried to think of a way to say it without being insulting to the dress or the model.

"It's very lovely, but I'm not sure this one is for me," she said.

Gloria nodded and swished her hand in a curt dismissive manner to the model. The girl turned on her heel and went quickly away. A surprisingly short time later, no more than 30 seconds, the girl returned wearing a form fitted black cocktail dress. This dress definitely had sparkles, sequins were sewn all over the bodice and in a swirling pattern that dipped down from the waist onto the hipline. But the spaghetti straps and very low cut neckline made Ro a little nervous. She didn't want to come across too sexy at her first official office party.

This time Gloria read her expression and Ro barely had to move her head before Gloria was sending the girl away. Quick as a wink she was back, this time in a gold gown. Ro smiled to herself. She couldn't go gold. It would be too weird.

After four more attempts Ro was beginning to think she might need to be less picky. Maybe she should have tried on the light blue dress or the very first one they showed her, the green one. Maybe it was all too much after her long day and the incredibly eventful last few days of flying here and getting the job and everything. Perhaps she was hopeless and would have to wear her cotton sundress to the party.

Then she saw the red dress.

Ro was immediately drawn to the color. A poppy red, bright and fresh, yet still sexy. Sleeveless, with a scoop neck, the cut was relatively simple. Fitted to the body without clinging or being too tight, the dress was fuller starting at the knees, which gave it a flirty kick when the girl was walking.

The feature that really got Ro's attention, however, was the beadwork. Sewn in overlapping patterns using diamond shapes of different sizes, the dress almost looked like something from the 1920's, the way it shimmered in the light. Ro sat up straighter as the girl turned in front of her, giving her the best view of the back, which was much lower than the front and showed off the girl's shoulder blades and smooth skin.

"I think perhaps this is your dress," Gloria said. She nodded at the girl and within minutes Ro was in the dressing room looking at her reflection. The dress was on and fit almost perfectly. Any alterations were being efficiently calculated, discussed and pinned by the three boutique ladies. Gloria watched from a comfortable chair in the corner of the dressing room, smiling widely.

"This is perfect for you. It's elegant, beautiful and fun," Gloria said.

Ro agreed. Looking in the mirror she was filled with the kind of excitement she used to feel when her parents were taking her to the amusement park in the summer, or when they left on a trip early in the morning. Her stomach filled with that same fluttering thrill and she marveled at how she'd ended up here, in this dress, preparing for the biggest party she'd ever been to in her life. She'd never had a dress like this. She'd never been able to afford it.

The fluttering in her stomach suddenly twisted into a knot and made her feel sick. She hadn't thought about how much this dress would cost. This kind of boutique was so high end. Even if they gave her a good deal because Gloria was obviously a good customer, she doubted she could afford this beautiful dress.

Gloria and the head boutique lady spoke rapidly in Spanish. Sealing the deal no doubt.

"They will make the alterations and deliver it to the hotel tomorrow before noon," Gloria informed her.

"I'm sorry, I didn't think to ask about the price," Ro said. "I'm not sure I can afford such a beautiful dress."

Gloria waved away Ro's comment, "We will charge it to the hotel. Your hiring bonus, yes?"

Too stunned to answer immediately, Ro finally swallowed hard and answered, "Yes."

Yes. Absolutely.

Before she knew it, her mind conjured up an image of Cooper in his gold tuxedo jacket, and she smiled. Red and gold went well together.

Chapter Seven

Winston looked excited and nervous, like a little boy about to embark on a new adventure. He was paying strict attention to Zander's instructions, his eyes bright with the new challenge of scuba diving.

Ro, on the other hand, wasn't really listening. Zander was going over the rules of diving, the things to look out for, the possible dangers, how to safely ascend, decompression sickness, but it was going in one ear and out the other. She had only come with Winston to see him off, intent on getting to her office on time today and, hopefully, spending some time with Cooper before the big party. Of course it would be work time, not like a date or anything, but still.

"What do you think?" Winston asked. He posed in the wetsuit he'd pulled on over his board shorts.

Ro eyed him up and down. The slick black look flattered him, actually. The way the material clung to his body accentuated his build and she was surprised to see that Winston had fairly wide shoulders. She had never noticed that when he was in his everyday clothes. He looked bigger in a wetsuit.

"He looks like a shark!" Zander exclaimed. He was

carrying scuba gear to a low empty table, getting it ready to haul to the boat.

Zander's dive shop was actually a garage, with a cement floor and metal walls and roof. But it was clean, with all kinds of scuba and snorkeling gear hanging on iron bars that looked like they'd been built specifically for this space and then attached to the metal walls. The front door, which was a garage door, was fully open to the beach and the dock where his boat waited, allowing the full sunrise of Playa del Carmen to shine into the building.

Ro had been taking a morning stroll on the beach with Carlos and his family when they ran into Winston on his way to Zander's place. It was just a short walk down the beach to the dive shop, so Ro had joined him to offer her support.

"You sure you don't want to come?" Zander asked her, his piercing blue eyes glittering with fun.

"No, I can't. I have to work," she answered. She tried to look disappointed, not wanting to insult Zander. In truth she was thrilled to go to work today. Not only would she probably, maybe, hopefully, see Cooper, she had the added pleasure of knowing that the day would end with her wearing her gorgeous new dress to the New Year's Eve party.

"On a day like this? It's the last day of the year and it's gonna be a beauty," Zander said. He swept his arm towards the sand and water and sunrise outside the open garage door as proof. "All work and no play..." Zander grinned at her.

"Well, in all fairness, I've only worked at the hotel a few days, I don't think I could ask for any time off just yet," Ro explained. The ocean was enticing there was no doubt about it, but she wasn't just a tourist here. She had responsibilities...and plans.

"Right, you're working for Coop aren't you?" Zander asked.

Winston gave Ro a look, raising his eyebrows at the

mention of Cooper's nickname. She scowled at his silent teasing.

"Yes, and we've got the big party tonight and everything," she answered.

"Ah, yeah, he puts on a great party," Zander mused. He chuckled to himself, remembering parties past no doubt.

"Are you going?" Winston asked Zander.

Zander shrugged.

"Are you?" Zander asked Winston, "You're staying there, aren't you?"

"I might," Winston looked at Ro, checking her reaction.

"You don't need my permission," Ro said. She never said he couldn't do whatever he wanted to do while he was here.

Now it was Winston's turn to shrug.

"I just want to be sure not to interrupt you at work," Winston said. He looked at Zander and indicated Ro with a tilt of his head, "You don't want to get in her way."

Ro rolled her eyes at him, "Don't be silly."

"You're on the career track, then?" Zander asked.

Winston nodded emphatically even though Zander had directed the question towards her.

"I guess if doing what you've been hired to do means you're on the career track, then yes, I'm on the career track," she responded. She didn't want to seem like a stick in the mud, but she also didn't want them to think they could convince her to go out on the water with them when she was supposed to be getting ready for work.

"Nothing wrong with that," Zander said. Then he chuckled again, "You may find yourself disappointed with Coop."

Ro cocked her head, interested in finding out more about Cooper from wherever possible, "What do you mean?"

Zander was leaning over a scuba tank, inspecting the gages, "Coop's a great guy, I love him. But he is definitely not

on the career track. He couldn't care less about business."
Finding the gages to his satisfaction, Zander lifted the tank
and placed it on a flat cart that he apparently used to transfer
the heavy equipment to the boat. He straightened and gave
her an amused smile, "Why would he worry, though, with the
kind of money he's got, he doesn't have to work another day
in his life."

This wasn't shocking news, but something about hearing
it from a completely unbiased source made her feel...what?
Excited? Nervous? She couldn't tell. She looked at Winston
who seemed to be preoccupied with making adjustments to
his diving mask.

Ro felt antsy. She looked out at the rising sun and thought
it was probably time for her to find Carlos and Josefina and
get back to the hotel.

"I'm gonna get going. I've got to get ready for work," she
said.

"Thanks for walking with me," Winston said. His hair had
gotten messed up with all of the scuba preparations and he
still looked a little nervous. But in an adorable kind of way.

Ro smiled as she reached out and squeezed his arm, "Have
fun, I'm sure it's going to be amazing."

After saying their goodbyes, Ro stepped back onto the
beach. She took a deep breath of the fresh ocean air then
took off towards where she'd left Carlos earlier.

There were a few more people on the beach than when
they'd first arrived. Still, it was a nice walk along the water.
The little tidbits Zander had provided about Cooper were
mulling around in her mind. How wealthy was Cooper? What
would it be like to work with someone like him? What would
it be like to be with someone like him romantically? A small
smile played on her lips when she let her thoughts linger
there.

"Good morning!"

A man's voice brought her back to the here and now. She looked up and focused on him. It was Cooper.

Ro hesitated a moment. Was he a mirage? Had she conjured him up by thinking about him as she walked?

"Getting a little beach time before work?" He asked as he approached her. Her heart skipped a beat.

It was definitely Cooper and he was definitely real. He had on another pair of his slim fitted bathing trunks. This time they were pale blue with white cording around the waist. He wasn't shirtless, but wore a salmon colored short sleeve linen shirt, unbuttoned. He had a knack for appearing half clothed a lot of the time. Not that she was complaining.

"Hi, good morning," Ro answered, trying to focus on not staring at the way the ocean breeze made his shirt flutter open.

Cooper glanced behind her towards the dive shop in the near distance, "Did you come from Zander's?"

"Yes, I was just there."

"Going diving?" He asked.

"Oh, of course not, not today anyway. I've got so much to do to get ready for the party tonight," Ro wanted to sound both competent and convey her excitement at the upcoming party.

"Great, I'm glad you're on top of everything. Too bad you're not coming with us, though, it should be fun," Cooper said with a dimpled smile.

"Us?"

"Yeah, Zander said he's going out this morning, so I thought I'd go with. Get in some scuba time on the last day of the year."

Ro felt her jaw clench, but she managed to hold the smile on her face as she spoke, "You're going scuba diving this morning?"

"Yeah, if you didn't have so much to do you could come

with us. Maybe next time?" Cooper said as he gave her a half nod and moved past her towards the dive shop.

"Right...sure...next time," she said. With a half-hearted wave she watched Cooper turn his back and walk away. The urge to chase after him and say that she'd changed her mind was strong. Her pride, however, was stronger. She trudged back to where Carlos and Josefina were waiting. Kicking herself all the way for making such a big deal about her workload.

Her mood did not improve greatly for the rest of the day. Overrun with work, focusing hard on trying to overcome the language barrier that was ever present, and plagued with thoughts of Cooper having a great day in the sea and sun with Winston of all people, kept Ro in a sour disposition. The only thing she had to look forward to was when she finally had the time to take a bath and slip into her new dress. Then she would feel elegant. Then she would feel exotic. Then she would feel like she was starting off her new year with a brand new life.

Before that, however, she had to help at the desk and in the dining area and the adjoining ballroom, which had been opened up for the party. The ballroom wasn't quite as big as it sounded, but it was definitely luxurious and impressive enough to earn its name. The activity was non-stop and completely engaged her until just before dinner. Politely refusing Gloria's invitation to sit with her and eat, Ro excused herself to her room at half past seven to prepare for the evening.

When she entered her room she found her beautiful new red dress hanging in the small closet. She grabbed the hanger and pulled it out of the closet. Holding it up, Ro turned the gorgeous garment around, inspecting it completely to ensure nothing had happened to the delicate beadwork during the delivery process. It looked perfect. She sighed and took the dress to the full-length freestanding mirror that stood in the corner. She held the dress up against her body and her long, busy day melted away. This was going to be an amazing party and an amazing night.

After a long bath in the soaker tub, which included sumptuous jasmine and orange bath salts that were part of the spa products provided in the hotel, Ro worked on her hair. Using a set of sparkling crystal hairpins, she was able to sweep her not very long hair up. She didn't go for the sleek look, but rather a messy do with lots of bounce and wave.

She applied her eye makeup a little darker than her normal day look, it was New Year's Eve after all. The extra attention to her eye makeup paid off. Ro was impressed with how much it made the blue-grey of her eyes stand out even more than normal. Waiting to apply lipstick until after her dress was safely on, Ro went to the closet and pulled it out.

Slipping it over her head was easy. Zipping up the back was not quite as simple. She had to do a few twisting, acrobatic moves in order to get the job done. As a result her hair needed to be adjusted. Not only that, but the humidity in the air made her break out into a light sweat. Ro decided to lay on the bed under the ceiling fan to cool off. This took a long time. So long she was worried her dress was getting wrinkled.

"Well, this isn't working," she said out loud. With much care, Ro pushed herself into a sitting position then stood. She would have to get ready in the humidity and hope she didn't melt in the process.

Finally, with hair fixed, lipstick applied and a pair of strappy black high heels she was thankful she'd packed on her feet, Ro arrived at the party. Officially off the clock, she was free to take in the beautiful flower arrangements and candles that lit the long table full of delicious food from the hotel's kitchen.

Wait staff, dressed neatly in all black, some of whom she'd

worked with earlier in the day, walked the room with silver trays carrying bubbling champagne or deep red Sangria. Men in tuxedos and women in a variety of colorful cocktail dresses and evening gowns filled the space. Under the twinkling lights strung along all of the ceilings, arches and posts, the black tuxedos looked like the ocean at night and the women's dresses flashed and shimmered like tropical fish.

All of the glitzy guests were laughing and talking over the live band that were set up in the corner of the ballroom playing traditional music from Mexico. Though the rooms pulsed with excitement, all of the extra bodies in the enclosed areas made the already warm air more than Ro could handle. She wandered around the party, sipping on a glass of champagne and searching out the least hot and humid area in the whole place. This, it turned out, was the tiled area by the pool. With the lights from the party glinting off of the shining surface of the water and the roof of the courtyard open to the night sky, it was both beautiful and cooler than inside.

Ro peered into the growing crowd and searched for any familiar faces. A few of the wait staff nodded at her in greeting, but she didn't speak Spanish and they knew that, so there was no conversation. With only Spanish being spoken all around her and nobody, not Gloria or Carlos or even Alicia, nearby, Ro was feeling a little uncomfortable.

A flash of gold caught her eye through the open doorway to the crowded ballroom. She cursed her short stature when a group of partygoers passed in front of her, blocking her view. She wasn't tall enough to see over them. It might not have been Cooper. There could be a woman wearing a gold dress in the ballroom. Or a different man with a gold tuxedo jacket. Ro thought again. Never mind, that was unlikely.

Pressing forward towards the ballroom, she saw a figure

approach in her peripheral vision. A man. A tall man with solid shoulders who reached out and touched her elbow.

"Ro?"

A familiar voice, but not a gold tuxedo jacket. This jacket was black. Ro turned towards the voice and her eyes flew open.

Chapter Eight

"Winston?"

Yes, her eyes were not betraying her. It was Winston. Except better.

He held raised his arms up straight from his sides as if presenting himself for her approval. Decked out in a tuxedo, his face tanner than when she'd left him this morning, his hair styled, Winston looked taller, more sophisticated, and cuter than she'd ever seen him.

"Wow," Winston looked her up and down with appreciation, giving her a low whistle as he did. "You look amazing!"

"So do you!" She meant it, too.

"Yeah?" He flicked his lapels with his thumbs and gave her a sly smile.

Ro laughed, then asked, "Where did you get the tuxedo?"

"Your boy hooked me up."

"My boy?"

Winston tilted his head and leaned in towards her ear, "Your boy, Coop."

Ro stiffened.

"Cooper gave you that tux?"

"He lent it to me."

Eyeing Winston again, she thought she did recognize the black jacket as one of the two Cooper had held up for her inspection. With that mystery solved, the only other question she had was exactly how buddy-buddy Winston was with her new boss. She took a sip of her champagne and swallowed with pursed lips. Just as she was about to ask Winston to explain the situation, his attention shifted to something in the nearby crowd.

"There he is," Winston cupped his hand to his mouth and called out, "Coop!"

Ro turned her head just in time to see Cooper making his way through a group of party goers towards them. Her emotions ricocheted inside her like a ball in a pinball machine. Elation and excitement slammed into embarrassment and insecurity, the same kind of bashfulness she used to feel as a schoolgirl whenever she was around her crush.

Cooper looked like a movie star. The gold tuxedo jacket suited him perfectly, because he was far and away the best looking man in the room. And probably the wealthiest. As well as the owner of the hotel. Winston had been right. It was a good choice. It gave Cooper an air of being a prince, but a really cool, fashionable prince.

Cooper smiled and waved at Winston, then his gaze fell on her and he froze for a second. He looked at her intensely as if he'd just discovered a rare bird and didn't want to frighten it away. When he smiled at her it was a full-blown sexy smile, complete with a mischievous gleam in his eyes. Ro's heartbeat increased markedly. Then, still pounding, it dropped into her stomach when she saw that he had two gorgeous blonde women with him, one on each arm. They looked almost identical.

She kept her smile in place, which took every ounce of concentration she could muster. She was focusing so hard on smiling that the Barbie women went blurry and Ro could barely see Winston glancing at her out of the corner of her eye. She couldn't look at him. She knew that he must know what she was thinking, and she didn't want to risk catching his eye and falling apart right here in the middle of the party. Her focus on staying calm and pleasant made it impossible for her to speak or even to remember the names of the two women when Cooper introduced them. Not that it mattered. They were all Tamara to her.

The party went by in a blur. Ro had lost her appetite, but kept grabbing flutes full of champagne when they were offered to her, which was quite often. She lost count of how many glasses she had, the pleasant buzzing in her brain being the only thing she wanted to focus on.

Cooper flirted with her a little, told her he liked her dress, and she thought he said something about doing something together outside of work someday, maybe scuba. Or maybe she had misunderstood what he said because of the champagne.

His handsome face was in and out of her vision, as were the beautiful, perfectly made up faces of the two blondes. They ran into Gloria, who was gracious and elegant as ever. Zander showed up in the mix as well. Although she really wasn't sure if she was imagining things at that point, because she was quite tipsy. She clearly saw Alicia once, staring her down from across the room. Ro hoped that she was imagining that part of the evening.

The only thing that remained constant throughout the whole party was Winston. Even when Ro couldn't see him, she felt him standing just to the left and behind her. He offered her food and non-alcoholic drinks. He danced with her when she wanted to dance. He caught her elbow when she started to sway from too much champagne. He found her a chair when she said she was feeling tired. And he carried her high heels when she declared her feet were hot and abandoned them on the floor.

"I think maybe we should get you to bed," Winston told her when she tried to stand up, but felt dizzy and sat back down again.

Ro groaned. It was all she could do. The room was starting to spin and she was so hot she thought briefly about taking her dress off. That thought sent her into a fit of giggles.

"Yeah, I think it's bedtime for you," Winston said with amusement.

"No!" Ro shouted. A few of the partygoers near them took notice, but luckily the music and people were loud enough to mask her drunken shout from most of the room.

"C'mon, Ro, I'll walk you," Winston took her by the hands and pulled her to her feet.

"But it's not midnight yet," Ro whined. "I won't get a midnight kiss," she pushed her finger awkwardly against her lips, then started laughing again.

"I don't think you need a kiss right now," Winston said calmly as he guided her through the crowd.

"I do need a kiss," Ro argued. Her voice still too loud, "Where's Cooper?"

"Uh-oh," Winston said, picking up their pace. He was practically lifting her off of the floor to move her along more quickly.

Ro cupped her hands to her mouth the way Winston had earlier and called out, "Coop, Coop, Coop!"

More heads turned their way, but she didn't see Cooper's gold jacket anywhere.

"Whoop! Whoop! Happy New Year!" Winston called out, as if joining her in a cheer. He ducked his head down to her ear, "Come on, party girl."

He helped her out of the crowd into the gloriously cool

lobby. The tile was cold on her feet and this fascinated her. She stopped walking and stared down at her bare toes.

"My shoes!" She declared, the fact that she was bare foot just now registering.

"I've got 'em," Winston held up her black sandals for her to see. He had them dangling from two fingers.

The sight of Winston, her funny Winston, all dressed up in a tuxedo and carrying women's shoes struck Ro as the most hilarious thing she'd ever seen. She laughed so hard that she had to bend over and was afraid she would never breathe again. The laughing was so all encompassing she didn't even notice they were at her room until Winston was asking for her card key. At that point she was too drunk to argue. A little nap wouldn't hurt. She could sleep off the champagne and be back at the party in time for the midnight countdown.

She flopped face down on the bed, no longer concerned about wrinkling her brand new dress.

"Do you want some coffee or something?" Winston asked.

She mumbled into the pillow. Winston hunted around in the cabinets under her television and found some bottled water. He brought two over to the bed and placed one on the nightstand next to Ro. She turned her head so her face was barely visible.

"I need to take a nap," she said.

"Sounds like a good idea."

She rolled over so she was laying on her back and half of the bed was empty. Patting the bed next to her she said, "You can take a nap with me."

Winston hesitated.

She patted the bed harder, "Come on, buddy. I'm not gonna bite you."

"I think you need to sleep," Winston said. He looked towards the door then back at her.

"You're going to leave me on New Year's Eve?" Ro cried out in dismay.

"No, I'm not leaving," he said.

She giggled and patted the bed again, "Be my new year buddy."

He shook his head and smiled. Then he took off his jacket and hung it on the back of a chair, undid his bow tie so that it hung loose around his neck and unbuttoned the top few buttons of his shirt. He hopped up on the bed and laid back with his head propped up on the pillow next to hers.

Ro liked how Winston looked with his shirt undone and his nice, new tan. She smiled at him and he smiled back.

"You got tan today," she said, trying to act normal. It had just struck her that she and Winston had never been alone in a bedroom, let alone on a bed together.

"Yeah?" He looked at his hands and forearms for signs of a tan.

"Did you have fun scuba-ing?" She scrunched her face in confusion, trying to remember the right wording, "Or scuba...diving?"

"It was fun," he chuckled at her struggle. "It was so calm and beautiful under the surface. You should really try it."

"I will!" She smacked his arm in mock annoyance, "I've been working since I got here!"

"I know, I know."

They remained quiet for a few minutes. Ro could feel her eyelids getting heavy. She blinked hard and roused herself.

"What was Cooper like?" She asked.

"Coop?" Winston grinned at her and she smacked his arm again. He gave a little shrug, "He's a good enough guy."

"Is he?" Ro sighed dreamily.

"He's rich, that's for sure," Winston said. He stared up at the ceiling fan and mulled over his scuba diving adventure.

"For someone who has as much money as he does, he doesn't know a lot about tax shelters and investing," he added.

Ro didn't hear much of what Winston was saying, because she was lost in her own thoughts. She was thinking about Cooper being a good guy. About how he was tall, dark and handsome. How much he reminded her of...of...suddenly, tears welled up in her eyes and she started quietly crying. She sniffled and Winston looked at her.

"What's the matter?" He asked with concern, "Why are you crying?"

"You know who else was a good enough guy?" She asked. Her words slurring.

"Who?"

"Th-th-theo," Ro stammered out his name with a sob.

"Oh, no," Winston shifted so he could pull her head into the crook between his chest and shoulder. Ro pressed her face into him and had a good cry. Winston didn't say anything, he just pet the top of her head.

When she had cried herself out, Ro gave a shuddering sigh.

"Better?" Winston asked.

She nodded, but she wasn't better. She was exhausted and her head throbbed. The party was going on downstairs and she was going to miss out on all of the fun, and the midnight countdown, and on Cooper. Ro wanted to ask Winston what time it was and maybe get up and wash her face so they could go back down to the party. But instead of doing all of that, she got distracted and thought about how nice Winston smelled and how comfortable the bed felt. Then she sank into the warmth of his chest and fell asleep.

A half hour later, as the crowd downstairs counted down to midnight, Winston looked over at Ro's tear stained and mascara smeared face. She was in a deep sleep, her mouth open, a small snore escaping her nose with every breath.

"Four...three...two..." the noise of the crowd was a low murmur coming from below.

"One...Happy New Year, Ro," Winston said quietly. He carefully leaned over and kissed her on the forehead. Leaning back, he smiled at her non-response. Then he reached over to the lamp on the nightstand and turned off the light.

Chapter Nine

S he was at the dentist, sitting in a large chair that was
tilted so far to the back she could feel blood rushing to
her head. The dentist was talking to her, but it was all inco-
herent mumbling because he wore a surgical mask over his
face.

This was wrong. Ro wasn't due for a checkup and she
certainly didn't need oral surgery.

Indignant, she tried to tell him that there must be some
mistake. That's when she realized two things were keeping
her from communicating with the dentist. The metal tube
that sucked excess saliva during a cleaning was in her mouth.
She felt her lips close around it when she tried to talk, and
every time that happened the device dried up the inside of
her mouth. When she tried to reach up to take the stupid
thing out of her mouth, she realized that she was strapped
down in the chair. Not only could she not move her arms, but
she couldn't get out of the chair at all.

Panic filled her, making her arms and hands feel like pins
pricked along her skin. Ro's eyes widened as the dentist
moved closer to her, murmuring behind his mask, adjusting

the glaring light above her head so that it shone right into her eyes. She tried to close them, but the light somehow held them open. A sharp pain shot through her head, blinding her.

She woke with a start.

"Too much?" A familiar voice asked.

Ro tried to blink, but her face was squished into a pillow. She had to move her head in order to see anything, but when she did, a stabbing pain shot from her forehead to her temples to the back of her brain, making her groan.

"I'll close them," the voice said.

She heard a squeaky grinding sound that echoed in her ears, making her wince. The blinds. The voice was closing the blinds on her windows.

"Shh..." she tried to say, but her mouth was so dry she couldn't make the sound. Sucking in her breath to steel herself against the pain, Ro unburied her face from her pillow and turned her head so she was looking into the shadowed room. Then she lowered her head gently back down to rest on the pillow again, working her tongue around in her mouth as she did to try and build up enough saliva to speak.

"I brought you some coffee," the voice said. It was Winston. She could see that now in the dim light. He was sitting back down into a chair that he'd pulled up to her nightstand. Ro squinted because even the grey light of the room was too much for her tender eyeballs. There was a coffee carafe, cream and sugar, and a gleaming white cup waiting for her on her nightstand. He held his own steaming cup in his lap.

A jolt of fear went through her powerless body. Was she late for work?

"What time is it?" She croaked.

"It's just after nine," he answered, taking a sip of his coffee.

"Oh no!" She started to push herself up from the bed, but

was forced back down by the splitting pain in her head combined with a horrible queasiness in her stomach.

"It's Saturday," Winston reassured her. "You don't have work today. I double checked with that Gloria lady."

Relief flooded her, but was quickly replaced with dismay as the details of the night before became clearer in her mind.

"What did I do?" She groaned.

"In general? Or do you want specifics?"

"I hate champagne," she complained.

Winston grinned, "You could have fooled me."

"Oh God," Ro lifted her hand to her forehead and tried to rub the pain out of it. Her stomach roiled.

"I got you some ibuprofen," he leaned forward and poured coffee into her cup, adding cream. "Carlos is sending up a big, greasy breakfast with some kind of jalapeño or Chile pepper stuff he wants you to eat. Says it'll make you feel better."

The thought of food sent her stomach into another tailspin. She groaned again, shoving her face back into the pillow.

Winston chuckled, "Happy New Year, Ro!"

"No."

"C'mon, it's your first day off, and the first day of the year!"

"Do over," she mumbled. The hangover was bad enough, although she knew she would get over it...eventually. What Ro couldn't stop thinking about was what a drunken fool she'd been the night before. What did Cooper think of her now? And Alicia? She could lose her job.

Some of it was a blur, but she did remember Winston removing her from the party and bringing her to her room. She didn't remember a whole lot after that. He had been laying next to her on the bed. Then what happened? She gasped, jerking up to her elbows and looking down to see what she was wearing. She was still in her red dress, though it was rumpled and twisted around her thighs. She looked at Winston with wide-open eyes.

"Did we...?" She didn't know how to say what she was thinking.

She looked him up and down, his feet were bare under his trousers, his shirt was completely undone, as if it had been off then put back on again.

He creased his brow, wondering why she was flipping out. Then it hit him.

"No, we didn't do anything. We slept," he said.

"Oh, thank God," she flopped back down with relief.

"You don't have to be so happy about it," he said with mock indignation. He thrust his shoulders back and puffed up his chest, "I don't want to brag, but if we had done anything you'd remember."

"Oh, be quiet."

"Just sayin'," he cocked his head at her and took another drink of his coffee.

Ro decided to push herself into a sitting position and try to swallow the ibuprofen with some coffee. Winston watched her wobble around until she was sitting with her legs dangling off the side of the bed, her face screwed up with the pain and nausea of it all. He handed her two pills and her coffee.

"Why are you here now?" She asked, taking the pills and coffee from him.

He scoffed, "I'm taking care of you, you drunken mess."

She choked back a laugh, almost snorting the coffee out of her nose. A fresh sea of pain washed through her forehead, making her wince.

"I thought you might need some help getting ready," he continued.

She looked at him, confused, "For what?"

"We've been invited to go to the ruins."

She took another sip of coffee. It was hot and delicious and she hoped it would help her feel better, but she couldn't imagine being well enough to leave her room today. Let alone go on a day trip to the Mayan ruins.

Winston eyed her reaction and must have deduced that she wasn't thrilled with the idea. He leaned back in his chair and put his feet up on the bed next to her like he always did when he was feeling cocky. He knew something she didn't.

"What?" She asked.

"You don't want to go?"

"I will be lucky if I make it out of this bed today."

His eyes twinkled with amusement. Like a naughty little kid who's pulling a prank.

"What?" She asked, exasperated.

"Coop invited us to go to the ruins today," he annunciated Cooper's nickname so she was sure to understand.

Ro's heart leapt even as she was irked at Winston's teasing. Nerves sprung up in her already unstable stomach and she didn't know if she was going to laugh or cry or vomit.

Winston sighed, taking his feet off of the bed and the cup from her hands, which were trembling. He placed both of their cups on the nightstand. Leaning forward with his elbows on his knees, he took her hands in his. He looked into her eyes with affection, then squeezed her hands gently and said, "I know, I know...you changed your mind."

With Winston's support, Ro was ready for their day outing in less than two hours. He made her promise that she would drink water almost continually while they were out in the heat of the day.

"Dehydration is your enemy," he told her as he packed several bottles of water into a day pack for her and even more into his larger pack. Ro nodded in mute submission. She was depending on the fact that Winston was not a hot mess to get her through this day.

Her hangover had reduced to what felt like a thin film of glass covering her skin, which any wrong move could crack and send shattering to the ground. Still, she was dressed for the day with comfortable shorts, light hiking shoes, a white tank top with a thin, blue cotton button up shirt over top, a straw hat Winston insisted on buying her at the hotel shop, and sunglasses. She was up and moving, looked reasonably cute, and was determined to spend the day doing something cultural and fun. Something with Cooper.

Cooper, on the other hand, was cool, sexy and in control as he met them in the lobby. One of the two blondes was still on his arm. No explanation of where the other blonde had went.

"One down and one to go," Ro said under her breath as she climbed into the stretch SUV Cooper had called to take them to Chichén Itzá.

It was over a two-hour drive to the site of the ancient ruins. The vehicle was air conditioned, stocked with food and drinks, decked out with a killer sound system, and an absolute misery for Ro.

The floating sensation caused by being in the back end of a stretch vehicle only exacerbated her queasiness and she was practically green for the full two-hour ride. Cooper and Winston talked and laughed about topics Ro couldn't focus on. It turned out the blonde's name was Tomi. Her name fit her bleached hair, deep tan, heavy lipstick, skimpy tank top look. Tomi kept her oversized sunglasses on and was pretty standoffish, which was fine. Ro had little interest in knowing about her competition, even if she hadn't been hung over.

The ruins were amazing. Ro regained some of her energy in the fresh air as they made their way around the different sections of the site. Cooper had hired a tour guide named Paco to take them around and explain what they were seeing. Paco was funny and interesting. When he said her name, he rolled his tongue when pronouncing the 'r', making 'Señorita Ro' sounded more like 'Señorita R-r-ro'. Her name had heft when Paco said it and she liked that. Winston kept her supplied with bottles of water and, despite the heat and humidity, she felt like she was getting back to normal.

The Temple of Kulkulcan dominated the site. A massive pyramid structure that rose 80 feet into the sky. It had four sides, each equipped with narrow stone steps that led to the platform on top. Cooper and Winston wanted to climb the steps to the top. Tomi was bored with the idea, but Ro thought she could accompany them.

The steps were narrow and steep, and there was no handrail. Apparently ancient Mayans didn't build their stairways with modern codes in mind. After trying the first few steps, Ro felt dizzy and a little sick again. She decided to sit it out this time and instead stood at the foot of the stairway next to a huge snake head carved of stone, watching the two men climb.

When they reached the top Ro saw them high five each other. They waved to her and Tomi. She waved back and glanced sideways at Tomi, who didn't wave at all. Ro wondered if her own personality was too enthusiastic for Cooper's tastes. If Tomi was an indication of the kind of woman he liked, Ro might have to tone her naturally nice persona down a few notches to get him to notice her.

After soaking in as much mind blowing architectural accomplishment and ancient Mayan lifestyle stories they could in just a few hours, Cooper decided they should head out. He wanted to stop at one of his favorite restaurants in Tulum on the way back for a meal. As much as Ro was impressed with the ruins and enjoyed Paco's tour guide skills, she was thankful to climb back into the air-conditioned car. Knowing that she could revisit this site in the future whenever she desired helped her feel better about not being completely herself on her first visit.

The outing must have taken more out of her than she'd realized, or maybe it was the humming engine of the car, because on the drive to Tulum she dozed off. What was going to be another two hour ride where she might feel well enough and finally have time to chat with Cooper, turned into less than 20 minutes of awake time. Plus she had the added humiliation of having fallen asleep like a child while Tomi had, presumably, stayed wide awake, all blonde and busty.

"You have to try the grilled octopus," Cooper was saying to Winston as Ro blinked her eyes open.

"I don't know about octopus," Winston grimaced.

"You're joining the party!" Cooper smiled at Ro as she straightened up and tried to pretend she hadn't been slumped in the corner of her seat, probably snoring.

"How are you feeling?" Winston asked. He reached for his bag where she knew more bottles of water waited.

She shook her head at him, indicating she didn't want any water right now. She couldn't think about drinking anything at the moment, in fact. Her bladder was about to burst.

"I'm fine," she said. "And, yes," she gave Cooper the best smile she could muster, "I am ready for the party!"

The party, it turned out, was at Rosa Negra. An eco-chic, Latin restaurant and bar located on the main beach strip in Tulum. Despite the simple dirt road it sat on, Rosa Negra was a nice restaurant, very nice in fact. Ro knew immediately when they walked in that they were too dusty and casually dressed to justify the warm welcome they received. The manager approached with an ear-to-ear smile, shook Cooper's hand and showed them to a table with a fine view of the wide room. It was easy to be impressed by the reaction Cooper got wherever he went. He was well known and, it appeared, well liked.

The walls of Rosa Negra were made of rough, white stone. Finely woven baskets acted as hanging light fixture covers. They were strung from a ceiling made up of single sticks pushed tightly together like floor mats. This rustic edge was in contrast to the fine china and glassware that graced the tables and the funky lounge, almost disco, music that mingled with conversations of well-dressed patrons.

Ro excused herself to the ladies room. Tomi didn't join her, which was a clear sign that they were not friendly. Not that Ro needed more proof of the other woman's disinterest. Tomi was obviously into Cooper and nobody else. In some ways, Ro could completely understand.

After she took care of bathroom business, Ro splashed water in her face and dried it with the paper towels provided. She dug through her purse to find the small brush and makeup bag and took a few minutes to spruce up for dinner. At least she looked better than she had this morning. When she returned to the table the waiter, Hector, was placing wild looking drinks at each seat, including hers.

Slices of cucumber and lemon mixed with a clear liquid inside of a long stemmed wine glass. Wisps of what looked like smoke, but must have been caused by dry ice, filled the top of the glass and spilled over the side. Hector pulled out her chair with a flourish. Ro thanked him and took her seat, inspecting her cocktail.

"What are these?" She asked.

"Gin and tonic...basically," Winston said, lifting his to his mouth and blowing the smoky steam towards her. Ro laughed.

"To the first day of the rest of our lives," Cooper said, raising his drink up in a toast. They all clinked glasses and even Tomi cracked a smile.

From there, the evening got even better.

To say the food was remarkable would not have done the

chef, or the staff, at Rosa Negra justice. The presentation was enough to rocket this place into the most impressive restaurant Ro had ever entered. Truffle popovers, roasted corn with butter and chile powder served on skewers, tuna sashimi, Kobe beef steak, seafood salad, and grilled octopus, as Cooper had suggested.

Her appetite had returned with a vengeance just in time, as the portions were huge and everything was delicious. The octopus was served in tact, artfully presented in the center of the plate so that the tentacled arms appeared to be climbing towards the ceiling. When Hector placed Winston's in front of him, Winston grimaced at the sight.

Cooper laughed at his reaction, "Don't knock it till you've tried it!"

Winston made a stoic face and picked up his knife and fork, which made Cooper laugh again. He looked at Ro and jerked his thumb at Winston, "You've got your hands full with this one."

Ro's face went numb. Though she managed to hold onto her amused expression, inside she felt a rising sense of dread. What did Cooper mean by that comment? She shot Winston a look, but he was busy making faces while trying to cut up his octopus. Entertaining both Cooper and Tomi, who were charmed with him.

Ro's mind tumbled over the details of the past 24 hours. Winston hanging around her at the New Year's Eve party. Winston taking her up to her room. The fact that he'd specifically said, "*We've* been invited to go to the ruins." We? There was no *we*. But Cooper didn't know that. He thought she and Winston were together. An item. Dating.

She looked around the table. Tomi, gorgeous, silently sipping her third drink of the night. Winston chewing his first bite of grilled octopus and making jokes. Cooper slapping Winston's back and giving Ro a friendly smile, as if they were bonding through their mutual relationships with Winston.

The reality of her situation sunk in. This was a date.

Heat rose in her cheeks as the implications of the misunderstanding became clear. She and Winston were on a double date with Cooper and Tomi.

Cooper didn't like her romantically. Winston was undermining her attempts at a brand new life. She was nothing more than a dreamy eyed secretary with a huge crush on her boss.

Their dinner ended with a fantastic dessert. A huge chocolate sphere with a creamy filling. Hector poured hot caramel over the top of the sphere to melt through the chocolate so they could all dig in with their spoons. The sphere was large enough for all four of them to share. Ro barely ate a bite.

Chapter Ten

By Monday morning, Ro had determined an appropriate course of action to get her new life back on track.

First, she had to avoid Winston. That was clear. She couldn't have Cooper and the rest of the people in her new surroundings believe that anything other than friendship was going on between her and Winston. She figured she could just stay busy for the rest of the time he was in Mexico on vacation. Once he flew home it would be easy to put him firmly away in her past and move freely into her future.

She'd already successfully kept away from him all day Sunday. Feigning the need to recuperate from her hangover and their day trip, Ro had spent her Sunday off in her room, plotting and catching up on sleep. Besides a few texts in the morning checking in to make sure she was okay, Winston had left her alone.

The second thing she decided she needed to do was put herself in Cooper's path as much as possible. Ironically, being his secretary didn't equate with seeing him much during the day. His tendency to take off on adventures was something she must learn to take advantage of if she ever wanted him to see her as anything except his employee. Taking care of her administrative duties could be done quietly and efficiently so that the next time Cooper brought up doing something like scuba diving, Ro would jump on the invitation.

This realization led directly to the third task in her plan to create her brand new life. Ro determined that she must be as open and friendly, even flirtatious, with Cooper as possible. This change was more subtle and something she was going to have to concentrate on to accomplish. No moment between them could be lost to insecurity or the formalities of their working relationship. If Ro wanted to be with Cooper in her new life, she must make her desires clear.

At nine o'clock Monday morning she walked the short distance from her room to her office, ready to take on this new day of the new year in her new life with gusto. She had opted out of a morning walk on the beach with Carlos and Josefina today, afraid they might run into Winston.

Instead, Ro spent some extra time getting dressed. A pale blue cotton dress she had previously determined was too short for work, now seemed like the perfect choice. Tanned from her day at the ruins, Ro saw that the dress not only clung nicely, but showed off the blue in her eyes against her darker skin tone.

Making sure her hair was artfully tousled, she went to the dining room and grabbed a quick breakfast to take back to her room. She didn't want to run into Winston while she was eating. He hadn't texted her or shown up at her hotel room this morning. Hopefully he was off on some tourist adventure and would stay away all day.

Not surprisingly, Cooper didn't show his face at nine o'clock. Ro busied herself checking emails, reviewing his business schedule, which was pretty sparse, and opening the mail. She popped in to see Gloria mid-morning and did some filing and mail opening for her as well. Ro returned to her office to find the whole place dead silent. She was beginning to wonder if Cooper was even in his rooms and glanced at the closed double doors continually, waiting for a sign of him. The determination to enjoy her day was beginning to wane as the hours passed with no Cooper in sight.

Just before lunch, the slim desk phone that had sat quietly on her desk since she started this job last week, buzzed. Someone was calling and Ro froze for a second, not sure how she should answer the phone. She cleared her throat and picked up the receiver.

"Good morning, Cooper Rivera's office. How may I help you?"

"Nice greeting! You're a real professional."

"Cooper?"

"Yes, it's me. I have something I want you to see," he said.

Ro turned towards the double doors, "Do you want me to come into your office?"

Cooper laughed with gusto, "No, come to the dock."

"The dock?"

"Yes, by Zander's dive shop. You know where that is?"

"I do," she answered. She stood up, her nerves and excitement taking over, "Right now?"

"Yes, come now. The day is wasting away!"

Without another word, the call was disconnected. Ro placed the receiver back into its slim receptacle and smiled to herself. Standing up, she smoothed her dress. She hadn't expected her next opportunity to be with Cooper outside of the office to come so quickly. But she truly felt like she was ready.

Almost 20 minutes later Ro approached the dock by Zander's dive shop. Her stroll down the beach had been hotter than she anticipated. Every other time she'd been on the beach it had been early morning and not nearly as crowded as it was now.

As Ro picked her way through tourists sitting on blankets or under oversized beach umbrellas or playing Frisbee along the water's edge, she felt a bit uptight. Like Mary Poppins trying to walk across the fine, white sand, without getting it in her shoes or stuck in between her toes. Families and college students and lovebirds all romped around her in their swimming suits. She remained formal and stiff while everyone else played.

She tried to relax and remember that she was on a beautiful tropical beach, on her way to meeting her handsome, single boss who wanted her to join him. This could turn into the fun, flirty and intimate moment she'd been dreaming about. Briefly, she wondered if Tomi was going to be with him. Then she wondered if Tomi would be wearing a gorgeous revealing swimsuit, while she was stuck in her short, but comparatively conservative, blue dress.

As she got closer she saw that Zander was talking to a man wearing a white hat who stood on an impressive yacht that was tied to the dock. Ro looked around for any sign of Cooper. Zander spied her and gave her a full arm wave, motioning for her to come over. The man on the yacht turned to see who had Zander's attention, and the instant she saw who it was, her heart lifted.

Cooper.

His gorgeous face broke into a wide smile. He was beautiful. A tan over his already dark toned skin. A tight fitting polo shirt in variegated black and white stripes. One of his signature slim fitted swimming trunks, these in black, showing off his incredible physique. The white boating hat sitting jauntily on his head.

"Ro!" He waved at her from high atop the shining boat and Ro felt a thrill flip through her stomach.

This was incredible. Were they taking a yacht out onto the water? Throwing a party? She waved as her steps quickened as her excitement grew, imagining all of the possibilities. The bright turquoise water lapped against the clean, smooth white hull. Stunning. Her concerns about being too prim as she had walked through the crowds of tourists on the beach disappeared. Her dress was perfect for a yacht party.

Ro stepped onto the dock and noticed another person who had emerged out of nowhere to stand next to Cooper. Her toe hit a plank of wood that stuck up unexpectedly and she tripped forward, catching herself with the handrail.

"Whoa," Zander exclaimed and trotted over to offer her a hand. "Watch your step," he said.

Ro took his hand and steadied herself before looking back towards Cooper waiting on the boat. Maybe she had been seeing things and the person standing next to Cooper was not who she thought it was. Zander led her towards the yacht and Ro cringed.

Nope. She hadn't been seeing things. It was Winston's face she saw next to Cooper's on the yacht. Winston's grinning face.

Ro was speechless as the two men waved to her, which was probably a good thing. If she'd been able to say anything she may have had a few choice words for her old office buddy. What in the world was he doing here? On Cooper's yacht?

"It's a beauty, isn't it?" Zander asked. He thought she was astounded at the sight of the yacht, not who was on it.

Ro nodded mutely.

"Come aboard!" Cooper called happily to her as Zander showed her to the portable steps that stretched up from the dock and across to the deck. "You coming, Zander?" He asked the Aussie.

Zander shook his head, his blonde dreadlocks bouncing, "Not today, mate. I've got clients."

"Fair enough, another time?" Cooper asked. Zander said something she didn't quite catch. As she made her way up and over the steps, Cooper was distracted talking to Zander over the edge of the yacht.

Winston took Ro's hand as she reached the end of the steps to ensure she transferred onto the deck safely. She almost swatted his hand away, but felt a little unstable and was forced to take it to steady herself.

Winston had on a pair of long, white shorts and a loose fitting royal blue cotton shirt that hung casually past his waist. He, too, was nicely tan and if she wasn't so furious at him she would tell him that he looked good. Vacations suited him.

"What are you doing here?" She hissed at him.

His eyebrows raised in amusement at her tone. Before he had a chance to react, Cooper turned towards them.

"What do you think?" Cooper asked, spreading his arms wide to indicate the yacht.

Ro didn't know what to say.

"This guy," Cooper stepped to Winston and put one hand on his shoulder and one on his arm, pushing him back and forth like a big brother teasing a little brother. Like they were friends. "This guy is a genius!"

Ro looked at Winston then Cooper, not understanding.

"Not genius, really," Winston said humbly.

"What did he do?" Ro asked.

"He convinced me to buy this..." again, Cooper stretched his arms out like a game show host showing off the grand prize to a contestant, "...as a tax write off!" Cooper let go a great hoot of laughter, then slapped Winston on the back as he walked past him towards the bow railing.

Ro's mouth dropped open. She stared at Winston, in shock.

"We've been yacht shopping," Winston said quietly to her.

She smacked his arm, "What are you doing? He can't write this off...can he?"

He shrugged, "Actually, he can if he uses it for hotel events."

"Want a drink?" Cooper pulled open the door of a small fridge built into the bench seating at the bow. "Then we'll give you a tour."

Ro took the drink. She needed something to help manage her disappointment. Not that the yacht wasn't beautiful. It was splendid, with polished wood decks and handrails, a spacious cabin with a large living room and bedrooms, or berths, enough to sleep over a dozen people. A captain and small crew were there to handle the actual sailing and there was a chef and staff to cook for them and clean up afterwards. No, it wasn't the yacht that disappointed her.

It was Winston.

The way he kept sitting by her, looking at her. The way Cooper joked with him constantly. The way he had somehow infiltrated her new world and was having a better time than she was in it.

All of this was annoying. And disappointing. Then annoying again.

Ro sat gloomily on the white sectional couch that stretched around what Cooper had called the saloon. She thought it seemed more like the living room. She'd abandoned Winston and Cooper at the helm with the Captain. They were involved in looking at the controls and other gadgets that held no interest for Ro. The Captain was a middle-aged man with dirty blonde hair, a hard jawline, and intelligent eyes. He seemed competent, which was all Ro cared about.

To her surprise, Tomi entered the room from the door that led down to the sleeping areas. She wore a red bikini and her sunglasses, nothing else. She didn't speak to Ro, just went to the long, mirrored bar that filled most of the inside wall and pulled out two glasses.

"Hi, Tomi," Ro said, giving the other woman a small wave from the couch. Maybe she hadn't seen her when she came in.

Tomi turned her head towards Ro and smirked.

"I'm not Tomi," the blonde said.

Just then another bikini clad blonde emerged from the bowels of the yacht. Ro blinked. This one's bikini was black, but she was also wearing a pair of sunglasses and, to Ro's confusion, this one was also Tomi.

"Hi," the black bikini blonde said to Ro. Then added, "I didn't know you were here."

"Tomi?" Ro asked.

The blondes looked at each other and giggled. Black bikini threw her arm around red bikini and said, "Tara, this is Ro. Ro, this is my sister, Tara."

Twins. How had she totally forgotten seeing them together at the party?

A rush of disgust swept through Ro. Was Cooper actually dating twins? Like some kind of Hugh Hefner wannabe?

"When did you come onboard?" Tomi asked. She took the drink Tara had fixed at the bar and joined Ro on the couch.

"Just a little while ago," Ro answered. Flustered at their presence and what it meant, Ro fought the urge to make a dash for the door.

"Want anything to drink?" Tara asked.

"No, thanks," Ro lifted her not yet finished bottle of ginger beer that Cooper had given her earlier.

Tara plopped her barely covered rear end down on the opposite side of the couch. Ro was flanked by two blondes on a Austin Powers style couch in the saloon of a yacht in the Caribbean. At the very least, she realized, over the past week her life had become surreal.

"So, you're the girl dating Winston?" Tara asked.

"What? No, absolutely not," Ro responded.

Tomi furrowed her brow, "But, I thought—"

"I know! Everyone thinks we're dating, but we're not," Ro felt somewhat relieved at the chance to announce the truth.

Tomi and Tara exchanged a look.

"So he's single," Tara said. Ro could barely see her blonde eyebrows raise with interest behind those giant, crystal studded sunglasses.

"Yes," Ro answered. Her thoughts flew over the past five years searching for a moment when Winston had ever announced he had a girlfriend. She couldn't even think of a time when he said he'd been dating anyone. At least not seriously.

"So he's fair game?" Tara asked.

"Fair game?" Ro didn't quite understand.

"He's single, you're not dating him. So he's fair game?"

Ro was so surprised at the question, she couldn't give a straight answer. All she said was, "Winston?"

Tara and Tomi both giggled again.

"He's hot," Tara said.

Before Ro could think of an appropriate response, Cooper and Winston appeared in the windows. There were windows spread across the entire length of the saloon that looked out over the bow of the boat and across the bright blue ocean. The men were making their way down the stairway from the helm, laughing and talking. Cooper knocked on the window when he saw the three women on the couch.

"We're setting sail!" He declared, his voice muted through the glass.

Both of the twins lifted their drinks in a toast towards him. Ro stiffened. They were sailing? Into the ocean? The men entered the room. Cooper was beaming as he jogged towards the couch and sat down next to Tomi, putting his arm around her shoulders in a proprietary way. Winston, a little less boisterous, took a seat between Ro and Tara. Ro gave him a look of alarm.

"We're just taking it for a spin and eating dinner on the deck," he explained. He noticed her expression and asked, "Are you okay with that? Do you want to stay here?"

"Why would she want to stay behind?" Cooper corrected Winston. So sure of the appeal of his yacht outing, he was unable to entertain Winston's comment.

The motors that lay somewhere below them in an unseen place, kicked into life. A powerful humming sent a low-grade vibration through the floor, the couch, and Ro's body. Tomi and Tara giggled at the sensation.

"It's just dinner on the water, then we're coming back," Winston spoke quietly to her so the others couldn't hear. He was still concerned, she could tell. He looked out the windows as two of the crew appeared outside. He gave her a reassuring smile, "But if you want to stay here you better say something before we pull away from the dock. I don't know how long it takes to turn these things around."

Ro stood up quickly. Without looking at Winston or responding to what he'd just said, without making eye contact with anyone, she made her way to the door and left the cabin.

Chapter Eleven

It was warm outside. The slow, humid warmth of the tropics. But the breeze off of the ocean was refreshing, and the view was enough to take her breath away.

Floating directly on top of the crystal clear water made it seem like she was actually standing inside of a postcard, surrounded by the ocean that stretched, uninterrupted, to the horizon. Low waves reflected the sunlight like a million diamonds twinkling on top the brilliant blue water. The sky was mostly clear, with just a few white puffy clouds perfecting the picture.

Ro leaned against the railing, looking into the distance. The yacht undulated with the waves, creating a rolling sensation. Combined with the rumble of the engines below, it was hypnotic.

Winston appeared at her side. He leaned on the railing next to her so their elbows were touching, and joined her in looking out over the water.

"You okay?" He asked.

For the 15 or so minutes it had taken them to leave the dock and maneuver through the other boats and obstacles close to shore, Ro had stood alone at the bow. The fresh air and breeze on her cheeks helped clear her muddled thoughts.

"I'm okay," she answered, though she didn't look at him.

"This is crazy, isn't it?" Winston said with a laugh of disbelief.

Ro didn't answer. She kept her eyes trained on the sparkling water and the distant horizon. A minute went by and Winston cleared his throat. Ro continued staring at the horizon. Hard.

He tried again, "I guess you could tell that Coop and Tomi are a thing?"

"Are they?" Ro pursed her lips.

"Yeah, I think so. That's how they act anyway."

Winston turned towards her, leaning sideways against the railing. She was curious if Cooper was also dating Tomi's twin, but didn't want to talk to Winston about any of it. She didn't want to talk to Winston at all.

"Look, Ro, I'm sure you're disappointed. But honestly," he leaned towards her and lowered his voice, "I don't think you're missing out on a whole lot. I mean, Coop is nice and everything, but he can be a little..." he searched for the word.

Ro turned her gaze on him, "A little what?"

He shrugged and looked away. Uncomfortable under her stare.

"You know," he said, giving her a sideways glance.

"No, Winston, I don't know," she retorted. "I don't know much about Cooper or his relationships, because you are the one that is spending every moment of every day with him. Not me."

She turned back to glare at the ocean.

Winston let out a laugh that was more of a snort and asked, "What?"

When she didn't answer, he looked around where they stood, as if searching for the answer in the teak decking or the gleaming white sides of the cabin. Then he let out a frustrated sigh. Ro shot him a look. What did he have to be frustrated about?

"You know what you're doing, don't you?" Winston asked, all humor gone from his voice.

"What do you think I'm doing?"

"You're doing it all over again."

"Doing what all over again?"

"Theo," he said, locking eyes with her. "You're doing exactly what you did with Theo, and with a man who seems to be a lot like Theo," he gestured towards the cabin, but kept his eyes on her.

Ro sucked in her breath and held it. She didn't know if she was going to cry or yell, so she kept her lips clamped together. Winston shook his head and raked his hand through his hair. He let out an empty laugh.

"It's like you can't see past their show. You get all wrapped up in some fantasy of who they are and you can't see the truth," he said.

Anger bubbled inside of her. She glanced self-consciously at the cabin windows. Her cheeks and eyes were hot with emotion, and she worried those inside were watching.

"What are you talking about? What truth?" She hissed at him.

"That men like Theo, men like Coop, are always going to go for the Tamara's and Tomi's of the world. And that's fine, that's great! Let them have each other, I say. Except you think that means you're not worth anything," Winston had moved closer to her and was speaking low. His big, brown eyes looked deeply into hers and her stomach clenched with the intensity. There was something in his eyes that she couldn't name, a question, like he was pleading with her. His voice dropped even lower, rumbling up from his chest, "They don't see you because they're not looking. And that's their fault, not yours. You deserve someone who treats you like a queen, not an after thought."

With that, Winston left and the angry knot in Ro's stomach twisted into despair. It took everything in her not to burst into tears. Her eyes welled up and she turned into the wind, breathing fast to try and regain control. Ro stayed where she was as the yacht moved further and further away from land. Pretending to be enjoying the view until her urge to cry disappeared.

DINNER WAS AMAZING. The table was set up on an outside deck under the stars. The furniture and table dressings were the utmost in luxury with fine china, crystal glasses, and heavy silver tableware. This stately service seemed even more extravagant out in the open water. As if the power and money that brought it here had dominion over the very sea upon which they floated.

They had lobster, of course. What else would you have for dinner on a lavish yacht? They also had wine, lots of wine. Ro didn't partake. She was already experiencing a roller coaster of emotions, wine would only exacerbate her problems.

Winston drank. As did Cooper and the twins, who had changed into evening wear for dinner. Tomi wore a skimpy black dress and black stilettos. Ro thought this was silly and rather dangerous, considering how much Tomi was drinking. She could easily trip in those heels and topple over the railing if she wasn't careful.

Tara wore an even skimpier dress than her sister. Red, go figure. And she made sure to sit next to Winston at the table so she could laugh at his jokes, touch his arm whenever possible, and act basically like she was in heat. Of course, this was just Ro's personal opinion. She didn't share it with anyone.

She did her best to enjoy the dinner, even if by the end of it she was feeling like a third, no, make that a fifth wheel.

Afterwards they retired to the saloon at Cooper's insistence. Ro would have rather stayed on deck and looked at the stars and the deep, black ocean around them. But it was Cooper's party and he had something he wanted to show them all.

"Look what came with the yacht!" Cooper reached into a small cabinet behind the bar area and pulled out two microphones.

"Is that...?" Tara giggled and took one of them, holding it up to her mouth.

"Hang on," Cooper said, ducking behind the bar.

The flat screen TV that was mounted on the wall lit up. A bright purple background with plain white text in all caps read, "KARAOKE NIGHT".

Tomi and Tara squealed with delight as Tomi grabbed the other microphone. Cooper presented them all with a printout of the songs available on the machine. Ro groaned internally. Without the benefit of alcohol, she expected karaoke to be an excruciating experience.

She glanced at Winston. He was perusing the list of songs. He hadn't really engaged with her since their conversation on the bow. Drinking steadily all evening had made him funnier than normal, but most of that good humor had been directed towards Cooper and, to her surprised annoyance, towards Tara. Winston always gave Ro his full attention when they were together. But not tonight. She wished she could share her discontent with him and let him make her feel better, like he always did.

Ro went to the bar and grabbed one of the open bottles of wine. A nice Chenin Blanc. She needed a little something to relax during this evening's entertainment.

"Oh, good, you're trying it," Cooper said. He had joined

her, leaning both elbows on the bar and bending his head down so his eyes were even with hers. His breath smelled like alcohol and he was a little unsteady on his feet. Even drunk, Cooper was astonishingly attractive. Dark hair sexily messed up, eyes glinting with mischief, giving a hint of the unexpected, his voice deep and gravelly. He nodded towards the bottle, "You'll have to tell me if you like it."

"I will," she answered as she finished pouring a generous amount into a large wine glass, trying not to blush under his sudden attention.

"Let's get this show on the road!" Winston called out from the couch where Tara had settled in right next to him, or vice versa.

Tomi and Tara sang the first song, "We Are Family", an expected cliché. Then they pranced around to "Call Me Maybe". They convinced Cooper to go next. He chose "Do Ya Think I'm Sexy" by Rod Stewart. His performance was hard to witness. Ro stole a few glances towards Winston while Cooper sang slightly off key, gyrating his hips and pointing occasionally at an overly receptive Tomi. Ro was certain Winston would be thinking the same thing she was, that this was like being trapped in a horrible, tacky nightmare. She didn't catch his eye, because he was laughing with Tara and Tomi. For the first time in their years of friendship, Ro felt ignored. It wasn't a good feeling.

Cooper offered her the microphone when he was done, and she politely declined.

"I haven't picked a song yet," she said with a dry laugh. Hopefully they would be entertained enough with each other throughout the night so she could stay on the couch and out of the spotlight.

Tomi took the stage next with a not too bad, for a drunk girl, version of "Can't Help Falling in Love". Although, her overuse of pouty lips and Marilyn Monroe-like antics was cringe worthy. Then Cooper and the twins started "Sweet Home Alabama". They pulled a reluctant Winston up to sing with them while Ro smiled and clapped. Her plan to escape having to sing included being the perfect audience. It was no fun to sing karaoke to an empty room.

Next, Cooper turned on "Margaritaville", insisting the others stay and sing with him, aiming all of their talents towards Ro on the couch. Weren't they almost back to shore? Ro smiled and clapped at the appropriate moments, wondering the whole time exactly how much longer this evening was going to last.

Finally the song was over and Cooper and the girls tumbled, laughing, onto the couch. Cooper raised his hand as a high five to Ro and she smacked it with her palm. Her false enthusiasm seemed to be working.

"Your turn," Cooper said to her, offering her the microphone.

Ro opened her mouth to refuse, but couldn't think of anything to say. At this point refusing could be taken as an insult, after the others had all gone along with the fun. At the very least she would seem to be a real stick in the mud, as her mother used to say. Ro's throat went dry. Nerves.

"I'll go," Winston interrupted. He deftly took the microphone from Cooper's outstretched hand and went to the karaoke controls, punching a few buttons. The title "How am I Supposed to Live Without You" by Michael Bolton appeared on the screen. Tara gave a drunken squeal and clapped her hands together while Winston positioned himself center stage in front of the couch.

He had sensed her embarrassment and thrown himself on the grenade, as it were. Ro watched him, grateful to be saved.

The blue in his shirt looked good against his tan. He had rolled the long sleeves up on the cotton shirt and his forearm flexed as he lifted the microphone. Winston had a nice, muscular build. She hadn't always noticed this fact, but since he'd been in Playa del Carmen his masculinity seemed to have escalated. His hair looked good today, too. Windblown and messy, and somehow sexier than his normal put together look.

Something in the look on his face caught her attention. As he waited for the light, tinkling intro to play, his stance had the same appeal she'd seen in singers at rock concerts. She got the feeling that he was no stranger to performing. He kept his eyes trained on the floor in front of him, waiting for the lyrics to begin. When they did he didn't need to look at the TV screen to follow along. Winston knew all the words. Winston, it turned out, knew how to sing.

With the very first words of the song, "I could hardly believe it...", his voice captured her. Every bit as good as Michael Bolton, maybe even better. Winston's singing voice was smoky, which gave the lyrics an edgier feel. Cooper and the twins were just as drawn into his performance as Ro was from the moment he began. Each word carried a wealth of emotion as Winston put everything he was into this song. When he got to the chorus, his face twisted with focus and passion and he belted out, "How am I supposed to live without you..." As he sang he lifted his gaze to Ro and held her in it.

She couldn't move. Couldn't blink. Couldn't take her eyes off of him. Cooper started whooping and holding his arms up in the air as if they were at an actual rock concert. When Winston got to the line about the lost hope that one day they'd be more than friends, Ro blushed furiously.

He broke his attention away from her, turning it towards the rest of his audience. As the song's intensity grew, so did Winston's execution. Cooper, Tomi and, especially, Tara, were impressed, enrapt. Watching wide-eyed as he carried them through the ballad like a professional. If Ro didn't know better, she would have sworn a spotlight had turned on and was shining only on Winston.

Ro was blown away. More than simply impressed, she was physically reacting to him. Her skin tingled whenever he turned his attention to her, which was often. As he clutched the microphone and let his body move with the rhythm of the music, her attraction to him was undeniable. Deep in her chest, her heart was fluttering.

When the song finished Cooper gave Winston a standing ovation, gesturing to the rest of them that they should stand up and cheer as well. Ro did. Her cheeks still hot. Her skin still tingling.

"Damn, brother, you can sing!" Cooper exclaimed, stepping to Winston's side and throwing his arm over his shoulders.

It was Winston's turn to blush. When he looked to Ro, his eyes were glittering, still caught up in the moment, still full of intense expression. He held her gaze once again. She tried to smile, but suddenly, without warning, Ro felt the urge to cry. She ducked her head and wiped the wisp of tears from her eyes with the back of her hand.

A horn blast interrupted their revelry. This was the signal that they were returning to dock. The trip was almost over. Cooper asked Winston if he would come with him to the helm and Ro watched the two of them leave. Cooper still laughing and jostling Winston around in congratulations for killing it at karaoke.

Ro watched them go, hugging herself as if she was cold, which she wasn't. Tara and Tomi flanked her, like two life sized, slightly tipsy Barbie dolls. They also watched the men go.

Tara spoke up, looking wryly at Ro as she said, "Single." She scoffed, "I don't think so."

Ro looked at her with confusion, "What?"

Tara nodded towards the door where the guys had just exited, "That boy's got it bad for you."

Ro's heart sped up, "Who?"

Tomi and Tara shared a look before Tomi chimed in, "If you don't know who, sweetie, you must be blind."

Chapter Twelve

As usual, Cooper did not show up in the office the next day. He was probably cruising on his new yacht with the bombshell twins, Ro knew. Two days ago she would have been jealous at that thought. Today, however, she wasn't so sure.

Late morning, she was called into a meeting with Alicia. Gloria attended in all of her quiet grace, efficiently tapping notes into her slender laptop while Alicia covered her agenda. They sat in Alicia's office, which was not as grand as Cooper's, but close. Her space was sleeker with less pomp and circumstance.

This was the first time Ro had met with Alicia in her office. The older woman and general manager of the Hotel Diamante was not apt to suffer fools, Ro knew this much about her from what little time they'd spent together. That's why Ro should have been on her best behavior. She should have tried to remain alert and appear competent. Having worked here for only one week, now was not the time to fall apart.

And yet there she was, slumping in her chair, fighting the

urge to yawn so often and so hard that her eyes watered madly. Ro looked rumpled today, not having had the time or energy to put into her appearance after getting home so late last night from the yacht trip. Though her eyes were watering like crazy, every time she blinked her eyelids scratched them like the backs of her eyelids were made of sandpaper.

"Miss Murray, are you listening?" Alicia's voice, balancing precariously between frosty formality and annoyance, cut through Ro's foggy brain.

"Yes, I'm sorry," she answered. She wasn't. Listening, that is. She was sorry. Ro was sorry that she seemed to be having a difficult time focusing on anything after last night. After spending all of that time with Cooper. After Winston sang.

"Would you like more coffee?" Gloria asked, pausing typing and furrowing her brow slightly at Ro.

"No, thank you," Ro said, stifling another yawn.

"You had a long day yesterday," Alicia stated. Not accusatory exactly, but definitely with a note of displeasure.

"Yes, again, I'm sorry," Ro perked up a little. How did Alicia know about the yacht trip?

Alicia looked sharply over the top of her black-rimmed glasses at Ro, then shifted her eyes to Gloria. Gloria seemed to understand what her boss wanted almost immediately. She turned in her chair so she was facing Ro more squarely, then placed a cool, dry hand on Ro's knee.

"Little one," Gloria said with kindness in her eyes. "We are..." she looked for the right word, glancing to Alicia and back to Ro before continuing, "We are concerned that your emotions are overwhelming you."

Now Ro was completely awake. Fear and humiliation rushed through her system, overcoming her fatigue. Was she getting fired? How much did these two women know about her man crush issues?

"Wha-?" Her voice croaked like a frog. Ro cleared her

throat and started again, "What do you mean?" She straightened her back in an attempt to look as prim and in control as they did.

"Did you spend yesterday afternoon and evening with Mr. Rivera...away from the office?" Alicia asked.

Ro stiffened. Not sure if this was the hammer coming down about inappropriate behavior or if they assumed she hadn't been getting her work done.

"Yes, he asked me to come to the dock and join him," she answered carefully. She didn't want to sound like she was dodging blame for anything, but technically he was her boss, wasn't he? "I'm not behind on work or anything like that," she added.

"No, that's not what's troubling us," Gloria reassured.

Alicia let out a short sigh, like someone who has been through a trying ordeal a hundred times and is about to go through it again. Her shoulders relaxed and some of her professional demeanor slipped away. She took off her glasses and placed them on her desk, leaning forward as she did. Ro could see a small sliver of what it must be like to be friends with Alicia, instead of an employee at her hotel.

"With all due respect to Mr. Rivera, we want you to understand that he is a man who enjoys the company of women," Alicia's face softened. "Many, many women," she added, tilting her chin down and raising her eyebrows to try and make her meaning more clear.

"Oh," Ro said. Her fear of being fired dissipated, but it was instantly replaced with embarrassment. As if she had been the unwitting participant in a prank. The butt of a joke.

Gloria patted her knee again, giving her a kind smile.

"I am assuming your outing with Mr. Rivera went into the evening?" Alicia asked, leaning back and picking up her glasses. Back to business.

"Um, yes, we didn't get back until late," Ro answered. She

felt the urge to explain that she hadn't been alone with Cooper. Nothing had happened. But the words didn't come out.

"Then you will take this afternoon off," Alicia said, "I think you may need the rest?"

Ro nodded mutely.

❧

A RHYTHMIC WHIRRING FILLED her ears as the ceiling fan spun and sent a steady flow of barely cool air across her face, her chest, arms and legs. The only other sound in her room was the occasional filtered squeal or shout coming from guests, probably children or teenagers, playing in the hotel pool outside her balcony. None of those sounds penetrated her focus on the turning blades of the ceiling fan. Ro's mind was far away.

After the meeting, she'd come back to her room and crawled into bed. Thoughts and emotions were all jumbled up and pumping through her body so hard she couldn't single out any one of them, let alone sort them out. Eventually, Ro had fallen into a fitful sleep. For how long she did not know. When she woke it was to the whirring of the ceiling fan and nothing else. Face up on the bed and still fully dressed, she was alone. Deeply alone.

Two hot, fat tears welled up in her eyes so quickly that they spilled out almost immediately, leaving streaks of wetness on her skin before pooling at her ears. More followed. Ro didn't move. She let the tears come, feeling them slide almost continually down the small patch of skin between her eyes and her temples, wetting her ears and hair. Time wasn't registering with her, but she stayed like that until her nose was too stuffed up to breathe.

Ro sighed and sat up. Only then noticing that she held

her cell phone in one hand. The black screen looked dead. A lump of technology, grey and unappealing, ready to be brought to life by a quick swipe of her thumb. She moved to do just that, compelled to...to what? Check her emails? Get on Instagram? Find Theo's profile and start scanning through his perfect life again?

She dropped the phone onto the bed in disgust and stood up, stalking into the bathroom. Ro flipped on the bathroom light and stood in front of the mirror. Her hair was sticking out in all directions, damp at her temples. Her eyes were puffy and red from crying. She looked hung over. Snatching some tissues from the box on the vanity, Ro blew her nose and wiped her eyes, then paused. She leaned forward and stared into her reflection.

"What are you doing?" She asked out loud, her voice throaty and cracking. The puffy eyed, red nosed version of herself stared back. Eyebrows pinched together and mouth screwed up in an attempt to control the crying. She didn't look like someone who was starting a new, adventurous life in an exotic place. She looked like the same old, heartbroken mess she'd been back in Indiana. Maybe she should take a picture of her reflection right now and post it on Instagram. Ro barked out a humorless laugh at the thought.

A light knock on the door of her room sounded. She hesitated before answering, maybe they would go away. The knocking sounded again.

Ro sighed and called out, "Hang on." She turned on the cold water and splashed her face with it, drying it on a thick, soft hand towel as she walked to the door. She peered through the peephole and saw that it was Carlos. When she opened the door to him, she saw that he had a rolling cart stacked with several covered dishes.

"Buenas tardes," Carlos said politely as he pushed the cart in through her door. If he was surprised at her appearance, he didn't show it. One side or Ro's mouth lifted in a half-smile. Carlos was a good sort of man. "Señora Alicia says I bring you food, because you do not eat," he explained as he parked the cart near her balcony doors. He turned and looked at her with his smiling, dark eyes. His brows furrowed slightly, "Is everything okay for you?"

"I'm fine, thank you, Carlos," Ro assuaged his concern. When his expression didn't lighten, Ro managed a smile and said, "I'm just a little tired."

This didn't do much to change his mind, but the promise to join him and his family for their early morning walk on the beach the next morning helped. He had a point. Ro needed to get out and explore the beauty of this place more. That was, after all, one of the reasons she had moved all this way.

Carlos excused himself from her room with gallant flourish, insisting that she call him if she needed anything at all. She swore she would and closed the door after him.

Delicious smells of onion and Chiles rose from the cart, making Ro's stomach rumble. Lifting the covers revealed ceviche, shrimp tacos, pico de gallo, and fresh corn tortillas, hot and steaming. She moved the dishes to her small table and looked into the pitcher to find an ice cold, bright red drink made with hibiscus. Very sweet and satisfying. Thankful for the spread, Ro poured a glass for herself and sat down to eat.

Munching on her first bite of ceviche, Ro savored the taste as she squinted out the window into the bright afternoon. A surge of thankfulness came over her. She still had her job and this beautiful place to live, not to mention all of the perks of working at a luxury boutique hotel. All of this obsessing over Cooper ended right now. Her urge to get involved with him was taking over her original goal, which was to have a wild and adventurous life. Winston had been right. She had a tendency to latch onto the kind of men that took her for granted. That, too, needed to be part of her New Year's resolution. She was not going to settle for a boring life or a sub-par relationship. Period.

Winston. Her stomach clenched at the thought of him. What was she going to do about Winston? Before she could spend another moment pondering that question, another knock sounded on her door.

Ro shook her head with amusement. Carlos was so funny. His attentiveness was over the top. She should take her cues from him when looking for her next relationship. If she could find a man who worried about her every need the way Carlos did, she would be a lucky woman.

"Coming," she called out as she hopped up and hurried to the door. "I swear, everything is del—" Ro started to say as she swung the door wide open.

She stopped short when she saw who was on the other side.

Chapter Thirteen

"Hey," Winston said, giving her a small wave from his hip.

An electric shiver ran up her arms and shoulders, as if he had somehow charged up the air on the other side of the door then blew it into her when she swung the door open. The sensation took her aback.

He wore swimming trunks and a T-shirt that read 'I heart Riviera Maya' on the front. The heart wasn't spelled out, but a big, fat, red cartoon heart. Just like the 'I heart New York' T-shirts. His sunglasses were folded and hung from the neck of the T-shirt. His brown hair, lightened by days spent in the sun and sea, was thicker and wavier than Ro had ever seen it. Tall, tanned and fit, he looked relaxed and confident, and sexy. To Ro's surprise, her stomach did a flip-flop.

"Carlos said you were off for the afternoon," he said. "I thought maybe you'd want to go swimming...with me," his voice broke a little at the pause.

Ro suddenly remembered how horrible she looked, and ducked her head as she half turned away from him.

"I was eating..." her voice trailed off.

Winston looked past her into her room, then back at her, "Smells good. I can wait for you, if you want to go." He smiled at her with a twinkle in his eyes, "There's a cenote about 20 minutes away from here that everyone says is really cool."

Ro had read about cenotes when she researched moving to Playa del Carmen. Of course, she had yet to explore one of them. She couldn't think of a snappy come back or a reason she shouldn't go with him. Actually, she kind of wanted to go with him.

"Sure," she shrugged and opened the door, stepping back so Winston could come in. As he walked by, the scent of him overwhelmed her senses. He smelled like sunshine and salt-water, like the beach with a little bit of coconut sunscreen mixed in. He smelled good.

"Good, you need to get out and experience some paradise!" Winston announced.

Her earlier feelings of gloom and doom weakened.

Soon she had finished her late lunch, sharing both the food and the delicious hibiscus drink with Winston. Then she changed into a yellow bikini and matching sarong she'd bought brand new before she moved here, but had yet had the chance to wear.

When she walked out of the bathroom in her new ensemble, Winston's hand froze at his mouth where he'd been about to take a swig of his drink. He swallowed hard and Ro felt a surge of that same crackling electricity.

"You look beautiful," he said.

Ro tried not to blush, but she wasn't sure it worked. She put her sunglasses on to avoid looking at him.

Winston insisted she slather on sunscreen. She couldn't reach her back, so he helped. His fingers were warm and firm as they made circles across her shoulders and down her spine.

His body so close behind hers, his fingers on her naked skin, the deep tones of his voice speaking so close to her neck as he talked about the cenotes in the area, all of this woke a hundred butterflies in her stomach.

When she was sufficiently covered in sunscreen they left. He took her downstairs and out the back entrance of the hotel into the alley where a small, beater of a car was parked haphazardly next to some trash cans.

"You're driving?" She hesitated, eyeing the two-door rust bucket Winston was unlocking.

"Yeah," he opened the passenger door for her and made a gallant sweeping motion with his arm to indicate she should enter.

"Where did you get this horrible form of transportation?" Ro asked with a laugh as she climbed in.

"It's Zander's. He leant it to me," Winston closed her door carefully and got into the driver's seat. When he started the engine it sputtered and belched out a plume of exhaust. Ro was certain the engine was about to die, but it chugged for a few seconds then settled into a more consistent puttering sound.

Winston wiggled his eyebrows at her, pulling his sunglasses out from his T-shirt and putting them on as he said, "We're off on an adventure!"

Ro laughed, then squealed as he put the car in gear and raced it recklessly through the alley into the street.

Despite crowds of pedestrians darting in and out of the streets, and honking cars, trucks and taxi cabs that were not following most, if not all, of what Ro considered basic traffic rules, Winston navigated Zander's funny little car successfully through the more populated city area. Soon they were on a two-lane highway that headed out of town towards El Jardin Cenote. Their destination.

There was no air-conditioning in the little car, so they

kept their windows down. The warm, humid air pummeled them from all directions and made conversation impossible. To combat the noise of the wind, Winston turned the old radio up and blasted Mariachi music from a local station. Ro's hair whipped around her face. She stretched her arm out the window and let it ride the pressure wave of speed against the fresh, heavy air of the countryside.

They buzzed past huge, ropey trees with deep green plumage, broken down buildings that may have been snack shops or small grocery stores, but Ro couldn't read the Spanish on the signs to know for sure, and a gas station that looked like it had seen better days. A lone Mexican man, who looked like he must be at least 80-years old, pumped gas into an ancient light blue pickup truck. This was the only way Ro knew the gas station was still operational and hadn't been condemned. Further past these roadside landmarks there was only a sea of dark green trees that extended into the far distance.

She looked over at Winston, whose own hair was being tossed around by the current inside of the car. He looked back and grinned widely, giving her a thumbs up.

"You okay?" He shouted over the noise.

Ro nodded and gave her own thumbs up in return. As chaotic and rough as this excursion was compared to her other experiences in Playa del Carmen, she was enjoying it. This was probably closer to the real Playa del Carmen anyway. Being away from the protections of the hotel and the watchful eye of Alicia, Gloria and Carlos, not to mention the over the top luxury of Cooper's existence, made it all the more exciting.

At the highway sign for Barcelo Maya Beach Resort there was another hand painted sign on the opposite side of the road, It read 'CENOTES – El Jardin del Eden – The Best – El

Mejor'. Winston slowed the car and turned onto a sandy road lined with fat palm trees that led them into the deep green of the surrounding jungle. Another hand made sign, on this one the message, 'Welcome, Eden Cenote' was burned into the wood instead of painted. The sign leaned against a stone wall where an open iron gate ushered them further down the bumping sandy road.

When they finally reached the cenote, Winston shelled out 200 pesos for each of them. They picked out snorkeling gear and a bottle of flavored water offered by the friendly attendant. Then they made their way along one of many pathways that led to the edge of the cenote.

Cenotes, Ro had discovered in her research, were naturally formed sinkholes that occurred when the limestone collapsed ages ago. These large openings exposed groundwater and became open to entrance from the top. They were especially found here, in the Yucatán peninsula and renowned as places to snorkel and scuba dive worldwide. She had always thought of them as something like a pond or a large, deep swimming pool. Standing directly next to one, Ro realized that they were much, much more than that.

"Wow," Winston said. He leaned forward and peered over the rocky edge and the sharp drop towards the water, "This is pretty cool."

"It is, isn't it?"

A thrill shimmied down her spine. They had seen a huge cenote at the Mayan ruins, the water level more than 30 feet down. So deep that anyone falling in would not be able to get out without assistance from the top. Paco had told them that the cenote was probably used for human sacrifice, which was chilling.

This one, however, was much more inviting. It had what looked like a cliff side, maybe 15 feet tall, where you could jump into the deep water below. But it also had stairs that had been built to take you from the top to the surface of the water, as well as several areas along the edges where the stones were easier to navigate. There was not beach to walk serenely to the water's edge, but you could climb easily enough in, and out again, from many points along the edge.

Surrounded by the jungle with sandy ground underneath, the park was punctuated by areas with picnic tables and benches so you could rest between swimming. Large rocks protruded up through the water of the cenote, offering places for swimmers to sit and rest while still sitting waist deep in the cool water or just out of its reach.

"Ready?" Winston asked as he pulled his T-shirt over his head, revealing his tan, muscled chest. Ro was temporarily distracted from their surroundings by this view, but pulled herself together and nodded with enthusiasm.

They spent the next hour swimming and snorkeling through all of the nooks and crannies of this beautiful place. Tiny, colorful fish surrounded them then swam away. Lazy iguanas watched them from the shoreline where they warmed themselves in the sun. Throughout the adventure, Winston would often turn to her and offer his hand to pull her towards a particularly interesting place, or swim so close to her while they were snorkeling that their arms or legs would gently tangle and untangle as they moved through the water.

Ro found these moments tantalizing. Being underwater with Winston was delicious, their bodies softly skimming one another's warm skin in the cool water. She wondered what it would feel like if he slipped his hand purposefully around her waist, or up her exposed stomach and along her ribs toward her bikini top.

She found that her own hands wandered naturally and freely in his direction, often coming into contact with his well formed biceps, or the muscles of his back and shoulders. She noticed how his abdomen flexed and moved as he swam and wondered what it would be like to run her finger along those muscles. She didn't do it, of course. But she couldn't stop herself from thinking about it.

"Want to take a break?" Winston asked.

"Sure."

They swam to one of the flat rocks that lifted out of the water in the center of the swimming area. Abandoned by a group of teens who had been sunning themselves on it earlier, it was the perfect size for Winston and Ro to stretch out on their backs next to each other and rest.

The sunshine felt good after being in the cool water for so long. And the exertion of swimming had tired her out in the most relaxing of ways. All of the worry and emotion she'd felt earlier in the day had simply been washed away by this beautiful cenote. Ro let out a contented sigh.

"I could get used to this," she said.

Winston chuckled, a pleasing, deep rumble from his chest, "You can get used to it. You live here, now, remember?"

"Oh, that's right," she answered with delight, as if she'd just realized this fact.

"There are tons of cenotes all around this area. Each one has its own, unique characteristics. Some of them are more underground and you're swimming in a huge cave," Winston explained with obvious interest. "You could map them out and go to each one if you wanted," he added.

Ro considered this for a moment, then answered, "Maybe I will. That sounds fun!"

"It would be fun," he answered. There was a wistful note in his tone and Ro turned her head to look at him. Tiny beads of water still clung to his skin. Because it was wet, his hair looked almost black, and it stuck out in all directions as it dried in the sun. She gazed at his profile. She'd never noticed how strong Winston's nose was, how his jaw was square and firm, how his lips were full. She'd only ever noticed how easily he smiled at her, and how much fun they had together.

"You seem to enjoy being on vacation," she said.

He turned his face to hers, it was only inches away. If she leaned in his direction, just barely, their lips might touch.

"I'm going home in two days," he said quietly.

"What? I thought you were staying for a month?" She was shocked at his news. More than that, she was disappointed.

"Nah," he turned back to face the sky, effectively avoiding eye contact, "I figure it's about time I go home."

His words sounded empty, not fully formed. Or not fully informative. Ro continued looking at him, her face twisting into a scowl. She didn't like being lied to, and she could tell that Winston was, at the very least, not telling her the whole truth.

Her gaze bored into him long enough that he turned back to her, exasperated, "What?"

"You know what. You're not telling me everything," she said.

He coughed out a laugh, "I'm not? What's my big secret?"

"I don't know, it's your secret," she answered. She meant for it to be friendly banter, joking between buddies, the light-hearted way they'd always been together. But the words came out softer than she intended, filled with sadness.

The jocular smile on Winston's face faded as he looked into her eyes. She wanted to say something more to him, make him tell her what he was thinking, explain why he was leaving, but there was a lump in her throat. Winston's jaw flexed. His deep, brown eyes traced her cheek and landed on her mouth where they lingered until Ro could feel blood rush into her lips, anticipating a kiss.

With no warning, Winston turned his face back to the sky with a frustrated sigh. He made fists with his hands and pressed them into his closed eyes, turning his head back and forth in an exaggerated 'no' motion.

"Okay, okay, okay," he said. He moved his arms back to his sides where they stayed, stiff and unmoving. "I can't believe this," he mumbled, more to himself than to Ro. He took in a deep breath and blew it out of pursed lips, calming himself. Then he cleared his throat and began, his face still aimed towards the sky, "I have something to tell you. Because, you know, I'm going back home and you're staying here and if I didn't tell you then I would always wonder what would have happened if I did." He turned back to her and Ro's heart started thumping in her chest. "You know I've never taken vacations," he paused, waiting for her to indicate she knew this was a fact.

"Right," Ro said quietly, nodding once.

"And you know that I always said it was because I loved my job so much. That I loved my career and my office and the work, everything."

Ro nodded again.

"The thing is, Ro, you have to believe me on this, I really thought that was true. All these years I thought I loved my job."

Ro furrowed her brow, "You don't?"

"No. The work is fine," Winston explained. He lifted his hand and flicked it in the air as if shooing away a fly, "That's not the point. That's not what I want to say."

Ro waited. He seemed to be building up to something and she didn't want to interrupt him.

"But then you left."

Ro's heart thudded even louder. A tingling dizziness flooded through her head and chest.

Winston sighed again and dipped his head so when he looked at her, he was looking up through his still damp locks of hair. Confessing a secret.

"You know why I never used my vacation time? Because you were there, at work. And I didn't want to miss a moment of time that I could be with you. When you left everything was empty. I was empty. That's when I figured it out. After all this time I finally figured it out. It's not the job I love...it's you."

Chapter Fourteen

Ro knew he was telling her the truth. As soon as the words left his mouth, she realized that she'd known Winston was in love with her for a long time. This fact had silently drifted in between them for years. She had grown used to it. Counted on it.

In the moments after he told her the space separating them seemed to solidify. Locked them in. Held them both captive to the other so that neither of them moved. Ro's heart seemed to beat out of her chest as she gazed into his beautiful, searching eyes.

The people playing in the water nearby, the sunshine of late afternoon, the shimmering water that lapped at the edge of their rock, all of this slipped away. What remained was a bubble that surrounded them, protected them from the outside world.

For a moment.

That moment was full of truth and love and possibilities. But the soaring feeling Ro had first felt upon hearing Winston's words soon faltered, stalled out and started to drop. And though truth and love remained floating around them, the feeling of possibility waned.

She watched him realize this. Observed quietly, meekly, as the expected response never came from her lips and the look in his eyes shifted from love and adoration to pain. There were no words that would ease this pain. So she said nothing. After what felt like forever and no time at all, Winston, her best friend, her confidante, withdrew his heart from the table.

Without saying a thing he turned away and sat up on the edge of the rock. Using his hands to support his weight, he lowered his body off the edge and sank into the water, pushing off and swimming away from her.

A piece of her heart tore off and left with him. Still she could not speak. Could not call him back. She didn't know why, but the words wouldn't come. All that came were hot, silent tears.

Riding back to town in Zander's crappy little car, the windows down, the wind whipping around them once more, there was a void between them. A chasm. Winston was silent, stony. Ro took every nuance of his mood as a punch in the stomach. She didn't want to be the cause of his pain, but she couldn't return his confession of love.

When he pulled up in the street in front of the hotel she mustered enough courage to ask, "Do you want to grab dinner?"

He shook his head and mumbled, "I've got to get Zander's car back. Not very hungry, anyway."

Ro nodded. There was a heaviness in the pit of her stomach, like she had swallowed some of the smooth stones along the edge of the cenote. She stepped out of the car onto the sidewalk in front of the hotel. Before closing the door, Ro bent down to say goodbye. When Winston gave her a begrudging glance his eyes were dark and distant. She couldn't form any words. She tried to smile, but even that seemed wrong. Crooked and awkward.

Winston looked down at his hands holding the steering wheel. An impatient taxi behind them honked their horn. Winston turned his head and glanced back at the taxi, then at Ro. His face softened slightly.

"I better get this thing moving," he said.

"Yeah," she felt tears pressing at the back of her throat and eyes. "Thank you for today," she managed.

He pressed his lips together and nodded, "Yeah, anytime. Bye, Ro."

"Bye," she said.

She shut the car door and Winston pulled away. The stones in her stomach started rolling and crunching together and Ro thought she might throw up.

That night she went to bed early, skipping dinner. She couldn't eat with the heavy weight in her stomach, and in her heart.

As she lay in her bed wishing sleep would come, memories of Winston played through her mind like movie clips. The way he always took her out for lunch on her birthday. That time he'd drawn her name for secret Santa and spent more than he was supposed to buying her the entire Harry Potter series in hardcover. She loved Harry Potter. All of the times he'd noticed when she got a new hairstyle or a new outfit. The laid back Friday afternoons they goofed off at work. The way he made her laugh in boring meetings, and over texts on the weekends, and just about any time she needed her mood lightened. The way he'd fussed over her when her engagement ended and she thought her heart was broken forever.

The memory that floated through her mind right before she fell asleep was of him today in the sunshine. Laying next to her on the rock in the middle of a cenote in the middle of the Yucatán Peninsula, where he'd come to make sure she was safe. She had never known anyone to care for her any better than Winston. This was the last conscious thought that drifted across her mind before sleep finally came.

THE NEXT MORNING Ro joined Carlos and his family for their routine sunrise walk along the beach. The brilliant pinks and oranges of the Caribbean sunrise filled the sky. The ocean was transitioning from its deep turquoise of night to the sparkling bright blue of day. Waves rolled rhythmically onto the sand. She normally found that sound relaxing. Today, however, Ro was wrapped in melancholy.

"Mira, Señorita, mira," Carlos' son and daughter called to her, showing off as they ran to the very edge of the water and waited for a wave, then raced as fast as their little legs would carry them to escape the water.

Ro smiled at them. But her smile faded as soon as they looked away, inviting Carlos' special brand of concern.

"All is good for you, Señorita?" His face was full of worry.

"Yes, yes, thank you...gracias," Ro said, trying to give him a reassuring smile.

Josefina, quiet and sweet as always, hooked her arm in Ro's as they strolled. Ro was almost positive Josefina understood she was having man trouble. Women understood women, and some things crossed language barriers.

A shout of recognition reached them from a short distance away. They all turned in unison to see who was calling out. Two figures moved towards them. At the sight of them, Ro's heart jumped into her throat.

Winston and Cooper.

All politeness, Carlos paused and waited for the men to catch up. Ro had no choice but to wait as well. When they reached them, Cooper was all smiles.

"Good morning," Cooper said, his exuberance about whatever adventure he and Winston were starting off on was obvious.

"Señor Rivera, Señor Winston," Carlos ducked his head in a half-bow kind of greeting. Josefina smiled and blushed, averting her eyes under Cooper's toothy grin.

"Anyone up for some scuba diving today?" Cooper asked with enthusiasm. "That's where we're headed," he indicated Winston with a quick jerk of his head.

Winston didn't respond. He stood a little behind Cooper with his hands shoved into his pockets. He didn't even glance in Ro's direction.

Cooper, on the other hand, focused in on her and said, "Your boy is quite the diver for a newbie."

Her boy.

The phrase ignited heat in her cheeks and a sickening feeling in her stomach. Ro shook her head and said something unintelligible, all while trying to avoid looking at any of them, especially Winston.

She felt Josefina's grip tighten on her arm. She knew. Everyone knew. How could they not? Body language was easier to understand than the spoken word. And the body language between Ro and Winston right now was the most awkward, painful interaction imaginable.

Of course, Cooper was unaware. Either that, or he just chose to push his way through the awkwardness to get to what he wanted.

"Not today, gracias," Carlos said. As if he would ever give up his post at the hotel to go on a random scuba diving trip. Carlos was the most dedicated worker Ro had ever met.

"Maybe another time, then," Cooper said. She was sure he knew Carlos would never go, no matter how many times he was invited. Cooper zeroed in on her, "Ro?"

She looked up. She had to. She couldn't ignore her boss.

And even if he wasn't her boss he wasn't the type of man that got ignored.

"You coming with us?" Cooper asked.

Ro flicked her eyes between Cooper and Winston, every time they landed on Winston she felt a stab of anguish in her heart. She shook her head 'no'.

"I'm helping Gloria today," she said. It wasn't a total lie. Most days she did help Gloria.

Cooper shrugged and they said their goodbyes. Cooper with gusto. Winston more quietly. She let her gaze follow them as they made their way towards Zander's dive shop. Melancholy wrapped more firmly around her, like a boa constrictor. Winston would never be, as Cooper had put it, 'her boy'.

At work the same dull sadness persisted, following her around like a little grey cloud. After she completed her meager tasks at her desk, she moved to Gloria's office to help her with some data entry and bill paying. While they worked Gloria tried to engage Ro in conversation. And Ro attempted to be perky.

"We missed you at dinner last night," Gloria said.

"I went straight to bed when I got back. I was really tired," Ro responded.

"Oh? What made you so tired?"

"We went to El Jardin Cenote to swim."

"Oh, how nice," Gloria smiled. Then asked, "Who did you go with?"

Ro had to swallow to keep up her perky voice, "Winston."

"Mmm," was all the older woman said. After a few moments she added, "He's a nice young man, isn't he?"

Ro nodded and managed a bright, chirpy, "Yes."

Gloria gave a small grunt of approval and continued working. But Ro struggled to focus. Her mind continually drifted to Winston and fogged up her concentration.

"Is he moving here like you?" Gloria asked, keeping her eyes on her computer screen.

"No. He's leaving," her cheery facade almost cracked. But she managed to explain, "He has to go back to work."

"I see," Gloria sounded a little let down. They worked silently for a few minutes until Gloria spoke again, "I was married for 37 years to my wonderful Fernando." She looked at Ro with soft eyes when she said his name. So sweet. "He had a good job at his father's ranch when we met. And he fell in love with me right away. He always said he was crazy in love with me before I even knew his name," Gloria chuckled quietly at this memory.

Ro listened with interest. A good love story might cheer her up.

"But I was young and full of adventure, and I didn't want to live in the country. I thought it was boring. I wanted to do other things besides have a husband and children," Gloria continued.

"You did?"

Gloria nodded emphatically, "Oh, this was a very unpopular view for a young lady to take, especially back then."

"I bet."

"But Fernando loved me with passion anyway. I left my family and moved to Playa del Carmen and started working as a maid in this hotel," Gloria tapped a pointed finger on the surface of her desk.

"Really?" Ro was impressed. Though she couldn't say she was totally surprised. Gloria may be small, but her strength was palpable.

Gloria nodded, her eyes glowing with happiness at the memory, "And do you know what my Fernando did?"

"What?"

"He followed me," Gloria leaned toward Ro and placed her hand on the young woman's knee, patting it warmly. "He told his father to give his place at the ranch to his younger brother because he was not returning, and he followed me here. He got a job at a construction company and we were married," she turned back to her work, giving Ro another meaningful look as she did.

Ro loved this story, and she was sure Gloria was telling her for a reason. Anyone with as keen an eye as Gloria's could tell something was going on between her and Winston. But the older woman refrained from looking at her again, leaving her to her thoughts. Ro was thankful for that, because her mind was whirling. A flurry of butterflies filled her stomach as well, as if revived by a cool, fresh breeze.

The door to Alicia's office opened and both Gloria and Ro looked up. Alicia, though calm, held the air of an emergency around her. She was holding her cell phone and her eyes were eagle-like behind her black-rimmed glasses.

"Mr. Rivera just called. There's been a diving accident and he's en route to the hospital."

Chapter Fifteen

Gloria immediately went into action, smoothly picking up the receiver of her slim lined desk phone and dialing a number. Any activity seemed impossible to Ro. Sitting stupidly in her chair, her face was frozen in shock. All she could do was ask short, stilted questions.

"Is Cooper okay?"

"He is fine, apparently it was someone on the boat with him," Alicia answered, her gaze moving swiftly to Ro then back to Gloria.

An invisible hand gripped Ro's heart. If Cooper was all right, then who was injured?

Outside, the cabbie who had taken them to the dress shop sped up to the curb and parked in front of them. The old gentleman hurried out of the driver's seat and ushered Ro and Gloria into the back of the cab.

"Where's the hospital?" Ro asked dumbly. Her tongue was almost numb. She gripped her hands tightly in her lap to try and keep them from trembling.

"It's close," Gloria said.

Just she and Ro would go to the hospital. Since the injured

party was not Cooper, Alicia remained behind to await updates from Gloria.

The ride felt like an eternity. The fingers that had slipped around Ro's heart earlier turned icy cold and squeezed. If Cooper wasn't hurt, it was possible that Winston was the one being rushed to the hospital. She could text or call him to find out, but something deep inside of her was too terrified. What if he didn't respond?

Every time a thought of him being pulled out of the water, or carried on a stretcher, or in a hospital bed with tubes and machines hooked up to him, entered her mind, the icy fingers gripped her heart even tighter and she couldn't breathe. She had to put any thoughts out of her mind and concentrate on breathing. In through her nose, out through her mouth.

When they arrived and walked through the front doors of the modest two-story hospital building, Gloria began speaking to a young woman at the receptionist desk in rapid fire Spanish. Ro couldn't understand a word of it. She waited behind the older woman as information was exchanged, breathing in through her nose and out through her mouth. A man in scrubs approached and led them into the hospital.

Not only were the conversations around her in Spanish, it seemed to Ro that the voices were echoing, getting deeper and slower. Their footsteps were muffled, like from a dream. For a hallway in a hospital, the space seemed dark and narrow. Ro blinked hard and the darkness receded. Tunnel vision. Her knees felt wobbly.

Just ahead Ro saw a man stand up from a dark blue plastic chair that was set outside a hospital room. It was Cooper. There was nobody with him.

Ro tried to speak, but her lips wouldn't move. Winston wasn't waiting in the hallway. He must be in the hospital room. She watched Cooper's expression change from the relief of seeing them to panic as his gaze moved past Gloria to her. He lunged forward just as the blackness filled her vision.

A strong hand held her around the waist. She was leaning on something warm, very warm. A body. A person. A chest. She sucked in a breath and smelled sunshine and sea salt and coconut sunscreen.

"You all right?" The voice rumbled into her ear. A familiar voice. Winston's voice.

Her vision began to clear. Her cheek was pressed firmly into a man's chest. She turned her eyes up and into Winston's face, so close to hers, full of concern.

Winston had one arm around her waist and was holding her firmly to his body, leaning his torso away from her slightly in order to support her shoulders and head. In his other hand he was holding a steaming cup of coffee.

Cooper stood in front of them. He'd lunged forward in order to catch her as she fainted. But Winston had been faster.

"Here's your coffee," Winston handed the cup to Cooper.

"Thanks," Cooper said. He was eyeing Ro warily, "Are you okay?"

Embarrassed, relieved, her head still spinning, Ro tried to nod 'yes'. Winston took hold of her upper arm with his newly freed hand. Suddenly, Ro was overcome with emotion and she pressed her face into his chest, letting him wrap his arms around her completely as she wept quietly.

"Hey, hey," Winston said softly into her hair.

"I'm sorry," she sniffled into his T-shirt.

"Everything's okay. Here, let's get you a chair," Winston said.

She shook her head defiantly and stayed pressed into him, his strong arms surrounding her. She didn't want to sit down, she only wanted him to hold her and know that he was safe. That she was safe with him.

She did sit, after all. There were two plastic chairs and as soon as she'd calmed down Winston made sure she sat in one of them. Gloria had the other one. Winston left to get them both something to drink from the vending machine where he'd found the coffee. Ro was wiping the wetness from her eyes with the backs of her hands as he left, watching him.

Just before he disappeared around a corner, Winston turned and walked backwards so he could look at her. She met his gaze and smiled through her drying tears. His face lit up into an ear-to-ear grin that was so bright it melted the cold fingers of dread that had held her heart on the way to the hospital, leaving her warm and tingly all over.

"Who is the injured diver?" Gloria was asking.

Ro felt like a real jerk. Overcome by relief that Winston was okay, she'd forgotten all about whoever was in with the doctor.

"Zander, but he's fine," Cooper answered.

Gloria sniffed, "Not too fine if he is here."

"What happened to him?" Ro asked.

"He got stung on the elbow by a Scorpion fish. He was trying to make an adjustment on his camera and jabbed his elbow back into the thing," Cooper explained.

"He'll be okay?" Ro asked.

"Oh, yeah. He definitely needs to be treated. They're poisonous. But now that he's here, I'm sure he'll be fine."

Cooper sipped his coffee. He'd obviously been in the ocean water and looked even more handsome because of it. He wore his normal style, James Bond crossed with yacht club chic. It looked good on him, as everything always did. He had been watching Ro carefully and out of nowhere crouched down in front of her, putting his free hand on her knee. The movement surprised her and she leaned back a little.

"Are you sure you're okay?" Cooper asked. His eyebrows were knit together and he rubbed small circles on her knee with his thumb, the motion making his hand edge further up on her thigh.

"Oh, I'm fine. I just got a little woozy in the car and...and I always feel a little weird in hospitals."

"Me, too!" Cooper said.

When he spoke he shifted his weight slightly and used Ro's leg to steady himself. This moved his hand even further up her leg. It was in the middle of her thigh now, his fingertips under her skirt, his forearm rested against her knee.

Ro became very aware of Cooper's physical presence. His sea tossed hair had dried in that way that only happens on the beach. This close up, the width of his shoulders almost made her claustrophobic. The muscles of his arm flexed. His fingertips grazed her bare thigh, tickling her skin. She couldn't tell if he was making a move on her or had gotten too close by accident, out of concern.

"Well, we'll be out of here soon. And hopefully not be back!" He said, laughing.

Ro nodded and laughed with him as he leaned forward to get in a position where he could straighten up. As he leaned in, his mouth came very close to her cheek. Close enough he could have kissed her if he'd been inclined. Flustered by this thought, Ro giggled. Just as Cooper stood, she glanced down the hallway and saw Winston halted abruptly, holding two steaming cups of coffee. Confusion filled his eyes.

From that distance he could easily have assumed that Cooper had just kissed her. And that she had responded with a flirtatious giggle. Ro made a move to stand. She wanted to go to Winston, to make sure he understood that wasn't what had happened. Before she could, the door to the hospital room opened and the doctor and two nurses stepped out.

From that point on there was a flurry of activity surrounding Zander, who lay irritated and restless in the hospital bed. Between Cooper taking over and asking questions in English while Gloria tried to interpret, and Zander declaring his fitness to be released from the hospital, then enduring bouts of pain bad enough they made him curse, the whole situation was rather chaotic. Winston silently delivered the coffee to her and Gloria, avoiding eye contact as he did.

She wished he would look at her. She wanted to somehow reassure him that she hadn't been flirting with Cooper. But he was busy offering Zander help and friendship, and she couldn't very well interrupt just to appease her own feelings. Zander was the one in trouble here, not her. After making such a scene with her fainting spell, she refused to follow Winston around like a needy, insecure girlfriend. She would wait until they were back at the hotel, alone.

That, it turned out, wasn't going to happen for a while.

It was decided that Gloria and Ro were no longer needed at the hospital. Nor was Cooper. Winston volunteered to stay with Zander and escort him home safely when he was released. Cooper was relieved to be released of the responsibility, which bothered Ro. Zander had been Cooper's friend longer than Winston's. Now that they all knew Zander was going to be fine, Cooper was bored with this scene and ready to get back to something more fun. They left Winston standing next to Zander's hospital bed and Ro was embarrassed for Cooper's lack of maturity.

She made sure to say to Winston as they left, "I'll see you back at the hotel?"

Winston nodded and gave her a small wave. Although he was looking at her, it felt like he was looking right through her.

Back at the office Cooper wanted to review his emails and actually give her some administrative tasks to do on his behalf. This was the first time he'd taken much of an interest in any real hotel business. Ro tried to concentrate, but found it difficult. Checking her phone discreetly every few minutes for any kind of message from Winston. None came.

Winston was a no show at dinner as well. After sweeping the dining area for him, Ro went to Carlos at the front desk.

"Has Winston come in yet?" She asked.

Carlos made a tsk-tsk sound and shook his head, "No, Señorita. He is not come by here this night."

With nowhere else to sit and wait, Ro took a stool at the hotel bar. The same dark shining wood that graced the rest of the hotel made its mark here as a long bar and floor to ceiling shelves set against a floor to ceiling mirror. The top of the bar was made of white marble, with veins of black and silver running through it. Ro ran her hand over the smooth, cool surface and ordered a citrus wine spritzer.

Hotel guests filled the room. They sat at the small tables or leaned against the bar, talking and laughing and sipping elaborate frozen concoctions. Mostly couples. Mostly in love, or at least on their way.

She sighed and took a sip of her drink. Bitter fizz ran over her tongue.

"What's a nice girl like you doing in a place like this?"

Ro saw him in the mirror first. Standing behind her, dressed to kill in a tight fitting, French blue shirt, no tie.

Cooper. His dark eyes gleaming, his perfectly shaped mouth curled into a sexy smile.

Surprised to see him, her spritzer went down the wrong tube, making her cough and splutter into her cocktail napkin. When she recovered, thankful none of it had sprayed out of her nose, she returned Cooper's smile.

Sliding onto the school next to hers, he nodded at the

bartender to bring him his usual. Leaning into the space between her shoulder and her ear, his breath brushed her skin.

"How are you, stranger?" He asked.

His breath wreaked of booze. Ro glanced behind him into the crowd.

"Is Tomi with you?" She felt the need to remind him that he had a girlfriend.

"Pfffft," Cooper blew a raspberry into the air, sending a fine spray of spittle onto Ro's shoulder. "She's not ready yet. Can you believe that? It takes her hours to get ready to go out, it's ridiculous," he slurred the last few words of his sentence just as the bartender placed a heavy crystal glass in front of him full of amber liquor.

"Are you two going out?" Ro tried to steer the conversation. She wasn't Tomi's biggest fan, but she also wasn't interested in talking nasty about her behind her back.

"Probably...gotta get out of this rat hole," Cooper took a swig of his drink then his eyes widened. "Did I say that out loud?" He asked in mock horror, dropping his forehead until it leaned on her shoulder and laughing.

Ro didn't know what to say. Cooper had never been this physical with her, nor showed her this kind of attention. He lifted his head, but kept his arm on the back of her bar stool, shifting so their bodies remained close.

Just a few days before she would have been thrilled at this new development. Sitting close together in the sensual light of a bar, alone, no Tomi, no Winston in sight. But now everything was different. Ro glanced uncomfortably around the people milling in the bar, hoping that Winston didn't show up while Cooper was all over her and sloppy drunk.

The truth of her situation rippled through her body making her shiver. She didn't want Cooper anymore, not at all. She didn't want him because she already had Winston.

And Winston was the best thing that had ever happened to her. The instant that thought solidified in her mind, Ro's heart soared.

How could she have missed it all of this time? How could she have left him hanging after her told her that he loved her?

Ro gave her head a quick shake, brushing off the guilt. Yes, she'd been confused and surprised. But now she wasn't, and the moment Winston walked back into this hotel, she would tell him. She couldn't wait to see the look on his face.

"You look extra beautiful tonight, Ro," Cooper dripped the words into her ear, making her feel slimy. He let out a fluid chuckle and started singing quietly, "Row, row, row your boat, gently down the stream." This sent him into another bout of the giggles and he dropped his head onto her shoulder again.

Just as Ro was wondering how she was going to get rid of this overly friendly version of her jet-setting boss, a miracle happened. Tomi walked into the bar.

"Tomi!" Ro shouted at her over the noise and waved happily. Cooper sat up straight and looked in the direction she was waving. Ro had never thought she would be so happy to see the bleached blonde, Botox injected, lipo-suctioned vision of Tomi as she was in that moment. She was saved from Cooper's drunken advances and full of the knowledge that she finally knew what she wanted. Who she wanted.

Hours later, her excitement was more subdued. After being saved from Cooper by Tomi, she had waited in the bar for over two hours. Winston never showed up there or anywhere else at the hotel. Nor did he respond to her text asking if everything was okay. It got too late for her to walk down to Zander's dive shop and see if she could find him. Too may drunken partygoers in the streets at this time of night. Plus she didn't know if they were at the dive shop. She didn't know where Zander lived. Left with little alternative,

Ro went to bed. She would find him first thing in the morning.

That night she dreamed.

Standing on the beach, looking at the sunrise. Fine, white sand soft and warm under her bare toes. Her pure white gown billowed, light and gauzy, in the ocean breeze and Ro realized that she was getting married. A beach wedding. So romantic.

Under a pink sky, the turquoise water glittered and Ro walked down the sandy aisle that led to a grand arch. The arch was decorated with pink and white flowers growing thick on vines. Two men waited for her. One was her groom. The other was a preacher.

Ro floated past faceless guests seated in white folding chairs and finally arrived at the arch. Her groom turned to her with a charming smile. It was Cooper in a gold tuxedo.

"Wait," she said, but it came out as a whisper and nobody seemed to hear her.

The preacher started speaking in a monotone voice, so low she couldn't understand what he was saying. Her arm wouldn't move and she looked down to see that Cooper had a tight grip on her. Shaking her head, she pulled on her arm. It didn't budge.

Ro looked up to plead with Cooper to let her go and she heard someone giggling. Turning around to see who was laughing, she was greeted with the vision of Tomi and Tara in neon pink bridesmaid dresses. They had their hands over their mouths to try and muffle their laughter.

"No," she said in her mind. But no sound came out of her mouth.

She whirled around towards the preacher. Surely she could refuse to marry Cooper? Nobody would force her, would they?

The preacher's mouth opened and closed as he spoke.

Still, none of the words made sense. Cooper's grip tightened on her arm and Ro began to struggle to get away.

She looked beyond the preacher at the beach that stretched for miles and the shining blue ocean. If only she could free herself from Cooper, she could run past the preacher and escape.

Ro blinked into the shimmering orange ball that was the sun sitting on the edge of the horizon. A silhouette appeared from the center of this bright light, standing where the waves kissed the beach.

Everything went into slow motion. The preacher's mumbling, her bridesmaid's from hell giggling, even her arm trying to twist free from Cooper. The silhouette moved closer and closer to her as she watched. As she hoped.

Then, miraculously, her arm was free. She stumbled past the preacher, away from Cooper and towards the silhouette. It was a man's silhouette. It was Winston. Coming to save her.

She ran.

She could see Winston clearly now. He opened his arms wide. A smile full of joy on his face.

"Winston!" She cried out and her voice was no longer stuck in her throat.

Ro woke with a start. She had slept so fitfully that most of her covers had slipped onto the floor and her arm had become wrapped up in her sheet. Still, she was exuberant as she practically leapt out of bed.

Glancing at her window she could see the early glow of sunrise. This was a new day. She would find Winston today and they would start their life together.

Chapter Sixteen

Despite Ro's excitement to talk to Winston, she wanted to take a little time getting dressed. After all, if she was going to declare her love for someone she may as well look good while she did it. Besides, it was still early in the morning and she had plenty of time before she had to be at work.

Running a bath in the soaker tub, she poured in some of the jasmine and orange bath salts. As the tub filled and the scent permeated her room, she went to the closet and pulled out the white cotton lace dress she'd bought just before flying here. It was mid-length, with a sweetheart neckline and adorable puffy sleeves. She had bought it on a whim, thinking it would be perfect to go out to lunch or shopping in Playa del Carmen. But she hadn't had the chance to wear it anywhere yet. It had seemed too romantic to wear to the office.

"Romantic is perfect for today," she said out loud.

Smiling as she laid the dress out on her bed, butterflies in her stomach, she checked out the window. The sky was turning its glorious pink, meaning the sun would be completely up soon. Ro hurried into the bathroom to sink into the warm scented water.

It was not yet 8 o'clock when she approached the front desk. In her flirty white lace dress, thin leather sandals and a dainty gold heart necklace with matching bracelet, Ro felt feminine and ready for romance. Carlos was already at the desk.

"No beach walk this morning?" Normally he arrived at the front desk at 8:00 am sharp.

"No, Señorita, not this day. Josefina takes children to see their abuela...grandmother," he responded.

She nodded in understanding. Glancing around the lobby as casually as she could, Ro tried to ignore the nervous ball of energy trembling in the center of her belly. Without looking at Carlos, she asked nonchalantly, "Have you seen Winston this morning?"

Carlos sucked in his breath, making Ro look at him with concern. His normally warm and friendly expression had fallen. Giving her sad eyes, he clucked his tongue and shook his head slowly.

"He not tell you?" Carlos asked.

"Tell me what?" Ro's stomach dropped at the shift in his demeanor.

"Señor Winston left this morning."

"Left the hotel?"

"To the airport," Carlos delivered this last bit of bad news with a heavy heart.

The romantic bubble she'd been in all morning burst, shattering all of her intentions into a hundred pieces. She didn't know what to do. She simply stood there staring at Carlos with wide eyes.

Carlos rummaged for something on an unseen shelf behind the counter. He pulled out an envelope and placed it on the counter. She recognized the Hotel Diamante stationary. Her name was written in the center of the envelope in Winston's handwriting. 'Ro' looked small and lonely in the center of the thick, gleaming paper.

"He say to give this to you," Carlos pushed the envelope towards her and shook his head sadly at what a shame the whole drama was.

Carlos knew this was not a love letter. So did Ro. She stared at it for a moment, not wanting to touch it because then she would have to open it and read Winston's last words to her. That was not something she wanted to do.

A family of tourists, Mom and Dad with four children, converged on the front desk and Carlos turned to help them. Ro reached up and slid the envelope off of the counter, surprised it didn't burn her fingers when she touched it.

Overcome with the need to get the pain over with as quickly as possible, like ripping off a Band-Aid, she sat down on the nearest Victorian loveseat. The envelope was light. Not much to be said, she guessed. She sighed and slid her finger into the top corner to tear the top open. Her hands trembled slightly as she pulled the neatly folded paper out and opened it.

Ro,

Sorry for the handwritten note drama. This was too much for a text, and I couldn't talk to you in person about it. I was afraid nothing would come out right. So, handwritten note it is.

I've gone home. I was able to get an early flight this morning and took it. I don't want to intrude on your new life any longer. I know you love me as a friend, but that fact doesn't make watching you fall in love with someone else any easier. It might even make it harder. I might be able to move on if you hated me.

Scratch that. I hope you don't. Hate me, that is. I don't hate you for not loving me the way I love you. You can't help how you feel. And you should know that being your friend has been one of the greatest experiences of my life. Thank you for that. You're the funni-est, kindest, most beautiful person I've ever known. You're the best, Ro. Don't ever forget.

I've got to get to the airport now. Best of luck on all of your new adventures. I hope you find everything you've ever wanted.

Love Always,
   Winston

The noise in the busy lobby hushed. All Ro could hear was her heart pounding, sending blood rushing through her head. She breathed in, listening to the air filling her lungs. Staring at the words on the paper without reading them, she saw a fat tear drop onto the top of the letter, smearing her name. Her throat tightened. What had she done?

Ro ran her thumb across Winston's signature. So familiar. She choked back a sob and tore her gaze away from it, looking up towards the ceiling then letting her eyes wander across all of the tourists and staff bustling here and there in the lobby.

Had she really only been here two weeks? It seemed like a lifetime ago that she'd first entered the hotel. Yet it had only been days. She'd been so excited, so sure that this was what she wanted. And now as she took in the weekday morning rush knowing she had a place here, could build a new life here, she didn't know if she wanted to stay. Did she really belong here? Did any of her big plans to move to Mexico and live in paradise mean anything if she lost the most important person in her world?

Without Winston in her life nothing else seemed to matter.

She groaned and looked at the letter again. Slumping against the wall, she read his words over and over.

"I'm such a fool," she whispered to nobody.

"You're not a fool," a voice answered.

Ro jumped at the sound. Blinking, she looked up into Gloria's gentle, round face.

"Oh, Gloria," Ro's expression crumpled as tears spilled down her face.

"Now, now," Gloria sat next to her and put her arm around Ro's shoulders. Ro dropped her face into her hands to try and hide her break down from the general public. "Carlos says you are having a problem with your young man?"

Ro nodded emphatically, emitting a small moan from behind her cupped hands.

Gloria tsk-tsked as she tried to discreetly console Ro's blubbering.

"Perhaps we should find him and you can speak with him about how you're feeling?" Gloria offered.

Ro let her hands fall into her lap, the letter now crumpled and tear stained. She shook her head morosely and tried to stem her crying long enough to explain.

"H-he-he is g-g-gone," she wailed, turning her face into Gloria's shoulder.

"Gone to the airport, yes?" Gloria asked.

"Mmhmm," Ro sniffled.

"Carlos said he left one hour ago. I think, perhaps, his plane is still here?"

Ro stopped crying. She sat up and looked at Gloria with instant understanding.

"Of course!" She exclaimed, "Why didn't I think of that? I'm so dense!"

Gloria chuckled and shook her head, answering, "Love does that to us."

Time was of the essence. Ro's mind was whirling with how to get to the airport, how to figure out what flight he was on, and how to get him off of the flight if he'd already boarded. Frantic energy took over and she stood up quickly.

"I need to get a cab," she said urgently, looking from left to right and back again as if a cab could be found somewhere in the lobby.

"Yes," Gloria stood up next to her and calmly gestured towards the grey haired, mustached cabbie who was ever present whenever Gloria was around.

"Your chauffeur!" Ro could have cried tears of joy if she had the time.

Gloria steered Ro and Carlos to the cab that waited outside, and climbed in after them. She and Carlos would go along for "assistance", she explained.

Grateful for their help and consistently solid presence of mind, Ro tried to remain calm. Her mind bounced between all of the possibilities; they find Winston and she confesses her love for him, or he has already boarded the plane and they have to get someone in authority to inform him of her love for him, or his plane has already left and she doesn't get a chance to tell him how she feels, and he goes back to his old life and realizes what a ridiculous emotional wreck she really is, then forgets about her.

That would be bad, but there was one worse possibility.

What if they did find him and she was able to confess her love only to find out that she was too late? What if he'd changed his mind?

She shook her head sharply, willing that thought away. She felt a little sick after considering this outcome. Or, perhaps she was getting carsick.

They were racing, more like careening, towards the airport. Ignoring traffic signals, signs, pedestrians, the rights of other motorists, and maybe even the laws of physics, Gloria's chauffeur was doing everything possible to get them there swiftly. When they were finally on the highway that was a straight shot to the airport, Ro was afraid to look at the speedometer to see how fast they were going. Sitting in the back seat left her feeling queasy, but hopeful they might make it in time.

When they reached the airport, the cab screeched to a halt at the curb. Carlos jumped out to intervene with airport security, which was ample, while the chauffeur helped Gloria and Ro out of the back seat. Gloria took Ro's elbow firmly and directed her inside.

Gloria had been on her cell phone almost the entire drive. The one sided conversations all in Spanish had gone over Ro's head. But now that they were in the airport she got the idea Gloria had been requesting important flight information, because the older woman steered Ro decisively through throngs of travelers and past all of the airline ticket counters.

Finally, she stopped. A middle aged, barrel chested man with a double chin wearing a dark blue suit and tie, stood at attention at what appeared to be an empty gateway leading into the bowels of the airport. Upon seeing Gloria, the man's face lit up and he greeted her in Spanish. A gold nameplate pinned to his suit jacket read, "Eduardo Durazo, Director de Seguridad".

Carlos, breathing hard from running to catch up, appeared behind them. He gave Ro an encouraging smile and a thumbs up. After a few short exchanges of information and a gallant bow from Señor Durazo, they were ushered through the abandoned entryway into a long concourse with digital signs showing airline names and flight numbers. Permanent signs, each showing a gate number, went on and on down the concourse, until they were so far away she couldn't read them.

"What gate number? Do we know?" Ro asked, overwhelmed at the sheer number of them stretching into the distance.

Gloria nodded, "They said gate number 65."

All three of them looked up. They were standing under

the first gate number in the concourse. Gate number 28. They looked at each other in dismay.

"What time did they say it was leaving?" Ro asked with a sinking feeling in her stomach.

Gloria's eyes saddened, "Five minutes."

"Cuanto?" Carlos asked.

"Cinco minutos," Gloria told him again.

Ro knew it was an impossible task. By the time they got to the gate there would be no time left to stop the plane. It would already be pulling away from the building. The hope she'd held onto in the cab slid off of her and fell into a puddle on the floor.

"You love Señor Winston?" Carlos asked her, passion in his voice.

Ro looked into his eyes, her heart already crumpling from disappointment. He knew the answer because he'd watched her and Winston together, and he was a romantic at heart. Carlos truly felt her pain in this moment.

Ro nodded, barely able to say it out loud, "Yes. I love him."

A huge smile spread across his face and his eyes danced as he grabbed her shoulders, "We run, Señorita. We run!"

Lifted by his encouragement, Ro felt a thrill surge through her.

Gloria's eyes lit up and she nodded enthusiastically, "Go, go, go!"

So they ran.

Ro's sandals slapped the smooth, shiny floor as she sprinted down the concourse. Her puffy lace sleeves and skirt fluttered madly in the breeze caused by her body's momentum. Carlos weaved through the crowd a few steps in front of her, leading the way towards Gate 65. The joy he was experiencing taking part in this dramatic lover's reunion was apparent in the way he shouted encouraging comments to her over his shoulder as they ran.

Ro ran as fast as she'd ever run in her life. Her legs flew under her skirt and she followed Carlos with single-minded focus. She had to get to Winston before he left Mexico. She had to tell him she loved him, that she was in love with him. Every minute that went by and he didn't know that fact was a tragedy.

By the time they reached Gate 65 they were both winded. Breathing hard and sweating in the humidity, Ro and Carlos broke through the last wall of people blocking their path. As they burst into the waiting area they were greeted by absolutely nobody.

"Oh, no!" Ro cried out.

No passengers milled around waiting to board. No airline employees perched behind the counter assigned to Gate 65. The digital sign was turned off and the door leading out to the airplane was shut tight.

They hurried to the giant windows. The airplane carrying Winston out of her life had already pulled away from the edge of the building and was turning to get in line for take off on the runway.

Placing her palm on the smoke tinted glass, she leaned her forehead against the back of her hand and watched helplessly. Still breathing hard, the glass began to fog up in front of her face. A strong hand rested lightly on her shoulder. Carlos, as dejected and upset as she was, shook his head in dismay as he patted her shoulder in condolence.

They watched in silence as the plane moved out of their view. Ro squeezed her eyes shut against the sight, and against the tears that threatened to come. Her throat tightened as she held down the frustration that wanted to burst out.

She'd pushed him away. Sent him back to Indiana and out of her life. Of course he wasn't dead and she could talk to him over the phone. Maybe everything would work out in the end. Maybe.

They made their way back up the concourse and ran into Gloria on her way to meet them. Upon seeing Ro and Carlos, who was almost as upset as Ro over the matter, Gloria gave them both a soft, sad hug. Winston had gone back to America and they had failed in their mission to stop him. The three of them trudged back through the concourse with the air of people who had just watched a romantic movie that ended catastrophically.

Cloaked in gloom, her eyes cast down to the floor just in front of her, Ro concentrated on taking one step at a time. She could do nothing more. If she tried to speak she was afraid she would cry.

The trip back to the main section of the airport where all of the gift shops and restaurants were located seemed much longer than when she and Carlos had been racing the clock. Of course they'd been running and filled with a powerful sense of hope.

Ro had no such feeling now.

There was only emptiness. Longing. A vague sense of loss every time they passed people reuniting with their loved ones or arriving in Mexico for a fun filled vacation. Ro scowled at the obvious honeymooners disembarking from their flight. The sickening displays of love were like barbs in her heart. Even Michael Bolton's "When a Man Loves a Woman" played loudly from a nearby airport bar. The irony was almost too much.

She sighed. She had to get a grip. She had to stop comparing her love life to the rest of the world and get on with her life. Besides, it wasn't even Michael Bolton singing. It didn't sound like him. It sounded edgier.

Ro paused mid-stride, tilting her head to listen more carefully. She turned her attention to the chalkboard sign outside of the bar. Scrawled in multi-colored chalk under the heading 'Cancún Beach Bar', written in all caps, was one word, KARAOKE.

The words of the song wrapped around her and pulled her towards the open door of the bar. Stepping into the airport version of Cancún, complete with fake thatch roofed bar and a mural of scuba divers exploring a vibrant coral reef, Ro saw him. He stood on a small stage set aside for live music. Belting out the chorus to the song with his eyes closed and the microphone held expertly to his mouth, was Winston.

"Señori–" Carlos began, stopping short just behind her as he caught sight of Winston singing.

Ro tried to say something, but her heart was in her throat. She tried to move, but her feet seemed glued to the floor. She tried to wrap her mind around what she was seeing and found herself feeling dizzy and unable to catch her breath. For the second time in as many days Ro thought she was about to faint.

"Go to him, hija," Gloria said, placing her hand on Ro's back. Carlos, bless him, took hold of her elbow to try and steady her. Emboldened by their encouragement, Ro took in a shuddering breath and stepped towards the stage.

It took Winston a few moments to notice her as she emerged out of several groups of tourists who were killing time in the bar. It took a few more moments for him to register what he was seeing. When he did, Winston froze. The accompaniment track kept playing, but he was no longer singing along. He had stopped on the 'please don't treat me bad' line and was staring at her.

All eyes turned to Ro. Her white lace dress glowing in the stage lights, her face turned up towards Winston. She responded to his surprise with a steady gaze, so happy to see him, so relieved that he was still here.

"Ro..." he said. Her name reverberated through the room

and Winston glanced down, noticing he still held the microphone to his mouth. Flustered by her presence, he fumbled with it as he put it back in its stand. He cocked his head at her, a puzzled smile on his face, and said, "What are you doing here?" But the swanky background music still pumped through the bar and his words were lost.

Ro couldn't find her voice. The whole bar looked back and forth between her and Winston, waiting for something to happen. Heat rose in her cheeks and she looked at her feet.

Carlos, unable to contain his romantic nature, called out, "She come to stop you, Seńor Winston!"

A group of middle aged men on their way home after vacation, sunburned and half drunk, stood closest to Ro. They watched with amusement.

One of them shouted, "Don't leave her standing there!" They all cheered in agreement.

Ro blushed furiously, uncertain what to do next.

Fortunately, she didn't have to wait long.

Winston hopped off the front of the stage. The crowd parted for him. When she lifted her eyes and saw the look on this face, a shudder went through her body. He watched her evenly as he walked through the crowd, a smile playing on his lips. And something else. Determination.

Winston, her best friend, her confidante, her love, moved towards her so directly, with such intent of purpose, she was helpless in his sights. Her heart pounded in her chest and a tingle moved across her shoulders and up her neck. Her breath came more quickly the closer Winston came, because she knew from the look on his face that he was going to kiss her. As Ro's lips parted ever so slightly in anticipation, Winston reached her.

He placed one hand on her waist, his touch sending a charge of electricity across her skin. Lifting his other hand, he brushed the back of it along her cheek, searching her eyes.

"I got your note," Ro managed to say. Her voice was almost a whisper.

He raised his eyebrows, grinning, "You did?"

She swallowed and nodded, the sensation of his body being just inches away was overwhelming.

"And what did you think?" He asked, letting his eyes wander across her face and lips.

"I wanted to say—" she started.

"Kiss her already!" One of the drunk tourists called out. The rest of the room cheered.

Winston pulled her into him protectively. He held his gaze locked to hers, ignoring the rest of the world. There was nothing but love and desire in his eyes. She wanted to sink into them and stay there forever.

"What did you want to say, Ro?" He asked again.

She ran her hands up his arms and over his shoulders, delighting in the feel of him under her fingertips. Clasping her hands behind his neck, she stood on her tiptoes so he would be sure to hear her over the music and the shouts of encouraging crowd.

"I wanted to say that I love you, Winston."

His arm tightened around her waist as she spoke the words. With great care, he pushed the fingers of his other hand lightly over her ear and into her hair. Ro felt the tension of his body against hers. All of the controlled strength holding her ever so gently made her dizzy with pleasure.

As he bent towards her, his eyes glittering with passion, he whispered, "I love you, too."

And they kissed. With the whooping and hollering of the bar crowd, the happy applause of Carlos and Gloria, and the last notes of the Karaoke song swelling in the air, they kissed.

"Están enamorados!" Carlos shouted, his joy only outdone by their own.

৯৯

THANK you for reading New Year in Paradise! If you enjoyed this book you may enjoy the other books in the series...
    Enchanting Eve - Halloween Romance
    Love is at the Table - Thanksgiving Romance
    Mistletoe Madness - Christmas Romance

৯৯

OR YOU MAY ENJOY Darci's Dream Come True series. The first book, Her Scottish Keep is a fun and flirty romance set in the Scottish Highlands...a clean and wholesome contemporary Scottish love story :)

Epilogue

A sweet smelling breeze touched Ro's cheek as she turned to look at the sunrise over the ocean. Her dress lifted and seemed to float as she moved towards the altar. There were no flamingos like in her dreams of Mexico, but the pink in the sky was the same color as those tropical birds. Just like in her dreams, the turquoise water, pristine and clear, shone brilliantly and winked in the morning light.

But this was not a dream.

Her father, dressed in the same sand colored shorts and white gauze shirt as Winston and the groomsmen, looked a little pale and out of place compared to her and Winston, and all of the locals who were present. Still, he was bursting with pride and Ro was thrilled that he and her mother, and the rest of her family, had made it all the way to Playa del Carmen to share in this special day.

Ro's dress had a sleeveless lace bodice and a floor length chiffon skirt, thus the floating on air. They had decided on a beach wedding, of course. Cooper had offered them the use of his yacht, but both she and Winston knew the beach was the right place for them to become man and wife. Just as they'd known that New Year's Day was the right day for them to get married. The yacht would come in handy for their honeymoon weekend, however. They didn't need any more than a long weekend for their honeymoon, because they woke up to paradise every day.

Winston had wasted no time in proposing to Ro after that fateful day in the airport when he'd decided not to get on the plane, but instead drown his sorrows in a cheesy airport bar that happened to offer Karaoke for entertainment. Their love, already settled after knowing one another for so long beforehand, didn't need to be tested out over time for them to know it was true.

Winston had enlisted Carlos' help in helping him plan the proposal. Carlos had suggested taking Ro on a gondola ride through beautiful canals that led to Xcaret park. Winston had popped the question on the gondola and they were met with a romantic dinner for two when they arrived at the park.

Because Carlos played such a big role in their romance, and because he had a huge heart, they had asked him to officiate their wedding ceremony. He had been thrilled at this request and so overcome with emotion Ro had wondered if he would be capable of getting through the wedding without bawling. So far he had been okay, but the day was not yet over.

They had spent the last year getting Winston moved to Playa del Carmen and setting up his business as an accountant to expats living in the area. Ro stayed on at the hotel. How could she leave it after everything Gloria and Carlos, as well as Cooper and Alicia, did to change her life?

She and Winston spent their free time exploring the cenotes and underground rivers in the area. And Zander had taught her how to scuba dive. And, of course, they had been busy with wedding plans, which included this gorgeous beach wedding followed by a reception at the Hotel Diamante.

All of the guests stood as Ro and her father approached. He squeezed her arm and smiled down at her. She gave him a kiss on his cheek, loving him and her mother and this entire day. But most of all, loving Winston.

Winston shook her father's hand and took her arm in his to face Carlos, who was already clearing his throat and fighting back tears. Ro held onto Winston's arm, strong and steady, and thanked her lucky stars that he had come to Mexico to check on her one year ago.

He looked down at her with twinkling eyes, "Ready for this?"

Ro nodded, "I'm ready for all of it."

Winston leaned over and kissed her on the forehead as he covered her hand with his and she lost herself in his warmth and love. A life of adventure was theirs as they became man and wife and the sun rose on a brand new year.

THE FINAL END

Also by Darci Balogh

<u>Dream Come True Series</u>

Five childhood friends vow to live the life of their dreams...without men to mess it all up.

1. Her Scottish Keep

2. Her British Bard

3. Her Sheltered Cove

4. Her Secret Heart

5. Her One and Only

<u>Lady Billionaire Series</u>

1. Ms. Money Bags

2. Ms. Perfect

3. Ms. Know-it-All

<u>Sugar Plum Romance Series</u>

Christmas, cooking, and chefs falling in love!

1. Charlotte's Christmas Charade

2. Bella's Christmas Blunder

<u>Love & Marriage Contemporary Romance (Box Set - best bang for your buck!)</u>

Steamy, emotional stories with relatable characters. These older woman, younger man romances are both racy and romantic.

1. The Quiet of Spring

2. For Love & For Money

3. Stars in the Sand

About the Author

Darci Balogh is a writer and indie filmmaker from Denver. She grew up in the beautiful mountains of Colorado and has lived in several areas of the state over her lifetime. She currently resides in Denver where she raised her two glorious, intelligent daughters to functioning adulthood. This is, by far, one of her highest achievements. She has a love-hate relationship with gardening, probably should dust more, adores dogs and is allergic to cats.

Darci has been a writer since she was a child and enjoys crafting stories into novels and screenplays. Big surprise, some of her favorite pastimes are reading and watching movies. Classic British TV is high on her 'Like' list, along with quietly depressing detective series and coffee with heavy cream.